W9-BXD-298

THE FAMILY JEWELS

THE FAMILY JEWELS

A gay comedic mystery

Book one of the trilogy
Glamour Galore

Iory Allison

iUniverse, Inc.
New York Lincoln Shanghai

The Family Jewels

All Rights Reserved © 2004 by William Iorwerth Allison

No part of this book may be reproduced or transmitted in any form or by any means, graphic, electronic, or mechanical, including photocopying, recording, taping, or by any information storage retrieval system, without the written permission of the publisher.

iUniverse, Inc.

For information address:
iUniverse, Inc.
2021 Pine Lake Road, Suite 100
Lincoln, NE 68512
www.iuniverse.com

This is a book of fiction, and none of its characters are intended to portray real people. Names, characters, and incidents are either the product of the author's imagination or are used fictitiously and any resemblance to any actual persons, living or dead is entirely coincidental.

ISBN: 0-595-33025-8

Printed in the United States of America

This book is dedicated to Leo Romero
because he is gentle of heart and generous of spirit.

"Wise men feel impossible loves"

WHAT THE READERS HAD TO SAY

LILLY'S BLURB

Lilly Linda Le Strange
Star of Glamour Galore
Club Crazy, Boston

Hi there you darling lumps, this is Lilly Linda LeStrange and I just have'ta get my two cents worth in here!

The Family Jewels is not the story I would have written, but hey, I'm a lazy Bitch, so who's surprised? I'll tell you one thing the climax, which, by the way, has nothing to do with sex, is still pretty dammed incredible. This is not to say I didn't like it, far from that, I'm in the story from beginning to end so who's arguing? But my one gripe is this: with a talent like mine, don't you think it's kind of a waste to be providing only the comic relief? Not that this story doesn't need a little comic relief, after all, with a slob like Nagib Iskander and that little rodent, Wisner Chilton working their wily ways the whole thing can get pretty heavy. And while we're on that subject, if those ugly lugs think they can mess with my daughter Valisha then think again 'cause I'll tear their faces off…"

L.L.LS. has been called away to Mc Clean's Hospital for a command performance of "Shock Therapy" in which she stars as the nurse who gives head, "Whorozine"

BA BA'S SCATHING DISH

Ba Ba Rum Toddy
The Charma Karma Ashram
Pun-jab, India

After attempting to impart the wisdom of the ages to this author over many laborious years with regular recitations of the pre Vadic saga, "Razzle Dazzle Raga", I fully expected something more spiritual from Mr. Allison. His current offering of, "The Family Jewels", and here I am joined by His Holiness, Dilly Dally Rimpoché, when we say, "this is clap trap in the extreme".

TILLY WINK PUTS UP A STINK

Tilly Wink
Literary Critic
The Bumble Bee Beacon
Bumble Bee, Arkansas

Having raced through the narcotic pages of "Family Jewels" I am frankly shocked! This book is rife with homosexual antics that would keep the major saints rolling in their graves like a heavy load in the clothes dryer. The characters are so vivid I had to slam the book shut just to keep them inside the cover! Talk about jingles you can't get out of your head, now I am constantly humming the refrain, "Into each life a little glamour must fall" and how can I explain that to my husband? If this weren't enough, I even missed the last episode of Seinfeld because I was madly tearing through the pages like a junky. This book is addictive, watch out!

VOICES FROM BEYOND

Lillian Hellmann
As channeled through the ouija board by
Madame Sonia Schnable
Literary critic for
Mystic Messages

If Mr. Allison thinks he can nuzzle his way onto the NYT best seller list with this worthless dribble, then he has more imagination than I would have supposed from reading "Family Jewels". I must admit I learned more about the "Gay" life than I had ever hoped for or needed to know. In my day the Queens around the round table were so closeted they chased the furs into the cold storage vault for the whole summer.

I will admit to an irrational attraction to Tatiana Sarkisian, "the dusky beauty in the sable coat" I mean really, but when she uttered that immortal line, "You little shithead, Chilton! Play games with me, and I'll break you like a dry bone" I had to chuckle. Other than that, this book is nothing more than frothy entertainment.

BOSTON AS IT IS

Bunko Lestrad
Editor of *The Police Blotter*
Boston, Massachusetts

The Family Jewels, a new mystery thriller just published by Iory Allison reads like an archeological dig of the Boston social stratum. The clear detailed prose paints a portrait of the city in vivid colors and the characters we meet promise to walk off the page and into our lives. The mysterious treasure hunt at the center of the story careens around the avenues and alleys leading us from shadows cast over hidden tombs to the absurd hilarity of the "Club Crazy".

My favorite character in the book is the socially savvy Cornelia Chilton who as the chair person of the Police Benevolent Society Ball gets free parking in front of Precinct 34, the now defunct South End Station. Will the perfect crimes committed by Cornelia's ancestors and family be discovered after the smooth maneuvering by her Uncle, the powerful lawyer, Eben Chichester? This officer of the law wouldn't dare stir up the ashes.

THE LAST WORD

Shirley Slurp
Avid Reader for
Silos and Commoner
On line hawker of excessive literary output

I know a good book when I read one and this gem is one ada best! The powerful explosive prose flows like lava from a volcano, irresistible! I couldn't escape being swept away by the fast pace excitement of the story. And who knew all that stuff about creepy Egyptian tombs and spooky heathen gods such as Anubis? Watch out world. Here comes "Family Jewels".

CHAPTER 1

▼

The young antiquarian from an old Boston family and his sister had just inherited their aunt's Back Bay town house. As they walked through the home they felt the sorrow and excitement of new heirs and they reminisced about their childhood days in this antiquated residence where nothing had changed for years. Upstairs in a shuttered bedroom, an ornately enameled chest lured them by its barbaric splendor, and they were compelled to open it. Inside they found a key.

Old houses collect all manner of objects as generations pass. Why were these things brought together, by whom and for what purpose? These are the mysteries that linger after death and ignite passions in the living who may not know the true meaning of their inheritance.

*   *   *   *

A tall thin man arrived by cab at 138 Newbury Street in Boston's Back Bay. He carelessly flung a black cashmere overcoat over his broad shoulders. Around his neck was draped a flowing white silk scarf. Hesitating a moment on the sidewalk, he looked up to admire the newly steamed limestone façade of his building. At the street level the empty shop windows stared hungrily at the man whose thoughts were crammed full of antique furniture.

Just then, the streetlamp shuddered from a blast of cold wind. The light dimmed struggling against the darkness, and somewhere in the neighborhood a dog howled sounding like a jackal in the desert.

The man remembered having seen somewhere a monstrous half human, half canine demon of an ancient god. As if to bind that menacing vision inside him, the tempestuous wind tossed the white scarf over his face. As he unwound it he thought of mummy bandages unraveling to reveal a desiccated corpse. Disturbed by this image he checked his reflection in the shop window glass. But all he saw was his own familiar self.

The wavering light cast contrasting shadows on his sculpted face making the deepset eyes look mask-like beneath thick brows separated by an aquiline nose. He slowly revolved his head, inspecting his clean-shaven jaw that was distinguished by a deep cleft in his square chin. He stroked his newly clipped mustache and smoothed his black curly hair back in place.

Inserting a new latchkey into the lock of the shop door he leaned against its weight and eased it open slowly. Inside, a bluish half-light filtered through the large plate glass windows, bathing the space in a monochromatic gloom.

The center of this cavernous room was dominated by a carved and gilded Baroque table with a marble top. Behind the table was a tall Chinese screen of nine panels.

The heels of his man's patent leather shoes made hollow noises as he walked across the faux-marble floor. Suddenly the quiet of the shop was disturbed by the ringing of a telephone. The man's eyebrows arched with surprise as he went to his desk behind the Chinese screen.

"Hello, Chilton's Antiques and Interiors. This is Gyles speaking." He recited his rehearsed but untried line, even though at this late hour it was unlikely to be a customer calling.

Gyles had arranged to meet his sister Cornelia at their shop before they went to the Dynasty Ball. He had been away for most of the month on his annual buying trip to England. Now, home again, he was excited to picture how the new space would look when filled with his antiques. He had also made this arrangement to give himself something to do while he waited for Cornelia.

Patience was an indulgence he was more than willing to afford her because he knew that their collaboration would be profitable on many levels. Gyles could trust Cornelia's abilities as an interior designer because she had already been tempered in the fire of China Trade Interiors. That venerable Boston firm was synonymous with taste and discernment catering to a demanding clientele who were used to sparing no expense when thinking of themselves.

Gyles had been pleasantly surprised by the complementary direction their individual tastes had led them in the past few years. But, after he thought about this, he ascribed these similarities to their shared childhood in Aunt Florence's townhouse in Back Bay. Even more subtly they possessed a family sensibility, for their entrenched clan had long enjoyed the leisure to cultivate artistic interests.

"Gyles, thank the Goddess you're there."

"Oh hi, Cornelia, the phone startled me. I didn't even know we had it in yet. Were you here when it was installed?"

"Gyles!" the voice interrupted with unquestionable command, "My scarabs have disappeared—vanished—evaporated. What am I to do? We are due at the Dynasty Ball in an hour! I can't be late. I've slaved on the planning committee for the last three months, and I'm supposed to be there now!" Cornelia spoke on the phone from her cluttered bedroom where she paced back and forth madly gesticulating as if she had an audience. "I'm going to kill myself. I'll jump out the window—" Towards that portal she lunged, but stopped short. "No, I can't do that. I'm on the first floor and all I'd do is run my nylons." She plopped herself onto the pouf before her dressing table with resigned chagrin.

"Oh my Goddess, Monique Lafarge is going as Alexis Colby, and you know what kind of a fabulous gown she'll have on. All month long she's been making comments about real women, as if that stoned queen would know a real woman if she fell over one. So I said, 'Real? You want real, Monique? I'll give you real.'" Cornelia wagged an aggressive finger at the absent Monique.

"That's when I thought of going as Cleopatra. It was Aunt Florence's necklace and tiara that gave me the idea. You know, the ones we found in the safety deposit box?" Cornelia changed the phone to her other ear in order to touch up her makeup. "Gyles, those are solid chunks of lapis lazuli," furiously dusting her cheeks with a mink brush, "and they look as if they've been soaked in embalming fluid. They must be ancient."

Talking with his sister Cornelia, Gyles was sometimes amused, often stimulated, but frequently mystified. However, he occupied himself pleasantly by thumbing through the new Sotheby's catalogue.

"By the way, can you believe it? Rita actually wanted me to declare them to the IRS!" Cornelia finally got down to the arduous task of sorting through the heaps of objects that weighted down every surface of her bedroom. While she sorted, she continued, "I told her, 'Forget it, gorgeous, that safety deposit box was in my name, and no one would ever know that the old dear had stashed the loot there.'" Coming across a rhinestone bracelet, Cornelia held it up to the light, idly admiring its sparkle without interrupting herself. "I didn't know myself! Well, Rita nearly had an apoplectic fit. You know, ever since she got her CPA, she's become so proper. It's a good thing we don't live together or it would be instant divorce. Then she said that she wouldn't go to the ball if I wore 'those gems.'" Cornelia mugged a haughty face at herself in the mirror. "Quaint phrase, don't you think?"

Gyles smiled to himself at the picture of Rita, his sister's lover, fuming over the jewelry. The two women had an intense and devoted relationship. He acknowledged her bit of mischief with a noncommittal "Uh huh," but otherwise he did not comment. Long ago he had learned not to involve himself too deeply in Cornelia's monologues, which could ramble on at an alarming rate. And on she did ramble.

"What a relief that was, because I didn't quite know how to tell her that the Dynasty Ball was going to be so outrageous. I mean, Rita is the soul of social conscience, and the AIDS Action Committee is very important to her, but you know, I don't think she could politically tolerate being in a room where hundreds of men dressed as Alexis Colby and Krystle Carrington tear each other to shreds.

"So here I am in what every woman would die for—an original Fortuny pleated silk sheath." Cornelia luxuriated in saying these words, stringing them out as she stroked her sensuous dress. "But Gyles, it's so dull without those scarabs," here she pouted for emphasis, "and without that tiara I look like Whoopi Goldberg, which I can thank Charles for, since he insisted that the latest word in Egyptian hairdos was ten thousand little braids strung with faience beads." She strummed the line of beaded braids as she spoke. "All very well for Whoopi, who has a lot more body to her hair. For me, it's like having a volleyball at the end of a rope, and every time I turn my head I get slapped in the face with these blasted beads. Coming home from Newbury Street this afternoon someone called my name from a passing car. Well, naturally I turned quickly to see who it was and bop, I nearly blinded myself." She squeezed her eyes shut and shivered with the memory of the pain. "I know that male hair dressers are supposed to harbor seething resentments against their female clients, but really this is too much."

Having dug through the sediments encumbering her bureau down to Paleolithic revelations, Cornelia finally hit pay dirt.

"Gyles, the scarabs, I found them! Right here underneath my *Casa Vogue*, and a few other items. I'm in ecstasy—"

"You're what? You've taken ecstasy! Cornelia, we're supposed to go to the Dynasty Ball. No wonder you can't find your jewelry," Gyles despaired.

"I didn't take ecstasy. I'm in ecstasy."

"Oh! Well, I hope you can handle it."

"You ninny. Just watch what I can handle. I'll be over in seventeen minutes. Ciao, amore." Click.

With a gentle sigh, Gyles replaced the receiver on its cradle. He knew that Cornelia would eventually find the missing jewelry, but because she subscribed to the never-throw-anything-out method of disorganization, it might be a lengthy task. Meanwhile, he made some notes in the margins of the auction catalogue and had consequently developed a serious lust for a silver wine cooler of the Louis XVI period.

*   *   *   *

Gyles grew restless as Cornelia's allotted seventeen minutes stretched beyond three-quarters of an hour. He sat at his mahogany desk, a brass lamp spotlighting only a small patch beneath its green glass shade. He looked about the dimly lit shop, imagining where he would place his antiques coming from England next week. He stood up and paced, stopping in front of an Edwardian dressing mirror, where he adjusted his black bow tie. He was startled to see an eerie ectoplasmic form emerge from within the wiggly old glass. With apprehension, he spun round on his thin-soled shoes, and sure enough, gliding silently towards him was an apparition that spoke in a wavering voice.

"I am Isis, Queen of the Underworld."

"Jesus Christ, Cornelia. You nearly scared me to death sneaking around here like a cat burglar. I didn't even hear you come in." He interrupted himself with a catcall whistle. "When you said real woman, you certainly meant it. Where'd you get that dress? And you're right, the tiara is perfect—the necklace—the hair—all those braids—Elizabeth Taylor's rendition of Cleopatra looks like a Kewpie doll beside you."

Cornelia stood beaming with pleasure, absorbing Gyles's astonished praise with the quiet dignity of a princess receiving tribute. The Fortuny sheath fit her like a second skin, beneath which could be seen every nuance of her body, from her pert breasts to her dimpled buttocks down tapering calves to tiny ankles. On her feet she wore delicate sandals, and her nails were painted salmon pink. Any slight movement of her head set in motion the myriad beaded braids, which made a rippling noise. Round her head was a tiara of gold mounted with lapis lazuli scarabs. In the center of her forehead a hooded cobra reared its bejeweled head, diamond eyes staring with scorn at a world doomed to decay.

"I found the dress in Great-aunt Florence's trunk room, although I don't think it belonged to her. It's an original Fortuny. It was carefully packed inside the most elegant Hermès suitcase, pasted with labels from Shepheards Hotel in Cairo. Too fantastic! When we came across the Egyptian jewelry in the safety deposit box, I thought it was natural to put them together."

"Well, it certainly makes a complete ensemble. However, it looks as though it might slide right off you. Is that dress anchored in any way?"

"Not really, that's the beauty of Fortuny. He invented the secret process of pleating the silk so it hugs the body."

"You better hope that it hugs your tits a little tighter than it's doing right now, or you'll end up the Minoan Flasher. No wonder you were relieved that Rita wasn't going to the ball. I seem to recall she has a slight problem with possessiveness."

"Oh, you're just jealous, Gyles."

"By the way, what were you doing rifling the goods at Great-aunt Florence's? I thought we agreed we'd wait until Lucy Ann was settled in her new place before disturbing anything there. You know, Cornelia, I don't want to upset her. She's not used to change, and she's been tending to that house all her life."

"Will you stop? That's all very sweet and considerate of you, but she asked me."

Gyles cast a doubtful look at his sister knowing that it would get her goat and delighted that he knew exactly how to do this without saying a word.

"That's right, Gyles, so don't look at me that way. I am not a conniving female. Lucy Ann called me up last week because she needed help in deciding about her suitcases. I went over to help and we went through the trunk room. In the process of finding her some appropriate cases, we came across this dress. I also found this perfectly marvelous topper and I brought it along especially for you." Cornelia retrieved an impeccable silk top hat from the floor where her coat lay, and handed it to Gyles.

"Well, thank you, little sister, it's just what I needed. I'm glad you found your designer original. It suits you. And better you should be wearing it than it being locked in an old suitcase."

As he said this conciliatory line, Gyles was closely examining her, intrigued to find his own familiar sister underneath the Egyptianesque makeup. Her eyes were ringed with pharaonic kohl, the lids dusted a greenish blue, which brought out her remarkable green eyes. Her braided hair just brushed the bottom of her delicate jaw, covering her ears and showing to advantage her long neck.

With as much nonchalance as he could muster, Gyles asked, "So, uh, what happened to the Hermès bag?"

"Oh Gyles, you're too much. And I'm such a fool. Here I am thinking that you were gazing with wonder deep into my eyes, but all this time you're thinking of the dusty piles in the attic. Listen, sweetheart, you've got antique-itis. Come on, let's go to the ball and see if we can't find a handsome stranger to pluck your heart strings."

While Cornelia was speaking, she picked up her coat from the floor where she had shed it and slipped into its furry depths.

"Cornelia, you look like an Erté showgirl in that old mink."

"Well thank you, Gyles. You look rather like Ramón Novarro in a Noël Coward play."

"Ramón Novarro was never in a Noël Coward play."

"Oh pipe down, handsome, and take my arm. These sandals will be the death of me."

Sometimes we say in jest what may prove to be, in part, an awful truth.

CHAPTER 2

▼

Cornelia and Gyles left their shop, walking arm in arm down Newbury Street. A phantom double followed them, reflecting in the polished glass of the fashionable shop windows. They made an exotic pair, the Egyptian princess in mink and her dashing escort in top hat, white tie, and tails.

After walking two blocks Gyles asked, "Corny, where on earth did you park?"

"At the Ritz of course. George juggles my M.G. around and I give him ten bucks."

Another half a block and they achieved that El Dorado of elegant addresses, the Ritz Hotel. They were greeted by a smartly uniformed doorman, who waved a leisurely salute to the couple. Cornelia replied with what Gyles thought to be overbubbly cheer. "Hi, George. May I have my M.G. please?"

"Sure thing, Miss Chilton, coming right up." With screeching speed Cornelia's convertible M.G. was brought to a rocking halt at the Newbury Street entrance to the hotel. The parking attendant hopped out, and Cornelia hopped in. Gyles folded himself into the sports car and George closed the door quietly behind him. Cornelia distributed largesse all around and spun away from the curb, zipping down the stylish street, where couturier boutiques and art galleries were evenly spaced between chic hairdressing salons. They passed crowds of beautiful people strolling the broad sidewalks and window shopping.

"Cornelia, isn't that a rather extravagant method of parking this windup toy?" asked Gyles, holding on to his black silk top hat in the blustering night air.

"It sure beats paying seventy-five-dollar tickets for parking in handicapped spaces. You know, Gyles, I'm all for minorities, but I think it's only fair that there should be stickers awarded to specially challenged car owners who have failed to find legal parking for one year or more. Hell, I'll be willing to pay a reasonable fee for the privilege. After all, George is not available everywhere I go."

"Very creative, Cornelia," was Gyles's dry reply.

The M.G. covered the short distance to Boston's South End in a flash. There, much to Gyles's horror, his sister aimed right for and nestled between two police cruisers in front of Division 4 headquarters.

"Well, here we are," she chirped, switching off the motor and swinging open her door, which banged into the cruiser parked beside her.

"Oops! Oh well, they're all so butch here, they'll never notice a tiny little scratch."

"Cornelia! You can't park here!"

"That's where you're wrong, hot stuff. I can't park anywhere else. Look around you."

She made a broad gesture towards the surrounding neighborhood, a marginal area crowded with every imaginable conveyance, all converging upon the Cyclorama auditorium, where the Dynasty Ball was being held.

"Now don't fret, brother dearest. I know all the boys at Division 4, and they wouldn't dream of having me park anywhere else."

"Sounds a little suspicious, Cornelia. Since when have you been cavorting with the constabulary on such a chummy basis?"

"Oh Gyles, where have you been? Don't you remember, last month I was the honorary chairwoman at the Police Retirement Fund Ball? Why do you suppose I do those things?"

"Perhaps you were looking for a butch girlfriend," suggested Gyles.

Cornelia sailed on. "I mean really, someone has to cash in on the absurd burden of toting around a Mayflower name. After all, why else did Obadiah and Naomi Chilton languish in the belly of that barge for so long?"

"Naomi and Obadiah Chilton sailed in the Mayflower in 1620 in order to get you a parking space at the police station?"

"Well, there have to be some benefits." Cornelia slipped a blue cardboard sign underneath her windshield wiper. It read: "Police No. 45." She commandeered her brother's stabilizing arm and marched with him around the corner to the ball.

People were arriving at the ornate kiosk that stood in the small square in front of the auditorium. There were several long, black limousines purring at the curb. Two uniformed chauffeurs were trying their best to look bored with the crowds. A highly polished black Packard eased into a reserved parking space. Immediately a crowd formed, shamelessly gawking at this glamorous arrival. Cornelia and Gyles joined them.

From the driver's seat of the Packard hopped out an immaculately uniformed chauffeur. He wore shiny black riding boots, dove gray jodhpurs accentuating massive thighs, and a double-breasted jacket struggling to contain bulging shoulders. He moved like a panther, fluidly graceful and dangerous. His massive hand took hold of the chromium handle of the rear door and opened it with studied slow motion.

The crowd recoiled from the car with what would have been a gasp had not all audio perception been eclipsed by the deafening wails of Donna Summer declaring, "I'm your Venus, I'm your fire," blasting forth from the quadraphonic sound system in the limousine. Following this alarming disturbance came almost visible waves of Chanel No. 5 perfume, which made several of the spectators cough.

There emerged one, and then two of the most curvaceous gams this side of Radio City Music Hall, sporting black seamed stockings and a pair of silver spiked heels. The appearance of these mysterious limbs inspired lewd whistles and catcalls in a crescendoing chorus that climaxed with thundering applause and commands of "more, more." The chauffeur extended a Herculean paw, which was grasped by a black-gloved hand encircled with numerous rhinestone bracelets. As if catapulted into action, Monique Lafarge fairly sprang from the automobile. Ice Queen of the Arctic, she froze her audience with astonishment.

From his breast pocket Gyles withdrew his cigarette case, offered a cigarette to Cornelia, who refused, and lit his own with a vintage Cartier lighter. He was wondering silently why all drag queens are six feet tall or over. Monique Lafarge, who did all things in a big way, had added four inches to her towering appearance with the aforementioned pumps, in which she was prancing about the curb striking poses, first against the limo, then mauling her chauffeur.

Blue smoke from his Sobranie cigarette encircled Gyles's head. He contemplated Monique with a wry smile. He had to admit that she was a stunner. Like all showgirls, she had an artificial beauty, a mask of the night that was calculated to dazzle. Her scarlet lips, so delicately shaped against blue-white skin and glistening porcelain teeth, were held in a perpetual smile, as if she had just been handed the Miss America crown. A cascade of auburn hair swung about her head in heavy waves when she moved, and above her high cheekbones dark eyes brazenly scrutinized the world as if it were all a contemptible joke.

Monique interrupted her acrobatic fanfare long enough to saunter up to Gyles and Cornelia. She towered in front of them, slowly gyrating, her gloved hands resting on her hips. She plucked the cigarette from Gyles's lips and let it fall on the pavement, where she ground the butt beneath her shoe and softly purred in a contralto drawl, "Don't you know smoking will stunt your growth, handsome?"

"I wanted to see if you'd notice," Gyles replied. Cornelia sighed deeply, raising her left eyebrow.

"You'd be hard to miss with this gorgeous broad at your side," growled Monique.

"Who's been writing your lines, Monique? Damon Runyon?" asked Cornelia in her most casual tone.

Monique's eyes half-closed, like those of a cat not sure what to do with its mouse. Again she purred, "Well girlfriend, I've got to hand it to you. You've got real furs, real jewels, real tits, and a real man."

"Monique, this is my brother."

"Yes, yes, I read about you Egyptian queens. Very kinky. Brother/sister, father/daughter, very cozy, girlfriend." Monique's tones were dripping with innuendo. Cornelia let all this slide by and with a slightly resigned grimace said, "Well, Monique, you're looking dazzling this evening. Who's the gorilla in the knee britches?"

"Jodhpurs, darling, and the name is Butch."

"That's original. Is he?"

"Not really. He wears black lace panties, and yesterday I caught him slipping out of one of my negligées."

"Well, at least he looks the part, and it's so important to keep up appearances, as you well know," Cornelia lectured cheerfully.

Monique gazed silently at Cornelia, her eyes glowering behind a black veil of mascaraed lashes. Just at this moment Butch glided over. He took Monique in his arms in a tangolike dip. Sweeping her off her feet, he marched towards the front door, Monique easily cradled in his arms. Her red-sequined sheath fell open, exposing the incredible length of her fabulous legs.

"Such a pretty girl, and they seem to be a perfect match," Cornelia mimicked with Junior League locked-jaw drawl.

Gyles exploded with rare, unguarded laughter and said, "Come along, Vera Viper. Forward into battle." And off they marched, arm in arm.

CHAPTER 3

▼

At the front door of the Cyclorama two flatbed trucks were mounted with enormous klieg lights. Their blinding columns pierced the starless city night. Around these beacons of glamour hovered the arriving crowds.

Gyles and Cornelia merged with the revelers who were squeezing through the double doors. They slowly climbed the stairs toward the enormous domed auditorium that had once housed the Boston Flower Market but now was used for flea markets and the less staid events of Boston nightlife, such as the serio-comic Dynasty Ball. Gyles surveyed the crowd around him. His eyes were irresistibly held by a scarlet-clad Lucifer with a long, provocative tail sprouting from the most perfectly formed muscular buttocks the Metropolitan Gym had ever produced. This demonic appendage was neatly tucked between its owner's legs, the serpentine length emerging before him. He held his tail's spaded head, and playfully, almost absentmindedly, bludgeoned his companion before him on the stairs. The companion, a gladiatorial hunk in full football regalia, gazed with besotted submission at his handsome devil.

Many of the men and women wore black tie and tuxedos, and a few wore white tie and tails. Amongst them was an androgynous beauty who wore a tailcoat of black sequins with rhinestone buttons. The Beauty's platinum blond hair was swept back from an angular face on whose upper lip was painted a thin mustache. As Gyles was puzzling over what sex this provocative darling might be, their eyes met. Gyles gave a silent nod of admiration and received a flirtatious wink in return.

There was of course a bearded nun, who kept drawling, "Oh Mary, oh Mary" while genuflecting, a performance that made forward progress sluggish. But the crowd accepted this with good grace as a necessary benediction along the pilgrimage of the absurd, on which gay people have an intimate perspective.

The Holy Mother was surrounded by a gaggle of leather queens, whose flesh was ferociously encased in black leather and bound with innumerable chains. Here and there the slashed leather coyly revealed an inch or two of pallid skin textured by neglected stubble. Their collective demeanor was scowling menace, an attitude completely eclipsed by the antics of a gender fuck drag queen wearing naught but a black corset stuffed with balloon tits, and a garter belt supporting fishnet stockings over hairy legs. He had a face painted like a cartoon Lucy, with fire engine red lips, eyelashes like the prongs of a garden rake, a Bozo the Clown wig, plus a bushy red beard liberally sprinkled with red glitter. This personage had already been partying long and hard as evidenced by his inability to balance on his roller blades. He was, however, amidst hysterical screams and general pandemonium, ascending the stairs by the determined effort of the crowd around him. They thrust him forward with helpful shoves and an occasional grab at his bulging black lace crotch. This latter encouragement magically levitated him a step or two at a time to the accompaniment of ariatic screeches.

Gyles turned to Cornelia and with feigned candor inquired, "Cornelia, wasn't that Butter Brickle, the famed gay Olympian?"

"No Gyles, that was Betty the Bounder on a prolonged binge, a dreary routine that has lasted the better part of a decade, but people put up with her because you know what makes a legend most."

"Her mink?"

"Wrong again. Her stink. Betty works at Filene's Basement in cosmetics, and she can always be counted on for free samples of leftover perfume."

"Oh I see," replied Gyles in a complete deadpan. "I should have known she was in the world of fashion. It's so influential, and she certainly has many eager supporters."

"Yes, you have to keep Betty on her toes, otherwise you might be inadvertently crushed."

By this time Gyles and Cornelia had reached the top of the stairs and were confronted by a welcoming committee composed of a natty Joel Grey-type maitre d' in white tie drag and painted mustache, who clicked her heels and snapped a "Velcome to zee Dynasty Ball," while all around cameras popped and clicked. They were passed on to a matronly dowager with trembling jowls and masses of sparkling rhinestones cascading over her bosom like a frozen Niagara Falls. In a tremulous voice she uttered the enigmatic greeting, "Think happy thoughts, my children, think happy thoughts," to the accompaniment of more flashing cameras. Cornelia, ever mindful of her opportunities, donned her sweetest expression of amused enthusiasm and surprise. Gyles stood by Cornelia, his immaculate black evening clothes a perfect foil to her pretty brilliance.

"Gyles, I'm going to the girls' room to freshen up. Will you check my coat?"

"Sure, I'll meet you at the bar." Gyles stood patiently in line holding Cornelia's vintage mink, which he could now see had a much mended lining, a rather limp fur.

"Good evening, my dearest boy, you're looking splendid but remarkably staid." Gyles looked up from the coat and saw a Chinese Mandarin in a dragon robe of aubergine-colored silk, richly embroidered with bright colors and gold thread. Around his neck were long ropes of jade and cloisonné beads and on his head a black hat with an upturned scarlet brim. Across his eyes was a plain black satin mask, and on his upper lip was glued a mustache with long, drooping ends. Gyles was amazed at this apparition, as he immediately recognized that all the component parts of this costume were of great quality and value.

"My dear boy, what can Cornelia mean by wafting about half-naked with all those expensive jewels on, and in this of all places? Anything could happen." Gyles recognized the voice as belonging to his uncle, Wisner Chilton, who, although well into his seventies, still got about quite a bit.

"Wisner, what a vision you are. Positively royal, or I should say, imperial."

"Never mind me, darling child, it is Cornelia I'm concerned about," Wisner replied, although while he dismissed Gyles's compliments a certain flutter rippled through him, like a cosseted cat luxuriating in a lap. "This is hardly the place for her to be risking life and limb displaying family jewels. Look around you, dear boy. Does this look like polite society to you?"

At that very moment a seven-foot-tall hard-on shuffled by, sporting a clown face painted beneath an enormous mushroom-shaped head, from which flowed streamers of silver Mylar. This helpful citizen was promoting safe sex by distributing condoms.

"Wisner, I think your evaluation of this crowd is a little harsh. After all, you're here, aren't you? That must add some tone to the proceedings. And while we're at it, what do you mean by family jewels?" Gyles picked up on this detail, confident that where the Egyptian crown had come from was known only to Cornelia and himself. It was all he could do to keep his acquisitive Uncle Wisner at arm's length and away from Great-aunt Florence's house in Back Bay, which Gyles and his sister had so recently inherited.

"Don't be ridiculous, I mean the jewels Cornelia is wearing are family heirlooms that came from 283 Commonwealth. You forget, dearest child, that I know a great deal by virtue of having survived the vicissitudes of life's drama."

During this last regal speech, Gyles had reached the head of the line. He checked the coats with the stylish character wearing a huge brimmed hat with a mysterious veil encircling her face. Having overheard Wisner's rather heated retort, she sympathized, "Dish, dish, dish," rolling elaborately made-up eyes, and added with overcasual disinterest, "Dump Charley Chan, honey. Let's go and boogie." Gyles was distracted from following up on this invitation by violent tugs on his sleeve.

"Would you please pay attention, this is important!" Wisner insisted, thrusting his diminutive self between Gyles and the veiled hatcheck girl. She dismissed Wisner's sputterings with a wave of her hand as if to brush away a fly and said to Gyles above Wisner's head, "Honey, these queens will do anything for attention." On the counter she snapped down a red plastic chip printed with black numbers. While examining her perfect manicure, she muttered, "Looks like the winning number to me, sweetheart. Come back after the dance and claim your prize."

"Wisner, I think we could both use a drink. Let's mosey up to the bar, where Cornelia will undoubtedly find us, and you can register your complaints directly with her."

"Young man, if that is a hint that I should be paying for your cocktails, I'm having none of it."

"Well that's gracious of you, Uncle, but no, I wouldn't dream of depleting your dusty coffers. You must be my guest and tell me all about this beautiful costume you're wearing."

"Oh I see, trying to ply me with liquor in hopes of purloining my mandarin robe. Well I wasn't born yesterday."

"That much is evident, but I won't hold it against you. Now come along and stop being such a fussbudget."

Wisner glared at Gyles but allowed himself to be gently herded towards the bar. However, navigating the sea of humanity that surged through the entrance of the domed rotunda was a perilous venture. For a while they had to drift with the currents that brought them towards the dance floor at the center of the hall.

CHAPTER 4

▼

Wisner and Gyles bobbed along with the jostling crowd. They were drawn irresistibly towards the dance floor of the Cyclorama, where all manner of beings gyrated with hysterical glee to the practically visible hammerings of a punk heavy metal band. The musicians were blasting forth from a stage constructed of building scaffolding draped with black plastic. The band members, five serious wymin, were climaxing their serenade by crescendoing from outrage to raw rage. One of their members was indulging in a reenactment of Jimi Hendrix's nihilistic farewell to his guitar, causing a flurry of panic as jagged bits of laminated instrument flew into the crowd.

Suddenly the other end of the hall was ignited in a blaze of light, which, in a more reverent age, would have been reserved for the appearance of Apollo. A grand sweeping staircase had been constructed there. Its uppermost balustrades terminated in a curtain of fringed silver Mylar reflecting the blinding lights focused on it.

From behind this shinning curtain the hostess with the mostest made her entrance.

She had been sewn into a silver lamé gown entirely covered with rhinestones. The effect was as if the Hope Diamond had gone cancerous and threatened to expand beyond the continent.

Lilly, as our gracious headliner was known, slowly spread forth her arms and opened her mouth wide in a gesture reminiscent of King Kong yawning. She mimed her way into the song "I Am What I Am, I Am My Own Special Creation" from La Cage aux Folles.

Simultaneously an army of dancers tangoed out from behind the shining curtain at the bottom of the gigantic staircase. Their identical half-man half-woman costumes were flawlessly executed in black sequins and blazing rhinestones.

This fanfare brought down the house, and the crowd joined in the rollicking chorus, proudly proclaiming, "I am what I am, and what I am needs no excuses."

"It's amazing how much delight an old drag queen and a little glitter can produce," Gyles said to Wisner.

"Oh, isn't she beautiful?" Wisner's hands were clasped, pressing the area on his upper chest where presumably an ancient heart lurked. "I saw Lilly at her debut, you know."

"Was that at the court of Agamemnon?" asked Gyles.

"No, it was at the Punch Bowl in Bay Village, which has tragically been demolished. She was performing that immortal ballad 'You Can't Get a Man with a Gun.' Ah, those were the days! But look, here she comes!"

The accuracy of this statement could not be denied as towards them steamed the resplendent Lilly. The crowd, who had resumed dancing, parted like the proverbial Red Sea, and she, not unlike the patriarch of old, led her tribe of half and half dancers toward the Promised Land at the bar.

"Oh Lilly, you-hoo, Lilly, it's Wizzy, over here, darling Diva…" Wisner projected a surprisingly penetrating falsetto warble, which reached the performer's ears like a puzzling echo. She searched her immediate vicinity with a myopic squint, attempting to discover the source of the vaguely familiar voice. "Lilly, here I am." At this point the grand dame had all but trampled Wisner, who had foolishly shoved his way directly into her path.

"Ah…ah…I hear voices."

"Lilly, damn it, down here!" Wisner stamped his foot to emphasize his position.

"Oh there you are, Wizzy, you charming little lump." She pecked the air three feet above his head with kissing noises.

"Diva, you were glorious!" replied Wisner in his most theatrical tones. "Lilly, I want you to meet my nephew, Gyles Chilton." Wisner lunged back into the crowd, got hold of Gyles's hand and hauled him forward for presentation. Lilly had increased her ample proportions with the aid of sturdy platform pumps easily capable of supporting the Mystic River Bridge, and from her lofty vantage point she inspected Gyles with keen interest.

"Ah Wizzy, this is your…ah…nephew?" She directed this question somewhat vaguely towards her feet. "And such a handsome boy he is." She continued to give Gyles the once-over.

"I liked the show, Lilly. You certainly were swell. Uncle Wisner was just telling me of your illustrious past."

"Oh?"

"Yes, he was saying how much he enjoyed your rendition of Annie Oakley."

"Oh my." This latter comment was uttered with a decidedly deflated tone. "Darling, that's ancient history. Let's talk about you," and here she gave Gyles an alluring gaze, which may also have been a small attack of epilepsy.

With his impeccable timing, Wisner grasped them both by the arm and directed them to the bar, saying, "Gyles, dearest child, has just invited me for cocktails. I'm sure he'd be honored if you would join us."

"Well yes, I think I could use the tiniest little drinky poo. Darling, how sweet of you."

Lilly fluttered her eyelashes at Gyles, who laughed and said, "By the time we get to that bar, we're all going to need doubles." The procession swept onward, followed by shuffling and giggling chorines.

The arrival of Lilly's entourage at the bar was like a caravan descending upon the last desert oasis. The principals and chorus elbowed their way forward. A grateful coterie of fans extended their hospitality, so that in the end every one of the girls, including Gyles and Wisner, had been bought drinks.

Gyles sipped his bourbon Manhattan and drew deeply on his Sobranie cigarette as he listened to the frothy chitchat of the chorines. One of them, a particularly shapely and muscular beauty, was poised in an alluring slouch, talking with Wisner while brazenly stealing glances at Gyles. Intrigued, Gyles raised his glass in a silent toast. Aware of the youth's divided attentions, Wisner instantly surrendered the modicum of interest his companion afforded him by turning on his heels towards the bar and demanding another drink.

Without visible regret, the demi-gendered chorine sauntered up to Gyles and announced in a pleasant baritone, "Hi, I'm Mona."

"Hi, Mona, I'm Gyles."

After these uninspired introductions, the two were at a loss for words. Because their smiles said so much, they resorted to sipping their cocktails and staring at each other. For Gyles this moment stretched into eternity as he squirmed with delight and tried desperately not to show it. Finally, he hit upon the brilliant idea of complimenting Mona on the production number.

"Gee, your performance was spectacular!"

"Oh, did you like it?" Mona launched into an impromptu encore: "I bang my own drum, some think it's noise, I think it's pretty…"

"I'm sure you do, but I'm surprised that you so readily admit it." Gyles teased Mona with lewd implication.

"No, it's a line from the song, you dope," and Mona slapped Gyles playfully with his feather boa.

"Well, whatever, I sure liked watching you." As Gyles listened to his own excited voice, he thought it might be time for another Manhattan.

"Well aren't we direct?" Mona drawled.

"There's one life and there's no return and no deposit, one life so it's time to open up your closet," Gyles quoted.

"Honey, as you can see, my closet door was blown away by a typhoon years ago."

Gyles laughed and offered to buy them another round of cocktails.

"Thanks, hot stuff, I'll have a sidecar."

"How deco," exclaimed Gyles approvingly. He deftly maneuvered himself through the crush at the bar and ordered the drinks. He was inordinately proud when he delivered Mona's sidecar without spilling a drop.

"My hero!" Mona enthused. Holding the glass by its stem, the chorine knocked back the cocktail with one gulp and absently tossed the glass over his shoulder.

"Ouch! What the fuck!" Angry sputterings could be heard behind Mona. Gyles was so surprised he choked on his drink. There appeared between them a very short fellow with a very bald head, who wore Mona's cocktail glass on his polished pate. Otherwise he was dressed as a cowboy. Looking up at Mona, he inquired with icy hauteur, "Have you lost something, Miss Dipshit? Other than your brain?"

"Sorry, but I just hate to have my hands full at a party." Having made this simple apology, Mona plucked the offending glass off the fuming cowboy's head and handed it to Gyles. Gyles, still coughing, was further confused by violent tugs at his sleeve.

"Oh my God, she's been murdered!" Wisner's trembling squeal compelled Gyles to look, and he froze with disbelief at what he saw. Through the crowd came a towering giant, arms outstretched, cradling a lifeless Cornelia. Gyles was hit with the fear that Wisner was right. He lunged forward, gasping, but he stopped short and yelled out, "No!" The rock and roll stopped. The crowd was silent. Hundreds of eyes were on Cornelia, who hung limp in the arms of Monique Lafarge, four-inch heels and all.

CHAPTER 5

▼

As Cornelia regained consciousness an hour later, she was bewildered to find herself in Rita's apartment. She had a roaring headache, and around her voices sounded strangely distant.

"If I get my hands on the monster who did this, they're gonna wish their mother had strangled them at birth. What did they give her? She looks half dead."

"Monique says it was angel dust."

"I should have gone to the ball. I had a premonition something like this would happen to her and I was right. She certainly shouldn't have worn those gems. But instead of following my hunch, I let her get under my skin and then she got mugged. Of course she looks about as ferocious as Tinkerbell, so I guess she was an easy target. But really, Gyles, you were with her, how could you let this happen?"

"I wasn't with her in the ladies' room, Rita," Gyles retorted dryly.

"Why not? Half the queens of Boston were apparently, including this, this, Monique Lafarge, or whatever he calls himself."

"Look, Rita, Monique found Cornelia on the floor of the ladies' room, and carried her out of that hole, granted, somewhat overdramatically. It was Monique who suggested bringing Cornelia to your apartment, and Butch drove us here, so lighten up."

"Now I have to be thankful to that drag queen because he used my lover for a prop in his tawdry drama. I'm going to scream!"

"Okay, Rita, okay! I'm going to live. Headaches I've got already. Yelling I don't need."

"Cornelia!" Everybody turned with surprise and stared at the waif lying on the couch. Rita reacted first. With complete change of tone, she fussed over her lover like a mother hen. As there was nothing else anyone could do, they all settled into various chairs around the room, their concern rapidly developing into curiosity as they saw Cornelia regain her color and resume normal breathing.

"Well, young lady, perhaps you can restrain yourself from cooing over my niece long enough for her to relate the details of this tragedy so that we might recover the missing property." Uncle Wisner could always be counted on to utter the least wanted suggestions prompting Rita to glare at him with threatening malice, which shut him up momentarily. Cornelia sat up and propped herself on pillows before she could say anything further. Rita's overprotective interruptions were shushed by exasperated sighs all around, and when she was finally quiet and seated next to her lover Cornelia resumed her story.

"I had been talking with Betty the Bounder, or I should say, she was talking at me, because of course Betty doesn't listen to a thing anyone says, including herself. But while Betty was rattling on and on, sliding all over the place on those lethal skates, she said that there had been a very classy dame, are you ready, wrapped in sable who was asking all about me, or about my jewelry, and wanted to meet me. Naturally I was intrigued. Then, as if on cue, a beautiful, foreign-looking woman joined us from where she had been standing at the bar. Her magnificent sable coat was draped about her shoulders. Betty took that opportunity to collapse on the floor in a thrashing heap. Tatiana took my arm and led me to safety at the other end of the bar, where she handed me a kir royale in a fluted glass. A conjuring feat that I was more than a little impressed with in those surroundings, but she seemed to know the bartender, whom she called Achmed. We chatted merrily along about jewelry, furs and fashion, and all that la la. She's married to a furrier from New York who is about to open a shop here on Newbury Street, and she's hunting for condos with Itzkan & Marchiel. Betty told her I was a decorator, and Tatiana invited me to look at the place she'd fallen in love with on the eighth floor of the Heritage Building overlooking the Public Garden. She said she felt an instant rapport with me because of my Egyptian interest and went on to explain that, although she was of Russian descent, she had grown up in Egypt during the last years of King Farouk's reign. Her father had been furrier to the queen. Her Egyptian husband started his career working with her father. Well immediately I had visions of Egyptian Deco interiors with lots of custom work, so I was very attentive. And it never occurred to me to question what this woman was doing at the Dynasty Ball. When we'd finished our drinks, Tatiana suggested we go to freshen up in the ladies' room and smoke a joint. I was pleasantly surprised by the offer, and off we went. We barricaded ourselves in one of those ancient wooden booths, and she lit up. Tatiana went on and on about the new apartment while she kept the joint to herself for quite a while. She finally offered me some, and I took a hit and passed it back, but she waved me on and said, 'keep it.' She signaled that she was going to brush her hair and squeezed out of the booth. That was the last I saw of her. I took another hit and passed out."

"I suppose I will be castigated if I observe that it may not have been the most prudent of gestures to have accepted drugs from a perfect stranger." Wisner offered this unnecessary comment, which drew total silence from the company, because they were all thinking more or less the same thing and also remembering times they had smoked a joint with a total stranger. "You can see the result of this indiscretion was the loss of yet another family heirloom, but in a family quite used to squandering its resources, it is to be expected."

Monique rose from the low overstuffed chair where she had been sitting and towering over Wisner said, "Okay, Charlie Chan, let's go for a ride. I can drop you in the river on my way home. Or if you're real nice I can take you home and Butch can tuck you in and kiss you good night."

"You most certainly may not. I wouldn't dream of going anywhere with you."

"Pipe down and get out the door, chump," ordered Butch.

With gasps and sputterings, Monique herded Wisner out the door and as a parting gesture blew them all a kiss from her gloved hand. "Hope you feel better, Corny. See you around the steam room, Rita." She took her chauffeur's arm and sauntered out.

"Gyles, why did you tell Wisner about Aunt Florence's jewelry?" asked Cornelia.

"But I didn't," protested Gyles. "I'm as puzzled about that as you. He came up to me even before I could get my coat off, carrying on and on about the family jewels. I asked him then how he knew about them, and he slithered out of it saying he knew a great deal by virtue of having survived the vicissitudes of life's drama. Probably it was just a lucky guess or an oblique probe to discover what we'd found. You know he's furious that Aunt Florence didn't mention him in her will. He did, I think, work for Aunt Norma, but that was decades ago, and anyway I think Aunt Norma did what she could for him herself."

"Yes, and apparently that wasn't enough for Wisner," commented Cornelia.

"Well, what could she do, really? After the Crash she didn't have very much except for the house, and I think it was Aunt Florence's money really that kept them going."

"Yes," agreed Cornelia, "that must have been a bitter pill for the grand dame art collector Norma Chilton. I really don't know very much about their lives. I should've asked Aunt Florence more."

"You wouldn't have been any more the wiser. I did ask her, because I was very impressed by the enormity of Norma's bequests to the MFA. It seems every other object in the Egyptian collection has her name as donor. But Aunt Florence would only sigh and say, 'Yes, that was before the Crash and the Depression.'"

"Hey wait a minute," interrupted Rita, who had been quietly listening. "I know Florence was your aunt, and I gather Norma was also, but where exactly does she fit in?"

"Oh, sorry, Rita. Norma and Florence were sisters. They were really our great-aunts," explained Cornelia. "As you know, Aunt Florence brought us up at her house in Back Bay after Mummy and Daddy died. She was the sweetest old dear in the world. I was her favorite because when I was eleven she and I were the same height."

"What Cornelia is trying to say is that Great-aunt Florence was tiny," Gyles interjected, "probably only about five feet."

"Great-aunt Florence had the whitest hair and the bluest eyes in all of Boston," continued Cornelia. "Everyone loved her because she looked for the good in everybody."

"Norma was her older sister," Gyles took over the narrative. "She died before we were born but she was legendary in our family. She was tall, strong-featured and haughty, to judge by her portrait in the front hall of 283 Commonwealth Ave. She has the questionable distinction of having lost an enormous chunk of Chilton money in the Crash of '29."

"It is all rather sad when you think of it," Cornelia said wistfully.

"How the mighty fall, huh, Corny?" Gyles's tone was more than slightly sarcastic.

"I guess I am being silly. After all, we have the things that matter. I have Rita—"

"For better or for worse," muttered Rita, nuzzling closer.

"—and you, Gyles, have—oh, I'm sorry, what a dope I am."

"I have you, Cornelia, and we have our new showroom and we have the big white elephant on Commonwealth Avenue, and you never know what goodies will be unearthed there." After a brief pause Gyles said, "Well Corny, I've got to go," and he rose from his chair. "I'm sorry about your pretty baubles. I think you can kiss them good-bye forever, unless you run into Tatiana again."

"I wonder if she really had anything to do with that," mused Cornelia.

"Woman, you are a dope. If you have one particle of doubt that that bitch stole those gems while you were making goo-goo eyes at her exotic beauty…. She was setting you up," Rita fumed.

"Well Rita, you might be right, but she didn't get what she really wanted."

"What do you mean? Do you still think she was after your decorating expertise? Or a piece of your ass maybe, along with the loot?"

"No, I mean I have the jewelry."

"Cornelia, that angel dust has really softened your brain."

"No, wait a minute, Rita," interjected Gyles. "What are you saying, Corny?"

Cornelia straightened herself up and gave them a mischievous wink. "I mean, there were two sets of jewels. One was real and the other costume. As you know, Gyles, this is not completely uncommon where expensive and rare stones are concerned. It still goes on today. When I was helping Lucy Ann in the trunk room, we found two old Hermès cases. One contained the dress and the other one the costume jewels. These were the ones you saw me wearing tonight at the ball."

"But why didn't you say so then?"

"Well, I guess it was vanity. I was so set to knock 'em dead that I didn't want even you to know."

"You almost got knocked dead yourself," interjected Rita with contempt.

"I am perplexed by Tatiana," Cornelia continued. "What an elaborate hoax. She seems like the real thing, but I guess her story was too good to be true."

"Perhaps not all of it was a lie, or even any of it. Perhaps everything was true except for her own motive in meeting you. Or perhaps she was entirely innocent," suggested Gyles.

"Yeah, well, what about the killer dope then? You're both chumps if you believe that woman was anything more than a crook."

"But she smoked the same joint I did."

"No she didn't. She smoked her half, then she handed you the half with whatever poison she'd laced it with."

"Oh, I never thought of that."

"No, but I did as soon as you said it. Don't be so naive, Cornelia, that bitch played you for a sucker."

"Well, maybe you're right, Rita, but she didn't get what she wanted."

"So where's the jewelry?" Rita and Gyles demanded of Cornelia.

"I put it in the safe at the shop. I knew it would be safe there, after all the trouble and expense I went through with the insurance company. You know, they insisted on us installing an expensive alarm system in addition to hideous security gates…. Oh my Goddess! We forgot. We didn't pull them down when we left the shop this evening! Oh well, it's still almost empty. No one's going to bother breaking in there. I guess everything will be okay. After all, I did lock the safe."

"Cornelia, what do you mean '*we forgot*'? I didn't even know we had a phone yet, much less security gates. When I went away to England last month, you said you could handle all that," Gyles complained.

"But I did," Cornelia defended herself, "and what a hassle it all was. The alarm people had to come back three times because the traffic vibrations would set the damn thing off. And anyway, you could just as easily have pulled down the grates yourself, Gyles. Besides which, they're so ugly they spoil the windows." Cornelia concluded her defense on this peevish and indulgent note. Both Gyles and Rita looked at her without sympathy.

"Well ugly or not, I'm going there on my way home and lock up. And in the future Corny, please, let me know about these things."

Rita's doorbell rang long and loud. "There's my cab, I've got to go. Good night, Rita, good night, Corny. And please, please take care."

Gyles's last remark was spoken with a tender concern that melted Cornelia's pose of indifference. She composed an expression of contrite chagrin on her pretty face. Rita, also warmed by Gyles's protective nature, put a chummy arm about his broad shoulders and escorted him to the door.

Just as Gyles opened the heavy paneled front door and emerged from Rita's apartment building, the Boston College trolley sped by, clattering loudly on its tracks. The trolley's bright interior lights and new cars were a marked contrast to the Victorian architecture of the boulevard.

A cold wind had blown up, tearing the heavy cloud cover apart to reveal a lonely and swollen moon. Bare tree branches whipped against the fortresslike buildings. The racing clouds momentarily shrouded the moon's light, casting spectral shadows down upon the huddled shrubbery. This changing light, combined with the turbulent wind, seemed to animate the night with an uneasy energy. Gyles shuddered involuntarily as he climbed into the waiting Checker Cab. Trying to conceal his spasm of fear, he heartily cursed the persistent cold. "Jesus, it's as cold as a witch's tit out there." He presumed this chummy bit of banter would elicit at least a grunt of agreement, but the cabbie just slouched behind the wheel in silence.

Gyles tried to arrange his long legs in some semblance of comfort behind the semi-collapsed front seat. Suddenly weary of the night and the loutish cabbie, he sighed and dropped his head back. He curtly ordered the driver to 221 Newbury Street. The cab pulled away from the curb and sped off, pressing Gyles against the cold plastic upholstery.

A long black Lincoln with tinted windows materialized from the shadows and noiselessly pursued the cab at an incautious distance.

CHAPTER 6

▼

Gyles watched the towering city with its perpetually lit canyons of glass and steel as his cab descended from the heights of Coolidge Corner. His thoughts were of different places, however, and a different time, as he searched his memory for images of Aunt Florence in her staid Victorian town house in faded Back Bay. He could not reconcile this drab but kindly lady with the exotic fantasies of the Egyptian tiara he had seen Cornelia wear earlier that evening. But Aunt Florence had only been an unwilling and temporary guardian of those expensive orna-ments, and she had secured them in the most innocent of places, a child's safety deposit box, where presumably they would be forgotten at least for her lifetime. What had Aunt Florence's accompanying letter said? He couldn't remember all the details because he had read it so fast, and since then he had been in England for a month. Gyles had assumed that, to Aunt Florence, Cornelia's old safety deposit box was a convenient and secure place for jewelry that she had intended Cornelia to have. There was a letter of provenance and family history concerning these pieces, as there were similar notes affixed to every object connected to "The Family." Gyles had promised himself to read all these inventory footnotes more carefully, but there had been such a lot to do lately, and of course it never rains but it pours, and Aunt Florence would have to die at the same time he was mov-ing and expanding his business. Gyles made a mental note to reread the letter about the jewels. Perhaps he should also pop around to Wisner's tomorrow and pursue a little family research. His uncle could probably do with a little coddling after tonight's ordeal. Rita had been none too tactful, and God only knew what he thought of Monique, although Gyles had a pretty good idea what Wisner thought of Butch. Well, it will be interesting to hear about Wisner's ride home, as well as the murky depths of the family history.

Gyles's thoughts were interrupted when the window separating him from the front seat dropped three inches. The cabbie spoke with a flat voice.

"Hey dude, we got company. You want me to ditch him or what?"

"I beg your pardon," Gyles asked lamely.

"Never mind the smart stuff, Einstein. Look behind you."

Gyles began to burn at this retort, but he reluctantly turned to look out the back window. All he could see were blinding headlights, so he turned back around, slumping down against the seat, and said nothing.

"I could lose him, you know," persisted the cabbie.

"Lose who? What are you talking about?" Gyles snapped.

"The heavy in the Lincoln behind us. Been sittin' on my tail since I picked you up."

With a grimace of undisguised skepticism, Gyles turned around again. The car behind the headlights was tailgating the cab mercilessly. Suddenly, the cab spun off Commonwealth Avenue, turning sharp right just in front of a trolley that bore down on the intersection with an angry clanging of its bell.

"Hey, what's going on?" yelled Gyles as he was thrown across the backseat.

"We're ditchin' the escort. I don't know 'bout you, but I don't like jerks leaning on me too heavy."

Gyles was too surprised to say anything as he struggled to sit up straight. The trolley rumbled on by, momentarily blocking any pursuer. The cab beat a hasty retreat up the side street. Clinging to the strap above the door to steady himself, Gyles looked back down the street below them. He caught a glimpse of a long, dark car making a screeching turn in the face of the oncoming traffic. Horns blasted all around as the powerful car roared up the street, just as Gyles's cab cleared the crest of the hill and disappeared from view. True to his boast, the cabbie almost immediately lost the Lincoln.

They charged around the winding streets of this dimly lit residential section of Brookline with a series of quick random turns. Gyles was not sure whether to be thankful or scared of this scruffy cabbie who was taking him into a part of town he only vaguely recognized. He peeled himself off the backseat and leaned forward enough to check the meter. It read $15.50 and was ticking fast. This was going to be an expensive digression, thought Gyles. But before he could worry too much about that the cab reemerged onto Commonwealth Avenue by Boston University and spun off in the direction of Back Bay.

"I won't ask any questions, but I'd say things are a bit thick for you, bud." The flat voice of the cabbie did nothing to reassure.

"Yes, you could say it's been an unusual evening," returned Gyles. But behind the bluff of nonchalance he was shaken by the very real threat of having been followed. He lapsed into a dull silence, a combination of tiredness and fear. The cab came to a rattling halt, double-parking in front of the shop. Gyles paid the fare and unfolded himself from the cramped backseat. As he collected his top hat, he became aware of his outdated formality, which increased his wary self-consciousness. He looked up and down the now deserted street. All seemed quiet except for the brisk wind, which whipped Gyles's white scarf in all directions.

Approaching the shop, he looked for the security gates and saw that they were cleverly concealed on the shop side of the glass, where they were recessed above the ceiling of the display windows. He would have to go inside to pull them down and lock them. He extracted a bunch of keys from his overcoat pocket, but they became tangled in the fringe of his unruly scarf. Standing in front of the shop, he became completely preoccupied with unsnagging them. After some time of fumbling, Gyles found the shop key but was unable to disentangle the ring from the scarf. Finally, in frustration, he left them tied together.

He slipped the scarf from around his neck and shoved the encumbered key into the lock. This method opened the door, but the whole mess got tangled around his legs and tripped him. He lurched into the shop knocking over a chair.

At that moment a charging figure leaped from the shadows at the back of the shop and collided with Gyles. A brutal arm swung a weighted leather sap at Gyles's head, and he collapsed with a heavy thud. The intruder fled, vaulting over the slumped body on the floor.

CHAPTER 7

▼

The next morning Gyles was seated at a table in Rebecca's Café on Charles Street. The white steam from his cappuccino was mingling with the blue smoke from his Sobranie. He nursed a fading headache caused as much by last night's knock on the head as by a lack of sleep. Fortunately, Gyles's top hat had taken the force of the blow. The local police cruiser on its routine patrol had stopped to investigate the open door of the antique shop. The cops found Gyles dazed and more foolishly concerned with the ruined hat than with his own condition. They considered his behavior very suspicious until he produced proper identification. Fortunately for Gyles, one of the cops was familiar with Cornelia from her volunteer work with the force and, recognizing the Chilton name, was inclined to be sympathetic. The process of reporting to the authorities and searching the premises revealed that Gyles had literally stumbled in on a robbery in progress. And although the thief had gotten away seemingly without anything, Gyles's desk area had been rifled. Apparently the intruder had only just arrived. Gyles did not get to bed until 2:30, but he returned to the shop by 9:30 the next morning putting everything right. He did not want to tell Cornelia about his encounter so soon after her own mysterious assault. There would be time enough for that in the coming days. He had a one o'clock appointment at Meindorff and Strobe, a wholesale dealer on Charles Street, so he would have to see Uncle Wisner this morning if he were to find out anything about Aunt Norma and the family jewels.

Now here he was trying desperately to clear the fog from his head with double cappuccinos. Gyles knew he would need all his faculties to deal with the slippery Meindorff, not to mention his eccentric Uncle Wisner. He was idly leafing through the Globe, glancing at the headlines. As he sipped his bitter coffee, he looked around the café. There were the usual lot of office-uniformed yuppies, men and women, tailored by Saks and Brooks Brothers. Some of the women wore running shoes over white socks, over black stockings. Some of the men had slouchy gym bags deposited on chairs beside them. There wasn't much conversation amongst the patrons, whose heads were buried in newspapers. Strains of Vivaldi could be heard now and again between blasts of hissing steam from the espresso machine.

As Gyles inhaled his cigarette, his eyes caught the sparkle of a tiny diamond twinkling in the ear of the waiter. He wondered why he had never had his own ear pierced. Of course now everyone had his ear pierced. It was too passé. But that wasn't really it. It was the same with tattoos. He'd considered a small swallow stained in his skin right above his left pec, but that idea had come to naught also. It had to do with being naked. Ornament was fine but when he made love he wanted to be completely naked—no rings, no chains, no tattoos, no diamonds, so that his kiss or his probing caress was unadorned. He wanted to be completely revealed and uncivilized and wild. He remembered those times with John when they pressed themselves together so tightly that he imagined they might melt into each other.

As Gyles's mind wandered back to the sweating romps of his first youth, his stare had caught the attention of the diamond-studded waiter, who now approached his table.

"Can I get you something else?" A perfectly innocent question, but it shook Gyles from his reverie.

"Ah…no thank you, I'm fine."

"Yeah I know, and I'm Mona."

"What?" snapped Gyles.

"I'm Mona," the waiter insisted.

"Well great, I'm Leonardo."

"No you're not, you're Gyles."

"Say, have we met before?"

"How soon they forget," the waiter disparaged while shaking his head. "Only last night!"

"Oh, you're Mona!" A light dawned in Gyles's memory of the shapely dancer in Lilly's company, and he was delighted to have found him again.

"That's me, but you better call me Chuck."

"Chuck?" Gyles asked with obvious disbelief. "Is that your real name?"

"No, but I'm embarrassed to tell you what is."

"You think I'm too uptight to call you Mona?"

"Percival."

"What?"

"Percival. That's my name."

"Oh."

"See, I told you you'd hate it. Well, just call me Val. Everybody does."

"Okay, Val." Gyles winked at him and felt a little foolish for having done so. "Your diamond is very nice," he continued, trying to regain his cool.

"Yeah, thanks, it was a gift." Val's hand tugged at the stone in his ear.

"Oh?"

The waiter laughed. "From my ex. Actually it was a divorce settlement. He got off easy."

"Oh?"

"Yeah. I got the diamond, he got my heart."

"Was that a fair exchange?"

"Not unless you consider emotional bankruptcy fair payment for slavish devotion."

"Oh."

"Yeah, oh."

"I don't mean to be so lame. It's just a little early in the day for me," quipped Gyles.

"True confessions, yeah, I know, it's probably a little tacky, but I can't seem to stop myself. That's how I lost him."

"Oh?"

"There you go again. Listen, you need another cup of coffee. Can I buy you a cappuccino? It'll get rid of the cobwebs."

"Well, I, uh—"

"Good. One of the best. Coming right up." Val was soon busy with the espresso machine. He returned with the perfect cup of cappuccino, its strong blackness contained beneath a white cap of frothed milk sprinkled with powdered chocolate. "There's an eye-opener for you," he pronounced with simple pride.

"Thanks."

"Waiter, can I have my check?" requested a determined-looking young stockbroker in a Brooks Brothers pinstripe.

"Sure, be right with you." Val walked off, scribbling on his pad. He busied himself between the coffee machine and the tables. He had an easy, attractive manner that appealed to everyone, and because of that he was often drawn into short conversations with his customers.

Gyles found himself staring at Val, because when he spoke he inevitably broke into a broad smile punctuated by the most charming dimples in the rosiest of cheeks. Gyles sighed for the blush of youth and sipped his coffee. Realizing with regret that he too had to be about his business, he reluctantly put his cigarettes in his pocket, downed the last of his cappuccino, and put a five-dollar bill under the cup on the table along with his card. He passed Val on the way out the door and said, "I left money on the table and also my phone number. Call me and we'll do something."

"Okay, Gyles, sounds great." Val smiled, giving a big display of the winning dimples.

CHAPTER 8

▼

Wisner lived on Chestnut Street on the hill, in a Federal brick house that was said to have been designed by Bulfinch, the eighteenth-century architect whose golden-domed State House crowns the beacon that shone so brightly throughout New England over the centuries. This was of course Beacon Hill, and Chestnut Street was decidedly on the right side of that hill, and Wisner's house, with its restrained façade, was on the sunny side of the street, an important distinction. Gyles ascended the short flight of granite steps to the recessed front door of number 28. He lifted the brightly polished brass door knocker, which was in the form of a ship's anchor. On the stock was engraved in worn letters Nefertiti, which as Gyles knew was the name of one of the clipper ships in the fleet belonging to Gyles and Wisner's common ancestor, Obadiah Chilton. The knocker fell against the mahogany-paneled door with a resounding thud that echoed across the narrow street.

While Gyles waited he admired the fanlight above the door. His attention was so fully given over to examining the finely molded leaden swags that decorated the window that he failed to notice the elegant figure wrapped in sable who noiselessly exited from the kitchen door underneath the stoop where he stood. At that moment Wisner opened the front door.

"Well darling boy, what a surprise. Come in, come in." And he fairly pulled Gyles through the door, closing it swiftly behind him. The woman in sable, who had been hesitating beneath the stoop, climbed the tiny circular stairs up to the brick sidewalk and, on tiptoe so that her high heels made no noise, she disappeared down the street.

Inside the front hall all the sounds of the city were excluded by thick brick walls. Only the measured tick of the tall case clock could be heard. Its polished cherry wood trimmed with brass had stood in that stair hall for nearly two hundred years, measuring the hours for generations of Chiltons who had never taken for granted or neglected this mechanical heartbeat. They intended for it to pass into posterity like their fortunes, unaffected by the ravages of time.

"Well my darling boy, let's have a look at you, come in and sit down. Mrs. Buckley has gone to market, so I can offer you very little. There is no tea at present. Perhaps a glass of sherry? No? Well, perhaps you won't mind if I indulge in the merest thimbleful of amontillado." Wisner poured amber-colored sherry from an old Waterford decanter into a tiny crystal glass, which he delicately sniffed before he carefully placed it on a lace doily protecting the black lacquer Chinese table that stood by his chair. During this ceremony Gyles was enjoying a look around Wisner's double front parlor. He noted that the originally restrained Federal decor had been swamped under an accumulation of ornaments, mostly Chinese in origin, with which Wisner had seen fit to crowd every available surface. Amongst all the usual export porcelain, Gyles was surprised to discover a lovely Chien Lung bowl on which was painted, with the most delicate shades, a butterfly alighting on a branch of blossoming peach.

"This is perfectly beautiful, Uncle Wisner. Where did it come from?"

From the depths of his wing chair, Wisner was glowering at Gyles over the rim of his sherry glass, which he held in the most shamelessly effeminate fashion. "Yes, it is rather unusual, is it not? Not very much in the Boston taste, however."

Gyles was painfully aware of the accuracy of this statement. He had tried to specialize in Chinese porcelain of the Chinese taste at his first shop, only to discover that his expensive merchandise was ignored by Boston collectors, who were exclusively interested in gaudy and coarse nineteenth-century export porcelain, with its snobbish appeal to armorial status. Gyles felt the sting of this subtle rebuke, for he knew that, to Wisner, everything that was not Boston taste was no taste at all.

"But you do like it. And you shall have it," Wisner pronounced.

Gyles was astounded and immediately suspicious, first of the cup itself. This probably meant that it was not Chien Lung period but a reproduction, probably Tao Kuang, because it really was exquisite and couldn't be any later. Second, he was suspicious of Wisner himself. What had prompted this sudden generosity? With pangs of remorse Gyles hypocritically said, "Oh, no, I couldn't take it, such a valuable piece."

"My dear boy, whatever do you mean?" Wisner could see the struggle Gyles had undergone to refuse his gift: only another collector would know the excruciating agony of possible loss and the exquisite joy of possession. He derived pleasure from toying with Gyles's sensibilities. "But it means nothing to me. I bought it at a junk shop. They thought it was Noritake, which, if you can believe it, they pronounced Nora-take, as if it were someone's old aunt receiving on the sly. Do take it. You will enjoy it, and I have so much."

The last phrase of this pronouncement was uttered in the grand tones of an abdicating monarch. Gyles was completely disarmed, which was Wisner's intention, because the cup was of the Chien Lung period and had cost him dearly. But Wisner was after bigger fish, and the ultimate rewards would be worth the sacrifices. Now he could proceed in total command.

"I trust that Cornelia is convalescing comfortably at her own flat this morning."

"No, as a matter of fact she's staying at Rita's. I called there before I left my house, and she was still asleep. Although we have lots to do at the shop, I agreed with Rita that it's more important for the kid to sleep in today."

"Lots to do at your shop includes a visit to your long neglected uncle?"

"Well, I had other business on Charles Street, so I thought I'd combine that with a visit to you. And I was concerned that you got home all right last night."

"My darling boy, you needn't concern yourself with my safety now. As you can see, I escaped the ordeal of last night entirely unscathed, although I must caution you to examine the quality of the company you have been keeping."

"Oh, you mean Monique and Butch. I thought they were rather sweet and helpful to us last night. She really is a stunner, and they've got such a terrific car."

"That would hardly be my appraisal of the characters in question. However, enough of them. I thank you for your belated concern. You are here for something other than news of my humble self."

"As a matter of fact, I was curious about a few points of family history."

"Hmmm. An odd moment for genealogical research, but is there something specific you would like to know? Perhaps you should read Charles Chilton's *Chronicles of a New England Family*. I believe our illustrious ancestor was the eloquent authority on the subject."

"Actually, it had more to do with your part in that history."

"You do flatter me, but what can I tell you? My part was a small one and very obscure."

"You knew Aunt Norma well, didn't you? You even worked for her at the Museum of Fine Arts?"

"Dear God, ancient history. Yes, I knew Norma Chilton, but I didn't work for her. Did you know that she was named for the Druid priestess Norma, from the opera by Bellini? Your great-grandmother had put her finger on that one, for Norma certainly was a priestess of sorts. Although she was perfectly capable of human sacrifice, Druids held no fascination for her. Her great obsession was for things eternal and monumental and Egyptian. Yes, in the summer of 1927 when I was at Harvard I helped inventory the artifacts that were being looted by Norma's archaeologists in Egypt. She was, you know, a great patron of the MFA, but they found her rather difficult to deal with because she wanted to keep most of the artifacts she paid to have exhumed. I suppose she wanted to sit on it, like some dragon coiled upon its horde, deriving mystical power by possession of the treasure. The museum took a dim view of her acquisitive nature, for they also were greedy to bask in the reflected glory of the ancients."

"But how was it that you came to be working at the museum?"

"I wasn't working at the MFA. I was on loan from Harvard, where I was studying art history at the Fogg. A political move to mollify the great patron Norma Chilton, who was becoming increasingly acquisitive."

"What was Aunt Norma like?"

"Norma Chilton was a vain and forceful woman." Gyles could not help smiling. Wisner was such a type. "She was also a great patron of the MFA, but only as an afterthought. She really intended to acquire artifacts for her own collection."

"But where is her collection? Other than a few insignificant items and the Egyptian jewelry, which of course is not ancient, there is nothing at the house on Comm. Ave. that even hints of Egypt."

"Consumed by fire, my boy. The Canton Wharf and all of Norma's treasures that had not been transported to the MFA by the end of that summer went up in smoke, a most tragic and mysterious affair. Beyond that I don't know, except that the bulk of the collection went to the museum. That summer I was cataloguing a great deal of the artifacts stored in a warehouse on a wharf that doesn't even exist anymore. It was a ramshackle building at the end of one of the ancient wharfs that our family owned from the China trade days. It was a gloomy place, full of dark shadows and rats that liked to nest in the raffia-filled packing cases. Scared me to death. And that, alas, was where I lost my virginity. Hardly the place to instill fond memories, and yet I was smitten, swept off my feet by that gigolo mortician Nagib Iskander." Gyles shuddered involuntarily at the thought of this grim picture.

"Norma Chilton arrived one afternoon in July to stroll amongst the ruins. By this time I was bored to tears cooped up in that warehouse. I was young and had wanted to spend the summer in Italy with my college chum, Ned. Ned, what a beautiful boy he was. He used to row on the Charles, rather like an Eakins painting. Alas, this innocent bliss was denied me. Instead I had to slave for Norma Chilton. You can imagine my excitement when she arrived that day with Nagib. He was dark and exotic, a perfect Mameluke pasha in a black frock coat and scarlet fez. His dusky skin was complemented by his blue-black hair, which he wore neatly cut following the perfect shape of his head. His powerful jaw was accentuated by an immaculately trimmed and brushed beard that parted in the middle of his chin and swept back towards his ears. His lips were deep rose and perfectly outlined by his beard and his teeth the whitest ivory. When he spoke or smiled they shone like a beacon on a moonless night."

Gyles wondered to what length Wisner's narrative of his antique passion would stretch and how florid it might become.

"As Nagib and Norma walked slowly amongst the ruins, they spoke perfectly accented French, and she pointed with her Malacca walking stick at certain of the artifacts, recounting with remarkable accuracy the dates and places of their origin and on which digs, and by which Harvard professors they were discovered. Nagib explained the religious significance of the pieces, if there was any, and read all of the hieroglyphics, translating those royal proclamations. I remember their attention was particularly riveted to what I thought was a rather insignificant shard that had some reference to Nefertiti.

"Although Nagib was scrupulously attentive to Aunt Norma, he would occasionally glance at me as I sat scribbling away at my inventories. His eyes were friendly and questioning and for me instantly compelling, so I had no head for my paperwork. And after a while I gave it up altogether. I simply stared at this fashionable couple walking among the ancient ruins in that dreary warehouse.

"It was not long after that fatal meeting that Nagib took to visiting the warehouse alone with the pretext of studying the hieroglyphics. Soon I was plunged into the abyss of passion whose deepest soundings could never be fathomed." Wisner took a sip of his sherry and produced a delicate handkerchief from his French-cuffed wrist. He daubed at his lips, a mannerism that Gyles found altogether lacking in charm, although he marveled at Wisner's shameless indulgence in studied affectation.

"Well dear boy, have I told you all that you wanted to know?"

"Yes, Uncle Wisner, that was a fascinating tale, rather more than I expected to hear. So your affair with Nagib ended unhappily?"

"Affair? You ignorant child. Ours was a grand passion, a drama enacted among the shadows of the pharaohs. Nagib's perfect body was hard as a granite stele, burning as the Sahara at noon. He poured the power of dynastic millennia into this imperfect vessel, and I, the pride of New England's gilded youth, shuddered with ecstasy to receive those flowing silver secrets of the ancient world." Gyles was completely surprised by this lyric revelation and not at all sure how to respond, but he was spared the effort of decision, for after Wisner had drained his sherry glass with swift dispatch and many fluttering daubs with the monogrammed handkerchief, he continued.

"Our joy was not long lived, as Norma took a dim view of Nagib's frequent and prolonged absences from her side, and was rather suspicious of our obvious growing attachment. I can remember soirées in her salon crowded with furniture and many rather suspect Old Master paintings as well as too many celebrities, most of whom harked from the world of music—although she was not above spicing her crowd with a baseball player or some other current personality intended to astound her Boston society guests. Norma was entirely encased in Battenburg lace over rustling black taffeta. She had draped herself over a chaise longue in what she took to be an attitude of seductive splendor. There she graciously received the adoring attention of several of her male guests, much to the consternation of their wives, who were left alone to admire the calculated gloom of the candlelit paintings that crowded the scarlet damask-covered walls.

"Nagib and I had strayed into the conservatory, where with smoldering passion we fell into each other's embrace, and the heat of his breath filled my lungs as the faint scent of patchouli and musk rose from his starched shirtfront. I was oblivious to danger in that dim twilight of palm fronds and orchids, but she had followed us and stood there like an avenging Medea, her black ivory fan held like a dagger in her clenched fist. Nagib, without apparent surprise, uncoiled himself from about me and in slow silence took his crisp handkerchief from his breast pocket, wiped my forehead and my lips, and pressed the immaculate linen, now stained with our kisses, into my hand, whispering, 'Au revoir, mon chéri.' With a slight bow he left me, calmly gazed at Norma, took her arm, and guided her back into the salon. I left the party immediately. I was badly shaken and afraid, not knowing what Norma would do.

"I returned home and drank half a bottle of brandy, at which point I must have fallen asleep, because the next thing I knew the maid was tugging at me and I awoke with a splitting headache, stretched out on the davenport of my father's study. Bridget was fussing about drawing open the heavy velvet drapes and chattering on about Aunt Norma's chauffeur having left me a letter. My head pounded with fear as I dimly remembered the events of the previous evening, and with trembling hand I fumbled with the letter. But Bridget snatched it from me and slit the envelope with a silver knife from my father's desk. I snatched the letter back from her and asked her to get me some coffee. She clucked and sputtered and left reluctantly, for she was a nosy servant who lived vicariously through us. When she had gone and my pounding head allowed my eyes to focus, I read:

"My dear nephew,

For some time now I have been gratefully aware of the kind service you have rendered by sacrificing your summer to the cause of archaeology and the glorious institution of the Museum of Fine Arts. I know that at your age there are more compelling interests to engage your attention, and I therefore am doubly grateful to you for having assisted me with my projects here in Boston. As a token of my esteem and gratitude I am sending you on a voyage to the continent, where I believe you can broaden your education in so many directions that we cannot offer here in the United States. Enclosed you will find a first-class return ticket on the *Mauritania*, sailing this coming Wednesday from New York. I also enclose letters of credit, which you may draw upon when you arrive in Europe. Again thank you, dear nephew. Bon voyage!

Aunt Norma

P.S. I sail immediately for Egypt for an indefinite sojourn. Please address all correspondence c/o Shepheards Hotel, Cairo.

"As I finished reading this surprising letter—calculated as it was to dispatch me to the ends of the earth and separate me from the man who had lit my darkness, casting a torch into the chasm of my loneliness, he who was my life, my love, Nagib—Bridget re-entered the room carrying a tray with coffee and scones and other enticements. With her characteristic backwards kick, she closed the study door behind her and placed the tray on a table before the davenport. In response to her silent, inquiring gaze, I handed her the letter and dissolved into tears."

As Wisner finished his impassioned narrative with the last bit of breath left to him, Gyles half-feared that the remembrance of this thwarted love affair would plunge his uncle into renewed paroxysms of grief. But Gyles need not have feared Wisner's emotional distress, because aided by liberal nips of sherry and a perverse enjoyment of the wounds of the past, Wisner's state could only be described as exhilarated. However amusing this digressive account had been, Gyles had learned little about the significance of the Egyptian tiara. Gyles was curious to know more about that affair, which seemed of greater significance than Wisner's macabre trysts amongst the rats and ruins. "So what happened to Iskander?" was his simple question.

"What happened to Nagib? How should I know? Didn't I tell you I was dispatched…sent away…banished? I should have hoped you would be more concerned with your dear uncle. Wasn't I the thwarted lover? Aren't you concerned about the injustices suffered by your own kind?" This last euphemism made Gyles shudder, as he hoped that he would never resemble Wisner's brand of closeted queen. But again his concentration had been diverted. He could not resist the retort "You appear to have been the other lover in this equation, and I don't know if anyone is required to muster up sympathy for that position. Not to mention the fact that your travels were rather comfortably providing you with your original intended—what was his name? Charles. No, Ned, wasn't it?"

"Yes, it was Ned, Ned Everest," Wisner shot back. "But lest I soil his blessed name in this conversation—" Wisner paused and with effort returned to his unctuous cordiality. "Let me simply state that Ned was the second great passion of my life."

"Wisner, what became of Nagib Iskander?"

"Nagib became a mortician in Watertown."

"Oh."

"Close your mouth, dear child. It's really not so surprising. He was Egyptian, after all. He did very well in that profession. They have studied the art since the beginning of time. He had the unusual task of preparing his former lover for her burial, which is to say that in death as in life he sucked the juices out of her, pumping her full of false hopes of eternal devotion." This revolting image was uttered with such withering acrimony that Gyles shuddered again.

"Well Uncle Wisner, this has certainly been an interesting morning. But I have an appointment and I must get going."

"Oh yes, the phantoms that fly from Pandora's box fill you with dread. Go then, and leave me alone with these dark shadows that you have unleashed."

"Well, uh, I guess I'll do just that." Gyles wondered from what ancient melodrama Wisner dragged these hackneyed phrases. But he did not linger with these conjectures long. While Wisner was refilling his sherry glass, he slipped from the parlor, but not without pangs of remorse for having to leave the beautiful Chien Lung bowl behind. He decided not to bring up that or any other subject again, fearing another lengthy diatribe. As Gyles shut the thick mahogany door behind him, the brass knocker sounded a hollow thud along quiet Chestnut Street.

Wisner put down his sherry glass and picked up the phone on the first ring.

"Hello? Who's that? What? So it's you. I trust you did not let him see you. You know that he's just left here. It would be difficult not to recognize you waltzing about in that absurd fur in the middle of April, perched on those stilts like a cheap harlot. I am not a jealous queen. You are about as inconspicuous as the temple of Karnak. No, I did not get the jewels. You were supposed to get the jewels. He was here to ask me about family history. He did not mention them. I have no idea. No? Let me tell you one thing. I will not be a part of any more of your crude intrigues. Good. Talk to your brother. And tell him this for me. The heart of his mother is lost, and only I can help him find it." Wisner hung up the telephone and quaffed another glass of sherry in one swallow.

CHAPTER 9

▼

Cornelia held her car phone wedged between her ear and her shoulder as she maneuvered through traffic, impatiently waiting for her call to be answered.

"Hello, Ross, this is Cornelia. What? Oh, I'm on the Harvard Bridge. What? In my car, you ninny. I'm running late, and I have a luncheon date with a client at the Bay Tower Room. I had a rather unpleasant evening and—oh, you heard? In the arms of Monique? Well, yes, something like that. Ross, Ross, what? No, I can't hold. Really! Whoever invented call waiting should be tortured." Cornelia downshifted and came to a reluctant halt for the red light at the intersection of Massachusetts Avenue and Commonwealth. She reached for the rearview mirror to check her makeup, but as she turned it towards her she caught the reflection of a black Rolls-Royce being driven by a striking-looking woman wearing a large-brimmed black hat, a black sable coat, and black gloves. "Sweet Goddess, it's Tatiana." Cornelia spun round in her seat, not quite believing what she saw, only to be confused by an old tank of a cab being driven by a creature closely resembling Cro-Magnon man. The cab blared its horn at her. The light had changed.

"Yoo hoo, Corny, I'm back," chortled Ross over the car phone. As Cornelia shifted into first, she scanned the horizon for the black Rolls. "Cornelia, are you there?"

"Listen, Ross, meet me for drinks at the Casa Romero about five," and with that sharp order delivered, Cornelia disconnected the call. She had located the limousine and realized it had not been behind her but directly to her left. But she had already overshot the intersection thanks to the insistent prodding of the none-too-glamorous cabbie, who at that instant was engaged in a death-defying maneuver of passing Cornelia on the left into oncoming traffic. It took some time to go around the block and regain the direction of the disappearing Rolls, and when she did turn, there was no sign of the elegant car. Cornelia cursed her bad luck in losing the mysterious Tatiana.

When she passed the Ritz, however, there was a black Rolls parked conspicuously by the front door. Cornelia swerved quickly curbside, although she was now due downtown for her luncheon with Julian Bannister to present her designs for his executive office and boardroom. Her window retracted into the door with a faint buzz. "Good morning, Miss Chilton, how are you today?"

"I'm fine, George, but in a hurry. Listen, tell me, who is the lady who was driving this car?"

"Lady, miss? But you must be mistaken."

"Well, you're probably right there. The woman who was driving the car, who was she?"

"Woman, miss?"

"Yes, George. I know the Ritz is the soul of discretion, but I am not the paparazzi. Out with it. Who the hell is the dame in the black hat?"

"But, Miss Chilton, this car belongs to a gentleman who is having lunch in the café." Cornelia recognized the implacable resolve of George to conceal what he knew. Or was he telling the truth, and this was another black Rolls? It was of course possible, but not so probable. "Shall I park your car then, Miss Chilton?"

"No thank you, George, I have another engagement." Cornelia's window cut short the last of this reply and she sped away from the curb. George watched Cornelia's M. G. merge with the traffic and disappear around the corner of the Public Garden. He smiled to himself as he fondled a crisp fifty-dollar bill in his pocket.

C H A P T E R   10

▼

At 5:25 that evening Cornelia's M.G. inched into a minuscule space on Glouces-
ter Street in Back Bay. She swung her door shut and activated the car alarm. The
alarm sounded two high-pitched screeches.

"Better lucky than rich," Cornelia muttered to herself, the cheerful phrase
commenting on the unusual convenience she had just enjoyed by finding a parking space so close to the restaurant. As she walked the brick sidewalk that hugged
the building down the narrow alley to the Casa Romero, she enjoyed the pretty
bed of lilies-of-the-valley and pansies. The entrance to the restaurant was marked
only by a wooden sign painted red and carved with the design of two Aztec war-
riors. The heavily coffered front door with inset Mexican tiles was recessed in an
alcove and almost hidden.

Cornelia pulled the iron ring that served as a doorknob and walked into a tiny
foyer, where the walls were entirely covered with blue and white tiles painted
with doves holding olive branches. She was greeted by the green, clean scent of
coriander mixed with the aromas of cumin and cinnamon issuing from the
kitchen, where passionate Mexican ballads could be heard from a scratchy radio
mixed with the hubbub of the dining room.

"Buenas noches. Welcome to the Casa Romero, Cornelia. You're looking very
pretty tonight," said Leo, the robust proprietor, his handsome face framed by an
immaculately trimmed gray beard. He radiated a warmth and vitality that melted
the cares of the world away.

"Buenas noches, Don Leo. Cómo está?" Cornelia replied with old-fashioned
respect.

"Muy bien, señorita."

"Leo, you have such a beautiful tan," gushed Cornelia.

"I've been out in my garden all morning weeding the iris bed."

"And now you're working all night. Where do you get your energy?" Cornelia asked with admiration.

"Oh, I love my garden. That's not work. It gives me energy. Cornelia, we were very concerned about you after the Dynasty Ball. Are you okay? We'd only just arrived by the time they were hauling you out feet first."

"Oh my Goddess." Cornelia put a hand to her forehead. "What a scene! Yes, I'm fine, really, fine. It's rather a long story. Um, Leo, have you seen Rosalind Wortheley?"

"Yes, she's here on the patio having a cocktail." Leo summoned a waiter. "Eduardo, please take Señorita Chilton to the patio. She is meeting Señora Wortheley."

"Is that the loco lady with the phone?" asked Eduardo.

"Yes. And," as an aside to Cornelia, "Señora Wortheley seems to be engaged in a leverage deal to buy out the entire Western Hemisphere. She's already offered me a million for the Casa, and when I declined she offered to buy my tuxedo instead. She's frantic to spend money, so please run right along and help out the dear lady." Leo rolled his eyes and shrugged his shoulders.

Eduardo led Cornelia through the busy restaurant. Because of its low ceilings and the tiles on the walls and tabletops, it had a cozy and exotic atmosphere. Because of its margaritas and spicy fare, the Casa enjoyed a boisterous conviviality that was unique in Boston and much appreciated by a loyal clientele. As Eduardo had said, Rosalind was completely absorbed in an animated conversation, her cell phone in one hand and a Neiman's catalogue in the other, while absently sipping a frozen margarita beside a mountain of chic shopping bags was piled on a chair beside her. Eduardo arranged a chair for Cornelia and asked, "May I get you a cocktail, Señorita Chilton?"

"Yes, Eduardo. May I have a Romerita?"

He gave her a winning smile and replied a lilting "Si."

"Yes, Chantel, my dinner date is here, so I have to go. You have my measurements, so I'll take the YSL suit and the five pair of Ferragamo heels—yes, the two-tone with the oyster ostrich leather as well as the sandals. Then, the Missoni sweaters—yes, I'll take all four of them, and the Klein strapless evening gown, and I guess you just better send me the Galanos also. What? Yes, I know it's passé, but I'm going to the Myopia Hunt Ball, and they'll think it's just the berries. Oh—and please ask Anne to accessorize everything in triplicate, because I don't know what I'm going to feel like tomorrow. Yes, send it all out by cab to my house in Chestnut Hill. What? You're in Texas? Well, put it on the plane. I don't need it until tomorrow afternoon anyway. Oh, you're a dear. I can't thank you enough, Chantel. By-eee!" Click. "Cornelia, why do you always look like a million bucks?" Rosalind unglued herself from the cordless phone. She swept her diminutive friend into her long and elegant arms and held her there for a moment.

Cornelia luxuriated in the fragrance of Rosalind's French perfume, which hinted at wild roses and honeysuckle. "Rosalind, what are you up to? Leo told me you tried to buy his restaurant, and then the shirt off his back. Really! Is this in the best of taste? And here I find you cleaning out the stockroom of Neiman's, in Texas no less! What's up?"

"No, darling, it is not in the best of taste. But there are some burdens that being nouveau riche carries with it. It is just in the nature of the beast, and I have to get used to it. George, my knight-in-shining-armor husband of all time, has been scolding me all morning that I haven't been spending enough money. Fool that I am, wasting my time volunteering at the Women's Union selling stationery, and in my spare time selecting pretty bargello patterns to needlepoint, while he's lolling about the sauna at Le Pli, having to endure the gripes of his chums as they enumerate their wives' expenditures! Well, I haven't heard the end of it, and I've been given an ultimatum, if you please! One word—spend! Do you know, Mummy told me I was getting into trouble by marrying George. But she is such a snob, I didn't think it mattered. Darling, what have you got on? You're so cute!" Rosalind interrupted herself to squeal at Cornelia.

"Rosalind, you are gorgeous, I'm cute. This much has been established. Don't rub it in."

"Oh, Cornelia, don't be cross. Everyone's cross with me today. I was only being nice. And besides, it's true—you do look marvellous!"

"Yeah, well, it's a designer original. Originally designed to fetch a hundred bucks. But I got it for twenty-five in the Basement. Betty the Bounder put it aside for me."

"Betty who?" asked Rosalind in disbelief.

"Never mind," said Cornelia. "She asks herself the same question whenever she looks in the mirror."

Eduardo returned with Cornelia's Romerita. "Muchas gracias, Eduardo. That looks just like pure heaven!"

"Looks rather ominous to me. What's in it?" Rosalind questioned primly.

"The Romerita? Oh, I don't know. Chartreuse and tequila, I think. They're just heaven. But definitely two-sippers."

"Two-sippers?"

"What are you, an echo?"

"Cornelia—"

"Oh, all right. I'll be nice. The first sip, you wonder. The second sip, you're hooked."

"Well, before you get entirely sloshed on those things, tell me why I have been summoned here. What's up? I know you're not pregnant, are you?"

"Rosalind, please! What kind of an idea is that?"

"Never mind. There's always room for hope—I mean, change—but—I'm not prejudiced."

"I know you're not prejudiced. Just a hetero pig."

"Why, thank you. That's sweet of you to say. I've been ripped away from an important personal dilemma in order to be insulted by a pip-squeak dyke in a tamale parlor."

"I'm sure it was the most exciting thing that's happened to you all week. But enough, please! Let me ask you a question."

"Ask away!"

"Have you met, or do you know about, a woman whose first name is Tatiana? I don't know the last name, but you would remember her if you saw her. She's very chic in a European style, hats, gloves, discreet jewelry, and a fantastic sable coat. She's—"

"Go no further. I know exactly who you're talking about. Tatiana Sarkisian. She and her husband, who amongst other interests owns Sarkisian Furs on Madison Avenue in New York, have just bought the old Hickox estate in Dover. She has contributed rather too generously to a half a dozen charities, and seems bent on making a direct ascent to the pinnacles of society. But she hasn't realized that goal. Boston is a far cry from New York. I hear she bought a condominium at the Heritage also. Her name has already appeared on the considered new members list at the Women's City Club. She hasn't got a chance, of course. She's been put forward by Connie Treadwell, who happens to be the chairwoman for the Brigham and Women's Cotillion this fall, as well as Tatiana's neighbor in Dover, but it will take a lot more than ten thousand charity dollars and Connie Treadwell to edge Mrs. Sarkisian through the front door of the WCC."

Cornelia was silently astounded by the snobbish malice that Rosalind loved to wallow in. "Well, you do know rather a lot about the mysterious Tatiana," Cornelia commented.

"I don't know why you say mysterious. She's really one of the more straight-forward social climbers of the season. How is it that you know her? Will you be doing her new house in Dover? That really is very clever of Mrs. Sarkisian, getting you to decorate. The Chilton name should add a lot of legitimacy to her formidable assault on Boston."

Rosalind was not far off the mark—or was she? Now Cornelia was more certain than ever that she had seen Tatiana in the Rolls-Royce that had been parked in front of the Ritz. But why had the doorman denied it? And what on earth did happen last night in the ladies' room at the Dynasty Ball? Cornelia really would have liked to believe that Tatiana Sarkisian had not drugged her and stolen her Aunt Norma's jewelry. Considering Tatiana's wealth and social aspirations, it now seemed highly unlikely that she would pull such an outrageous caper. On the other hand, it was rather unusual for such a person to be offering joints to anyone, much less getting stoned herself. But Cornelia needed a big job right now, and to design the interiors for Tatiana's condominium and possibly her house in Dover would be a blessing. She had been very anxious about leaving the successful China Trade Interiors and starting out in partnership with Gyles and his antiques business, and she needed the security of a big job right now.

"Darling, has that cocktail addled your brain? You're a million miles away!"

"Oh, I'm sorry, Rosalind. I was just thinking about—last night."

Rosalind jumped on this opportunity. "What is it that you know about Mrs. Sarkisian that the mere mention of her name makes you as silent as the Sphinx?"

"Funny you should mention the Sphinx. Doesn't she ask a rather dangerous riddle?" inquired Cornelia wistfully.

"Sphinx, shminx. It's just an expression, Cornelia. What happened to you last night? I heard a nasty rumor that you got drunk and had to be carried out of a rather questionable fete."

Cornelia interrupted Rosalind. "As to the questionable fete, I was at the AIDS Action Committee's Dynasty Ball. As to being drunk, I certainly was not."

"But you were carried out, limp and unconscious, as I heard it," Rosalind smugly retorted.

"I…I…I don't quite know. That is, I'm not sure…I fainted in the ladies' room," stammered Cornelia.

"Well, that does explain it. From what I hear, all the homos in the city were in there doing God knows what."

"Rosalind, I think we might be safer discussing the weather."

"Well, all right, darling. After all, it's your life. But—"

"Rosalind, why don't we redecorate your house in Wianno? That should cost George a pretty penny."

CHAPTER 11

▼

Gyles arrived at his great-aunt Florence's house at 283 Commonwealth Avenue after a long day of dealing with customs officials and the inevitable delays and frustrations inherent in international trade. As he walked up the several brownstone steps of the old town house, he realized for the first time that the entire facade was completely overgrown with ivy. It grew over windows and chimneys and dripped off the front porch like a tattered fringe. Although it gave a rather romantic and wild image to this most urban and formal of city boulevards, he knew the ivy was corrosive for the masonry and should be trimmed back, restoring the neat and dignified appearance of the family house.

Gyles opened the front door with his key but also rang the bell to alert Lucy Ann of his arrival. The outer door was a heavy wrought-iron gate lined with plate glass, composed of scrolling arabesques surmounted by an elaborate intertwined monogrammed CSC. These initials stood for Cosmo Stebbins Chilton, who was Gyles's great-grandfather and Norma and Florence's father. Old Cosmo moved from 28 Chestnut Street on Beacon Hill in 1879 to this house, which he had built in the newer, more fashionable Back Bay. In 1902 Cosmo built a house next door for his son, Gideon Bradbury Chilton, on the dual occasion of his twenty-first birthday and his marriage to his cousin, Helen Chichester. That house was later passed to a younger son after Gideon's untimely death in the second battle of the Marne during the First World War. Gideon and Helen had given birth in 1914 to one son, Gyles Stebbins Chilton, who was Gyles and Cornelia's father.

Inside the vestibule of 283 Commonwealth Avenue was a second door of solid oak panels, mellowed by age to a dark honey color. Inside the front hall, a dim greenish light filtered through the ivy covering the fanlight over the door. Augmented only by a Moorish lamp of dense fretwork and colored glass inserts, the general effect was of Pre-Raphaelite gloom. From the shadowy recesses Gyles could hear Lucy Ann's measured step on the back stairs and he waited for her to usher him into the house.

As the housekeeper crossed the front hall towards Gyles, he looked at her immaculate, proud, and ageless self with deep affection. Lucy Ann's light café au lait color was dignified by frizzy gray hair brushed into a neat bun at the nape of her neck.

Lucy Ann was more than Gyles' and Cornelia's nursemaid and Aunt Florence's housekeeper. She was the heart and soul of the family, and it was she who could give voice to her feelings in an atmosphere that would otherwise have been formal and stilted.

"Well, God bless my baby! Come here, child, and give your old Lulu a big hug. Lucy Ann took Gyles by the shoulders and, while she kept him at arm's length, they stood eye to eye, her tall, sturdy frame equaling his height. She inspected her "baby" with proprietary candor, to which he submitted without complaint. "Gyles, you look mighty hungry—and then again, tired too. Well, you've come to the right place, 'cause I've been fixing fried shrimp for Mr. Charlie. You're just in time. We're in the kitchen. You run right upstairs to your room and wash your hands. Lord, it's been powerful lonely around here since Miss Florence up an' died. Now I get my two men wanting dinner all at once." Lucy Ann kept up a running commentary as she disappeared down the back stairs.

Gyles mused with delight over his old Lulu, who had been everything to him and Cornelia since that summer so long ago when their parents had sailed for Europe, leaving them in the hands of Lucy Ann and Aunt Florence. The fashionable young Gyles Stebbins Chiltons never returned. Much later, when Gyles was prepping at Deerfield Academy, his godfather, Uncle Ted, a somewhat distant relative from the Hawaiian branch of the family who was visiting back East, told Gyles of the death of his parents in an auto accident on the Haute-Corniche above Nice on the Riviera. Apparently the couple had been to a wild party and had drunk rather too much for safety. The great tragedy was not only their own deaths but their having caused another car to plummet off a high cliff. The entire scandal had been suppressed as much as possible.

On the third floor, Gyles stood in the middle of his old room, and he felt nostalgia tinged with guilt, because everything was the way it had always been, and everything was clean and dusted awaiting his return, but he had stayed here only very occasionally since he went away to Deerfield, and that was practically twenty years ago. On his bed, leaning against the pillows, was George, the limp teddy bear whose missing button eye had been covered over by a red bandanna tied around his head, transforming this ailing friend into a ferocious pirate—or so said Aunt Florence to the then-weeping Gyles so many years ago.

Gyles turned the doorknob of the adjoining room. It had been Cornelia's, and this too looked as if she had just stepped out. Her dolls were in place on the shelves, and the huge Victorian dollhouse stood on the window seat of the bay window. Gyles walked over to it, still fascinated by the elaborate, diminutive furnishings that filled the many rooms. It was really this dollhouse that had started Gyles's interest in antiques. He remembered every article lovingly and marveled at his favorite piece, a walnut bookcase in the study that had glass doors and tiny books with handwritten stories bound in leather, made by Aunt Florence when she had been a girl. Gyles's concentration was so absorbed with the tiny books that when he heard a knocking at the window, he jumped. He was even more surprised to see a handsome, grinning face dumbly speaking to him from behind the double-hung windows. Someone was out on the fire escape, trying to get in.

"Good God! It's Val!" exclaimed Gyles to himself. He tugged at the old bronze locks of the window. Once released, the heavy frames with their thick plate glass rose easily on counterweighted chains.

"What are you doing in this strange joint?" asked Val indelicately.

"This joint is my great-aunt's house. That is, it was until she died last month."

"Wow! The old lady died? I used to see her walking down Commonwealth Avenue every morning, rain or shine, as I was on my way to work. She used to give a quarter to each of the bums. Poor bastards will be hurting this winter without your aunt."

"Did she really? I never knew that. She was very involved in her church. I expect that's where she was going when you saw her, to Trinity in Copley Square. What are you doing out there on the fire escape?"

"I'm the boy next door. I live next door. It's my day off, and I'm filling my bird feeder, and being a snoopy kinda fella, I was looking in the window and I saw you. Would you like to come over and have a cup of coffee or something?" Val asked, raising an eyebrow.

"I didn't know you lived on Commonwealth Avenue."

"There's a lot you don't know about me," Val said coyly.

"Well I hope we can correct that," Gyles replied as he looked at the fair hairs that curled over the neck of Val's T-shirt, which hugged his chest so tightly that Gyles could see Val's hard nipples perfectly formed beneath the soft jersey.

"No time like the present. Why don't you come on over now?" Val suggested.

"Well…actually…the present is in fact spoken for…I uh—"

"Don't tell me you have a date." This last comment was uttered with sarcasm and disbelief.

"Well yes, I do, but maybe you'll give me a rain check?"

"Busy, busy, busy."

"Gyles Chilton! Who are you speaking to? I had to drag these weary bones all the way up from the kitchen, looking for you. Mr. Charlie wants his shrimp. Come on, boy—food's getting cold! My, oh my—who's that? The boy who feeds the pigeons? Well, come on along, child—there's plenty for all."

Lucy Ann started plodding down the hall, not waiting for a reply.

"Well, I guess you're invited to lunch, Val. We're having fried shrimp with Mr. Charlie," said Gyles.

"Who's Mr. Charlie?" asked Val, climbing through the window and tucking his T-shirt into his shorts. He conspicuously rearranged his crotch in the process, a maneuver that did not escape Gyles.

"Mr. Charlie is Lucy Ann's gentleman friend. He drives a cab now, but he used to be Great-aunt Norma's chauffeur, although that was before my time. He takes Lucy Ann on her errands, and she cooks him fried shrimp in Creole sauce. Lucy Ann is…well, Lucy Ann is Lucy Ann. She takes care of us all."

Gyles led Val down the spiraling back staircase to the basement, where the old-fashioned kitchens were. An hour later, Gyles and Val emerged, satiated and glowing from the spicy Creole shrimp that Lucy Ann had heaped on their plates.

*   *   *   *

"Wow! Mr. Charlie and Lucy Ann are a trip and a half!" exclaimed Val, as he plopped himself down on the front hall settee, a formidable piece of furniture with a dark walnut frame writhing with grotesque gargoyles. "She really can cook. Are they an item, or what?" Gyles peered at Val with a severe and mystified expression. "You know—are they, um, an item? Like, married? Or, what?" stammered Val awkwardly.

"I know what you mean, but I can't possibly think of Lucy Ann and Mr. Charlie as 'an item.' It's just not an appropriate term."

"Okay, okay, never mind. But who is Mrs. Jackson?"

Gyles rolled his eyes in disbelief and said, with an edge of exasperation, "Mrs. Jackson is Lucy Ann."

"Oh. She's married? So, is Mr. Charlie Mr. Jackson?" Val prodded naively.

"There is no Mr. Jackson. It's a title of respect."

"Well, all right, I didn't know. They seemed like such a couple."

As Gyles looked at Val, he wondered how he could ever explain the subtleties of these relationships, which seemed of a different world than the boy who was sprawled over the old settee, which no one had sat on for at least a decade. One of Val's powerful legs hooked over the ornately carved arm of the piece and his shorts rode high on thighs that were covered with golden fuzz. Gyles could not help but enjoy the incongruous sensuality of his new friend in these old surroundings. "Never mind," said Gyles. "C'mon upstairs. I have a mystery to solve, and maybe you can help."

"Seems like this joint's full of mysteries," said Val. Widening his eyes and tip-toeing like a cartoon character, he followed Gyles up the stairs.

Gyles laughed at the hamming and casually rested his hand on Val's shoulder, and said, "You're quite a trip yourself, you know."

Val smiled and looked at Gyles's remarkable eyes. They were the color of the ocean just after sunset, an almost iridescent blue-green.

Gyles led Val to the third floor, where he opened a heavy mahogany door.

"This was my great-aunt Norma's room," he said as he opened the interior shutters, which folded neatly into paneling surrounding the windows. Outside, the ivy had sent clinging vines over some of the glass. The last window was completely covered by green leaves, so the daylight had a weird greenish cast. Gyles seated himself at a delicate writing desk, made of dark mahogany and light tulip-wood forming an elaborate pattern of flowers and plumage. He pulled the tas-seled cord of a silk-shaded lamp, which illuminated with a pink glow a letter that he spread on the desk. Gyles motioned Val to sit in a comfortable chair beside the fireplace in the inglenook, and said, "This is a letter that Cornelia, my sister, and I found when we opened an old safety deposit box which was in Cornelia's name at the Chilton Savings and Trust Bank. It was a box that Cornelia had forgotten all about. She had kept it as a child for all the coins that our parents had sent back to us from their travels. In addition to the coins, which were only of sentimental value, we discovered some rather spectacular jewelry and this accompanying let-ter. In our excitement, we had put off reading this letter just as we had put off reading the familial histories that are attached to the most of the items in this house. When you called this place a strange joint before—"

"I didn't mean—" Val tried to apologize.

"No, that's okay, you couldn't have been more accurate. This house is a strange joint, and a monument to generations of illustrious Chiltons, as well as— and I think we are about to discover—the infamous Chiltons. If you want to understand the extent of this obsession, just pick up any item and turn it around or upside down until you find its label."

Val was not at all sure what Giles was talking about, but he picked up a pretty cloisonné ashtray on the table beside his chair and, sure enough, glued to the bottom was an octagonal paper label with a red border. In tiny and exquisite script was penned the following note, which he read aloud: "Cloisonné, brought back from China, 1867, by C.S.C. onboard the clipper ship *Flaming Pearl.*"

"C.S.C. was Cosmo Stebbins Chilton, who was Aunt Norma's father. The Flaming Pearl was one of his fleet of ships engaged in the China trade, although at the time it was imported—what was that, 1867?—Cosmo's main interests had shifted to coal, railroads, and cotton mills, amongst other things. But let's find out more about the Egyptian tiara." And he read aloud from the letter in his hand:

My Dear Niece

During your aunt Norma's last illness, when she was very weak, she insisted that I send away the nurse and lock her bedroom door, as she had something to tell me. I was very alarmed by her fevered agitation, so I did as she asked. When we were alone, against all my protestations, she got out of her bed and went to the bookshelves in the inglenook, where she opened a concealed chamber hidden behind the woodwork where there was a large casket. She showed me how to open the compartment, and then she and closed it again. She made me promise to send the casket to Nagib Iskander after she had passed away. I had been so used to saying "yes" to Norma all of our lives that again I acquiesced in order to persuade her to return to her bed. Shortly afterwards, she slipped into unconsciousness, and the next day she died. When I returned from the funeral, the house had been burglarized, and Norma's bedroom had been all torn up. Although nothing much had been taken, everything had been ransacked, and the room was a shambles. I was very much disturbed, but relieved to find that the casket was still safe in its hiding place. Other than that, the rest of Norma's jewelry had been sold years ago, so there had been nothing of real value anyway. The presence of those barbaric ornaments weighed on my mind. They were somehow a menace that I wanted to rid myself of, so I have placed them here for safekeeping. Perhaps some of the Chilton fortune will be salvaged yet, and serve a more wholesome purpose.

"My aunt's assessment of the contents of this house—how did she put it?—'so there had been nothing of real value anyway'—is a very telling remark, and strikes at the heart of the conflict of my family," Gyles explained to Val. "My aunt Norma had somehow squandered, or lost through bad investments during the Crash of '29, her portion of the Chilton fortune. If we can judge what was lost by what remains, the loss was catastrophic, because this house was only one of several belonging to Aunt Norma. It is jammed to the gills with items of quality, although a great many of them are not in style right now, but what she means is that there are no Rembrandts or Hope diamonds lolling about the odd corner. For Aunt Florence, all of this," Gyles broadly gestured with open arms, "was a responsibility that with dwindling funds was difficult to maintain."

While Gyles was explaining the letter, Val had been examining the inglenook for the secret panel. Seated as he was, he could examine closely the details of the inglenook's design. This entire room-within-a-room was constructed of cherry wood. The surrounding walls were bookshelves, also of cherry, trimmed by elaborate low-relief carvings of Renaissance grotesque patterns. The fireplace was the focal point, surrounded by blue iridescent tiles. Over a mantel of handsomely paneled cherry wood hung a fine landscape painting in a gilded frame.

Val stood up by the fireplace, and, letting his fingers travel over the elaborate detailing, pushed and pulled all available protuberances from bursting pomegranates to dentil moldings. Gyles, by this time also attempting to unravel the secret, was beside Val, trying to remember how secret drawers were concealed in old furniture he had seen. But he was quickly distracted by a collection of art glass vases that sat on the mantel shelf. He picked one up and saw the ubiquitous paper label attributing this piece to N.S.C.—Norma Stebbins Chilton. Gyles carefully peeled the label back, revealing the mark he'd hoped would be there. L.C.T.— Louis Comfort Tiffany. He was astounded by this peculiar vessel, with its long, attenuated neck. He had never seen such an intense gold finish applied to glass. It looked like molten rock bubbling from a volcano.

Transfixed, Gyles moved to rest his elbow on the mantelpiece. But he slipped off the shelf, and stumbled, tripping over the fireplace fender at his feet. He reached out blindly, and grabbed hold of a hook that held fireplace tongs. As he struggled to regain his balance, he inadvertently tugged hard, releasing a secret latch that held a portion of the bookcase in place. A section of the shelves the size of a small door swung inward. The weight of the loaded bookcase was carried by wheels that traveled on a track inset in the floor.

Val caught Gyles as he careened towards him, and they both went crashing to the floor. Gyles, oblivious to what other damage he might have caused, had curled himself around the delicate art glass and landed safely, antique unharmed, nestled in Val's lap. Val, pleasantly surprised to discover Gyles right where he wanted him, was equal to his opportunities. He gently stroked Gyles's hair, and he gazed into those heaven-eyes with as much rapture as Gyles lavished on his cherished antique.

"Look—I didn't break it!" proclaimed Gyles with tremendous relief. Val sighed with resignation, realizing that Gyles only had thoughts for antiques. For a fleeting moment, he considered smashing the vase on Gyles's head, hoping to grab his attention, but he decided against it.

"You may not have smashed that blob, but somehow you managed to open sesame" muttered Val with exasperation, and his eyes pointed to the open bookcase.

"It is not a blob. This is a tear vial of Favrile glass by Louis Comfort Tiffany," declared Gyles haughtily.

"Yeah. Well, next time you're playing basketball with it, warn me and I'll jump out of the court." Val's neat bit of sarcasm went unheeded as Gyles untangled himself from Val's embrace, stood up, replaced the vase on the mantel shelf, and, stooping in front of the open door, peered into darkness.

Gyles's nostrils flared as he tried to identify the musty odor issuing from the long-closed space. "What is that smell? It's so familiar," he asked himself.

Val commented, "If that smell's familiar to you, sweetheart, it's only because you've been hanging around cemeteries. Can you see anything?"

Gyles looked askance at Val and said, "No, it's as dark as a tomb in here. See if you can find a candle. I think I saw one on the bedside table."

Val obediently began his search, muttering to himself in a mocking tone, "It's as dark as a tomb in here. It's not surprising. The whole joint is like a tomb."

"What's that, Val? What did you say? Did you say something?" came Gyles's voice from the darkness.

"Oh nothing. I was just saying what a lovely room."

"Yes, it is rather. Did you find that candle?"

"Yes, here it is. But I can't find any matches."

"Never mind. I have my lighter. Just hand it in to me."

Val handed Gyles the candle, stretching his arm out but not venturing beyond the threshold of the secret compartment, because something about it made him shudder. He could hear Gyles striking his lighter and see a dim glow growing brighter as the burning wick began to melt the candle's wax.

The chamber was quite a bit larger than Gyles had imagined. Beyond the thick wall in which the bookshelf door was set, the space opened up so that Gyles could stand. Three sides of the room were shelves mostly empty, and coated with dust from the ceiling hung an old gas lighting fixture. Gyles turned a knob on the light slightly and heard a faint hissing. He held the lit candle to the fixture, and there was a soft pop as the gasolier ignited, burning brighter as he turned the gas on full. "Amazing! This old gasolier still works," Gyles marveled.

"If you think that's amazing, wait 'til you get a load of Rin-Tin-Tin sitting on the TV," said Val from the doorway, pointing a thumb at what looked to him like a big, black dog with huge ears perched on a golden box covered with pictures. "He's a friend of yours? The family pooch, perhaps?" Val asked with mocking distaste.

"Good Lord! Anubis from King Tut's tomb!"

"Uh oh. Don't tell me—your illustrious ancestor Cosmo was King Tut's brother, and—"

"Never mind the smart stuff, Mona. Come here and help me carry him into the bedroom, where I can examine this extraordinary beast." Gyles's voice was filled with excitement.

"Ooh—no, I ain't toting no coffin around, no way José!" Val stood his ground, arms crossed over his chest glaring at Gyles.

"Val, this is not a coffin. It's a coffer, and if my guess is right, it is the very coffer that held Cornelia's jewelry which was once Aunt Norma's jewelry."

The wooden statue of Anubis, the wild jackal that roams the necropolis, sat sphinxlike upon his gilded shrine. He was all black except for his pointed ears, which were gilded on the inside. He wore a linen cord tied around his neck, from which hung a bronze ankh, amulet of eternity. His expression was menacing and alert. His lean body and pointed muzzle bespoke speed and attack.

"I hope you know what a creepy thing that is, 'cause I ain't touching it," Val complained.

"Look. I'll put Anubis over here." And with both arms Gyles tenderly embraced the wooden idol, lifting it off the pylon-shaped shrine and carefully placing it on the floor. "Now, grab those handles and help me carry this out into the light. Please, Val—for me?" Gyles gazed tenderly, head cocked to one side, shamelessly turning on all his charm.

"Oh, all right, tough guy. But save the goo-goo eyes for some other chump." Val reluctantly entered the chamber and, squatting before the shrine, his back to it, he grasped the poles that extended from the bottom as Gyles did the same from behind. Together they lifted the shrine and carried it out into the room.

"Now, that wasn't so bad, was it?" Gyles asked.

"Yeah, and now I've got a voodoo curse on me" came Val's retort.

Gyles walked around the shrine slowly, marveling at its beauty and fine craftsmanship. He realized by its perfect condition that it must be of modern construction, not ancient, but it still was old, he thought. He also could see where the front wall could be opened by sliding the center board of its carved and gilded panel up. Or at least he suspected that was how it opened. When he tried his theory, he was surprised to be challenged by a mysterious lock. After a while of poking and prodding the various intricacies of the design, he sat back on his haunches and stared at the gilded shrine.

Val, who had been watching Gyles's struggle, stepped up to the shrine, took hold of the cornice molding that edged the front panel, and with considerable pressure slid the piece to the right about two inches. Then, using the same cornice piece as a handle, he pulled straight up. Slowly the center board rose, sliding on tongue-and-groove fittings. Nonchalantly gesturing with his hand, he announced, "There you go!"

Gyles started with surprise and demanded, "How did you know how to do that?"

"I had a Chinese puzzle box when I was a kid, and I thought it might work."

"Well, bravo! It certainly did. Thank you. I couldn't figure it out to save my life." Gyles knelt in front of the shrine, reached into its dusty shelves, and withdrew several odd-shaped leather-covered boxes decorated with gilded borders of blossoming lotus. He opened the largest box. Its interior was lined with blue silk, and carved into the padding were indentations obviously intended to hold jewelry. The inside lid was imprinted in gold with the words "Karnak Jewels & Antiques, Shepheards Hotel, Cairo."

"So the mysterious jewels were from Karnak's of Cairo. One might have guessed that." Gyles was talking absentmindedly to himself as he envisioned Norma on her deathbed showing these jewels to Florence, and Florence taking them out of their hiding place and depositing them in the bank. Why had she removed them from these boxes? For that matter, why remove them from this seemingly impenetrable hiding place? Perhaps she chose to foil her sister's exoticism with prosaic good sense and lock the valuables in the bank, where they belonged. Undoubtedly the cases were too large to fit in the safety deposit box.

Gyles closed the shrine door and asked Val, "Would you help me put it back?"

"Yeah, well, okay."

Once the shrine was replaced and the gasolier turned off, Gyles pulled the heavy bookcase door closed. It made an ominous rumbling sound as its wheels rolled in their tracks. With a final tug and a click, the door locked into place, fitting flush with the rest of the bookshelves in the inglenook.

"Val, I want to find Cornelia and show her these boxes. She hasn't even read Aunt Florence's letter, and I need to do a lot of work at the shop. Can I drop you anyplace on the way?"

"How about out the window?" Val suggested with disgust.

"Oh, sorry—you live here—or that is, next door," Gyles stammered.

"Yeah, stop by and see me sometime," Val muttered wistfully.

"Seems to me I've heard that line."

"Well, yeah, I guess. I'll see ya around the steam room."

"What's that?"

"Oh, nothing. Just something Monique says. And what's the other line? 'Don't bother, I'll see my own way out,'" Val continued.

"Val, how will I get in touch?"

"I could give you my number."

"That would be great."

Val rummaged in his wallet for a piece of paper. He found a matchbook cover from the Lord Nelson Pub with an old phone number written on the back.

"I guess this is okay. Have you got a pen?"

"Yeah, here," and Gyles handed Val his thick-barreled Mont Blanc pen.

"Pret-ty snazzy, boss!" Val teased.

"Get over it," Gyles commanded playfully as he tousled Val's hair.

Val drew a line through the other phone number and wrote his name and number for Gyles. Gyles read the information and put the paper in his wallet. "You have my card with both my numbers, so please call me."

"Okay, I'll do that. Will you come by the café, and have coffee soon?"

"Okay."

Val led the way out of the bedroom. The two men descended the grand staircase together.

CHAPTER 12

▼

Cornelia walked into the new shop carrying two overflowing shopping bags, one from Decorator's Walk, the other from Scalamandré. Her open purse dangled from her right pinky. She had slung her purple nylon gym bag over her left shoulder, her sunglasses were perched on the very end of her nose, and her car keys were clenched in her teeth. She had pushed open the oversized oak door with her right shoulder. As she advanced into the shop, she shed her various encumbrances on the floor without concern, leaving an untidy trail. "Oh Gyles, there you are." She stood in front of him, the picture of simplicity in a pearl gray crêpe de chine dress complemented by a silk scarf that was decorated with a cascade of mauve wisteria. She wore the scarf tied loosely about her neck. Gyles sat on the floor surrounded by piles of shredded raffia and a growing collection of brightly colored Imari porcelain plates. As he removed them from a wooden crate, he carefully unwrapped and checked each one against his inventory sheet.

Cornelia kicked off her heels and searched her gym bag for a towel, which she spread on the floor to sit on. She plopped herself down beside Gyles and began unwrapping the elaborately patterned Japanese plates. After a while she said, "You'll never guess who I had dinner with last night at the Casa Romero." Knowing how much Gyles loathed Rosalind Wortheley, she somehow hoped to dodge his disapproval by affecting an overcasual manner.

"Don't tell me," Gyles said, gesturing halt by a raised hand. "Martina Navratilova, and she wants you to design her palimony paddock."

"Terribly witty," said Cornelia, "but no, although now that you mention it, there was some talk about a condo at the Ritz Tower, or was that Liv Ullmann?"

"Is Liv Ullmann a lesbian?" exclaimed Gyles with surprise.

"No, darling, but sometimes I think you are. It was Rosalind Wortheley, so there!"

Gyles groaned and said, "Well, I won't criticize the company you keep, since then I would sound exactly like her, God forbid."

"That's very mature of you, Gyles, and you're right, that's exactly what she said, or at least tried to, but I dismissed her disparaging remarks as mere claptrap, and you'll be happy to hear that the result of our meeting is that I will be completely redoing her beach house at Wianno."

"Why should I be glad to know that we have to put up with that driveling idiot for an unspecified length of time? Ye gods, what with special-order fabrics, wallpapers, and her complete inability to make the simplest decision on any subject, we may be subjected to her torture forever. It's surprising that the woman can even feed herself. I hear she has a shopping consultant to go to the grocery store."

"Gyles, she has a nutritionist, not a grocery store shopping consultant. And you don't need to tell me that, because I was the one who told you. But of course you've got it all ass-backwards on purpose. The reason you're going to be thrilled to death to see Rosalind Wortheley is that we are going to give her the English country house look."

"For a beach house on Cape Cod?" Gyles's question sizzled with scorn.

"Rosalind's husband, George—"

"I know who Rosalind is married to. Please, don't be so ruthless as to remind me."

"Yes, George—lovely, lovely George wants Rosalind to spend major money."

"Undoubtedly an occupation for which she was assiduously educated. It's a pity her capacities aren't equal to the task."

"That's just it, Gyles, and I know I can count on you to fill her enormous old rambling villa chock full of lovely English antiques."

Gyles's eyes flashed wide with horror. "I'd rather die."

"You know, Gyles, sometimes you really are a snob." There was a conspicuous silence as they both unwrapped porcelain.

"Cornelia, I've got something to tell you about Aunt Florence's. Something I found there. But first you should read her letter, because it really is your letter. It's the one that was in your safety deposit box at the bank." Gyles handed the letter to Cornelia, who was immediately absorbed in it, and as she read Gyles returned to his inventory list, checking off the plates that Cornelia had unwrapped.

"Wow, this is hot stuff!" exclaimed Cornelia. "Who on earth is Nagib Iskander? Thank the Goddess that Aunt Florence didn't fork over the loot to that creep."

"Apparently he was Norma's lover."

"What was he going to do? Waltz around town with a cobra and vulture popping out of his forehead?"

"It does seem odd, and more so to have been left to the last moment, so to speak. If it had been so important to Aunt Norma that Iskander should have the jewelry, why depend on Aunt Florence, who seems an unlikely messenger—"

Cornelia interrupted. "What do you mean, he was her lover?"

Gyles continued. "Well, according to Uncle Wisner, Iskander had something for everybody and a great deal for Norma Chilton." Gyles gave Cornelia the condensed version of Wisner's story about Nagib Iskander, but in the telling he realized he didn't have a very clear picture of how Aunt Florence was to locate the questionable beneficiary. "Wisner did mention something about Iskander ending up a mortician in Watertown, but I couldn't tell whether he was being literal or metaphoric. His humor, as you know, is completely warped."

"Let me get this straight," Cornelia puzzled.

"Heaven forbid!" Gyles gasped with mock horror.

Cornelia laughed and went on. "Okay, moving gaily forward, the gist of this story is that Wisner and Norma were having an affair with the same guy, one Nagib Iskander, who was some kind of an archaeologist that Norma had dragged back from Egypt. She catches the two love doves billing and cooing right under her nose and exiles the offending nephew to Europe, while she proceeds in courtly splendor up the Nile with Nagib. Then years later, as she gasps her last, she reveals the secret stash to Aunt Florence, begging her to give the jewels to Iskander. Florence of course foils Norma, probably for the first time in her entire life, and locks the loot in my bank vault."

"Essentially yes, that's the story, though you've certainly put a new twist on it."

"Well, it is a narrative that calls for a certain flair."

"So anyway, I went to the house and—"

"Oh Gyles, how could you? Without me?"

Because Gyles had not told his sister about being attacked at the shop that night, it was now hard to explain why he felt such an urgent need to know as much as possible about the Egyptian jewelry. He had wanted to keep her away from any further danger, so he had purposely avoided involving her until he knew it was safe. But now he was practically bursting with the news of his discovery.

"Let me finish. Yes, I went to the house and by the way, Lucy Ann sends her love, as well as Mr. Charlie."

"He's so wonderful. I bet he was there eating Creole shrimp."

"Cornelia—"

"So go on already."

"I went to Norma's room and with the help of Val—"

"Who's Val? Val went but not me?"

"You were probably shmoozing with the charming Rosalind Wortheley. Val is the self-proclaimed boy next door. But never mind, you'll meet him. And I think you'll like him."

"You mean you like him?"

"Well, he is very cute, although he doesn't think I've noticed."

"Well, have you?"

"What kind of a question is that? I just told you that he was."

"It's a rhetorical question, designed to make you aware of how you sound."

"How do I sound?"

"Like you're already trying to deny that you might be attracted to this kid."

"Cornelia, don't be tedious. Let me tell you what I found."

"I've got a better idea. Show me." Cornelia got up from the floor, stepped into her shoes, and, retracing her progress across the shop, picked up her purse and keys, slipped on her sunglasses, and headed for the door.

Gyles shouted after her, "Cornelia, it's Anubis—on the Golden Shrine of Tutankhamen." At that moment the door swung open to reveal Tatiana Sarkisian beneath a large black felt hat, her dusky complexion complemented by shimmering black sable. The two women froze in silence, staring at each other.

Tatiana's resonant voice broke the silence when she said, "Your brother is talking to you of the ancient gods." Cornelia involuntarily shuddered and found herself more than a little frightened.

"Anubis, the jackal, god of the western gate, he who also is Horus. He guards the entrance to the inner tomb." As she slowly walked toward the pair, Tatiana continued her exposition on Anubis. She had serendipitously arrived and overheard Gyles reveal a secret whose significance he did not fully realize.

In her speech he heard the tenacious hunger of the hunter, of Anubis the jackal, and Gyles was awed by Tatiana's intensity. "Yes, Anubis was…uh…on the postcard that I received from Cairo, where my aunt was…uh, had been visiting."

Cornelia immediately picked up on Gyles's diversion. "Gyles, may I introduce you to Tatiana Sarkisian. Mrs. Sarkisian, this is my brother and business partner, Gyles Chilton."

Gyles stood up and brushed the loose raffia from his hands, but instead of extending a hand he gave a slight formal bow, saying in a neutral tone, "How do you do, Mrs. Sarkisian. My sister's told me about her meeting with you."

"And by that you mean that you are surprised to see me here?" Tatiana's blunt reply was a challenge directed at Gyles, for the moment ignoring Cornelia, like the soldier attacking when even slightly threatened.

Cornelia, who was not at all clear about the events surrounding the Dynasty Ball, and wanting to give Tatiana the benefit of the doubt, or at least a chance for explanation, interposed a softening word. "As you can see, we're only beginning to move into our new shop, and everything is in disorder. But I do have a couple of chairs in my office. If you will please follow me." Cornelia led Mrs. Sarkisian to the small staircase that ascended a half flight to a gallery. The elegant woman followed at a maddeningly slow pace, examining everything in the shop as if she were a casual browser. In order to urge her on, Cornelia climbed the stairs and paused at the top. Halfway up, the lady stopped and scrutinized everything in the shop beneath her before continuing to join Cornelia.

The decorator opened the door and politely held it for her mysterious visitor. As Tatiana entered, her soft glistening fur brushed Cornelia's knee, and the scent of ambergris and heliotrope trailed after her. "Please have a seat," said Cornelia as she gestured towards a comfortably upholstered chair. She closed the door and found her own chair.

The interior of the office was painted bayberry green, ascot gray, taupe, and old ivory, with touches of gold. The sensuous Art Nouveau furniture constructed of blond wood, consisted of a desk, two upholstered chairs, and a loveseat. There was a glass wall separating the shop from the office salvaged from an old pub in London. Its frosted and etched design, of florid patterning was a wonderful complement to the fluid lines of the rest of the interior. On the wall behind Cornelia's desk hung a painting. It depicted an androgynously sturdy young woman draped in orange gauze. She was staring with transfixed gaze into the distance, while with uplifted arms of remarkable musculature she crowned herself with laurel and oak leaves. In this environment Cornelia felt confident and at ease to fairly judge what Tatiana might have to say about the Dynasty Ball. But she was resolved not to be influenced by the beauty of this mysterious woman.

"I'm very confused about the events of the other evening," Cornelia began. "I realize now that I was foolish to have smoked marijuana there, because it affects me strongly. I don't know if you know it, but I passed out in the stall."

"But so did I," broke in Tatiana excitedly. "There on that loathsome floor in that squalid toilet," and she jerked in her chair and shuddered. "When I came to I was alone and my purse was stolen. You were gone, and I was afraid. I carry a small revolver in my purse. I could have been shot with my own gun, and if my coat had been stolen my husband would have killed me anyway." Having painted this grim picture, she dissolved into tears.

Cornelia did not know what to think about this development. Generally she did not respond to weepy women. She felt uncomfortable and unsure of what to do. She didn't have a Kleenex to offer her guest and was relieved to hear the phone ring. "Hello, Chilton's Antiques and Interiors, this is Cornelia Chilton."

"Cornelia, be careful of that witch, she's dangerous," Gyles warned in a low voice because he was calling from his desk below.

"Oh hello, I'm glad you called, I've been meaning to tell you that I've been puzzling over our problem, and I have some new ideas to tell you about," Cornelia improvised.

"Yes, I know you can't talk in front of her, but if she tries any funny business, just scream. I'll come running."

"That's kind of you, Mrs. Wortheley, but I haven't yet completed the curtain designs, and I would prefer to show them to you after they're finished."

"Mrs. Wortheley? Yuck! I'll get you for that, Cornelia. Just make sure that Natasha doesn't finish you and draw your curtain. Now listen, I'm serious, I don't like this."

"Thank you for telling me that, Mrs. Wortheley. You can imagine how much I value your opinion. Good-bye now." Click.

While Cornelia was on the phone, Tatiana searched her purse for a handkerchief which she duly produced, daubing her eyes delicately. Cornelia was unmoved by this performance and she continued her story without acknowledging the other woman's tears. "Please excuse the interruption. As I was saying, while I was unconscious a friend found me and got me out of there, and she was kind enough to drive me home. When I came to, I was generally okay, but hung over. The most horrible part of it was that my jewelry was stolen." Cornelia stopped her narrative, looking directly into Tatiana Sarkisian's eyes, and she waited. There was a long pause and an unseen struggle that grew in tension as both women fought to maintain their inscrutable poise.

Tatiana broke the moment, gushing surprise and sympathy. "My poor Cornelia. Your wonderful Egyptian jewels. And they suited you so well, as if you had been born with them. A little princess of the Nile. Those beasts. How selfish of me to assume…that is, when I awoke I was alone. You were gone…I didn't know—"

"You thought I stole your purse," Cornelia said with shocked disbelief.

"And you thought I stole your jewelry." There was another pause. Tatiana hastened to add, "But it's my fault, I was so desperate to be accepted by this strange new crowd. Everyone seemed so Bohemian, and I had read that all chic Americans took drugs. When I first arrived I unexpectedly recognized one of the bartenders. He is the son of one of my husband's furriers. I asked him for a bottle of champagne, which he magically produced, and then I was foolish enough to ask him for some drugs. He laughed. Apparently I had not used the correct terms, but he produced that cursed cigarette which we smoked, and I am so sorry. My husband does not let me make many decisions, and now I see perhaps he is right."

Tatiana fought off tears. Her story was gaining credence with Cornelia. Her frank confession of wanting to belong struck a sympathetic chord. But this last submission to the tyranny of men, with its implicit assumption of the inferiority of women, produced an outraged and protective attitude in Cornelia for what now appeared to her as a cloistered and misused woman. Cornelia spoke in measured tones. "It would seem that we've both been foolish—no, indiscreet and impulsive, but it is the purpose of mistakes to teach us, not to make us chastise ourselves with guilt or to hide from the pain of learning behind masks of inferiority. I accept your explanation, and I'm sorry that we have both lost, but mostly I'm sorry to have condemned you without having heard you first." Cornelia magnanimously tipped the scales of objectivity as she basked in the glory of her own enlightened attitude.

Tatiana looked at her a little surprised and said, "Well thank you. Yes, you're right, that's very generous of you, very wise. I am even surer now of my decision, and I will ask you to help me with our new condominium. But first you must meet my husband, and I must prepare you that he is very old-fashioned and may not always have the greatest confidence in your…that is—"

Cornelia interrupted, "He doesn't like women in business. Is that it?"

"Well yes, you seem to understand."

"That is my job to understand both of you, so that I can create an atmosphere most appropriate for your lifestyle. I'm a graduate of Harvard Design School and the Boston Architectural League, as well as a fully accredited member of the

ASID." Cornelia enumerated her impressive credentials with casual assurance, and further suggested, "We can also, at your convenience, visit some of the houses and offices that I have done here in Boston."

Tatiana's misgivings were relaxed by this suggestion, and her attention became more animated. "Oh yes, I think that's a good idea. Let me speak to my husband and call you for an appointment." She rose and extended her hand, signaling the end of the interview.

CHAPTER 13

▼

"Hello, Percival? This is Wisner Chilton. Did you get into the house yet?"

"Piece of cake, Wiz. Mr. Gyles fell right into my arms."

"Yes, you are a very resourceful young man. After having seen you in action, I knew you'd be right for the job. But remember, my nephew is not a desperate old john at the Lord Nelson Pub."

"Keep your rug on, Wiz. No, he ain't like you, but you'd be surprised how easy some guys are."

"At my age I am hardly surprised by anything. Between us, there was a mutual hunger for which your lost soul sat up and barked almost immediately."

"Oh, you mean the money? Yeah, so what? I should maybe quiver with shame? Well, let me lay it on ya, Daddy, I want some more."

"You'll get my check as we arranged, every week, and you live at that apartment free."

"Never mind the check. I want cash."

"Then you'll get cash. Now what did you find out, other than the length of my dear nephew's member?"

"Member? Hah! That sounds like a club. How very English. We didn't exactly get that far. The dog's in the closet."

"What did you say?"

"The dog's in the closet."

"Are you sure we're talking about Gyles Chilton?"

"Yeah, the dude at the Dynasty Ball with the black hair and the shoulders, right?"

"And you find him unattractive?"

"No, he's a doll."

"Excuse my obtuseness, but who then is the dog in the closet?"

"Hey, beats me. Rin-Tin-Tin on a TV. He's in the closet behind the bookshelf."

"A glimmer of light is beginning to penetrate the darkness. Gyles found something in a closet at his aunt's house?"

"Yeah, a dog. A statue of a dog on a golden box covered with a lot of pictures."

"Anubis."

"Yes, that's the one. That's just what Gyles said."

"So he recognized the guardian."

"Yeah, he seemed to know a lot about it. But he didn't know how to get it open."

"But you did?"

"Sure, it was a cinch. I used to have a Chinese puzzle box that was just like it."

"And did you see what was inside?"

"Yeah, a lot of empty boxes."

"Empty boxes?"

"Yeah. Gyles said they were for jewelry. They were kinda lumpy."

"Kind of lumpy? How very interesting. And where is the dog now?"

"Behind the secret panel."

"Where are the lumpy boxes?"

"Gyles took those with him. He said Cornflower could use them."

"What?"

"He said Cornflower should see them."

"You mean Cornelia?"

"Oh yeah, that's it, Cornelia. That's his sister, huh?"

"Did you leave the window unlocked as I instructed you?"

"Like I told you, Wiz, it was a piece of cake. The sucker didn't even look back."

"Good. You did very well, Percival. I'll bring your money to you right now. I would like to see Anubis, the guardian of the western gate, myself." Wisner hung up his telephone.

CHAPTER 14

▼

Tatiana's Rolls-Royce came to an abrupt halt at the front door of Greenbrier Funeral Home in Watertown, which was the name that her grandfather, Nagib Iskander, had given his highly lucrative business. She flung her hat into the backseat, and her dark hair highlighted with henna bounced with her stride as she briskly climbed the steps to the front door. Her gloved hand pressed a mother-of-pearl button beside the oppressively ornate front door, and in response she could hear bass chimes intoning a doleful melody. She impatiently waited for the doorbell to be answered, and after a moment the door was eased open. Tatiana with a quick sidestep brushed past and without pause continued up the polished marble stairs towards the cavernous hall.

"Hello, Zaki, is my brother in?" She tossed off her curt question.

"I'm sorry, Mrs. Sarkisian. Mr. Iskander is with a client at the moment."

"Tell him that I'm waiting for him in the inner office." She issued this command from the top of the vestibule stairs as she removed her gloves one finger at a time. Her heels struck the marble floor with percussive stabs as she disappeared behind a heavy velvet portiere. The inner office was in the former library of this rambling pile, which had been the pretentious achievement of a now nameless industrialist. Tatiana tossed her sable onto an old leather sofa and seated herself behind a vast expanse of mahogany desk. Behind her was an impressive neo-Jacobean fireplace, over which hung a somber portrait of a distinguished-looking man with a carefully trimmed gray beard. He wore a black double-breasted frock coat with satin lapels and on his head a scarlet fez with a long black tassel. Tatiana shuffled through the papers on the desk, disregarding their meticulous order. She rapidly discarded various documents, bills, and letters. Some of them drifted to the floor about her.

Without a sound and without her realizing, there appeared before her a man in an elegantly cut dark suit of fine material that hinted at the powerful physique beneath. He stood with his hands in his pockets, revealing a heavy gold watch chain that looped from his alligator belt to his trouser pocket. Studying the woman at the desk impassively, he awaited her recognition. Eventually she became bored with her desktop perusal, and with an impatient click of her tongue she discarded a handful of papers onto the blotter. She looked up, a surprise rippling through her as her eyes came to rest on her brother's disfigured face. His features were of the same even, strong lines as the portrait above the fireplace, but the right side of his face was stained by a lavender-gray shadow, as if ink had been splashed there and left to fade. He wore this birthmark defiantly, and his demeanor had assumed a perpetual air of arrogance. He continued to stare at her in silence.

"So, Nagib, you are here." Tatiana's greeting was void of warmth.

"To state the obvious is to limit perception." Nagib's voice was a colorless monotone.

"Is that the wisdom of our revered grandfather?"

"It is the truth. You see only the surface of reality, the fleeting moment of today. I see eternity. I have always been here. I will continue." Nagib pontificated in sepulchral tones.

"That's all very well and good, but you will need far more than the wisdom of the ancients to get you through tomorrow if these bills are any indication of the general state of your finances." Tatiana pointed with contempt at the papers that she had scattered about the desk.

"You should know the pressures of underfinanced ventures if anyone does. The ravenous flames of your ambitions have, I understand, consumed the resources of that taxidermist you married."

A blush of repressed anger colored Tatiana's deep olive cheek. "My dear Nagib, as long as you are in this house of charnel, you're hardly in a position to cast disparaging remarks on anyone's profession. If you had not tied up all Grandfather's money by trying to control the Chilton Savings and Trust Bank, we wouldn't be in such a desperate situation."

"I have to regain my birthright. I am on the verge, the very edge of success. Do you think that whatever paltry sum we retrieve from the tomb will satisfy me? That is merely the seed destined to rise from the barren desert. It is the dismembered Osiris, who will come to life again as Horus. I am Isis, who collects the pieces. I am the great ennead, all of the old gods together."

His speech diminished to a hissing whisper that echoed through the dim room. Tatiana stared at Nagib with half-closed eyes, allowing him to rave. He fed his own passion with the Egyptian delusions that had been drilled into him by their grandfather.

Although her relationship with her brother was mutually contemptuous, Tatiana had a powerful grasp on Nagib's attention by virtue of their shared secret. He had no one else to proclaim his destiny to, and she would listen without censure, waiting for the moment when she could use his delusion to enact her own plan. Tatiana was not a patient person. Growing up in her grandfather's house, she had been pampered and spoiled, partly to compensate for her growing awareness that to be a child of a mortician was a stigma that would stain her as effectively as her brother Nagib's birthmark. But now she was compelled to cultivate an appearance of patience because Nagib quite fantastically had tied up all their assets in his grandiose scheme to take over the Chilton Bank.

Nagib and Tatiana had been brought up in a netherworld of ambiguous social status. Their lifestyle had been lavish with a certain Oriental excess. All the great families of Boston gathered periodically in the dim, solemn opulence of the Greenbrier Funeral Home, where, with quiet dignity, august persons were eased into their eternal rest. Although this profession provided a handsome income, which by investment had grown over the years into a sizeable real estate empire, it had always excluded the Iskanders from the society they most craved. It was this hunger that consumed both Tatiana and Nagib. The key to their acceptance was their past connection to the Chiltons, which might appear nebulous at present. But appearances would crumble as new forms emerged from the dust of the past; for that goal Tatiana conjured the patience of a sibyl.

Struggling to maintain a neutral tone, she announced, "I have located the real jewels." And she thought to play into her brother's Egyptian fantasies by adding, "The heart of our mother is in the hands of the heretics."

Nagib reacted to this proclamation like a starving predator riveted to its prey. But he fought to control himself, saying, "It is not hard to imagine where that might be, but I'm glad to have saved time and not risked any more bungled efforts. Where is the sacred scarab, the heart of our mother?"

"There is a safe in the back of the Chilton's new store, rather obviously hidden behind a Chinese screen. I am sure the jewels are there. Unfortunately, we will need someone to open it."

Nagib tapped the ends of his fingers together and said, half to himself, "I am sure that can be arranged. May I ask how it is that you have such easy access to the Chilton's shop?"

"That was quite simple. Cornelia is going to decorate my condominium at the Heritage."

"And that was quite simple? She was not disturbed by your administering drugs to her and stealing her jewelry?"

"I told her that I too had been a victim, that the marijuana had been given to me. I appealed to her sense of guilt and her greed. It wasn't difficult. I was not trying to convince her to like me, merely to take on a very lucrative job. She was only too willing. I am afraid in the end she will have no luck convincing my husband that her decorating schemes are necessary for his continued happiness, and I of course will be deeply saddened and embarrassed by his contrary dictates. But what can a poor, obedient wife do?"

Nagib smiled at Tatiana's intrigue, but inwardly he realized how very dangerous his sister could be. He remembered her easy lies of childhood, webs that had enmeshed him in unavoidable disasters. He thought to himself, when we return the heart of our mother to its tomb, Tatiana should enjoy the eternal reward and remain behind as companion to the departed. His smile broadened. "I will arrange for the safe to be opened and take the precaution of replacing the real jewels with the reproductions. That way the exchange will go unnoticed for some time."

"Wait, Nagib, I have an idea how we can accomplish this delicate task with speed and efficiency. At some point I will have to produce Mr. Sarkisian, but no one in Boston has seen him yet. Perhaps your friend who will assist us to open the safe can be persuaded to assume that role. As I have already told Cornelia, Mr. Sarkisian is very difficult, and in order for him to decide which of Gyles Chilton's expensive antiques to purchase, I will suggest that we be left alone at the shop for a while so I can soften his opposition." Tatiana gazed at Nagib with gloating eyes, and he continued to grimace.

CHAPTER 15

▼

Tatiana emerged from her Rolls-Royce and locked the door. Guided by her reflection in the window glass, she adjusted her hat minutely. She circled the car to the passenger side, where she took the arm of her distinguished escort, and with measured steps they progressed toward the front door of Chilton's Antiques and Interiors. They waited for someone to respond to the buzzer. As she peered through the window, Tatiana was surprised to see the shop so elegantly appointed. She recognized the Chinese screen that concealed the back of the shop, from behind which emerged Gyles, who was putting on his suit jacket as he briskly approached them to open the door.

"Mr. Chilton, this is my husband, Farag Sarkisian." Tatiana's escort was a scowling and reluctant-looking fellow with an enormous silver mustache and contrasting bushy black eyebrows. His black overcoat was trimmed with Persian lamb on the collar and lapels. He wore a black fedora hat and tight black kid gloves, and he carried a black Malacca walking stick with a gold knob. Tatiana also was a study in black. Underneath her ubiquitous sable she wore a severely tailored black suit, which was cinched at the waist by a black patent leather belt with an Art Deco buckle of silver inset with marcasites. As a couple, these two were reminiscent of the severely regal Dutch portraits of the late seventeenth century.

Tatiana's escort acknowledged Gyles by the slightest of nods and a distrustful silence. As the couple proceeded into the shop, Gyles was calculating what tack to pursue with the taciturn Mr. Sarkisian.

"May I hang up your coats?" he asked politely.

"No, I'll keep my coat if you don't mind," the man snapped and pointed with his rapier-thin cane at a Louis XVI gilded console table. He proclaimed, "This is a reproduction."

Tatiana interjected a diversion by replying, "Yes, that would be very nice of you, Mr. Chilton." She turned around, allowing Gyles to ease her out of her fur.

The grim gentleman admonished Gyles curtly, saying, "Be careful, young man, that is Russian sable. Don't put it on a wire hanger."

Tatiana, in conciliatory tones, urged, "Farag, please! Mr. Chilton is very careful. Now give him your coat and hat."

Gyles advanced and, with patient assistance, coaxed the overcoat from the man called Farag. Tatiana looked at Gyles with pleading indulgence and gratitude in her smile. Gyles began to sympathize with the melancholic beauty of this woman, as he saw her flawless deep olive complexion contrasted against the coarse, bushy frown of the man she fussed over.

During the few moments it took Gyles to return from the coatroom, he had decided the more successful tack was not to argue with Mr. Sarkisian's judgments about the antiques but rather to compliment the man on his keen observations. With this noble resolve, he said, "Yes, the console table is mid-to-late nineteenth century. It was made by Henry Danson in Paris. The carving is very sharp, and of course the legs represent quivers of arrows, and the stretcher is in the form of crossed bows. An unusual curving line for the period, but I think it serves the motif perfectly. The mask, of course, is Mercury." Here Gyles pointed to the handsomely modeled face that was carved into the center of the apron.

"Why do you attribute that rather nondescript decoration to Mercury?"

"Oh, Farag, please! Mr. Chilton is—"

Gyles good-naturedly interrupted Tatiana's objections. "You are right to be skeptical. I didn't notice at first either, but tilted back on his head, like a halo, he wears a helmet with the wings of Mercury."

"And does that make the maker Henry Danson?" Sarkisian relentlessly attacked.

"No, although there is a similar table at the Musé du Louvre that I can show you in a photograph. They are under the impression that their table was made by Henry Danson because they have half the label still glued to it. This table has the same label, but in its entirety. I am rather fortunate to have such positive identification. The green marble top is such a foil to the burnished gilding. It is a handsome piece, don't you think?" Gyles smiled, proud of himself for maintaining a pleasant tone and thanking his lucky stars for the unusual amount of documentation he had on the console table.

"Is this the table that Cornelia has suggested for our foyer at the Heritage?" asked Tatiana.

"Yes. We feel that in combination with the Empire mirror, as you see here, flanked by the porphyry obelisks, the Classical themes will be strongly established. Then as we enter the living room, we will update the period by using the Deco Ruhlman pieces, with their Egyptian references. The deep plum color of the porphyry and the forest green of the marble are the major color schemes of the apartment, echoed by the spectacular Unitarian Church steeple on Arlington Street, which you can see so well from the apartment. The steeple is carved from red sandstone amazingly similar in color and shape to the obelisks, and the various greens of the marble can be seen in the trees of the Public Garden."

"Oh, Gyles, it's marvelous. I'm dying to see Cornelia's watercolors of the apartment. I am sure that Farag will agree when he's able to see how the apartment will look when it is completed." Tatiana recklessly enthused, but Farag's approval was not forthcoming.

"How can you call such a hodgepodge marvelous? To begin with, the building is no more than a motel."

Tatiana tried to explain to Gyles. "Farag does not like the low ceilings at the Heritage. He's used to the tall rooms of Cairo. But Cairo is hot. In Boston, they don't need high ceilings." And here she came close to begging.

"What nonsense, Louis XVI and the monstrous grotesqueries of the Corsican usurper. Those are not Sphinxes, they are harlots on that mirror."

Tatiana took Gyles aside. "Oh dear Mr. Chilton, Gyles, I wonder if you could leave us for a while. I wish to speak to my husband alone, especially before he meets Cornelia. As I told you, Mr. Sarkisian is very old-fashioned. He's not used to women in business, and I fear an even greater upset if I cannot calm him now."

"Yes, yes, certainly. I'll just pop round to the Mirabelle Café, and have a brandy, and I'll arrange for Cornelia to meet me there. How long do you need? I mean, uh, when shall we return? In an hour perhaps?"

"No, no, not even that. Perhaps a half an hour. Yes, that will be enough, because I would not want to keep my husband waiting either. Come back, the two of you, in a half an hour. I am so sorry about this." Tatiana's apology was convincing to Gyles. He paused only long enough to go to his desk behind the Chinese screen to get his keys. Practically tiptoeing from the shop, he waved a silent good-bye to the elegant lady in black while Mr. Sarkisian lurked in the background, sulking.

As soon as the door closed, Tatiana hissed. "You certainly played that scene fast."

"You told me to," returned the man in a pouting tone.

"I did not."

"Yes, you did," he insisted. "You said we would have very little time and I would have to open the safe quickly."

"You didn't have to jump down his throat before you got your coat off."

"Where is my coat?"

"What do I care?"

"I care, and you better care, too. My stethoscope is in the pocket, which is why I didn't want him to take it in the first place. What if Mr. Chilton had seen that, huh? What would he have thought of a furrier who carries a stethoscope?"

"The implications are rather macabre," returned Tatiana casually. "Come along, the safe is this way."

"I need my stethoscope. You don't know what this is doing to me. I am too nervous, too upset. I won't be able to do it."

"Stop your sniveling. You will work, or you will never work again. My brother will throw you out of that hole that you cling to like a badger, out into the street."

"He can't do that. I've been a tenant in that building for thirty years. I have rights." Farag screeched and waved his fist at Tatiana.

"Keep quiet, you pathetic creature. You have no rights whatsoever. You haven't paid rent for over a year."

"The economy is down. Business is slack."

"It is not likely that you will be able to pay in the near future because your future is over, so you will do what you are told." Tatiana had reached the back of the shop, where on either side of the staircase going up to Cornelia's office were doors. She opened the right door first, only to find a broom closet stuffed with cardboard boxes. Slamming it shut she opened the left door, behind which she found their coats. Digging in the pockets of Farag's, she found the stethoscope.

"Here, now get to work. The safe is behind that screen." She thrust the instrument at him and struck him in the chest with her fist. He awkwardly fumbled to collect the stethoscope and his dignity. "You heartless bitch."

"Don't swear at me. It wasn't I who drank you into the gutter. You did that all yourself, so here, take your medicine and stop that trembling long enough to do the job." She handed him a pint bottle of gin and he grabbed at it with desperation. He sucked half the bottle down in a flash.

"You're lucky to have me here, Mrs. Sarkisian, to do your dirty work. You didn't even know that that table wasn't eighteenth century. Without me, this job would already have been loused up."

"Oh, please, what do I care how old that stupid table is? But it does not surprise me that you know all about forgery. Now get to work."

The man known as Farag shuffled off behind the Chinese screen. At first sight of the antique iron strongbox, he sighed with relief. He had been apprenticed to the Wheelock Company, the manufacturer of this type of office safe, at an early age. His uncanny ability to decipher lost combinations was based on a detailed understanding of the mechanism as well as a very sensitive ear and a light touch. If the mechanism were in good order, he should be able to hear the tumblers click into place after each rotation of the dial.

He drew the desk chair up to the safe and lowered himself unsteadily onto the seat. His body ached and his hands trembled, but the gin that burned inside his rumbling stomach began to anchor his drifting fear, allowing him to focus on the delicate task at hand.

He hooked the stethoscope into his hairy ears as he held the listening end to the safe. At that moment, a blast of fire engine horns exploded on the street. Farag jumped, dropping his stethoscope and uttering a pathetic screech. Tatiana, livid with disgust, stood over the trembling man with a lit cigarette in her hand. She waited for the fire engines to pass. Blue-gray smoke clouded the atmosphere as she said one word, "W-o-r-m," and then thrust the gin bottle at him. He grabbed at it with the precision of a diving eagle, catching the bottle in midflight.

"Now pull yourself together and open that safe." The last word came out as a prolonged hiss.

Tatiana grabbed the bottle away from Farag. He wiped his mouth with the back of his hand and cracked his knuckles, first his right hand, then his left, which was curiously larger than its mate. Tatiana shuddered at the sound and walked away from him. The booze had kicked in, and Farag returned his attention to the safe. Using the most delicate touch, only the very ends of his fingers, he rotated the dial slowly and smoothly. His entire concentration was directed inwards, guided by the slight signals he heard through the stethoscope and felt at his fingertips. He closed his eyes, forcing his mind to envision the combination of digits that would retract the steel dowels locking the door in place.

After a miraculously short five minutes, he had discovered all four numbers. He knew it was the final digit because the mechanism gave an infinitesimal click like the snap of military heels saluting him. His forehead immediately broke into a heavy-beaded sweat, as though the release of his concentration made his brain weep. He stood up and staggered away from the safe, his face buried in his handkerchief.

"Be careful, you lumbering ox, you'll break something," Tatiana barked as she lunged for the safe door. It opened easily, but before her she saw a black hole. Her rage burned uselessly as she stared into the emptiness.

"You little shithead, Chilton! Play games with me, and I'll break you like a dry bone." Tatiana's fury hit Farag like a shock wave, and he collapsed onto the desk chair, staring at her in silent terror. Tatiana dashed for the coat closet and threw open the door. Grabbing her sable, she fairly tossed it into the air, thrusting herself into it like a bull charging a matador's cape.

She screamed at Farag, "Get the fuck out of that chair and into the car."

The careful veneers of cultivated tones were torn from her speech by the blistering fire of her fury. She threw Farag's coat at him and stormed out of the shop. He stumbled after her.

CHAPTER 16

▼

Wisner did not like heights. Except for the exalted pinnacles of Boston society, he had an extreme aversion to higher altitudes. You might even say a disdain. He had attained the summit of his ambition at birth in his father's house on Beacon Hill, and, from that prominent rise, he surveyed the rest of creation with a certain proprietary assumption. He therefore had to force himself out onto the fire escape that connected 285 Commonwealth with 283. Gingerly placing one foot onto the black iron bars of the bridge, he made the overcautious mistake of looking beyond his well-polished wingtip shoe, and gasped at the five stories of uninterrupted void between his foot and the hard concrete that paved the laundry yards below.

"Don't shove me, you juvenile delinquent."

"I didn't shove you, I'm helping you."

"Yes, helping me fall to my death. Let me warn you, you'll have a hard time explaining any accident that may befall me."

"Hey, Wiz, chill out. It's no sweat. I'll go first, and you can hold on to me. Just don't look down."

Val hopped out onto the fire escape. His deeply defined, muscular legs, covered with soft golden hair, flexed beneath his cut-off jeans. He held out his hands for Wisner to follow.

"Is it absolutely necessary for you to traipse about like a half-naked hooker all the time?"

Val did not reply, and Wisner reluctantly took the boy's hands and allowed himself to be lifted up and out the window. Val placed Wisner's trembling hands on the railing of the fire escape and playfully raised the old man's chin with his fingers, cheerfully admonishing him to "Look up at the birds, Wizzy."

"Don't let me go" came the panicky reply.

"You'll be all right. I have to open the window."

"I'm going to fall and die."

"Stuff it, Miss Thing. You really are a pain." Val raised the window that he had left unlocked when he was in the house with Gyles. Then, after prying Wisner's hands from the railing, he practically carried the man piggyback into the adjoining house.

Once Wisner was safely ensconced in his late cousin's house, he struggled to regain his dignity by ordering Val to wait for him on the fire escape.

"Yeah and how will you open the bookcase to get at Rin-Tin-Tin?"

"I pull the hook that holds the fire tongs."

Val shrugged and said, "Yeah, well good luck, but even Gyles couldn't open the gold box."

"Silly child, you have already told me how to do that also. Now run along. I am perfectly capable of finding my way around this house. I've been coming here since before you were born."

Wisner brushed imaginary dirt from his immaculate dark blue suit jacket, turned on his heels, and walked away. From the other side of the glass, Val gave him the finger and returned to his own apartment.

Wisner tiptoed through the old nursery that had been Cornelia's childhood room. When he came to the hall door, he paused to listen if anyone was about, but, hearing nothing, he opened the door and stepped into the fourth-floor hallway. The light was very dim, coming only from the skylight above the stairwell. He noiselessly proceeded down the hall hung with grim portraits of deceased Chiltons. These shadowy ancestors alternated with their cultural trophies, which were sullen landscape paintings of the Barbizon school in elaborate gilded plaster frames.

As he was about to descend the stairs to the third floor, where Norma Chilton's bedroom was, he was momentarily distracted by a bookcase that loomed in the shadows. Its self-consciously Neo-Jacobean carvings guarded a collection of leather-bound books, which, at a glance, Wisner could see were early nineteenth-century editions of ecclesiastic treaties. Nothing could have been further from Wisner's interest, and he sighed with relief that he did not have the responsibility of these possessions. His eye came to rest on a volume of a different mark and size than the others. On the spine of this book, deeply tooled into fine Moroccan leather, was the title *The Egyptian Book of the Dead*. This was a subject that seized Wisner's imagination, and he plucked the tome from the dusty shelf. Wisner seated himself on a convenient but none too comfortable side chair, one of a pair that flanked the bookcase.

The front cover of the book was decorated with the wedjat eye of Horus, and around the edge was a border of lotus blossoms alternating with the stylized feather of Maat. Wisner opened the book and saw pasted on the flyleaf was a finely engraved bookplate. The central image was of Osiris enveloped in a tight shroud from which hands protruded. The mummy held a crook and flail and was adorned with the white crown of Upper Egypt. The face, stained green and wearing a false beard, was the unmistakable likeness of Norma Chilton. Boldly printed below this monstrous idol were the initials NSC Norma Stebbins Chilton. Wisner whispered to himself aloud, "Osiris, ruler of the afterlife, you call me and I follow. I hear you and I will obey."

He snapped the book shut and placed it deep in the shadows of the chair, where he could retrieve it on his way out.

Wisner mused aloud to himself. "*The Egyptian Book of the Dead* will make interesting bedside reading, a little gem that will never be missed by my dearest nephew. God knows how it got shoved in that ghastly bookcase to begin with. Probably that illiterate fussbudget Lucy Ann, with her eternal tidying. Oh well, it appeared at the proper time and to the intended heir. Yes, all goes well, and now to meet Anubis, the god of the western gate."

When Wisner arrived at Norma Chilton's bedroom door, he paused to listen, but all that could be heard was the familiar Westminster chime of the tall case clock that stood in the front hall below. He opened the paneled mahogany door of the bedroom and slipped into the darkness beyond. Locking the door behind him and leaving the key in the lock, he pressed the light switch on the wall, illuminating the lamps on either side of the great bed.

He crossed the room to the inglenook, where he found another wall switch. This illuminated two elaborate bronze sconces chiseled with designs of acorns and oak leaves, which were mounted above the fireplace. These lights shone with studied effect upon the golden iridescent Favrile art glass and the fine landscape painting. But Wisner's eyes were blind to their beauty, and his hand trembled as he reached for the brass hook that held the fire tongs. At first his efforts came to naught as he delicately twisted and wiggled the hardware. In his frustration a temper surged through him, and he yanked on the hook with all his might. He heard a metallic click, and then a rumbling like distant thunder, and watched with wide eyes as the bookshelf swung inward, traveling on the bronze track recessed in the floor. Like a warning or a threat, a gaseous, musty odor issued forth on a chilly draft. Wisner hesitated only a moment before he pushed the bookcase deeper into the darkness.

"Anubis, I am here," he chanted. "Oh my heart, which I had from my mother, oh my heart, which I had from my mother, oh my heart, of my different ages, do not stand up as a witness against me. Do not oppose me in the tribunal. Do not be hostile to me in the presence of the keeper of the balance."

Wisner was well prepared for his encounter with the god of the western gate. In addition to this spell from *The Book of the Dead*, he had brought a flashlight, which he directed into the hidden place. The focused beam of light traveled over the golden shrine upwards, illuminating the black jackal of the necropolis. Through the darkness the haughty stare of eternity glared at Wisner, who fell to his knees in ecstasy, tears bathing his eyes. He reached an impertinent hand towards the shrine, his fingers caressing and stroking the gold-covered pylon on which the god sat lean and poised. The cold, smooth touch of the precious metal made the old man's heart race.

He nervously searched his pockets for matches to light the gasolier that Val had told him about. Because of his nervous excitement, Wisner had to light several matches after turning the gas key. Suddenly, the antique fixture ignited with a mild explosion. Wisner uttered a repressed screech and dropped his matches. The flame had singed the hair on his knuckles, filling the small space with a nauseating odor of burnt hair. Beneath the flickering gaslight, the enthroned Anubis seemed to quiver with nervous tension. Wisner whispered into the erect and pointed ears of the god, "Your journey will soon be complete. We will return together to the western gate and join the great ennead in the world of eternal bliss."

Standing by the shrine, Wisner wrapped his arms around the jackal's neck, his head lightly resting against the jackal's head as one would embrace a trusted dog. Slowly uncoiling himself, he sought the entrance to the pylon. He held the crown molding in both hands and pushed to the right as Val had explained. Wisner was surprised at the ease with which the gold-encased wood slid smoothly on its track. Next he raised the center board of the shrine by pulling on the crown molding like a handle. Holding the flashlight and stooping to look into the shrine, Wisner was puzzled and surprised to see the old jewelry presentation boxes of irregular shape. He thought he remembered Val telling him that these "lumpy" boxes had been removed. Had Gyles, in fact, removed only some of the contents of the shrine? Had Gyles not told Val of all the contents? Is there more than one compartment to the pylon shrine and have I discovered a cache that was overlooked? Wisner's mind raced with the possibilities.

He staggered from the secret room, laden with treasure, and crossed over to the writing desk, where he carefully placed the three boxes. Wisner noted the simple gold border of lotus blossoms that was embossed in the leather of the cases and the tiny detail of the wedjat eye of Horus that decorated the round button catch that held the case closed. He pressed this catch and opened the case, which was shaped like an oversized scallop shell. Wisner gasped; his hands became moist, and he began to tremble slightly. Before him nestled in midnight-blue silk lay the tiara of the bejeweled cobra, its headband set with scarabs of deep blue lapis lazuli. The hooded serpent's diamond eyes with their cold flame glared menacingly up at him.

Unnerved by the formidable presence of the god, Wisner sought to diffuse his intimidation by commenting to himself as he picked up and examined the long-sought-after treasure. "Not exactly archaeologically accurate. You could never let well enough alone, Norma. Quaint touch, these diamonds. I suppose as Queen of the Nile, you are to be allowed your innovations."

He replaced the dazzling crown and closed the box with a click. The next case he opened held a pair of earrings fashioned of gold depicting birds with polychrome wings of cloisonné, enameling in rich shades of turquoise and lapis lazuli blue and carnelian. The birds had fringed tail feathers constructed of colored beads strung on gold wires.

The third case held a large pectoral amulet strung on a silken cord. Its complexity of gold cloisonné, and inlaid jewels was breathtaking. Its powerful dual imagery of the sun god was represented as a falcon with the body of a scarab, its wings outstretched and clutching in its talons the symbols of infinity. The falcon was surmounted by the delicate barge of the moon carrying the left eye of Horus and the wedjat eye, as well as the two cobras of Upper and Lower Egypt. All this Wisner took in at a glance, but his attention was riveted to the central jewel, the chalcedony scarab, the heart of the mother, that pale green-gold, pulsating gem that dominated the amulet, the scarab-god who would show the way to the western gate. Wisner lifted the amulet from its case. He held it reverentially before him, and gazing at it, transfixed, he recited from memory a spell from *The Book of Gates.*

"Rah, oh gods who are in the underworld who are behind Osiris who are stretched on their side who are sleeping on their supports, raise your flesh, pull together your bones, collect your limbs, unite your flesh, may there be sweet breath in your noses, loosing for your mummy wrappings. May your head masks be uncovered. May there be light in your divine eyes in order that you may see the light by means of them. Stand up from your weariness."

Through Wisner's hands surged a power invincible, which the innocence of Cornelia and Gyles could not conceive. To them the regalia had been but ornaments of vanity. Although they had great appreciation for the quality and beauty of the jewels, they were ignorant as to their true meaning. But Wisner knew that he held his eternity. Anubis, unfortunately, would have to stay behind, at least for now. He too would join the great ennead aboard the sun boat, but how that was to be Wisner could not tell. The heart of his mother lay in his hand, and now Nagib, the one who wears the shadow, would prepare Wisner for his journey because Wisner held the secret of the western gate.

Wisner returned to the concealed room and closed the golden shrine. He turned off the gasolier, and in the darkness he bid farewell to Anubis and then pulled the bookcase door closed with a rumbling complaint. He gathered up the three cases, stuffing the two smaller ones in his jacket pockets. The larger case containing the tiara he held under his right arm. He left the bedroom, and as he retraced his steps up the stairs, he could hear again the old clock chime far below in the front hall. But in his excitement he forgot to retrieve *The Book of the Dead* that he had left on the chair in the upper hall. When he reached the window in the nursery that connected with Val's apartment, he was panicked not to see the boy waiting for him.

"The stupid little whore, where is he? He's probably in there jerking off. How am I going to do this?"

Clutching the leather case that contained the tiara, he reluctantly climbed out the window and onto the fire escape, closing the window behind him. His body became rigid with fear. He inched his way along the iron bridge, hugging the brick wall behind him. In only a few moments, he reached the other house, but it had required all his will to force himself across the abyss. He rapped angrily on the window, which was almost immediately opened.

"What do you mean by locking me out on that death trap?" Wisner's blistering complaint did not conceal his spasm of fear as he slithered to safety inside Val's apartment.

"Hey, man, it's like wicked cold out there, you know."

"Your appalling jargon is practically incomprehensible. However, if you mean that you are cold, I would suggest that you put on some clothes."

Pointing at his shorts and tank top, Val said, "Yeah, well, what's this, chopped liver?"

"The identification of those garments escapes me at present, except to say that they appear to be the scanty rags of a streetwalker."

"Drop dead, bitch."

"Remember, you're in my house, young man, so keep a civil tongue in your head."

"Hey man, why don't you take your apartment and stuff it. I'm outta here."

"It's fine with me, baby vomit. You have served your purpose. I was wondering how I was going to dispose of you anyway."

"Hey, what's that under your arm and in your pockets? Shit, this queen's been robbing the house, and he's going to get my ass in the slammer." Val grabbed the jewelry case that held the tiara from beneath Wisner's arm. He clicked open the box, and his jaw actually dropped when he saw the diamond-eyed serpent glaring at him. With surprising speed and strength, Wisner snatched the leather box out of Val's hands. He snapped it closed and with the same motion withdrew a small pistol from inside his jacket pocket and pointed it at the boy.

"You contemptible guttersnipe. I was afraid I might need to defend myself from you one day. Get your paltry possessions and get out."

Val stared at Wisner in silence, and a cruel, hard look of the street masked his face. He was neither surprised nor frightened by the gun. He said nothing as he slowly unbuttoned his cut-off shorts. He let them fall to the floor and stepped out of them. He peeled his red jersey tank top off over his head. Standing naked before the older man, his taut, well-defined body casually curved as he leaned his weight on his right leg. Wisner's eye quickly traveled down the boy's naked flesh and stopped at Val's half-hard cock. He felt his heartbeat quicken, a chilled shiver rippled through his aged body, and he could feel his pulse pump hard at his thin temples and sinewy neck.

Val stared at Wisner with contempt as he pulled a pair of Levi's from the duffel bag on the bed. He pulled on the skintight denim, one hand protectively cupping his cock and balls as he zipped and buttoned his fly. He slipped a white jersey T-shirt on, stretching it over his square shoulders and swelling chest. He pulled on unknotted high-top Reeboks over white socks and completed his uniform with a black leather jacket.

Val swung his duffel bag over his shoulder, said, "Fuck off dick head," and slammed the door behind him.

CHAPTER 17

▼

Cornelia and Gyles were shocked to find the front door of their shop unlocked and ajar.

"Did you forget to lock the door when you left them?" Cornelia asked Gyles.

"No, I don't think so," replied Gyles without conviction. "But maybe I did. It was rather a tense moment. Perhaps Mrs. Sarkisian had to get something from her car and just forgot to relock the door."

"Yes, like her checkbook," suggested Cornelia.

"Shhh, Cornelia, she'll hear you. Wait a minute, the Rolls. It's gone." Gyles, with one hand on the open door of the shop, had twisted around, facing the curb, expecting to find the Sarkisian Rolls with its black lacquered elegance. But instead, he was staring dumbfounded at a shabby Ford Escort with a peeling bumper sticker that read, "Honk If You're Horny."

"I don't understand. That's where Tatiana parked her car. I watched her do it."

"How long did you leave them, Gyles?" Cornelia's question had an urgent edge to it.

"She told me to stay away for a half an hour. It's only been twenty minutes." Brother and sister pushed through the door together.

Cornelia called out cheerfully in a musical tone, "Hello, Mrs. Sarkisian? I hope we haven't kept you waiting." But her greeting went unanswered, and she tossed her coat, handbag, and portfolio, which held her watercolor sketches of the Sarkisian apartment, onto a chair by the front door. There was silence except for the impatient clicking of Cornelia's high heels on the wooden floor as she progressed towards the Chinese screen at the rear of the shop.

"Hello, Mrs. Sarkisian, Mr. Sarkisian? Maybe they've gone up to my office." Cornelia skipped up the stairs, two at a time. Gyles was still standing by the front door, and he could hear her open the glass door of her office. He felt sure now that she would find no one there. He gathered up Cornelia's things from the English Regency armchair and went to the coatroom closet by the mezzanine stairs. The door was open, and one of the wooden hangers was on the floor. Gyles stooped to pick it up. On the floor he found a peculiar chromium disk. He picked it up, slipped it into his jacket pocket, hung up Cornelia's coat, and placed her portfolio and handbag on the stairs leading to her office. At his desk Gyles was surprised to discover that his chair was lying on its back beside the second screen that made up the rear wall of his office alcove. He frowned with puzzlement as he righted the upset chair.

When he peered behind the tapestry-covered screen, everything seemed to be in order. The safe was closed as he had left it, but he wondered about the reason for this slight disorder in his otherwise meticulous environment. Returning his chair to the desk, he could hear Cornelia on the phone.

Gyles seated himself and lit a Sobranie. He picked a minute piece of tobacco from his tongue and carefully flipped it into the huge crystal ashtray on his desk. Reaching into his pocket, he withdrew the mysterious chromium disk and placed it on the blotter before him. He held an oversized magnifying glass by its ivory handle. Gyles enjoyed the puzzle of identifying objects, especially fragments. He had spent a lifetime studying the art and artifacts of civilization, the flotsam and jetsam of mankind that continually washed up on the marketplace beaches of auction houses, flea markets, and antiques stores. So much so that he had become a better-than-average detective with the odd bit. But this little chromium disk stumped him.

Cornelia stood at her office door with the expression of a deflated tire. She had kicked off her heels and descended the short flight of carpeted stairs with a heavy tread. Gyles looked up at her, magnifying glass in hand. He took a drag of his cigarette but said nothing. Without her fashionable high heels and suffering the disappointment of the Sarkisian decampment, Cornelia looked terribly young, small, and fragile. Without asking, she took Gyles's Sobranie from his fingers. She inhaled deeply on the cigarette and fought valiantly not to cry. She spied her portfolio on the stairs where Gyles had placed it, picked it up, and extracted several thick sheets of watercolor paper on which were painted her very impressive designs for the Sarkisian apartment. She tore all three sheets in half, but not without difficulty, as if the images themselves protested against this destruction.

Dropping the pieces into the wastebasket beside Gyles's mahogany desk, she dissolved into tears.

Gyles stood beside her, plucked the burning cigarette from her lips and crushed it out in the crystal ashtray. He pulled up a very pretty Louis XV bergére covered in yellow brocaded silk and guided her onto its elegant seat. After a while, Cornelia's sobs relaxed. She looked up at Gyles with a brave smile. Gyles waited for Cornelia to speak.

"I reached the Sarkisians on their car phone. They're on their way to Dover. Mr. Sarkisian is implacable and will not allow the services of a designer. He in fact will not allow her the apartment at all, so the whole job is down the toilet." Cornelia had to pause to keep her tears from returning. "Oh, Gyles, I'm so sorry," she said and grabbed his hand. He began to protest, but she shushed him. "You don't know the half of it. The executive offices I was doing for Sprague, Bannister and Pelham are cancelled also."

"But you went to the Bay Tower Room yesterday to clinch the deal."

"Yes, fool that I am. I should have known, the Bay Tower Room, what a kiss of death that place is. Julian Bannister was very kind and complimentary about my designs. He mentioned that his wife loved shopping at my brother's shop, but his board felt that a larger firm such as China Trade would handle the corporate needs more comprehensively."

Gyles squeezed Cornelia's hand reassuringly. "Never mind, Corny. Somehow it will all work out. Our expenditures have been a little steep opening this business and I've spent rather extravagantly, but wisely, too."

"Yes, and I had to spend a fortune on that silly office. A lot of good that's gonna do us now." Cornelia looked pleadingly at her brother.

"Never mind, I'm sure we could mortgage Aunt Florence's house to get working capital. At least until we can sell it."

"Oh, Gyles, do we have to? I know that was the general plan, but I really hoped we might…" Cornelia's pleading drifted into silence when she saw the pained expression that Gyles fought to conceal. Suddenly, she realized how much he, more than she, was attached to the old relic on Commonwealth Avenue. It was a familial responsibility that represented the mantle of adulthood, and what was he to do with that heritage? Sell and disburse it like a common commodity? There was something so opportunistic and undignified in the idea, to live off the crumbs of past grandeur. Gyles shuddered involuntarily and stood up.

"If by selling the house we can continue doing what we love," here Gyles warmed to his thoughts, resumed his chair, and faced his sister, "and what we are good at, and, Cornelia, we are very good at what we do" by affirming this, his voice gained conviction, and she smiled at him "then it won't be so much a loss as a metamorphosis. We will have revitalized the family and used our inheritance to create."

Cornelia smiled at Gyles and blew her nose. "I love you, Gyles. You're right, we are good at what we do, and you are a superb bullshitter. Or a consummate salesman. Take your pick and I'll pick you anytime."

"Well, thanks a lot, Pal. I was only trying to cheer you up."

"And you did. Look, I'm laughing."

"Right, and I'm the Mona Lisa."

"Do you remember that magazine article about how the Mona Lisa was a self-portrait of Leonardo in drag?"

"Yes, I do. It was an absurd idea but one that sold a great many magazines," Gyles commented.

"Maybe that's what we need. A little cultural shock treatment. You know, some mild icon bashing to increase our notoriety," Cornelia suggested.

"I should think that our notoriety level is quite sufficient already," said Gyles.

"Oh, you mean the debacle at the Dynasty Ball. Yeah, I guess you're right, Gyles. Do you think that's why Julian Bannister cancelled the deal at Sprague, Bannister and Pelham? I'll bet that's what his oblique reference about his wife being a customer of yours really meant. It's a small town and they had already heard that I was a dyke and now they know it."

"Cornelia, do you care?"

"Yes, I care. Passionately. I don't like being discriminated against because I'm a lesbian or because I'm a woman or because I'm a small independent businessperson. I am well educated, competent, and capable of prodigious amounts of work. I have an extensive portfolio of actualized designs, and I am ready to compete."

"Cornelia, you're projecting all of this. You don't even know if Julian Bannister knows or cares that you're a lesbian, and somehow I suspect that he does not follow the events of the Dynasty Ball very closely."

Cornelia crossed her arms in a tight knot over her chest and raised one eyebrow. "Yeah, and I suppose that Elizabeth Bannister doesn't know you're gay."

"Cornelia, when I see Elizabeth, the conversation centers on antiques, not sex of any kind. So I'm not sure what she thinks about me, but I assume that everyone knows I am gay. Listen, this is only upsetting you. Since there doesn't seem to be a hell of a lot of business, let's go over to Aunt Florence's house." Gyles changed his tone and imitating Tatiana said, "I'll show you Anubis, god of the western gate. I've been meaning to tell you that I've put your Egyptian jewelry back in its shrine for extra safekeeping. I figured no one had disturbed Anubis for the past forty-five years or thereabouts. So 'those gems,' as your dear Rita would say," Cornelia smiled at this phrase, "would be better there than in the safe at the shop."

"You certainly drop in and out of the old homestead with remarkable frequency."

"Well, there's a lot to do there, and I sure could use your help."

"So let's go. I can't wait to meet Anubis. I have to talk with Lucy Ann anyway."

Cornelia climbed the stairs to her office to get her shoes. "I'm just going to call Rita and ask her to meet us there after work."

"Okay, but chop-chop, time's a-wasting."

Gyles took up the mysterious chromium disk from his desk. He turned it over in his hand, but still its purpose eluded him. He pulled open his desk drawer and placed the piece in with his paper clips. Its identification would have to wait for another time.

CHAPTER 18

▼

Val trudged through chilly April rain. His soggy Reeboks dodged the puddles in the shabby alleys of the South End. He shifted his duffle bag from his right to his left shoulder. Like a turtle, he retracted his head into the tall, black leather collar of his motorcycle jacket in an effort to protect his ears from the cold. He slogged through the maze of side streets leading to the more obscure corners of this hinterland, leaving behind the gentrified renovations of the more fashionable squares. Here the buildings shrank to more humble proportions and were void of the embellishments that had been the hallmarks of the Victorian bourgeoisie.

Finally he reached Dartmouth Place, a cul-de-sac that ended in a flight of stairs descending to a footpath that followed a row of shabby backyards concealed behind high walls. An ancient and battered gas lamp cast a Dickensian twilight on the scene. Val stopped at a door painted a gay Bermuda pink, which was recessed into a stout brick garden wall. Over the wall grew a thick jungle of forsythia bramble trailing down one side of the door where early yellow blossoms frothed amongst unfurling chartreuse leaves. Deep inside this jungle, behind the wall, a swarm of sparrows could be heard. In shrill chorus they chirped, chattered, and cheeped at one another. Hanging beside the pink door was a rope wound with scarlet plastic beads. Firmly affixed to the end of this festive cord was one three-inch spike-heeled shoe entirely encrusted with screaming red sequins. On the instep, written with red nail polish, was the word "PULL." Val did just that.

From inside the garden could be heard a racket of tinny bells. There was an abrupt halt to the bird conference, and in the resulting quiet, mincing steps could be heard and a rich contralto voice softly singing, "I am what I am and what I am needs no excuses. I deal my own deck, sometimes the aces, sometimes the deuces.

There's one life and there's no return and no deposit, one life, so it's time to open up your closet." At that appropriate moment, the resplendent Lilly swung wide the portal of her gate, and in full voice with arms outstretched she concluded her song, "Life's not worth a damn till you can say, World, I am what I am."

Lilly's voluminous pink chiffon housecoat fluttered delicately about her hefty frame as she stood in the doorway warbling. The hem of this garment was shamelessly trimmed with pink feathers of mysterious origin, and on her feet clear plastic mules showed to advantage her impeccable pink pedicure.

"Valicia, darling, welcome to Lillyland. But, my pet, you are absolutely drenched."

"Hi, girlfriend. Sorry to say, but life's not worth a damn, and I am what I ain't and I hate it."

"My own little lump. What tragedy, what drama! Come, come, come, Mother will take care of her little wayward girl." Lilly's outstretched arms engulfed Val in an awkward headlock intended to be a maternal embrace. She slammed his dripping head against her ample breast and made ominous cooing noises. Just as suddenly she plucked the boy off of her and, holding him at arm's length, peered at him with myopic concern. "Sweet pea, you're a complete disaster. Where is that luster of youth, that dazzling smile, those sparkling eyes? Who has done this to you? A man? Never trust a man, they're all liars!"

"Miss Thing, if you've finished, may I come in? I am cold, I am tired, and my feet are wet."

Lilly lunged for Val's hand and dragged him across the threshold into Lillyland, slamming the door behind him. "Finished? Sweetheart, we haven't begun with you yet."

Inside Lilly's garden was a wilderness of rain forest lushness. A cavelike central arbor penetrated the dense jungle and was knotted with a tangle of wisteria and ivy vines forming a protective canopy. Woven into the serpentine tendrils were a collection of plastic Christmas tree lights in the form of red lobsters, pink flamingoes, and purple grapes. Representing the human interest in this fantastic landscape were gaily painted garden statues of all the Disney darlings, including Snow White and her leering dwarfs, Bambi, Mickey, and the gang. Through a haphazard vista in the foliage could be glimpsed a lurid grotto where lurked a vividly sanguine rendition of Jesus flashing a pulsing heart. Arching above this apparition, in cursive neon, was the compelling sentiment, "I love you, I love you with all my heart."

Lilly dragged Val along the proverbial garden path towards her basement apartment. Val, struggling with his duffle bag, tripped over a colorful rendition of

Daisy Duck and nearly fell flat on his face. He broke away from Lilly's hot grasp and with peevish tones inquired, "Excuse me, do you mind?"

"Oh sorry, darling, I should have known. You're not a well woman. Here, give me that satchel."

The gargantuan Lilly plucked the bulging duffle bag from Val's belabored shoulders with no more effort than carrying an evening purse. She wiggled down the path, her mules slapping her heels as she walked. She bumped the door of her apartment with her ample hip, and it went flying inward on squeaking hinges. Lillyland was an over-the-rainbow fantasyscape in early Technicolor, as seen through a kaleidoscope while smoking hashish. The dominant mood was Floridian Deco, with flourishes of Carmen Miranda. The entire ensemble could, at any moment, be used as costume material for Lilly or her troupe of sizzling chorines, including thirty-four stuffed baby alligators who were posed doing unnatural acts.

"Girls, my wayward daughter Valicia has returned to Lillyland."

Val complained with undisguised weariness. "I didn't know anyone was here."

Lilly dropped Val's duffle bag and posed herself in the middle of the room, her hands on her hips. Glaring at Val, she said, "Well, there's me, that's one, but I live here the last time I checked, anyway. Then there's Monique Lafarge and Butch. They are two and three, although you'll be happy to hear that they are only visiting. I nearly forgot Betty the Bounder, although she doesn't really count because she's forgotten where she is. So are you coming in to join us, or do you have a reservation at the Ritz maybe?"

"Sorry, Lilly. I didn't mean anything. It's just that I've had a rough day."

From a heap in the corner a wheezing complaint was heard. "That's nothing! I've had a terrible ten years."

"Don't scare the child, Betty. I've been trying to cheer him up," Lilly scolded in the loud voice one would use with a deaf person.

"My, look at what the cat dragged in. A M-a-a-a-n," Monique drawled.

"Don't get no ideas, gorgeese. You're with me!" Butch insinuated himself closer to Monique.

"Don't I know it, you animal." Monique gushed hot breath at her escort and flashed him a dazzling smile.

Val rolled his eyes and commented, "You've got a real chatty bunch here tonight, Lil. What do you say we play a little charades?"

"How about spin the bottle?" enthused Monique.

"Watch it, Miss Thing," rebounded Butch.

Lilly beamed benevolently on the assembled company and lowered herself onto a chaise longue upholstered with polished chintz that was printed with florid tropical flowers and monkeys climbing coconut palms. She thumbed the tufted mattress to indicate a place for Val to sit and said, "Valicia, sit here and let Lillita dry your hair. Come along, don't be stubborn, Mother knows best."

A petulant Val shed his coat onto the floor by the door, and lumbered over to the chaise. Lilly produced a pink, fluffy towel embroidered with spindly-legged flamingoes from a large willow basket, which she kept beside her chaise. She referred to this magical receptacle as her sewing basket, and although over time it had disgorged any number of remarkable and handy objects, ranging from hash pipes to plumber's wrenches, it had yet to offer up anything remotely related to sewing. Lilly worked Val's scalp vigorously with the terry cloth, and the boy began to melt beneath her ministrations. His rigid posture slumped backward, caving in his chest.

Monique idly sauntered about the room, her ultralengthy showgirl legs stretching the seams of her designer blue jeans. She stooped to pick up Val's jacket, and pointing her index finger through a steel ring that hung from the leather epaulet of the right shoulder, with her characteristic feline purr asked, "My, my, what do we have here?"

Val replied from beneath the pink towel. "That's my cock ring, Monique. What did you think it was, an eggbeater?"

Butch momentarily awakened from limbo to inquire, "Hey, you call me a wife beatah?"

"Is that a threat or a promise?" inquired Monique with relish.

The schizophrenic thread of this exchange was too exasperating for Val not to comment. "Not wife beater, bimbo, eggbeater."

"That ain't no eggbeatah, that's a cock ring. You da bimbo if ya don't know that, punk."

"Brilliant. Then why don't you model it for Monique? I'm sure we'll all be fascinated."

All eyes in the room turned on Butch expectantly, and with cheerful encouragement from the forgotten heap in the corner, Betty added, "Hey, strap it on, hunk. Show us a little beefcake."

Lilly primly admonished, "Betty, will you keep still?"

Butch answered the stares with belligerent defense. "Whatcha take me for, an exhibitionist?"

"There's always hope," slipped in Val.

Lilly hoisted herself out of the chaise and stabbed at her coif with agitated fingers. "Children, Mother is very cross with you. Monique, drop that jacket this minute and sit down. Butch, fluff up Betty and put her over here on the chaise. It's not dignified for her to be left on the floor all the time. Valicia, you come with me to the boudoir. I want to know just what has happened to you."

Lilly swept Val off to her bedroom in the rear of the apartment. This chamber was a cross between a naiad's grotto and Jayne Mansfield's dressing room. The bed was a heart-shaped affair draped with a shocking pink chenille spread that was skirted all about with tutulike netting. Looming over the bed, an oversized heart-shaped headboard was covered with pink tufted satin reminiscent of an old chocolate box. Affixed to the low ceiling was a mosaic of shattered blue mirror glass that multiplied any movement beneath it by fifty. This produced the illusionary effect of always being in a sizeable crowd.

Opposite the aortic bed was an alcove cheerfully encrusted with varnished tropical shells of gaudy colors. Recessed into the wall of this grotto was an aquarium. It gurgled away, revealing an aquatic world of neon bright fish, which darted hither and thither amongst coral fans and green plastic seaweed. More pink tufted satin encircled the lower half of the grotto, creating a cushion banquette that was further comforted with a collection of embroidered pillows depicting a variety of lewd subjects. It was to this cozy corner that Lilly led Val, and she flopped down her sizeable girth in a surprisingly graceful pose. Extracting a slim cloisonné case from the depths of her cleavage, she popped it open and offered Val a joint wrapped, of course, in pink paper. They smoked awhile in silence, and when the mood had mellowed to a point where Val was staring transfixedly at the fish in the aquarium, Lilly gently inquired, "Well, Valicia, was the fashionable Back Bay not all that you hoped for?"

"You could say that. You could also say that it sucked."

"But only a month ago you were on a chariot to the stars."

"Yeah, well only one of them turned out to be a star, and he doesn't even know I exist."

"But, my dearest lump, you have a nice little job, a nice little apartment, you must give these things a chance to develop and blossom."

"Dead on the vine, girl. No go."

"Yesterday everything was hunky-dory. Would you please tell me what could possibly have happened in twenty-four hours?"

"Your boyfriend the midget from hell pulled a gun on me and shoved me out the door after he involved me in a grand larceny scam that he cooked up to con the only person who ever trusted me and treated me like a human being, not just a piece of meat."

"I see. And who is this midget from hell?"

"Your old boyfriend Wisner Chilton."

"Ick! Don't blame that pip-squeak dwarf on me."

"Well, I met him with you."

"Darling, I didn't accept an apartment from him. And he was certainly never my boyfriend."

"Well, you acted pretty lovey-dovey with him."

"Yes, lump, and that's just what it was, an act. I don't even know the old fart."

"But you gushed all over the bastard."

"Right again. That's what he wanted, so I gave it to him. Valicia, I am an actress. That's what I'm supposed to do."

"You're a fuckin' drag queen."

"And you, sweetheart, are a hustler. And hustlers are supposed to take, not to give, Val. What do you care about this old troll?"

"I don't fucking care. See, I'm just a piece of meat. No brains, no heart, no soul, I don't care about nobody." Val shouted these last phrases and slammed his fist against the banquette. Hot tears streamed from his eyes. Lilly stared at the boy with wonder, and she felt a sob grab at her heart. His love and his hate and his frustration were all tied up in a storm that was so strong it threatened to explode. Afraid he might hurt himself, Lilly grabbed his fists, but he slammed them against her chest and knocked the wind out of her. She gasped and choked and went dreadfully white. Val stared with horror at his friend, afraid of what he'd done.

"Oh shit. Lilly, Lilly, say something. Fuck, what the hell did I do now? Lilly!"

Lilly flopped her forearms and hands like a penguin and, with her mouth wide, gasped with a horrible rattle. Val stood up and over her, and with an open hand he gave the actress a resounding thump on the back, with the immediate result of a prolonged inhalation sounding like a passing hurricane. Val ran to the bathroom to get a glass of water and when he got back, Lilly's color had returned and she was reclining in the grotto waving a dainty hankie about. Val administered the water with great care, gently holding Lilly's head as well as the glass.

"All right, girl, you don't need to drown me as well as knocking me for a loop," she sputtered.

"Are you okay, Lilly? Jesus, you scared the shit out of me. I didn't know if I should shove a popper under your nose or what! I'm so sorry, but that man has got me so crazed I might murder my best friend!"

"Calm yourself, my pet, and go over to my dressing table and douse this rag with eau de cologne."

Val ventured forth on this errand, happy to be of some use. Lilly's dressing table resembled a miraculous shrine as designed by Madame Pompadour to be installed at Filene's cosmetic counter. The general effect was softened by a voluminous canopy of lace that was coyly drawn back and held by gilded cherubs. Val lifted a succession of cut crystal atomizers and cautiously sniffed at them until he found a scent that he hoped might not asphyxiate them both. He spritzed the hankie liberally and returned it to the ailing Lilly. Then, settling down beside her on the banquette, he plucked a more than slightly bent joint from his sock, laboriously straightened it out, lit it, and passed it to his friend.

Lilly grimaced at the shabby looking reefer but bravely took a hit. "Thank you, darling. Now, having survived that outburst of passion, don't you think I deserve to know *what the fuck it was all about?*"

"Oh, uh well, yes, uh, Gyles. His name is Gyles." Val ducked his head and nervously played with the pink satin buttons of the banquette.

Lilly slapped his hand and said, "Don't pull apart the upholstery," and she handed him the joint. "Gyles who?"

"Uh, well, uh, Gyles Chilton. He's Wisner's nephew, and he had me spying on him, see?"

"No, I don't see. Gyles Chilton had you spying on his uncle?"

"No, it's the other way around. Gyles wouldn't spy on anyone. He's this big sucker, and see he just trusts everyone, or at least he trusted me," Val's outburst trailed off.

"Okay, let's get this straight. Wisner, the midget from hell, had you staking out his nephew Gyles, whom you have fallen head over heels in love with. But that didn't stop you from ripping him off."

"I didn't rip him off. That motherfuckin' Wisner did."

"What did Wisner actually do?"

"He took jewelry out of the house."

"Out of Gyles's house?"

"Well, no, it is, but it used to be his aunt's."

"So what was your part of this nifty affair?"

"I was supposed to hang out and meet Gyles and leave a window open. But I ran into him at the café, after we did our gig at the Dynasty Ball, and now he comes in every morning for coffee, and, well, I sort of got to know him."

"There's nothing illegal in that, Val, so what's the problem?"

"Yeah, see, the apartment that Wisner gave me was next door to Gyles's aunt's house. But she's dead now, and Wisner used me to get inside."

"Did you break in with Wisner?"

"No."

"But you have been in the house."

"Uh, yeah, I guess so, but that was with Gyles. He's a big chump, and he told me all about his aunt and their family, and he even read me her letter. And then we found this secret panel. Don't look at me like that. He asked me to help. Well, inside there was this Egyptian dog."

"And you let Wisner into the house."

"Yeah, but I didn't know what he was going to do. Then he pulled a gun on me, but the stupid faggot didn't even have the safety off, so I wasn't too crazed over that. I didn't like the whole setup, and I wanted out, so I packed my stuff and split."

"So what are you going to do now?"

"If you don't mind, I thought I'd hang out here for a while till I got my shit together, and then maybe I'll head out to P'town for the season."

"You're not going back to Rebecca's?"

"No way, José! Gyles goes there every morning, and when he finds out that he's been ripped off, he'll know just where to find me."

"But why should he blame you? Maybe he really likes you."

"That man doesn't even know I exist. Not like that anyway. He's from a different world. I mean, you know, it's like up there. You already called my number. I'm just a hustler. And if he doesn't know that by now, his slime-bag uncle will tell him."

"You mean you tricked with Wisner Chilton?" Lilly shuddered involuntarily.

"Well, he gave me a blow job and fifty bucks, but I thought he was going to have a heart attack. Anyway, that's not the worst thing that's ever happened to me."

"Spare me the details. Life on the street has never appealed to me. But I think you're wrong and you should tell Gyles."

"You don't get it, Miss Thing. I'm just street trash, but he...he...he's awesome."

CHAPTER 19

▼

Gyles and Cornelia had let themselves into 283 Commonwealth Avenue, as well as rung the bell to alert Lucy Ann of their arrival. Gyles stopped at the marble-topped hall table to look at the stack of mail that was piled up there. He shook his head at the irony that even death could not stop the stream of junk mail that flowed relentlessly from the ever-hopeful vendors of the useless. Cornelia went directly to the arched door beneath the front stairs and called out a cheerful melodic trill as a familiar greeting for Lucy Ann. By the time Gyles descended the kitchen stairs to join the women, Cornelia was sitting in a well-worn Windsor chair drawn up to the enormous old pine table that dominated the old-fashioned kitchen. Before her on the table was a plateful of cookies and a steaming cup of café au lait.

"Praise the saints, here's my boy now! I can see for myself he's too pale and smoking too many of those awful cigarettes." Lucy Ann produced a chipped glass ashtray and plunked it down in front of Gyles. "Crush the butt, boy. You're in my kitchen now, and I know what's best."

"But, Lucy Ann, this is fine Russian tobacco from Peretti's in Park Square. Old Cosmo Stebbins himself smoked them."

"Never mind the spooks from the past. You're gonna be one of them real soon if you don't mind your old Lulu."

Cornelia was giggling at Lucy Ann's scolding, and even though she wore a chic crêpe de Chine frock and three ropes of mauve baroque pearls around her neck, she looked for all the world like the naughty little brat that Gyles remembered from childhood.

"Well, if I have to extinguish a perfectly good cigarette, you can at least offer me a cup of coffee."

"Oh child, you've got such dignity, I'd hesitate to suggest anything like cookies, but yet and still, maybe I have some coffee left."

"Okay, you two, stuff the guff and hand over the cookies. And you, you old tyrant, I want café au lait just like Corny."

"Ooo-eee, that man's a caution." And the three old friends laughed and considered themselves very witty as Lucy Ann immediately produced a huge cup and saucer of Chinese export porcelain filled with steaming café au lait, which she had already made for Gyles, and an equally large plate of the latest batch of her own superb almond and pecan shortbread cookies.

"My old cup you do remember everything. Just for that you deserve a big hug," and Gyles fairly attacked Lulu with a bear hug that made her squeal. When she had disentangled herself from Gyles's embrace, she scolded: "Gyles Chilton, you sit your butt down on that chair and stop goin' about and crushin' an old woman like me."

"Lucy Ann, you're not old," insisted Cornelia.

"Child, I am seventy-five years old on June seventh, and if that's not qualifying for respect, then I have lost my marbles as well as my good looks."

"Seventy-five, wow! But you look terrific. You haven't lost anything. You don't even have any wrinkles. Maybe a little gray hair, but so what. On you it adds dignity." Cornelia was genuinely impressed, and she'd had no idea of Lucy Ann's age. She had never thought about it before. Lucy Ann had always looked the same: immaculately well-groomed and handsome with her wooly gray hair brushed back in a bun from her light toast-colored face. She had a timeless appearance because of her ubiquitous long skirt and crisp white blouse.

"You right about that, Corny. I haven't lost any of this weight. That's been creepin' up with my birthdays, and the doctor says my pressure's up too. But yet and still, I'm feelin' pretty good. And that's lucky, because I have a hankering to go traveling and see the world leastwise a little."

"But when will you go and when are you coming back?" asked Gyles.

"Well now, I'm not entirely sure. I thought I'd go to New York City and continue on to Washington, D.C. I read in the paper about a round-the-country railroad ticket, so I thought I'd go and see what's out there. After all, you know I haven't left this house since Miss Norma brought me here in 1930."

"Well, that sounds like fun, Lucy Ann. Will you write to us and keep in touch?" asked Cornelia.

"Why sure thing, honey, but between you two and Mr. Charlie being so sweet, I better just go or I'll never get out of here."

"What was Aunt Norma like, Lucy Ann?" Gyles asked.

"Child, Miss Norma was a very grand lady, and she was very particular. Everything had to be just so and then some. Yet and still she got her comeuppance, although she never lost her place in Boston."

"How do you mean, she got her comeuppance?" pursued Gyles.

"Gyles, you know you're not supposed to talk ill of the dead. I know you know that because I taught you so, but, honey, that woman, she was mean and she was vain. Miss Florence, she had to wait hand and foot on Miss Norma, and she took it. Even still, it was Miss Florence who paid all the bills all through the Depression. Ah yes, and Mr. Charlie, he had to work with no pay at all. Course I didn't expect nothing being part of the family. But here you got me talking about all those bad times before my babies came to stay with us. By then Miss Norma was long gone and nothing but a ghost. She didn't last the Depression out. If she couldn't have it the way it had always been, she didn't want nothing to do with life. It's a sin really, but I wasn't too sad to see her go. She wouldn't recognize her own flesh and blood. But here, what am I saying, my babies and I are here and all that's past and done with."

"Lucy Ann, do you know anything about the secret panel in Aunt Norma's bedroom?" Cornelia had grown uncomfortable listening to Lucy Ann relate times that obviously upset her, and she tried to stop Gyles from continuing.

"Child, there are some places in this house I just don't go, and Miss Norma's bedroom is one of them. Since that woman died I haven't been near that room. Miss Florence would dust that room herself, and she never asked me to go in there besides."

Cornelia guided the conversation toward more practical concerns in Lucy Ann's plans—when she intended to leave for her trip and when they would see her again. Gyles reminded Cornelia of the work they had to do upstairs and asked for her help, so they reluctantly left their old friend with promises to return for dinner when Rita arrived later that evening.

As the two were ascending the front hall stairs, Gyles asked, "What do you think Lucy Ann meant when she said that Aunt Norma wouldn't recognize her own flesh and blood?"

"I don't know, probably some old family scandal that she only partially remembers."

"I think her memory is as clear as a bell perhaps too clear, so much so that it just burst out of her as soon as she was reminded of Aunt Norma."

"Yes, it evidently wasn't a pleasant memory. Norma Chilton sounds like an arrogant bully to me. Did you hear Lucy Ann say that Norma took her away from her mother when she was fifteen?"

"Yes."

"How could that be, and what was Norma Chilton doing in rural South Carolina anyway?" asked Gyles.

"I'm glad Aunt Florence left her little income to Lucy Ann, even though it would come in very handy for us right now."

"Cornelia, listen to you! We're not exactly being shoved into the poorhouse. Look around you. The real estate values in Back Bay haven't been so high in eighty years. We can get a good mortgage on this house and have enough invested capital to help our business as well as maintain this place until we can decide what to do with it. But first things first. I want you to see Anubis and the secret chamber and the jewels as they were originally intended to be secured."

Gyles led Cornelia up the elaborate stairs towards the third floor bedroom of their great-aunt Norma. The old stairs groaned softly beneath the thick red carpet. Gyles's opened the door, and followed Cornelia into the dim chamber.

"Gyles, what is that awful smell?"

"What smell? I don't smell anything. Oh yes, maybe you're smelling the old gasolier in the secret panel. I remember I smelled the same thing when we first opened the secret panel."

"No, it isn't gas. It's more like burnt hair."

"Well, Corny, I have no idea what that may be, but you heard Lucy Ann. The only person to come in here since Norma died in the mid-thirties was Aunt Florence, and of course myself, and Val. So I don't know what you're smelling."

Cornelia wasn't listening to her brother, because as soon as he had turned on the lights, she had been enthralled by the bed that towered so grandly, almost scraping the tall ceiling of the room.

"Gyles, look at this bed! These draperies are all embroidered on linen, and I'll bet you anything these are designs by William Morris," she said excitedly. She continued, "Praise the Goddess! Maybe they were embroidered by May Morris, his daughter. Look at those acanthus leaves. They look as if they might wrap the whole house. Here's a little rabbit...and look, there's a pheasant...and a meadowlark. You know, I don't think I've ever been in this room. I certainly would have remembered this bed. Why, it's just an unbelievable fantasy."

"I hadn't been in here either, because Aunt Florence kept it locked when we were growing up. I found the key in Cosmo's office on the second floor. Look at this incredible collection of Tiffany Favrile glass. This place is a veritable treasure trove."

"Forget the Favrile baubles, Gyles. Look at that painting over the mantel. I absolutely adore it. What a beautiful meadow. What a gorgeous painting. I just want to peel off my stockings and go wading in that stream. And wouldn't you know it, it's by Dennis Bunker."

"Who's that?"

"He was one of the American impressionists. There are several of his paintings at the MFA. He only lived to be twenty-nine. And he studied with Gérome, of all people! But as you can see, he became an impressionist. Oh Gyles, do you suppose I could have that painting? It must be worth a fortune, but if I could have nothing else, just that painting, I could wander in that meadow whenever I wanted. Look at those willow trees in the background."

"And what about your May Morris bed?" Gyles teased Cornelia, but thoroughly understood her excitement.

"Oh well, that's lovely too, but I don't think Rita would like it."

"And since when does Rita dictate your interior design schemes, my pet?"

"Well, Gyles, there are some compromises you must make in a relationship. Besides, now that I look at it the bed is a little bit much. But still a sterling example of its type."

"I'm glad to hear you say so, because I think it's a piece of heaven. And besides, you don't have ten-foot ceilings."

"Dear Goddess, do you think that thing is really that tall?"

"At least ten feet."

"I'll gladly trade you the painting for the bed, dearest brother."

Cornelia stood on her toes and gave Gyles a quick peck on his cheek, which she hoped would clinch the deal about the painting. "So where's the mysterious room?"

"You won't believe this; it's right here in the inglenook. I only came across it by accident when I fell over Val."

"Oh, you fell over Val, huh? You stick to that story and you'll find somebody to believe it."

"But I did. I mean I didn't do anything with Val, like make a pass at him or anything. Not yet, anyway. Cornelia, stop looking at me with that smug know-it-all expression. I tripped over the fireplace fender with one of those exquisite pieces of glass in my hand. Oh well, never mind. If you don't believe me, there's nothing I can do. This is how the mechanism works."

Gyles tugged hard on the brass hook beside the fireplace, and they could hear a rumbling as the bookcase door rolled in on its track. Cornelia recoiled from the pitch dark passage, startled by the ominous noises. She wrinkled her nose at the unpleasant odor emanating from the darkness. Gyles stared with excitement at the concealed door so brilliantly crafted that even he, knowing it was there, could not detect its presence before the hook released the spring mechanism.

Gyles stepped into the dark recess, and Cornelia reached out involuntarily to hold him back, but he slipped by her. She held her hands to her mouth in a melodramatic gesture of helpless consternation. She didn't understand the intensity of her revulsion, but she couldn't disobey it. From inside there sounded a faint pop, and a flicker of bluish light from behind the half-open bookcase cast a peculiar shadow on the floor. Gyles had lit the gasolier, and he pulled the heavy door farther in, to the accompaniment of more thunderous rumbling. Here, in the shimmering, dusky light of burning gas, sitting sharply alert and glaring from atop his golden shrine, was Anubis. His haughty stare and pointed snout spoke of menace, and his sharp, erect ears strained to hear a summons beyond eternity. Cornelia gasped, and a shudder passed through her. A feeling of dread flamed around the periphery of her memory. Her strong instinct to run away was subdued by a compulsion to focus on Anubis, the black jackal of the necropolis, the embodiment of danger.

"Cornelia, Cornelia, what is it? What's happened to you? Corny!" Gyles had to shout to break her trance. He was afraid at how pale she had suddenly become and was cursing himself for giving her such a shock. He ducked his head under the low opening of the secret panel and dashed to her side. He led her to the overstuffed chair beside the fireplace and helped her to sit down. He returned to the secret room and with a fearsome tug pulled the panel closed. Then turning towards his sister he said: "Corny, I'm so sorry. I had no idea you'd be so affected. What—what happened to you?"

"Oh Gyles, gosh, I don't know. This is really silly of me. I was so frightened by that thing. I don't know. I felt like a deer frozen in the headlights of an oncoming truck."

"But that's silly. That statue can't hurt you. It's just wood and paint."

"I know, I'm just being silly, you're right. Rita says the same thing about me, that I'm too sensitive. But somehow I recognized that image."

"Well, I'm not surprised. It looks to me to be an exact copy of the statue of Anubis from King Tut's tomb. You're bound to have seen photos of it."

"No. I don't mean that. It's like déjà vu. Like someone remembering it for me. Oh, it's all too stupid."

"Let me get the jewelry and show you the original boxes. You don't have to come inside or look at Anubis."

Cornelia was about to protest, but Gyles's excitement was too much for her, and she dropped the hand that was reaching out to stop him and sighed with resignation. Gyles had reopened the bookcase but only enough for himself to enter, and he disappeared behind it. She could hear his rummaging about, presumably opening the shrine. There was a long pause, then she heard Gyles's voice raise in anger. "I don't believe it. What the fuck?"

A door was slammed, and Gyles emerged from the secret chamber empty-handed, looking as if he had been punched in the gut. He had searched the shrine inside and out, even removing Anubis from atop the golden pylon and tipping the shrine forward, hoping that the leather jewelry boxes would slide out, but all to no avail because they simply weren't there, a fact that Gyles could not accept. He had placed them there himself last week, just before all the antiques arrived from England for the shop. He had been proud to have taken such care with Cornelia's spectacular jewelry. He had taken every precaution for its safety but failed. He couldn't look at Cornelia when he said quietly, "I'm so sorry, Corny, it's all gone."

Without missing a beat, Cornelia replied, "Good. There's something wrong about all of this, something we don't know about, something that has nothing to do with us, and yet, I can almost remember something about it. No, I'm glad they're gone. I don't want those things."

While Cornelia spoke, Gyles held a pack of matches in his hand that he had picked up from the floor by the shrine. He puzzled over the pack, which had several matches torn out. On the cover was printed in gold embossed letters "Lord Nelson Pub." He slipped the pack into his jacket pocket, took out his wallet, and withdrew from it the tattered matchbook cover that Val had given to him with his phone number. It was also from the Lord Nelson. Gyles noticed for the first time another number scratched out on the back side. The scratched-out number seemed familiar, and he puzzled for a moment before it dawned on him: 523-7667 was the phone number of Wisner Chilton.

CHAPTER 20

▼

Wisner closed and locked the door of his study. He crossed the room and tenderly placed the three jewelry cases on his desk. He then recrossed the room to the south wall, where, standing in the shadowy corners and being careful not to be seen from the two windows, he lowered the Venetian blinds. Minutely lifting one of the wooden slats of the blinds a fraction of an inch, he peered out. Parked across the street was a large, conspicuous black Lincoln limousine. A dark-complected man dressed in a dark suit sat at the wheel smoking a cigarette. Wisner considered himself very clever to have evaded this surveillance by entering his house through the back garden, accessible only to the initiate by a labyrinth of back alleys and further protected by a series of locked gates.

He seated himself at his delicate Louis XV writing desk. He drew the desk lamp close so that its light shone directly on the jewelry cases. The first one he opened contained the scarab amulet. He gazed at the gaudy brilliance of gold cloisonné, and inlaid gemstones. He was mesmerized by the green-gold chalcedony stone carved in the form of Ra, the sun scarab at the center of the amulet. This gem eclipsed the complex iconography of the greater part of the amulet. This was the heart of the mother, for which he had been searching so long. The map to the tomb that would lead to his own eternity.

He took a very fine needle-nose pliers and a tiny steel screwdriver from his desk drawer. With these delicate tools he carefully loosened the scarab from the gold prongs that held it at the center of spreading wings. Wisner turned the amulet over and shook the scarab into his palm. His fist closed around the smooth, polished surface of the cold stone. He squeezed it so hard that it began to absorb the heat of his body. Clasping his fist to his breast, he held it like a lover dearly sought after and rapturously treasured.

Finally, after a long moment he reluctantly uncurled his fingers and placed the scarab on the blotter beneath the lamp, where the light refracted back a golden glowing green from within the gem. On the flat underside of the scarab, within an encircling cartouche, were exquisitely carved hieroglyphics. Wisner examined these with the aid of a large magnifying glass. He referred to several textbooks to translate the encoded message. He wrote these translations on a thick piece of his monogrammed stationery.

When he had finished, he stretched his arms above his head to pull out the tension that his concentration had caused. He admired his handiwork and read the inscription aloud to himself: "The lotus path within the necropolis, from the tower of the mountain forest, Anubis sits astride the tomb. At the gate he is looking back. With the ankh he will pierce the wedjat eye." After committing this cryptic message to memory, Wisner folded the paper in thirds and slipped it into an envelope. This he sealed and addressed to himself at the Union Club at 8 Park Street in Boston. That impenetrable bastion of Brahmin respectability would faithfully hold his mail for him from now until doomsday, if need be. And how prophetic that date would prove.

Wisner took up his phone directory. The elegant, thin blue pages with gilded edges rustled as he flipped through them rapidly. He found the number he was looking for—Stoddard's Lapidary, Gem Cutting & Fine Engraving, a firm he and his family had used for generations of congratulatory occasions. He dialed the number.

"Good morning, Stoddard's. How may I help you?" The polite greeting was a standard of the old-world firm.

"Good morning. I would like to speak to Pelham Stoddard."

"Yes sir, who may I say is calling?"

"Wisner Chilton."

"Thank you, Mr. Chilton. Would you please hold?"

"Yes, I will." While Wisner held the line he was entertained with phone Musak. He was feeling triumphant enough to forgive this lapse in taste with condescending good nature, realizing that Stoddard was, after all, in trade and therefore tending towards the unctuous.

"Hello, Mr. Chilton, this is Pelham Stoddard. How may I help you today? It's been quite a while since we've seen you, sir. I hope all is well. Let me see, I think the last job we did for you must have been the engraving for Jonathan Stebbins' gold watch. Wasn't that his eightieth birthday? My own eightieth birthday approaches rapidly, and I don't mind telling you I'm looking forward to that day with relish. Yes sir, I never felt better. And do you know what I ascribe my vigor to? Cognac, sir. Yes, cognac, and only the best. Never stint on yourself, that's my motto. And never stop working. But how is Mr. Stebbins, fine old gent that he is?"

"My cousin died two years ago." Wisner replied curtly.

"Oh—I am...that is...I...well...at our age—I didn't know. Sorry."

Wisner left Mr. Stoddard sputtering, an unnecessary cruelty in which he delighted. "I have a job for you, Stoddard."

"Yes, yes of course."

"I'm sending you now, by messenger, an envelope containing a chalcedony scarab. It has a heathen inscription on the reverse side, some Arab fantasy of hieroglyphics that spoils the piece, and I would like you to polish it smooth and return it to me as soon as possible this afternoon."

"Hmm, this afternoon...and you say the stone is chalcedony?"

"Yes. Is there a problem?" Wisner inquired with a slight edge to his voice.

"No, no, I'll have to do the job myself, as I am the only lapidary left at the firm. You know, times have changed, and it's now cheaper for cutting colored stones and cabochon work to be done in Germany or, of course, the Orient—"

Wisner interrupted, "I assumed you would do the work yourself. That's why I called you, and I hope it is not necessary for me to ask for discretion in this matter."

"No. No, not at all. I will receive your package myself and proceed with the work immediately. I will not be disturbed. I have my own workroom."

Wisner's self-serving nature had long ago cleared his character of misgivings. He concluded his instructions thus: "Make sure there are no raw or unpolished edges. I wish the stone to appear as if it had always been blank on its underside."

"Yes, I understand, Mr. Chilton. There should be no problem with that."

"Good. And return it to me by special messenger immediately after you finish."

"Yes Mr. Chilton."

Click. Wisner did not wait for Mr. Stoddard to finish his good-byes or offer any of his own before he hung up the phone. He dialed again. This time his purpose was to summon the courier to pick up and deliver the heart of the mother. The dispatcher at Sir Speedy promised to have a bicycle messenger there within the half-hour.

An excitement bubbled up inside Wisner like the humorless joke of a madman. He leaped from his desk, pacing the room for a moment. His thoughts drifted towards the sherry bottle, and he fairly skipped down the stairs to the front parlor, where amontillado filled the old Waterford crystal decanter. After two glasses, he daubed his lips with his handkerchief. He was startled by the sound of his own front doorbell. Quickly recovering his dignity, he picked up the padded envelope that contained the scarab and went to the door.

The messenger, a rather ragged urchin in Wisner's eyes, sported mud-spattered sweat pants layered over with shredded and cut-off blue jeans. On top of these he wore a hooded sweatshirt. Strapped over one shoulder was a large black nylon bag crammed with envelopes and a couple of mailing tubes.

Wisner stood at the front door clutching his package against his chest in a posture more often observed in twitching squirrels guarding a precious peanut. His obvious misgiving about the appearance of the messenger was rallied back upon him when the boy asked with sneering scorn, "Wis-ner Chill-ton?"

Wisner stared in silence, not comprehending the mockingly attenuated pronunciation of his name.

"Hey man, you got a package for Stoddard's or not?"

The sharpness of this challenge snapped the older man out of his paralysis, and he thrust the package at the messenger.

"Mind your manners, young man! Make sure that you go directly to Stoddard's and deliver this personally to Pelham Stoddard!"

"Yeah, sure thing, Gramps. It ain't likely I'm going to Bermuda just yet, so I guess it'll get there. Sign here."

Wisner began to sputter at the rude rejoinder, but he was interrupted by a clipboard being pushed at him as the messenger grabbed the package, stuffing it into his pack. Without further comment the boy collected the clipboard and took off down Chestnut Street on a fenderless mountain bike.

Wisner stared contemptuously at the disappearing messenger and then at the man in the Lincoln across the street. Returning to the safety of his front hall, he slammed the door.

Wisner plopped himself down into the feathered cushions of a large wing-back chair. There the comfort of silk brocade upholstery and the mellow warmth provided by several more glasses of sherry lulled him into a sweet and dreamless sleep.

He awoke two hours later, stiff from his exertions, and returned to his study, where yet another glass of amontillado revived his flushed excitement. He dialed the heavy, old-fashioned telephone. Resuming his seat in a decidedly more pensive mood, he listened to a man with a slight Middle Eastern accent say, "Hello, this is the Greenbrier Funeral Home."

"Let me speak to Nagib Iskander," commanded Wisner curtly.

"Mr. Iskander is with a client now. May I tell him who's calling?"

"Wisner Chilton, and it is very important, so put me through right away."

"Thank you, Mr. Chilton. I will tell him you are waiting to speak with him."

A muffled confusion of voices could be heard, as if someone were holding a hand over the mouthpiece, and then Wisner heard a woman's voice crossly hissing, "Give me that phone."

"Wisner? This is Tatiana. Who the hell do you and your bloody nephew think you are dealing with? Both Nagib and I have played all the games we're going to."

A cold, commanding voice broke in. "Hang up the phone, Tatiana."

"I will not. I want that scarab and I want it—"

"Shut up, you foolish woman."

A struggle could be heard and angry voices, Tatiana yelling, "Let go of me, slime!" Click.

Quiet was restored to the phone line as the extension was disconnected, and Nagib's calm voice said, "Now I think we can converse in a civilized manner without interruption. Good afternoon, Uncle."

"Don't ever call me that."

"But it is my right. You are my uncle. We share the same blood."

"We share nothing. The connection is distant, if not oblique, and surely morganatic."

"Not very gracious of you, Uncle. Still, let us not quarrel. I believe that you have something I want."

"I have the heart of the mother, and neither you nor your raving sister is going to benefit from it unless you do precisely what I tell you."

There was a long pause and then Nagib said in measured tones, "I see, and what exactly would you have us do?"

"Nothing." Wisner gloated over the irony of this command while sipping delicately from his sherry glass, allowing Nagib to squirm. Finally Nagib controlled his mounting rage long enough to say, "If I am to do nothing, then why have you called me? You need me, Wisner, for it is I who will prepare you for your journey beyond the western gate."

"Yes, Nagib, that is entirely correct. You were always a quick lad and one who could see to the heart of the matter. Oh, pardon my pun. You impressed your grandfather with your abilities, and that is why you were instructed to be the guardian. But you also seem to have digressed from your intended purpose. You have been plotting to overthrow your masters, using your privileged and sacred knowledge to betray the great ennead, we who have raised you. Therefore I have taken certain steps to assure your compliance with our intended purpose."

"And what steps have you taken, Uncle, to protect yourself from harm, an old man living by himself, a bachelor without immediate family, no one who follows his daily life, no one who cares?"

"That is where you are wrong, Nagib. I have followed the same daily and weekly routine for decades, lovingly attended by my most loyal housekeeper, Mrs. Buckley, who allows me the luxury of a very busy schedule of commitments, starting Sunday with Church of the Advent. I am during the week a regular diner at my several clubs. Monday it is the Union Club, Wednesday tea at the Athenaeum, Friday lunch at St. Botolph's. I also attend periodic board meetings, one being the vestry of the Church of the Advent, as well as Massachusetts General Hospital, the Harvard Corporation, the Boston Symphony, and the Horticultural Society. So you see, far from not being missed, my absence would be most conspicuous. So please, reserve your murderous fantasies for your less prominent victims."

He continued, "Although I do not involve myself in business very much, Nagib, I do attend to one old family connection, albeit rather distantly, through proxy of my solicitor, who is of course my cousin. I assure you that I have always read his reports with great interest. It would seem that our venerable institution the Chilton Savings and Trust Bank is threatened by a certain real estate entrepreneur who is about to absorb us into his empire. Aside from the grotesque presumption of this takeover, it seems that the vampire is only after the lifeblood of our institution and intends to dispose of the carcass as so much dead weight.

"Simultaneous to this transaction, but from an entirely different quarter, I am informed by my agents who comb the market for me, of a sale in London of an important diorite head of the god Amun from the Temple of Mut in Asher, from the reign of Taharqa, Dynasty XXV, 690 to 664 B.C. This god's head was knocked down a £850,000 pounds in London. In addition to the unprecedented price paid for an ancient Egyptian sculpture, over the past year a dozen other artifacts of Egyptian origin have appeared on the market in different parts of the world, their combined price amounting to in excess of $15 million.

"The curious aspect of these transactions is that without exception the pieces are familiar to me as having been part of the collections of Norma Chilton. These collections had been assembled at the Canton Wharf, a Chilton family property where I was employed one summer in the tedious task of cataloguing them. I was dispatched to Europe later that summer as a reward of sorts for my labors in that endeavor. But when I arrived in Paris, I read in the *Herald* of the tragic fire which had consumed the Canton Wharf and destroyed Norma Chilton's entire Egyptian collection. All of those artifacts were awaiting transport to the Museum of Fine Arts.

"Well, my dear Nagib, picture my surprise to see these very same artifacts reemerging from the dust of eternity to be sold to none other than the Boylston Real Estate Development Corporation. And who should be the guiding light of that corporation but yourself! Let me congratulate you on the creative brilliance that you displayed in using the newly acquired ancient art collection as partial collateral for your purchase of the Chilton Savings and Trust Bank.

"The most surprising thing about all of this convoluted transaction, I fear, is a confidential disclosure by an old and dear friend of mine, who works at Northber's International Auction House. He told me that the original anonymous owner of the thirteen Egyptian pieces was a prominent mortician from Watertown, Massachusetts, a fact that was not so easily learned, and, I must say, was costly for me to obtain. So it would seem that the owner of the admittedly valuable artifacts has increased and established their worth tenfold or more at a cost of ten percent plus buyer's fee by selling them to himself, and now he intends to use them to acquire a major financial institution, which in turn he intends to liquidate for God knows what enterprise.

"In addition to all of this, I fear you are seeking further capital in a desperate attempt to extend your overmortgaged properties, which I am told are valued at an incredible $80 million on paper. I am happy to learn that you have prospered, Nagib. As your grandfather before you, it is essential for the perpetuation of our destinies that you have the means to maintain your ability to fulfill your obligations. If it is necessary for me to clip your wings, I do so without malice, even with a certain admiration for your lethal ambition. But be sure of one thing: You cannot usurp the throne of Horus!"

Wisner's soliloquy was interrupted by a loud knocking at the front door. "I must go now to attend the messenger who bears the lost memory. There will be a meeting of the board of Chilton Savings and Trust Bank at 10:00 a.m. on Thursday. You will be expected to attend, and to assure us of your abandoned intentions to gain a controlling interest. Then we will elect you to our board, where a closer eye can be kept on your creative endeavors." Again a loud knocking could be heard in the front hall. "But, Nagib, your house of cards stands on no foundation. Your salvation in this matter is a gift. It is because of me that you will survive. You will prepare me for the journey beyond the western gate."

"Yes, yes, uncle. You are right. That is just what I will do."

Wisner hung up the phone without further ceremony. He quaffed the remainder of his amontillado and with deliberate leisure ambled towards the incessant knocking. When he opened the sturdy mahogany door there stood before him a figure whose over-casual pose bespoke exasperation. The messenger, aggressively ignoring Wisner, spoke into a walkie-talkie. "The dude did show, so I can deliver the goods, then I'm out of here. Like gonzo, man. Yo, Wisner, Chilton, gotta sign here."

Wisner could hardly answer. His attention was fixated on the adolescent figure before him, clad in a black spandex bicycling costume with Day-Glo yellow lightning bolts slashing the sparkling surface, accentuating every nuance of the boy's body, which was lean with a certain menacing elegance.

"What's the matter, dude? Are you Chilton or what?"

Wisner roused himself and looked up at the boy's head. He was alarmed to see the features of an archangel spoiled by a shaven head wearing a spiked mane of hair down the center, and on the right side of his pallid scalp were tattooed in the ugly blue of wasted blood more jagged lightning bolts. Wisner said nothing; he took the proffered clipboard and signed his name. The boy thrust the package from Stoddard's at Wisner, and turning on the balls of his thin-soled biking shoes, he sauntered down the stone steps. The older man was totally transfixed by the retreating figure who wore a bolt of screaming yellow lightning stitched into the shimmering black spandex accentuating the cleavage of his buttocks. Wisner stood staring at the boy while he mounted his sleek multispeed bicycle. The messenger spat on the sidewalk and muttered "faggot" before he disappeared in a flash of yellow, black, and steel.

CHAPTER 21

▼

Wisner felt very pleased with himself because he had gotten to the scarab before Nagib or Tatiana, and now the map was his secret alone. He had also prevented disaster from befalling the Chilton Savings and Trust Bank, a power play that his cousin Eben Chichester would be relieved—and mystified—to hear of. But Eben need not know all the details of that battle. Being in a celebratory mood, Wisner decided after another nip of sherry to make an excursion across the Common to Park Square. There he might find some pleasant company at the Lord Nelson Pub. Perhaps he might splurge and allow himself to be coaxed into buying a drink or two, maybe even dinner, for the right amusing companion. If such a person were not to be found, well, there were always the boys on the block, whose rates could be negotiated. So thinking, Wisner left his front door without regard for the dark sentry in the Lincoln opposite his house, assuming that he had effectively defused any threat from Nagib's henchmen. But, like other of Wisner's assumptions, this one would prove rooted in the arid soil of self-delusion.

Wisner strolled across the Boston Common, where he paused to observe a German shepherd who had chased to exhaustion a motley squirrel. This blood sport between a mighty hunter and a weak and sickly prey was a contest that Wisner relished. Thoroughly refreshed by the diversion, he proceeded on towards Park Square. He walked briskly by the Greyhound bus terminal, taking note of the several young men loitering about. He would first try his luck at Lord Nelson's, which occupied several old carriage houses along a neat, secluded mews in Bay Village.

Wisner entered the street drinking in its clandestine atmosphere along with the scent of sea salt that billowed in on an early evening fog. He failed to notice the limousine that turned into the mews behind him. The powerful engine made hardly more sound than a gloating purr. Two men stepped silently out of the automobile. Instantly they overpowered Wisner, securing his hands behind his back and gagging him with a white handkerchief. Lifting him off the pavement, they packed him into the rear seat of the waiting Lincoln.

At the other end of the mews, a slouching figure in faded jeans and untied Reeboks loitered inside a doorway. When he saw Wisner enter the street, he had retreated deeper into the shadows and pulled the black leather collar of his motorcycle jacket up to hide his face. He watched with surprise but then a certain satisfaction as the old man was roughly hustled into the black limousine. The figure in the doorway memorized the license number of the car as it slipped by him and disappeared into the fog.

Wisner was outraged by the infamy of Nagib's thugs, for the identity of his abductors was immediately apparent to him. Didn't they know that he had them all by the balls? It was only by his mercy that they were not rounded up and thrown into the nearest jail. The old man struggled against the shackles that secured his arms behind him. He stretched his jaw wide, pushed with his tongue, and rolled his head against his shoulders, furiously trying to loosen the humiliating gag. All the while he yelled unintelligible threats at his captors, one of whom responded by jabbing him in the gut with enough force to make Wisner retch in agony, turning his anger to terror. He lapsed into silence, overcome with pain and nausea.

The limousine came to an abrupt halt not fifteen minutes after they had left Bay Village. Wisner was too sick with fear and injury to notice the direction they had been driving or speculate on their destination. He was completely unprepared to be dragged from the car so shortly after the punch that still had him reeling. He was led, half dragged, over a footbridge spanning the roaring traffic of Storrow Drive, and for one horrifying moment Wisner thought that his captors were going to throw him off. He stumbled over his own feet in the middle of the bridge, and the men on either side of him aggressively lifted him from under the armpits, forcing him on towards the strip of park along the Charles River known as the Esplanade. There, trees with lifeless black branches stood in even rows, sentries in shadow beneath a broken streetlamp. An oversized granite balustrade edged this formal plantation interrupted by monumental stone plinths, between which broad granite steps led down to the murky river. At the bottom of the stairs, moored by a rope, was a vintage wooden Chris-Craft speedboat. Its varnished teak decking and polished brass hardware gleamed dimly in the billowing fog.

Wisner was hurried to the waiting boat. As they approached the river, the sound of their footsteps routed a pair of mallard ducks, who noisily took flight. This startled Wisner so that he swallowed back a gasp of fear, which, with the gag in his mouth, sounded like a sob. Again the men lifted their hostage, this time into the stern of the Chris-Craft, where he landed sprawling on the deck. Almost immediately a dim shadow at the helm started the boat's engine. A cloud of exhaust mixed with the heavy briny mist. One of the men who had deposited Wisner in the boat cast the slimy rope into the vessel so that it landed on the old man cowering against the gunwale. Wisner recoiled with horror, mistaking the serpentine mass for some further tormenting monster. The boat's engine revved up to full power, and the sharp prow mounted the dark river water, cutting it into dirty, foaming waves. The stern dipped, and Wisner was thrown against the back bench as the Chris-Craft, with a tremendous surge of power, sped off toward the center of the river.

After some minutes of black despair, Wisner struggled to his knees. Dazed, he tried to balance against the back bench, which was covered by canvas cushions. A cold wind blustered over him. He could only half-focus his eyes on the rapidly receding city lights. But far down river he could recognize the neighborhood of Beacon Hill by the brightly lit golden dome of the State House. Looming above this antique quarter of the city like a phantom about to devour its prey was a mountain range of steel, glass, and concrete towers ablaze with lights. An overwhelming dread seized Wisner, and he turned away from that vision of the rapacious metropolis.

The boat cruised rapidly up the Charles. The towering buildings of the center city were left behind, and the low banks of the river were dark with thick, overgrown woods. Occasionally traffic along the Soldiers Field Road could be glimpsed through last year's dried and broken reeds. They once passed another boat slowly making its way down the Charles. Otherwise the river was deserted, and the black-hulled Chris-Craft was but an unidentified shadow, passing without notice.

A half hour passed, and suddenly the engine slowed. Its deafening roar quieted, and the bow fell level with the water. Wisner was shivering uncontrollably. Spasms of cold rippled through him, and his dentures clicked like castanets. He struggled to his knees again and could see two figures standing at the end of a wooden dock, which the Chris-Craft stealthily approached. As soon as the boat was within reach, Wisner was seized by strong hands and unceremoniously hauled ashore. Again he was half-dragged, this time towards a long, black vehicle, the distinctive silhouette of which was somehow familiar to Wisner, but in his present condition he could not identify it. The abductors opened the tailgate of this conveyance and tossed their terrified charge into its heavily draped and thickly upholstered interior. They slammed the gate shut. Wisner jerked with abhorrence, realizing that he had been thrust into a hearse. This last surge of outrage and horror proved too much for him. He collapsed in an unconscious heap.

*　　　*　　　*　　　*

Wisner's awakening was not a revelation of joy. The throbbing agony of a steel vise around his skull roused him to consciousness. But the source of the headache was an illusion, unlike the leather straps that bound his four limbs to the stainless steel slab on which he lay. He was strapped to an operating table, and from his left forearm trailed a clear plastic tube joined to his vein by a needle secured with surgical tape. The tube was connected to a plasma bag that hung above him on a steel hook. As his head began to clear and his eyes focused on the white-tiled room, he was at first alarmed by the intravenous apparatus. Then he relaxed and sighed with relief, supposing that he must be in a hospital and that all was well.

He tried to get up to shake his infernal headache and call a nurse. This bed was hardly to his liking, and he wanted a pillow and a blanket because, although he had stopped his convulsive shivering, he was far from warm and comfortable. But Wisner's efforts to rise were thwarted by the leather straps, and his former terror rushed back in on him. He writhed against his bonds in a futile attempt to break away. Then, with an audible sob, he gave up his struggle, his whole body going limp. His clenched fists relaxed, his jaw dropped, and he opened his tightly clamped eyes. They streamed tears of self-pity. It was then that his gaze fell upon the desiccated cadaver that lay beside him on a similar steel table. Adorning this mummified shell was the regalia of Norma Chilton. The gleaming perfection of that jewelry was in such mocking contrast to the decayed corpse beside Wisner that his dreams of beautiful immortality were shattered.

He screamed a cue that brought forth his tormentor. The double stainless steel doors of the mortuary flew open, slamming against the tiled walls with tremendous clamor. In the doorway stood the god Anubis, his hairless, dusky skin ripely contouring a symphony of rippling muscles. He emanated a beauty of unearthly perfection. Clad only in a pleated gauze kilt and elegant sandals, he held an ankh. Mounted above broad, powerful shoulders was the black head of the jackal. Glaring eyes fixed Wisner with haughty disdain. From beneath this mask a strong but muted voice demanded, "Give me the heart of the mother."

"Aaaaaa!" Wisner's reply was a piercing scream of terror, and he began chanting a spell from *The Book of the Dead*. "O my heart, which I had from my mother, o my heart of my different ages, do not stand up as witness against me. Do not oppose me in the tribunal. Do not be hostile to me in the presence of the Keeper of the Balance."

The man-god-jackal Anubis came close and, towering over his prey, demanded, "Where—is—the scarab?"

Wisner began his chant again. "O my heart—"

The massive hand of Anubis clamped over the old man's mouth, and he said, "We—are witness against you. We are hostile to you. The scale has lost its balance. Your heart, leaden with lies, plummets you into hell." The sharp snout leaned close to Wisner's face and whispered, "Where—is—the scarab?"

The god slowly lifted his hand from Wisner's mouth. "The scarab is there, on the amulet!" was the trembling reply.

The overbearing presence bellowed. "Lies!" And as if his anger tore it from him, the head of Anubis flew across the room, exposing the sweating and convulsed face of Nagib, his birthmark splashed across his features like the shadow of hell.

Wisner recoiled from the slavering rage of Nagib. His unmasked head was, if anything, more horrific than the jackal mask, the discolored dead blue blotch a livid disfigurement which had infected the man's sanity. Nagib swung his fist toward the pinioned coward on the slab, stopping inches short. The fist unfurled, fingers stiff with tension, and on the broad palm sat the chalcedony scarab. With barely repressed violence Nagib hissed, "What—have—you—done—to—the—scarab? Tell me the message!"

Wisner's eyes dilated with fear. He shook his head and croaked, "No-o-o!"

Nagib lunged for the old man and plucked him from the slab so that the shackled arms strained against their bond. Just as suddenly and with a gargantuan effort, Nagib suppressed his passion and dropped Wisner with a thud. "Do you know where you are? Do you know what this is?" and here Nagib gently stroked the intravenous tubing. "This is my final means of persuasion. It will drain you drop by drop of that thin blood that throbs so hesitantly through your shriveled flesh. If you do not tell me the message of the scarab, then with hardly more than a whimper the measure of your life will ooze from you until you die."

"You won't kill me. You won't dare. I could have you arrested for your fraud and your lies. You have broken every rule of banking, and your falsely inflated real estate is not worth a particle of your debt. Far from taking over anything, it is you who will take orders. The golden sarcophagus of Norma Chilton's tomb is not for your thieving grasp!"

Nagib slapped Wisner with the back of his solid hand, reducing the bravado speech to whimpering sobs. He wrenched the plasma bag from the plastic tubing and threw the open end into a basin swirling with water that made ugly sucking noises as the waste disappeared down the drain. With slow and deliberate pressure, Nagib opened the valve that would allow Wisner's blood to flow. The clear plastic tube filled with a trail of red as the old man's heart pumped his blood down the drain.

"Now, dear Uncle, it is time for you to speak. Tell me the message of the chalcedony scarab. You have perhaps fifteen minutes, at this rate of flow, as your precious blue blood empties into the sewers of Watertown. You will not be the first of our family to be cleansed of vital fluids here in the Greenbrier mortuary. I think you have already seen our great ancestress, Norma Chilton, although you may not have recognized her. She has been languishing these many years in a vat of natron, awaiting the delivery of her jewels and crown. She had so cleverly concealed the map and key to her tomb in that scarab. But she was not really so clever, because she has been unduly delayed on her journey beyond the western gate." Nagib grabbed Wisner's head and wrenched it towards the mummified corpse. "Look. Look well upon the fury of her impatience. She will not suffer your interference any longer, Uncle. Tell us the inscription on the scarab."

"I am not your uncle," Wisner retorted with surprising vigor.

"You idiot. I am the grandson of Norma Chilton and Nagib Iskander. I am Anubis, guardian of the western gate. You are not one of us. The great ennead, the nine gods of Egypt. This is your only life. Save yourself and tell me, where are the tomb and the key?"

"No. I am Horus. My mother is Isis. I will be pharaoh of all the world, and you will prepare me for the journey. I will not be condemned. I know the way." Wisner's last defiant statement was spoken in a whisper as his weakened body strained no more against the ravages of time and abuse.

At that moment, a disheveled Tatiana staggered through the double swinging doors, her olive face drained of its full color. She clutched the doorsill for support and stared at Nagib, shocked to see him half naked here in their grandfather's laboratory. She looked at the old man on the operating table, and when she recognized Wisner she yelled, "You fool! You will kill him and spoil our chances of ever finding the tomb." As she spoke she approached Nagib, who had been standing between the tables, but now he stepped away, and Tatiana saw Norma's wasted and mummified corpse. She screamed and lurched backwards. Tripping on her high heels she fell to the floor, landing beside the oversized jackal's mask. When she saw the black dismembered head glaring at her, she screamed again and kicked the head away from her. At this moment two of Nagib's henchmen rushed in, seized Tatiana by her arms, and lifted her from the floor. She struggled violently, yelling, "Slime! Let go of me!"

Nagib had recovered the mask and placed it again over his head. The effect was magnificent, making him a seven-foot god, and he commanded, "Silence, you stupid woman. Take her to my office, and this time, DON'T LET HER GO! Soon all will be finished here." Nagib returned his attention to the fading Wisner. He closed the valve on the plastic tube. Wisner's eyes fluttered and half-opened. His irises had rolled up, showing the blind whites only. Slowly, like waxing moons his irises returned, and Wisner again saw Anubis, this time as a beatific vision. Now beyond concern for this life, Wisner began to whisper softly, and the jackal deity hovered over his lips, straining to hear. But all he could make out was "the tower of the mountain...forest...Anubis sits astride the tomb." There was a wheeze and gurgle, and an awful stench escaped from the parched lips. Black corruption trickled from the corner of the dead man's mouth.

CHAPTER 22

▼

At 6:30 p.m. Gyles stormed into Rebecca's Café, his forehead damp from the exertion of his march from Back Bay across the Public Garden to Charles Street, a distance of about a mile, which had taken him exactly thirteen minutes. The café was in the midst of a bustling dinner, and it was difficult to catch anyone's attention. His agitation was glaringly apparent when he uncharacteristically forced himself in front of several people waiting to be seated. Gyles blocked the way of a scurrying waiter.

"Excuse me. The hostess will be right with you." The waiter glared at Gyles with drop-dead loathing.

"I'm looking for Val," Gyles blurted out.

"So are we. And when you find him, tell him he's fired. Now excuse me." The waiter sidestepped Gyles and slithered off into the dining room. Gyles surveyed the crowded restaurant, looking for the manager.

A gray man in a dark suit and a too-short khaki raincoat tapped Gyles on the shoulder and said, "Line forms at the end, pal."

Gyles glared at the man with ill-disguised exasperation and replied, "I'm not here for dinner. I'm looking for someone."

"Terrific. Why don't you read the personal ads in the Phoenix?"

Gyles responded with a murderous, silent stare. The man's girlfriend, shamelessly clad in pink polyester satin with cascades of wiry curls frothing about her small skull, pulled him away. As the man was about to renew his assault, he was interrupted by the hostess, who said, "Mr. Westlanger, I have your table now."

Gyles watched with amusement as the hostess smiled warmly at the couple while she showed them to a small table against the wall by the back stairs. She then recrossed the dining room towards Gyles, ignoring the sputtering protestations of Mr. Westlanger.

"One for dinner?

"No. Not really. That is, I'm looking for someone, someone who works here, as a waiter. Val. Do you know him?"

"Val? Why yes, but I'm afraid he's not here."

"Do you know when he'll be working again?"

"He's supposed to be here now, but he never showed up this morning. When I came in at 3:30, I called his apartment, but there was no answer."

"Ah. I see. Well, thank you," Gyles mumbled.

"If you see him, please tell him to call the manager right away, because he's very angry."

"Yeah. Sure. I'll have him call." Gyles liked the tone of concern the hostess had for Val and found his agitation turning to worry. A second ago he had been pissed as hell with Val because he suspected him of having stolen Cornelia's jewelry. What else could he suppose? Val was the only other person who knew about the secret panel. And Val had Wisner's telephone number. And who else could have dropped the Lord Nelson Pub matches on the floor inside the secret chamber?

Gyles had trusted Val. But so had the hostess, and her reaction to his disappearance had been concern. Now when he saw Val in his mind's eye, he began to hope that there was an explanation other than his worst fears.

It was time to pay another visit to Uncle Wisner and find out what he knew about Val. The idea of Val even knowing Wisner made Gyles angry again. He left the café, striding rapidly up Charles Street and, turning right on Chestnut Street, he climbed the hill.

Gyles stood for the second time in a week at the front door of 28 Chestnut Street. This time, however, he was not idly musing over the decorative details of the architecture. His stare was glazed over with heavy concentration, and he automatically repeated, "Nefertiti, Nefertiti, Nefertiti," the name that he read from the brass door knocker. Suddenly realizing what he was saying, he stopped the chant and puzzled over yet another Egyptian reference. At that moment the front door opened, and Mrs. Buckley, looking quite old and fragile, stood there, her round, wrinkled face aquiver with tears.

Gyles stepped into the front hall. Closing the door behind himself, he took a crisp, clean handkerchief from the breast pocket of his jacket and handed it to his uncle's housekeeper, urging her to sit. After a moment Mrs. Buckley quieted down and blew her nose. "Oh Mr. Gyles, I'm so worried I am. Himself is gone without a trace, and haven't I been worried half to death!"

"Uncle Wisner is gone? What do you mean? Where'd he go?"

"Mary Mother of God, if I knew that, I sure wouldn't be blubberin' here like a schoolgirl."

"He didn't come home last night?" asked Gyles.

"Oh no sir, his bed hasn't been slept in, and he's nowhere to be found."

"When did you last see him?"

"He left here yesterday morning, bound for his club."

"Where does he go after lunch at the Union Club?" Gyles softened his voice.

"Why sure, he'll be goin' to tea at the Athenaeum. But haven't I called both those places and been told he never arrived there a-tall." At this point Mrs. Buckley had to choke back more tears, and Gyles patted her shoulder, which made her really break down and cry.

Gyles knelt beside her, took his handkerchief, which she had crumpled up in a ball, and wiped at her eyes. This kindly old woman had done a lot to soften his heart towards his fussy and difficult uncle over the years, and he hated to see her so upset. "Come on now, Mrs. B. We'll find him, I'm sure. Don't cry now."

Mrs. Buckley smiled through her tears, not quite so afraid now that Gyles was here. "I hope Mr. Chilton will be forgivin' me, but I went 'round to the Paulist Center this mornin', and after Mass I lit a candle for himself and said a prayer."

"But that's very kind of you, Mrs. B. Why should Uncle Wisner have to forgive you?"

"Oh Mr. Gyles, himself is very much against Rome and His Holiness. Him bein' a proper Bostonian and all."

"Well, I don't know anything about Wisner being proper, but it sounds like the bigoted old fool." Mrs. Buckley frowned disapprovingly at Gyles's criticism. "Has he ever stayed away like this before? Gone out of town, or stayed over with a friend?"

"Oh no sir. Mr. Chilton never sleeps anywhere but in his own bed. He's very set in his ways, he is, and would never leave his collection unguarded. You know how attached he is to his antiques. No, never in thirty-six years have I known Mr. Chilton not to come home."

"I see. Well, in that case I think we'd better call the police. And while I'm at it, I'm going to call Cornelia and ask her to come over and stay with you, at least while the police are here."

"Thank you, sir."

Gyles stooped to enter the small telephone room that fit snugly beneath the front hall stairs. He felt like a giant seated on the diminutive Gothic chair inside this cubicle. A heavy, old-fashioned black phone sat on a shallow mahogany shelf, and beside it was a pad of paper printed with Wisner's initials, WWC, for Wisner Wilder Chilton, as well as an old chipped Chinese mug filled with an assortment of pencils and pens. The top sheet of the pad had doodles drawn on it of meandering fretwork that exploded into stabbing abstractions, which hinted at agitation and anger. In the middle of the page was the name "Greenbrier," and a phone number. As Gyles dialed the number for his Aunt Florence's house, he absently glanced at this name, Greenbrier, wondering why it sounded so familiar. At that moment Lucy Ann answered.

"Hello, Chiltons' residence."

"Lucy Ann, this is Gyles. May I speak to Cornelia?"

"Sure thing. Hold the phone, she's right here."

"Thanks."

Cornelia's voice came over the line. "Gyles, where are you? You tore out of here like a madman, and you know Lucy Ann is making us all dinner. Rita's here and we're going through some really interesting family papers in old Cosmo's office."

"Cornelia, hold on. I'm over here at Uncle Wisner's, and he's disappeared, or at least he hasn't been home in quite a while. Twenty-four hours, to be exact, and Mrs. B is a basket case. Now listen, I have to call the police, and I thought it would be better if you came over to be with her. You know, for moral support."

"Good Goddess, what on earth do you suppose has become of him?" exclaimed Cornelia.

"Almost anything, I guess. He is getting on in years. Maybe he had a heart attack in the street or something. In any case, would you please come right over?"

"Yes, certainly. Rita's car is right out front. I'll just tell Lucy Ann to put dinner on the back burner, and we'll be right over."

"Good. Because I have to leave, and I'm going to call the police now."

"Gyles, where are you going? I can't face the police by myself. I don't know anything about Wisner."

"Cornelia, you won't be alone. Rita can handle the police. You just be a support for Mrs. B. She knows everything about Wisner. There isn't time to tell you about anything else. Just come right over."

"Gyles, if you're chasing all around town because of the Egyptian jewelry, forget it."

"Cornelia, just come." Gyles hung up the phone. Something about the agitated doodles and the name Greenbrier on the phone pad bothered him. He reached for the white pages from a stack of old phone books on the floor and looked up the name. There was only one listing for the Greenbrier Funeral Home in Watertown. He wrote the address at the bottom of Wisner's scribbled note and tore off the sheet. Neatly folding it in half, he put it in his wallet.

Gyles emerged from the phone room, ducking low to fit through the door. Mrs. Buckley sat forlornly quiet on the chair where Gyles had left her. She looked up at him with pleading eyes.

"I've called the police, and someone should be right here. I also called Cornelia and asked her to come over and stay with you while they're here."

"But praise be, I've never spoken to a policeman in my life. What am I to tell him? No, Mr. Gyles, you do the speakin'." Mrs. Buckley had a healthy fear of authority, which under the present circumstances was amplified to something akin to terror, and Gyles realized how right he had been to ask Cornelia and Rita to be there.

"Now, Mrs. B., don't worry. You just tell them what you told me, and everything will be okay. I'm sorry I have to dash out of here, but Cornelia will be here shortly with her friend Rita. You remember Rita from Aunt Florence's funeral."

"Is that the girl who was tellin' me about women's suffrage?"

"That sounds like Rita, yes, although I'm surprised that she called the women's movement suffrage."

"Oh, she didn't say that exactly, but I forget the words she used. My, but she has a powerful conviction."

"Yes, Rita is a very take-charge kind of a gal, and you'll be in good hands with her. Okay then, Mrs. B, I'm off, and don't worry. I'm sure Uncle Wisner will show up where we least expect him." Gyles could not know how prophetic this simple statement of consolation would prove to be.

He left Wisner's house with only a vague idea of how to find Val but stubbornly determined to do so. Gyles could be obsessive about getting what he wanted, and the seriousness of Wisner's disappearance hadn't really registered in his brain yet. His real intent lay in finding Val. He regained Charles Street quickly and waded out into the traffic with as much disregard for his safety as the speeding drivers who swerved around him. With an ear-shattering whistle, Gyles hailed a cab, but several blocks away he could see a gleaming black Packard limousine. Even as he stood, arm raised, in the middle of the street, his eyes followed the slow progress of the elegant automobile.

He was rudely awakened from his reverie by the blaring horn of a cabbie, demanding, "Yo buddy, cab or what?"

As if on cue, the limo eased to a purring crawl in front of Gyles. The rear window, obscured by reflection, slowly lowered, and a deep, breathy voice asked, "Hi, Dollface. Going my way?"

"Monique! Just the person I need to talk to." Gyles was thrilled to see her. Butch sat silently at the wheel and guided the enormous bulk of his antique machine closely in front of Gyles, completely blocking the waiting cab.

"I hope we can do something more than talk," suggested Monique.

"I won't ask what you have in mind, because there are some things beyond the power of words. But if I ride with you, will you help me find someone?"

Monique struck a pose, turning her provocative profile towards the sky. Whether this was to signify rumination over Gyles's request or petulant indifference, there was no time to decide, because Butch leapt from the automobile and, opening the rear door, fairly shoved Gyles inside.

Monique wore a submit-or-die outfit so low cut and high hemmed it hardly qualified for lingerie. But this was not the most alarming aspect of her appearance. That was the skintight black vinyl gloves that entirely encased her hands and arms. To coordinate this stunning accessory, she also wore high-heeled black vinyl stretch boots that traveled the length of her extensive legs. Without disturbing her languid repose, Monique turned to face Gyles as Butch maneuvered the limousine into traffic.

"Well, Dollface, where are we going?" asked Monique.

"I hoped you could tell me."

Monique's eyes opened wide with suggestion, but she said nothing.

"Do you know a guy who dances with Lilly by the name of Val? He was one of the chorus in the *La Cage aux Folles* number Lilly did at the Dynasty Ball."

Knowing full well, Monique asked, "Hm. What does he look like?"

"He's about five-eight or nine, and maybe a hundred and fifty pounds. He's tight, with lots of definition, and shaped like a V. You know, with broad shoulders and tiny hips. He's got blond hair, at least it is now, but I suspect that could change with the seasons. He has incredibly deep brown eyes with flecks in them."

"Flecks?"

"Yes, like sparks of a fire." Monique raised one long penciled eyebrow as Gyles went on. "He's clean-shaven—well, not exactly. That is, he often wears two days' stubble that shadows his cheeks like an El Greco painting. His mouth is rather pouty and full, and he has a couple of dimples in each cheek, like quotation marks. He never stands straight, he's always leaning on something, and he wears a motorcycle jacket."

"With a cock ring in the right epaulet?"

"Now that you mention it, yes. I think so. So you know him?"

"Well, Dollface, not as well as you do, apparently."

"Monique, I have to find him. This is urgent. It's not what you're thinking."

"Who says I'm thinking?"

"Well, that's a point," admitted Gyles mischievously.

Monique snuggled up to Gyles and took hold of his right biceps with both of her black-gloved hands. Butch glared at her from the rearview mirror. "Dollface, Butch and I were just going home to freshen up before my performance tonight. Why don't you come up for a smart cocktail and forget about your little lover boy?"

"Monique, this is urgent." Gyles untangled his arm and reached in his pocket for a Sobranie. No sooner had he produced his cigarette case than Butch offered a light from his stainless steel Zippo, reaching over the front seat with one powerful arm. Gyles had to shift over to one of the jump seats in the cavernous limo to accept the proffered light, and he was relieved to have escaped Monique's pawing.

"Ain't that the kid who's hidin' over at Lilly's, Mo? I think the cops are afta him, or somethin'."

Monique examined her manicure and muttered, "Dumb lug. You spilled the beans again."

"Hey, watch your mouth, woman."

Monique plucked a plastic compact from her purse and threw it at Butch with athletic precision. It bounced off of his crew cut, making Gyles cringe. But Butch was completely oblivious to the missile.

"Monique, where does Lilly live?" asked Gyles.

"Oh, I don't know," she replied lamely, and stared out the window.

"The broad lives in this scrungy little alley in the South End. I'll take you dere if you want, but Mo is right, you'd have a much better time over at our place. I got a whole bunch of new CDs. There's this really good one, Alicia de Larrocha playing Granados, I just got yesterday." Gyles turned and stared at Butch, who caught the look of surprise in his rearview mirror. "Yeah, yaw not da only queer who knows about culture, ya know," Butch said defensively.

"No. I, ah, that is, uh, you're absolutely right, Butch, uh, but maybe some other time. Right now, if you'd take me to Lilly's, I've got some important business."

"Have it yaw way, Buddy. But don' expect Madonna, the beautiful, 'cause da kid's a mess."

"What do you mean, Butch?"

"He's been ballin' for days." Gyles straightened up as if an electric shock surged through him. "No, chill out, man! I mean he's been cryin' an' watchin' soap operas."

"You mean to say that he's been sobbing over afternoon TV?" The edge of Gyles's voice veered towards outrage.

"No, dope, it's a man! The Irma la Douce story," interjected Monique.

"What do you mean, Monique?" asked Gyles with mounting anger.

"Oh, honey, it's the hooker with the heart of gold. You know, she finally fell for one of her tricks."

Gyles stopped asking questions and smoked in silence while Butch drove them deeper into the South End.

CHAPTER 23

▼

Gyles stood at Lilly's garden door and yanked at the sequined shoe that hung from the bell cord. In his present dark mood, he was blind to the attractions of the cheery and vivid shade of Bermuda pink that adorned the sturdy wooden door. When the clanging and clattering of the doorbells went unheeded, he hauled at the cord repeatedly, sending up a racket that could be heard two blocks away. Still no one answered. He vented his frustration on the bell cord once again, pulling with such force that the sparkling slipper came off in his hand. The clamor of the bells diminished, and the door went flying inward as if torn open by a cyclone.

Confronting him and filling almost the entire doorway was the formidable and fuming Lilly. One hand on her hip, she stared with murderous intent at Gyles's hand holding the festive pump. He felt absurd with the shoe in his hand. This further inflamed his agitation, which Lilly's hostility did nothing to extinguish.

"I believe this is your shoe. I'm here to see Val." Gyles handed the shoe to Lilly and tried to pass by her into the garden.

Lilly ignored the pump and with one sturdy finger jabbed at Gyles's chest and ordered, "Hold on, chump. This is my house, not the fuckin' Back Bay. I don't care if you're Miles Standish. No one comes in here without an invitation from me."

"Look, Lilly, I know Val is here, so just let me in. And here, take your damned shoe!"

Lilly smiled at Gyles without joy and folded her arms akimbo. "Val who?"

"Oh come off it, Lilly, you know very well Val who. Monique told me he was here, so don't deny it."

"Monique Lafarge is certainly a reliable source of information. Did she tell you this fairy tale before or after she smoked her daily dose of angel dust?"

"Lilly, this is serious. You don't know what Val's done. Don't make me come back here with the cops." Gyles tried the stern and sober approach, attempting to contain his anger.

"It's okay, Lilly. I'll talk to him."

Lilly swirled around to face Val without budging from her guard post. Gyles could spy him just behind the bulky diva, and he was shocked to see how wiped out the kid looked. "Sweet pea," began Lilly, "you don't have to talk to this pushy eleganza queen."

"Thanks, girlfriend. I know I don't have to, but I want to anyway."

"Have it your way, darling lump. But don't let that man into my house with those dirty shoes on." Having proclaimed the limits of her tolerance, Lilly grabbed the ruby slipper from Gyles and sashayed down the garden path towards her back door.

Left alone, the two men stared at each other in awkward silence. The feelings generated in them by being together were so different from the hard resolve that each had made about the other that neither knew what to say.

"Do you want to come in?"

"I want to talk to you."

"Well, you'd better come in, then."

Gyles stepped inside Lillyland, and even in his distracted state the overwhelming frivolity caught his attention. Val closed and bolted the door behind them and led the way beneath the arbor hung with strings of blinking lobsters, grapes, and pink flamingoes. After depositing Gyles's shoes at the door, they entered the apartment and found themselves alone, Lilly having retired to her inner sanctum, from whence wafted the strong odor of Maui Wowie and the melancholic wail of Billie Holiday. The antique dealer's gaze came to rest on a phalanx of stuffed baby alligators performing unnatural acts with GI Joe and scantily clad Ken dolls inside an enormous TV cabinet.

Val's courage deserted him as Gyles stared inside the gutted TV, and he fled to the kitchen, saying, "I'll go make us some coffee. You make yourself at home." The unlikelihood of Gyles being at home in Lillyland confused Val, and he corrected himself. "I mean, have a seat. I'll be right with you."

In spite of himself, Gyles was fascinated by the bizarre array of objects that crammed the room. The pink, mauve, and fuchsia color scheme that divided prismatically into numerous shades on the walls, ceilings, and floor was a dazzling effect, one Gyles had never seen before. Everywhere was a surreal mixture of the naive and the reptilian, best exemplified by a Little Lulu doll lolling about the inside of an armadillo skin basket hanging from the doorknob of the coat closet.

Val returned to the living room, and Gyles was standing inspecting a tubular steel chair covered in faux leopard upholstery. "You know, I think this is a Frank Lloyd Wright. Lilly must have paid a fortune for it," he said with surprise.

"Well, actually, she just got it at the Morgan Memorial in Roxbury. There's a dude there that saves that junk for her. He's the one with the pins in his ears. Have you ever seen him?"

"Pins? No I'm afraid I haven't had the pleasure," Gyles replied with a grimace.

"Yeah, safety pins. He's got a whole collection of 'em. They go from big to small. It's sorta cool, I guess." Val had placed a tray holding a coffee set on the low blue glass table in front of the sofa. Gyles seated himself on the tubular steel chair, and Val sat on the enormous mohair sofa, his legs curled up beneath him. Gyles stared at Val as the boy poured coffee from what appeared to be a pregnant flamingo into the gullet of a yawning hippopotamus. Gyles shook his head in disbelief.

"Too much, huh? Lilly bought them on vacation at Safari Land in Florida," Val explained.

"You know why I'm here, don't you?" Gyles asked. He couldn't bring himself to accuse Val. He loathed confrontation and this more than most because the boy's palpable presence disarmed him. Beneath the turquoise tank top, he could not help noticing the graceful curl of Val's collarbone and the swelling pectoral muscles where soft golden hair fringed the taut jersey.

"Yeah. You think I stole your jewelry," Val mumbled into his coffee cup.

"Well, didn't you?" Gyles persisted stubbornly, but losing conviction as he stared at Val's blond hair shining in the lamplight.

"You think so, so what does it matter?"

Gyles jumped on Val's evasion. "The truth matters a great deal to me, Val."

"Yeah. Too bad I don't," the boy replied sullenly, his heavy golden hair now covering his eyes as he tried to retreat inside his coffee cup, as if the weight of Gyles's accusation sat crushingly on his head.

"What's that supposed to mean? Am I supposed to care for you? I trusted you, Val. What did you do to me?"

"Bullshit you trusted me!" Val's head shot up, and his eyes shone with anger and hurt. "You didn't trust me! You don't even know me! You didn't even bother to find out who I was! You just figured I was no one, no threat, so why bother!" Val shouted.

"Val, did you take the jewelry?"

"No! Your fuckin' Uncle Wisner did. But you'll never believe me!"

"Believe you? Why should I? How would you know such a thing, even if it were so?"

"Because I was there, asshole. Yeah, I was there. I tried to stop him. But he pulled a gun on me. Well, it's a long fuckin' story, and you wouldn't be interested, so why don't you just get out?"

Gyles was confused by Val's counterattack. The idea that Wisner would pull a gun on anyone was ludicrous. He knew that Wisner was deathly afraid of mice, let alone carrying a gun. Surely that vindictive curmudgeon would not resort to firearms. No, it was too fantastic. As far as what Gyles felt about Val went, well, that was irrelevant now that he had been betrayed. It had never occurred to Gyles that anyone he had befriended would steal from him. Besides, it wasn't Gyles's property that had been stolen: it was Cornelia's. Gyles had taken the responsibility of protecting her from any harm, but he had failed.

"I'll be glad to go after you give me the jewelry," he said with elaborate calm.

"Hey dude, are you deaf or what? I don't have your lousy jewelry. That old fag Wisner stole it. So why don't you go bother him?" Val leapt up and paced about the room. Stopping at the kitchen door, he leaned on one arm, his sleek hips cinched into worn jeans. His right leg bent at the knee and rested on his left foot, a pose not unlike a Renaissance bronze of a young warrior.

Gyles stared, trying to maintain a stern exterior. Inwardly he was wondering whether Val ever stood up straight. And how studied were these poses, anyway? "Then perhaps you should tell me the 'long fucking story,' as you call it, because I don't believe for a moment that Wisner Chilton is a jewel thief."

"You're so wrapped up in your goddamn antiques. What do you know about anyone? All right, you want to know? Fine. I'll tell ya. I'll burst your little bubble that you float around in. First of all, I'm a hustler. That's how I live. It's not the greatest, but you gotta do what you gotta do. It's not always so bad, the money's easy, and sometimes the johns are kinda nice to me. Except your dearest Uncle Wisner, who's a joke on the block. Yeah, don't look so high and mighty, 'cause he's a regular with us, and everyone runs in the opposite direction when he comes, 'cause he's so cheap, and a crook to boot. Yeah, well that may seem funny to you, but the bastard doesn't have a car, and he won't get a cab, so if you're so desperate that you have to go with him 'cause there ain't no business on a cold night in January, well, ya have to walk to his house. My friend Billy actually caught him stealing dough from his wallet while Billy was in the bathroom. And that's another thing. He won't let you take a shower afterwards 'cause he won't take you upstairs. No, he thinks he's so clever, and he takes ya to this scrungy little hole in the basement. He thinks no one knows that he lives upstairs. But of course we all do know.

"Anyway, I was in a real bad way this last winter and I had to go with him, and yuck, what a drag that was. He wanted to give me a blow job, but I couldn't get it up. He's such a toad. But surprise surprise, he didn't take me to Beacon Hill, but to an apartment on Comm. Ave. Afterwards he told me he wanted me to stay there as a super 'cause he owned the building. I told him I wouldn't have sex with him, and he said I didn't have to, just clean the halls and take out the garbage. Well, that wasn't all he had in mind, 'cause after a month or so he started telling me about you, and how I should meet his real hot nephew, and that I would like you, and all that crap. Okay, so I was interested. I decided, now that I have a place I don't need to turn tricks, so I got that job at Rebecca's, and then I got real horny 'cause I wasn't trickin', and I never did have a boyfriend before. Well, who would want a hustler for a boyfriend? Tough shit, huh?

"So anyway, Wisner set it up for me to meet you at the Dynasty Ball, and then you started comin' into the café, and I thought Wisner had told you where to find me. But it turned out it was just an accident. Then of course the old bastard laid it on me that I was supposed to get into the house next door, your aunt's house. I was supposed to ask you like I was curious or something. Then as luck would have it, I saw you inside from the window. You know the rest. Oh, except that I was supposed to leave the window opposite my apartment open so Wisner could get in."

Gyles scrutinized Val with mounting anger. "No, I don't know the rest, Val! Why would Wisner Chilton bother to concoct this elaborate ruse in order to steal jewelry worth maybe five thousand dollars? That may sound like all the money in the world to you, but it wouldn't pay his last year's income taxes. Do you know who Wisner Chilton is? He is a rich old man. Rich old men do not climb in and out of fourth-story windows in order to pinch some insignificant jewelry!"

That the boy would be so brazen as to assume that Gyles was another gullible john, willing to believe any absurd story in order to trick with him, wounded Gyles's vanity. He felt foolish for having been attracted to Val, and he suddenly realized that he wanted to be far away from this unsavory scene.

Cornelia was right. There was something tainted about Norma Chilton's Egyptian jewelry, something that lured one into a labyrinth of deceit.

"I don't know why the old fart stole the jewelry, and if you're all so rich and famous, why the fuck do you care anyway? I told you, you wouldn't believe me, so call the cops. That's what you threatened Lilly with. I don't have your shitty jewelry, but why should you believe a hustler? Sure, you can trash around with us at the Dynasty Ball, but we're not the type you'd invite to your 'A' gay dinner parties!"

In the middle of this last speech, Gyles got up and went to the outside door. He opened it and slipped into his tasseled loafers, their perfect polish soiled by drying mud. He retraced his steps through the garden to the pink door, where he turned and looked back. He saw Val standing in the doorway, all his weight resting on his left hip. The arbor, a garish tunnel of flashing lights, seemed an endless distance between the two men.

Gyles put up the lapels of his tweed jacket and thrust his hands deep inside his pockets against the damp, cold air. He climbed gritty stone steps, leaving the shadowy alley. Behind a dilapidated wooden fence, a dog barked hysterically, and Gyles quickened his pace.

He reached the high front stoop of his brick town house on Union Park in a short ten minutes, but the distance between Lillyland and Gyles's condo on the well-kept square, with its venerable elms and carefully raked lawn encircled by a Victorian cast-iron fence, was amplified by contrast. Inside his flat, Gyles shed his jacket and sank into an overstuffed chair upholstered with an antique kilim rug. He dialed the phone, sitting with the instrument held to his ear. He wasn't really listening, but in his mind's eye he replayed the confrontation with Lilly and Val. Gyles struggled with the realization that he must give up the jewels. The phone in his hand rang on and on unanswered. He roused himself with some effort and hung up, rubbing his eyes with both hands, pushing hard as if to break the crust of exhaustion that held him in a trance. He dialed the number for 283 Commonwealth Avenue, and this time his call was answered on the first ring.

"Hello?"

"Hi, Cornelia, this is Gyles."

"Gyles! Where on earth are you?"

"I'm at home. I just got in."

"Well, I hope you've eaten, because we went ahead without you. Do you know it's eleven o'clock? What happened to you?"

"I'm sorry, Corny. I should have called. No, I haven't eaten a thing since breakfast, but now I'm too tired. I'm just going to fall into bed. What happened with the police?"

"Oh my Goddess, the police. What a scene that was! Mrs. Buckley was hysterical. Rita was belligerent. The cops were by turn condescending and dismissive. I had to mediate between them all, which was exhausting. So far as anyone can gather, Uncle Wisner has simply disappeared. He isn't in any of the Boston or Cambridge hospitals, and he hasn't been arrested, at least not in Massachusetts, which is not surprising but they did check. He was not in any of his usual haunts, his clubs, the Athenaeum, or the church, no one in the family has heard a peep out of him in a dog's age, except for Cousin Eben, whom he consulted on business matters last week. So now we wait."

"Wait for what?" asked Gyles.

"I don't know. For whatever the police do for a missing person. Investigate, I guess. He's not someone they will likely ignore, not with Eben Chichester for a lawyer. By the way, they want you to call Detective Sergeant Pooler at this number. Have you got a pencil?"

"Yes, go ahead," and Gyles scribbled down the number that Cornelia read to him.

"Okay, Gyles, I've got to get going. Rita's waiting for me, and we were just leaving when you called."

"Good night, Corny. I'm sorry that everything was such a hassle for you, but I'm grateful you were there for Mrs. Buckley. Please tell Lucy Ann that I'm sorry I missed her dinner. I'll see you at the shop tomorrow. What time will you be in?"

"I have to be there early to work on my designs for Rosalind Wortheley's house, and I have to talk with you about that, so please be there, and Gyles, don't tell me how awful she is because I already know it."

"Did I say anything?"

"No, but you were about to, so don't."

"Well, I guess I've been told. Okay, sis. Nary a word disparaging our grand patroness. I just thank my lucky stars that the vulgar trollop has bucks to burn."

"Gyles…"

"I'm sorry, it just slipped out."

"Well stow it, and good night."

CHAPTER 24

▼

Rosalind Wortheley was eagerly perched on an undulating art nouveau chair in Cornelia's office. She had assumed a pose that hovered between languid ease and charged anticipation, much like the scintillating portraits of the Edwardian painter Baldini. She wore a Bill Blass suit of wool crepe in a subtle pearl-gray color, its impeccable tailoring following the line of her elegant body, without being prim or severe. Her silk blouse, the color of old ivory, was trimmed with an exquisite French lace that fell softly on the lapels of her suit, revealing a slight décolletage.

Cornelia sat behind her desk examining the perfection of her client as they talked about the decoration of the rambling old house on the beach at Wianno. She assessed Rosalind's appearance from all critical points of view and decided that the master stroke of this discreetly expensive fashion plate wasn't the platinum and moonstone pendant that hung on a fine chain about her neck but rather the faded bayberry green stockings Rosalind wore on her long, shapely legs. Cornelia couldn't help wondering whether this gorgeously insipid creature was not more calculating than she'd given her credit for, as it dawned on her that Rosalind was dressed in the same delicate colors as the office where the two women sat.

Rosalind was corralled by piles of bulging shopping bags from all the expensive stores in Back Bay. Having taken to heart the admonition of her commanding husband to spend major money, she had launched a career of conspicuous consumption that promised to rival Imelda Marcos. From one of her designer bags she produced a sample of glazed chintz printed with a vast herbaceous border in the style of Gertrude Jekyll. This design epitomized the fussy and crowded patterns that interior designers lavished upon their more gullible clients with intentions of evoking the English country house look. However, it more closely resembled a horde of botanical gluttony. Cornelia watched with dismay the flushed excitement that lit up Rosalind's easily ignited sensibilities when she presented this predictable example. She remarked with guarded understatement, "I see you've been to Romayne," referring to a popular furniture store on Newbury Street.

"Well yes, but how did you know? Oh silly me, of course, the bag gives it away," chirped Rosalind, and she continued. "But don't you think it's too fabulous, so English. Reginald, you know, the fellow at Romayne—isn't he the cutest? Well, Reginald assured me that it was very English and that Lario Dota used just reams of it for Elsa Fassbinder's cottage in the Cotswolds."

"Elsa Fassbinder's cottage is in Palm Beach," Cornelia contradicted with telling emphasis.

"But Reginald said—"

Cornelia interrupted. "A furniture salesman will tell you almost anything to sell a sofa."

"But Reginald is a designer," insisted Rosalind.

"I'm sure he has designing ways, but wish fulfillment will not get him to Wianno," Cornelia remarked with blatant snobbery that Rosalind could easily relate to.

"Oh. You don't like it." Rosalind's deflated remark teetered on the brink of resentment.

"Rosalind, it just won't do." Cornelia's firm dismissal was a risk but she felt she really had to put her foot down. "One of the principal drawbacks of this fabric, apart from its esthetic shortcomings, is that it's affordable."

"Huh?"

"Anyone can buy it." Cornelia stared at Rosalind, raising both eyebrows.

"You mean the stuff's cheap?"

"Far be it from me to dish that rag, but in a word, yes. Listen, Ross, George told you to spend in a big way, and I'm here to assist you. But more than that, I'm going to give you a home that is both classic and unique, a showplace that will appear to have evolved over generations. It will be credentials of old money clothed in culture, an environment that you can wear like a privileged birthright. It will be comfortable and familiar to you and suit you like your beautifully tailored suit. You will be the ultimate adornment of this lush interior, the jewel of George's crown." Cornelia, drunk with the power of her words, could not resist this last very English reference to empire. Rosalind, not immune to the effects of flattery, was somewhat mystified by the specifics of Cornelia's speech, but she caught the gist of the argument and was swayed by the designer's conviction.

"Oh well, it was just an idea. Reginald is such a dear boy, and I hate to disappoint him. Perhaps we can use it in the maid's room."

"Rosalind." Cornelia's one-word reply was implacably firm.

"Oh all right, if it's so important, there." Rosalind tossed the offending chintz into the waste basket and straightened her skirt unnecessarily, dismissing the incident like an unwanted wrinkle. Cornelia used the moment to present her beautifully rendered watercolor designs for the beach house. This house had been commissioned by Rosalind's grandfather and designed by Mr. Mead of McKim, Mead & White. But it had suffered neglect as a result of dwindling fortunes. It had escaped being sold and torn down thanks to Rosalind's timely marriage to George Wortheley. George liked to make money, and he fully expected his money to answer all his needs. It was this expectation that Cornelia intended to fulfill with panache and genuine quality. Rosalind looked at the pictures with childlike fascination, not realizing that the rambling and somewhat shabby barn of a place where her grandmother had gathered the clan over countless summers could ever be transformed into such a pretty house. The effort to concentrate on Cornelia's designs proved too onerous for Rosalind's fractured attention span, and she sought relief in the filed bits of gossip that hovered at the dim periphery of her conscience.

"Cornelia, these remind me that I've been meaning to tell you more about your Mrs. Sarkisian."

"She's hardly my Mrs. Sarkisian. And how on earth do my designs remind you of her?" Cornelia's question was tinged by slight but perceptible exasperation, which Rosalind perceived with satisfaction.

"But darling, you are decorating her condo at the Heritage, aren't you? You told me so yourself."

"Actually I didn't tell you that, although you assumed it. As it turns out, I'm not doing any work for Tatiana Sarkisian."

"Oh, I'm so sorry to hear that." Rosalind gushed with unnecessary sympathy, as if she were condoling a young widow. Cornelia was beginning to agree with her brother's harsh assessment of her old school chum, and she decided to add on a hefty percentage to the Wortheley bill for having to endure such exasperation. "Well, it's just as good that you aren't," continued Rosalind, "because Mrs. Sarkisian's grandfather was a mortician, and she grew up in his funeral home. Not exactly the kind of person you'd want to chair the Save the Children Ball, not to mention the Cancer Foundation Luncheon. After all, there might be a conflict of interest." Cornelia shuddered at Rosalind's macabre snobbery, suspecting this fantastic story to be a fabrication of some warped viper. She failed to find any humor in it.

"Rosalind, Tatiana Sarkisian was born in Egypt. Her father was a furrier to King Farouk, and she was married to a man who appears to be her father's partner. He is in any case a great deal older than she."

"Nonsense. Farag Sarkisian is a handsome Armenian hunk somewhere in his late forties. My cousin Dottie, you remember her, she went to Holyoke and she used to date Debbie Chandler's brother, well, Dottie has bought every fur coat she's ever had from Farag Sarkisian, and, darling, you know Dottie is draped in the stuff year round because she has that circulation disorder. How do you suppose I knew about Mrs. Sarkisian in the first place? Anyway, George and I were at the Brigham and Women's Ball last night at the Ritz, and who do you think was at Connie Treadwell's table but Farag and Tatiana Sarkisian? She was looking very New York in a black Yves Saint Laurent gown cut practically to her navel with a load of diamonds from Dorfman's and of course that sensational sable coat. But the husband, my dear, no wonder Dottie is head over heels. I can tell you, Cornelia, that I'm seriously thinking of scrapping this whole decoration project and spending a positive fortune in fur." Rosalind had no intention of carrying out this threat because George had already bought her a full-length silver mink last winter, and George needed to know that nothing threatened his supremacy. So more fur was out of the question, but she wanted to get back at Cornelia for not allowing the flowered chintz.

"George and I were sitting at Mummy's table with Aunt Harriet and the Slatterlys. Mrs. Slatterly and Aunt Harriet were remarking on the diamonds that Mrs. Sarkisian was wearing. Mummy thought they were vulgar, and she said so too. Mrs. Slatterly remarked that Tatiana Iskander hadn't changed much since their school days at Dana Hall, except that she was thinner now and not as striking. It seems Tatiana made up wild stories even then about how she was the orphaned daughter of a Russian princess and similar rot. But they found out that she was just the granddaughter of a mortician."

The telephone intruded on Rosalind's scathing discourse, and Cornelia grabbed for it. "Hello, Chilton's Antiques and Interiors. Oh Gyles, Rosalind Wortheley is here in the office, and we're going over the designs for Wianno. When will you be here? Yes of course I'm sitting down. What? Oh, good Goddess. Where is he? In bed? No. Yes, yes. Yes of course, I'll be right over. No, I'm all right. How's Mrs. Buckley? Oh the poor dear. Yes, right away. Good-bye."

Rosalind glared at Cornelia like a starved cat. Her appetite for scandal was tantalized and she pounced on Cornelia before the phone reached its cradle. "Darling, what on earth has happened?"

"My Uncle Wisner has died," Cornelia replied automatically, dazed by the news.

"Oh no. I'm terribly sorry." This time Rosalind's condolences were at least appropriate to the occasion. Unfortunately she couldn't leave it at that and inquired, "Were you close with your uncle?"

"No, not really. He had—" Cornelia was about to say that Wisner had disappeared two days ago but caught herself in time, aided by Gyles's admonition not to tell Rosalind anything.

"He had—?" pumped the gossip.

"Oh nothing. Rosalind, will you forgive me? I must go join Gyles at Uncle—"

"Darling, of course you must. And Mrs. Buckley?"

"Yes, she is or was my uncle's housekeeper."

"And Mrs. Buckley found—" Rosalind continued her relentless inquisition.

"What? Oh Rosalind, please, I'm sorry, but I really must leave."

"You know it's good to talk about these things, Cornelia. It gets it out and over with. But never mind, my car is out front. Let me give you a lift."

"No! That is, thank you, but so is my car out front. I don't want to impose on you."

"It's no imposition at all. What else are old school chums for?"

"Thank you, Rosalind, but no. I'll need my car to drive home." Cornelia voiced this firm resolve as she rose from her desk, slinging her small Hermés purse over the shoulder of her suit jacket. She held the door open for her client and stood with calm patience as Rosalind wriggled into her Trigére coat and scrambled to collect the shopping bags piled around her.

"My dear, I know you're in a hurry, but give a girl a chance."

"Take your time. If you'd like to leave some of those things here I'll make sure they're delivered to your house tomorrow."

"Would you? Oh, that would be marvelous. But I don't want to be a bother."

"It's no bother, Rosalind. Our new shop assistant will be here. I'll just have her drop them by." Cornelia smiled to herself as she envisioned the meeting between the very upfront feminist Pat DeScenzo, and this dependent professional beauty who referred to herself as a girl.

The two women walked out onto busy Newbury Street together. Cornelia paused to set the shop alarm and lock her front door. They both threw kisses into the air somewhere in the vicinity of each other's cheek, and then they parted.

CHAPTER 25

▼

It was a strange day for death. A bright day, when no cloud could eclipse the swelling bloom of life. No shroud could muffle the bustling clamor of a city rejoicing after a winter interminable. But death had come, an unwanted visitor with all his artificial importance, compelling and drear.

Cornelia drove towards Beacon Hill with the top of her M.G. down. Warm spring breezes played with her hair and carried the scent of magnolia blossoms. May sunshine had brought all the flowers out at once, as well as bikini-clad sunbathers and hoards of noontime office workers. All the tree-lined streets of Back Bay and the Boston Common were either covered with thin green leaves or aflutter with billowing white blossoms. A gentle shower of blossoms rained down on the fragrant grass of the Public Garden.

Cornelia parked on Charles Street and turning the corner, walked up the hill on Chestnut. She was surprised when Eben Chichester opened the door instead of Mrs. Buckley. Her cousin Eben mistook her confusion for grief, and with a gesture of courtly protection, he linked arms with her, leading her through the front hall into the antique-filled double parlor. There she was more surprised to see a small group of Chiltons and Chichesters already assembled and deporting themselves with poise and decorum. In their midst, a primly uniformed Mrs. Buckley was passing a well-polished silver tray laden with old Waterford stemmed glasses filled with sherry. Unlike the rest of the company, the old housekeeper was hardly able to conceal her grief. Her eyes were red and puffy and her features drawn and pale. She approached Cornelia and Eben. Cornelia slipped her arm from her cousin's protection and took hold of the proffered tray with both hands. Mrs. Buckley weakly protested, "Oh no, miss!"

Cornelia said, in a gentle but insistent tone, "Mrs. B." This was enough for the servant to relinquish her burden. Cornelia took the tray and pressed it upon Eben. She put her arm around the older woman's waist and led her from the room.

Eben's aunt, Julia Chichester, came to his aid. She took the tray and deposited it on a side table, disrupting but not harming a display of porcelain snuffboxes. She commented with a sniff, "The clutter in this house is discouraging. Wasn't that Cornelia Chilton? Poor girl. She never did have a mother to draw boundaries for her."

Cornelia had taken Mrs. Buckley downstairs, where a cheery kitchen opened out onto a walled garden with a delicate pink dogwood in full bloom. Cornelia poured Mrs. Buckley and herself a cup of tea from a Spode teapot that had been keeping warm beneath a quilted tea cozy. Mrs. Buckley dried her eyes on a plain linen hankie.

"Here now. Drink this. It's nice and hot," said Cornelia.

Mrs. Buckley smiled wanly and asked, "May I have sugar, miss?"

"Mrs. B, only if you stop calling me 'miss.' We went through this the other day. You've known me all my twenty-nine years. My name is Cornelia."

The two women sat in comfortable silence for a while, sipping their tea.

After a while Mrs. Buckley spoke. "Himself was so terrifying. There on the pillow shams that I had ironed for him just last week. I was so surprised to see him, I dropped all the towels, and I must have screamed, because the day girl came running. When she poked her head in the doorway and saw himself staring at her, she let out such a shout and a holler that was like to bring the neighbors round. We couldn't have that, so I had to pull myself together and shake some sense into the girl. I sent her downstairs to call for Dr. Wallace. Then I went back to collect the towels I dropped and close the shutters and draw the draperies. I hope you won't be angry with me, but I did say a short prayer. It only seemed proper, himself being all alone and such."

Cornelia was a good listener, giving all her attention with nodding agreement, never probing or interrupting. When Mrs. Buckley was finished with her narrative, Cornelia asked the natural question. "What did Uncle Wisner die of?"

"Dr. Wallace says it was heart attack," replied the old housekeeper without conviction.

Cornelia had been brought into the world by Perkins Wallace. He had tended to her medical needs throughout her childhood, as he had done for Gyles and Aunt Florence, and the entire Chilton-Chichester clan. It had been a radical departure from custom when Cornelia had begun to consult another physician, and a woman at that, Gloria Birnbaum. Cornelia's older cousin Julia Chichester, who was Perkins Wallace's aunt, had called to remonstrate with her on such a slight. Cornelia had been politely firm. She didn't doubt Dr. Wallace's competence. She simply wanted her own family doctor, now that Rita and she were lovers. Rita would never dream of going to a male doctor.

For Cornelia, if Dr. Wallace said that Uncle Wisner had died of a heart attack, then so it must be. But she heard doubt in Mrs. Buckley's voice and wondered what could have caused it. Mrs. Buckley was encouraged by Cornelia's permissive silence and continued, "Forgive me, miss, uh, Cornelia. But himself looked like one of the holy martyrs, so pale and drained, almost blue, and the agony frozen in his face. His wrists were burned and scarred, like a tortured saint."

Cornelia gently stroked the bent shoulders of the older woman as she sobbed. She assumed that Mrs. Buckley was suffering from shock when she equated Wisner with the holy martyrs. She thought she understood the housekeeper's Catholic imagination enough to edit the overdramatic and macabre embellishments of her story.

Gyles entered the kitchen as Mrs. Buckley was tucking her handkerchief into her apron pocket. Cornelia stood by the window, looking out at the garden. "Oh, here you are." And he added politely, "Mrs. Buckley, I am terribly sorry. I know I speak for the whole family when I say how grateful we are to you for your devotion to my uncle."

"Thank you, sir."

Cornelia stared at Gyles, amazed at how true to type he was in this setting and how much the crisis of death brought that out in him.

"Cornelia, may I speak with you? That is, if you've finished here."

"No, I have not finished here, Gyles," she replied with annoyance.

"That's quite all right, miss. I must be tending to the guests."

"Mrs. B, I am Cornelia, not 'miss'!" the younger woman snapped.

Gyles intervened and forcibly guided Cornelia out into the garden. "Cornelia, pull yourself together! I know it's a shock, but the old boy was getting on. In any case, he's gone now, and it would be better if you returned to the parlor. The family is assembling, and asking after you. Please let Mrs. Buckley do her job. It was good of you to console her, but now your family needs you. Oh hell, Cornelia, I need you. Those people are asking me where you are!"

"Where's Uncle Wisner?" Cornelia asked with more than an edge to her voice.

"To wherever they take them. Don't be morbid. Eben Chichester arranged it all."

"Who are 'they'?"

"The undertakers, of course. Who else, Bela Lugosi?"

"Eben certainly is on top of this situation."

"What do you mean, Cornelia? Of course he is. That's his job. He was Wisner's lawyer. Would you like to make the arrangements? Do you know anything about funerals?"

"Who said anything about funerals? Uncle Wisner was a missing person until a few hours ago. Aren't you curious about where he's been?"

"Well, unfortunately we're too late to ask him about that. But from what I know, you don't want to hear any more about it."

"What do you mean?"

"I mean that our dear Uncle Wisner died in the saddle."

"What?"

"I told you not to ask."

"Don't be a male chauvinist pig with me, Gyles. I'm not one of those hypocritical drooping lilies upstairs in the parlor. What the hell happened here?"

"The short version, which I caution you is purely speculative, is that he died of a heart attack while having sex with a person or persons unknown."

"But that's disgusting! It's absurd! Uncle Wisner was at least seventy-five years old!"

"Disgusting and absurd, maybe. But that's only the half of it."

"Well, what's the other half? For godsakes, Gyles, out with it!"

"Apparently there was bondage involved, as well as drugs."

Cornelia flashed on Mrs. Buckley's story about the scarred wrists of martyrs and the agony in Uncle Wisner's face. "But Mrs. B found him in his bed."

"Yes. Apparently that had been arranged. I didn't inquire too deeply."

"Why not? Gyles, this is a matter for the police."

"No! Absolutely not! Listen, Cornelia, don't be angry, but I've called Rita, and she's on her way to pick you up."

"Go to hell, Gyles! I'm getting to the bottom of this." Cornelia whirled around to leave, but her brother caught her arm and held her. She froze and with seething rage ordered, "Let go of me, Gyles!" He obeyed her, and brother and sister stood facing each other.

"Cornelia, wait," pleaded Gyles.

"This better be good," she replied with utter disgust.

"Wisner was in the habit of using hustlers for sex. Whatever you and I think about that, it doesn't matter, because this time he went too far. There were drugs, as I told you, and apparently some kind of S&M. The result is that the man is dead. Nothing is going to change that. Now, do we get involved in a huge scandal and drag this pathetic lonely bastard through the muck? The man died of a heart attack. What does it matter how it was caused?"

"How do you know this? Is this what they're all talking about upstairs?"

"Good God, no. Eben Chichester and Perkins Wallace reported to me the circumstantial evidence they found, and I filled in the missing pieces."

"What do you mean, missing pieces?"

"I told them about the hustlers."

"Gyles, how do you know about hustlers? I suppose you'll tell me that you've been hiring them by the dozens for years."

"Hardly, but I know someone—God, now I sound like Eben. Val is a hustler, Cornelia. He told me that Wisner's well known on the street, and from what he said, I believe him."

"Val who? What street?"

"Val the guy I met at the Dynasty Ball. I told you about him."

"Apparently not enough, Gyles."

"Well, I just found out myself. I'm not exactly thrilled, but there you have it."

Cornelia sat down rather abruptly on an uncomfortable iron garden bench. "So what's going to happen now?"

"Nothing. Wisner's been taken to the funeral home, and Dr. Wallace made out a death certificate stating that his patient died of a heart attack, which is entirely true."

"Oh." Cornelia's monosyllable was an act of resignation that spoke volumes. Gyles seized his moment.

"So please come with me upstairs and say hello to a couple of the relatives, and by then Rita will be here and you can go home and forget all about this. I'm sorry I dragged you here. It wasn't necessary. I didn't know you would be so upset. Eben was calling all the relatives in the neighborhood, so I thought I should call you."

"Okay, Gyles. Okay. I guess the whole house just gives me the creeps."

"Corny, this business is unfortunate, but it's not our concern. Let's let the professionals handle it."

"Yeah. That crowd upstairs are certainly professionals at dispatching the dearly departed to their just reward and dividing the spoils. I remember them all from Aunt Florence's funeral."

"Cornelia, just thank your lucky stars that we don't have to deal with this place as well as Aunt Florence's. We must concentrate on our business."

"Well, I'm glad to hear you say that, Gyles, because, as I told you, I had Rosalind Wortheley with me at the shop this morning. I think she was pleased with my designs for her grandmother's house. She better be, because they really are beautiful. All of your antiques are going to look terrific. You know, it really is a great old house. By the way, didn't you tell me that Farag Sarkisian was an old curmudgeon with bushy eyebrows and hairy ears?"

"Yes, he is rather grisly. But don't you think we could talk about him later?"

"Gyles, Farag Sarkisian is a handsome forty-five-year-old hunk. So who did you really meet, and why?"

Gyles looked at Cornelia, his eyebrows puckered with concern as he considered what she was telling him. At the same time he deftly maneuvered her through the kitchen and upstairs.

"Where did you learn this?" asked Gyles.

"It's a complicated story, and I know you're going to object, but suffice it to say I believe her."

"You believe who?"

"Rosalind."

"Oh. Well. If you say so. But the man Tatiana introduced me to was no playboy."

"I didn't say playboy, Gyles. I said hunk."

Cornelia and Gyles had reached the first floor. Cornelia spotted Rita talking with Eben by the fireplace in the front parlor. Various other relatives were scattered about the adjoining rooms, sipping sherry and chatting quietly. Before Cornelia could join her lover, she was waylaid by Julia Chichester.

"There you are, Cornelia! We wondered where you disappeared to."

"I should have thought that was quite obvious, Julia. I was taking care of Mrs. Buckley, a concern that apparently has escaped everyone's keen sensibilities."

"You remind me so much of my grandmother Gwendolyn Chichester. She was something of a bluestocking, you know, and an ardent suffragette."

"Your grandmother could afford to be a suffragette. She had twenty servants and a rich husband."

Julia smiled and said, "Your friend Rita arrived about fifteen minutes ago. She certainly has charmed Eben. Is she socially conscious too?"

Cornelia knew the unlikelihood of Rita bothering to charm any male, let alone one as cocksure of himself as Eben Chichester, so with amused irony she repeated Julia's question. "Is Rita socially conscious? Oh yes, she's a radical feminist lesbian."

"I see. And have you known her long?"

Cornelia was piqued by her cousin's blandly polite reaction, so she decided to really let her have it. "Let me think." Cornelia mimed concentration. "I've known Rita about five years, although we've only been lovers for three of them."

"I see. And where did you meet, at college? I remember having a terrific crush on one of my sorority sisters when I was at Smith."

"No, actually she picked me up at a BLAB festival in Vermont."

"Blab festival?"

"Yes, Bicycling Lesbians Around Boston. Our fall weekend that year was in Bennington."

"I see. Don't you just love Vermont? You know, George and Harriet Chilton had the most divine house in Woodstock, Vermont. What's Rita's last name? Maybe they know her family."

"Rosenstein and they live in the Bronx, New York, not Woodstock, Vermont."

"Oh I see."

"What is it exactly that you see, Julia?" Cornelia raised her voice above the subdued tones of the rest of the company, and everyone stopped in midsentence to listen. "You keep saying 'I see.' And I'd like to know just what it is that you see, because I don't think you see a goddamn thing."

Rita shelved her untried sherry glass on the mantelpiece and swiftly made her way to Cornelia's side. Gyles had warned Rita that Cornelia was upset, so she had arrived alert to her rescue mission. Having had to endure fifteen minutes of Eben Chichester's pleasantries did nothing to subdue her protective passion. Rita encircled Cornelia with her sturdy arm. She gave Julia a confrontational frown but said nothing.

"Oh hi, Rita, I'm glad you're here." Cornelia turned to her lover and rising on tiptoes conspicuously kissed the taller woman full on the lips. "Rita, this is my cousin, Julia Chichester. She was just asking all about you. Julia, this is my lover, Rita Rosenstein."

Totally nonplussed, Julia extended an openhanded greeting, which Rita grasped reluctantly. The older woman enthused, "Hello, Rita. I think it's marvelous how liberated your generation has become. Now in my day, we were taught the limits of social behavior, but I can see you've thrown all that to the wind. It fairly takes my breath away to see you together. I suppose when each of you is married you'll have fond memories of your passionate youth."

Cornelia said indignantly, "We are married."

"Oh really? To whom?" the gossip persisted obtusely.

"To each other," they said in unison.

"I see. How modern of you."

Rita took the lead then. "Not really so modern, Julia. After all, there was Sappho, and of course, in Boston's more recent past, Amy Lowell. I should like to have said I enjoyed meeting you. Good-bye now." Rita escorted Cornelia into the front hall, where they encountered Gyles and Eben.

"Gyles, we're leaving now. Did you bring your car with you?"

"No, Cornelia. What's up?"

"Would you drive my car home? It's down on Charles Street. I'm going to take the rest of the afternoon off and spend the night at Rita's."

"Sure thing. As a matter of fact, I was just about to leave myself. I have to get back to the shop. If you'll wait half a minute, I'll walk with you down the hill."

"Oh, Gyles old man, there's something rather important that I must speak with you about. It'll only take a minute."

"Well, if it really can't wait, Eben. But I have an appointment with an important client."

"Maybe I should come with you after all and fill you in on Rosalind and Wianno," said his sister.

"It's okay, Cornelia. You go relax with Rita, you've done more than your share today simply by putting up with—that is, taking care of Rosalind Wortheley."

"I think you had it right the first time, Gyles. Mrs. George Wortheley is a great deal to put up with."

The two women said their good-byes and left. Eben Chichester's expression was doubtful when he asked, "George Wortheley is your client?"

"In a manner of speaking, yes. Although so far we've been spared actually dealing with the great man. He is, however, paying the bills. Cornelia went to Dana Hall with his wife. Why, is George one of your clients?"

"No, he's not actually our kind of customer. But he's very much the upcoming man on the market."

"Well, I'm glad to hear that, because Cornelia has a rather ambitious project planned for their house in Wianno. But what was it that you wanted to speak with me about, Eben? I do have a customer waiting for me who's lusting after a French silver wine cooler, or at least she will be when she sees the one I've selected for her."

Eben led Gyles upstairs and into their Uncle Wisner's library, lined with four matching Georgian mahogany bookcases. Behind their delicately mullioned glass doors, an impeccable collection of fine leather-bound books filled the shelves. Although the room was rich with detail and crammed with Wisner's important collection of furniture and art, Gyles's eye was riveted to the leather-covered jewel cases that littered the desktop. Eben did not say anything as he assumed his place at Wisner's desk chair without hesitation. Gyles stared with disbelief at the empty boxes that Val had said Wisner had taken from 283 Commonwealth Avenue. Sure enough, here they were. But now Wisner was dead, and the jewels that must have been here were gone.

Eben watched Gyles carefully and said, "I found these empty boxes here when I arrived this afternoon. I assume that whoever was with Wisner when he died took the contents, which must have been jewelry of some kind. As I said earlier, there were no signs of forced entry, and all the doors were locked when Mrs. Buckley arrived this morning. So it appears that Wisner invited his companions into the house. Do you know what these boxes contained, and how important a loss it may have been?"

"Uh, no. At first I thought I recognized them. Aunt Norma had something similar. Some costume jewelry, souvenirs from Egypt. Yes. See here on the inside lid, Karnak Jewels, Cairo. Probably these were similar. Nothing of importance, considering the contents of this house. I would say whatever baubles may have been in these cases would have been inconsequential." Gyles did not know exactly why he was lying to Eben Chichester, except that the Egyptian jewelry of Norma Chilton had led from one unpleasant mystery to the next, and here it had reemerged to haunt him once more. He only knew that he wanted to be away from this house, to forget the desperate and pathetic loneliness that had led to his uncle's death.

"I'm relieved to know that the missing articles were of no importance," said Eben. "We want to avoid any unpleasant complications. I knew that because you and your uncle were alike, sharing similar interests, so to speak, that you would be able to advise me on the matter. So I could in turn protect your interests."

"Eben, what the hell are you saying? That because I'm gay I can tell you about Wisner's sordid sex life? I am not similar to Wisner. He was a prissy, closeted old queen of the worst type. We did not share similar interests. For one thing, I'm not interested in pubescent children, nor am I into playing the hypocritical role of a Boston Brahmin. So save your condescending bullshit. Yes, I happen to know quite by chance that he hired hustlers. If you tell me he died having sex and being tied up in his bed, you know more about it than I do."

"Gyles, Gyles! Please! I mean nothing of the sort. Forgive me if I expressed myself poorly. We are of different generations, and we don't know each other well. But let me assure you that I would never allude to your private life. I am a lawyer, not a judge. I have to gather information in order to protect my clients, nothing else. Apparently you do not know, but Wisner Chilton has named you as his single heir. This house, its contents, his other properties and investments, excluding certain bequests, all go to you. I assumed that because you and your uncle were both avid collectors of art and antiques and therefore shared certain interests, that you were his most simpatico relative and confidant. I'm only trying to avoid any official inquiry and ensuing scandal by having you advise me on the importance of anything that may be missing from this house."

Gyles was struck dumb by this revelation. He could hardly believe it. Surely Wisner had closer blood relatives. Who, after all, were all those people downstairs in the parlor? He felt foolish and naked for having berated Eben about being gay, and his harsh words about Wisner reverberated against Gyles's conscience like hammering steel. "No, Eben, these things don't matter. We won't mention them again. Thank you for your concern, and please forgive my outburst. I, uh—"

"Think nothing of it, old man. These are trying times. Go back to your shop and work. Work is the best antidote for grief. Tomorrow come have lunch with me at the Union Club at twelve noon, and we'll talk some more. I will be happy to represent your interests as I did for your Uncle Wisner and as my father did for his father."

"Okay, Eben. Yeah, sure. Tomorrow. Lunch. Twelve o'clock. I've gotta run now. Good-bye." Gyles left Eben Chichester sitting at Wisner's desk. The lawyer's eyes narrowed, his thin lips pursed together and he stared at the jewel cases.

CHAPTER 26

▼

Cornelia kicked her heels off immediately upon entering Rita's apartment and dropped her gym bag in the foyer. She plunked her handbag and portfolio down on the living room carpet and draped her silk scarf on a table lamp. Shedding her alligator belt on the floor, she collapsed onto the sofa in a dramatic pose with her forearm covering her eyes. Rita entered, completely absorbed in leafing through her mail. Having completed this editing job, she looked up to discover Cornelia's littering trail. She commanded, "Neil, peel yourself off that sofa and pick up this junk. I don't have any servants handy to pick up after you, and I'll be damned if you're going to cast me in the role of lady's maid."

"Ree…"

"What?"

"C'mere…"

"What for?"

"Ree…"

"Neil!"

"Ree…"

"Oh, this is stupid."

"C'mere…"

"I don't know why I should. What do you want? Maybe I should give you a back rub?"

"Mmm…"

Rita sat down reluctantly on the edge of the sofa and continued to rant, although her protestations were losing steam. "Look here, Neil, we can't just loll about here all night."

"Ree…" Cornelia slid an arm around her lover's waist and pulled her towards her.

"Neil, I have to get supper ready so we can get to bed at a decent hour."

"Let's skip supper and get to bed at an indecent hour." Cornelia raised herself into a sitting position with a fluid and sure movement. Without hesitation or force, she brought her lips to Rita's and silenced her lover's complaint. Cornelia eased them back into the soft comfort of the sofa. There the scent of sandalwood cologne mixed with the secret warmth of their bodies as they sought, with exquisite delicacy, the pulse of happiness.

Several hours passed, consumed by dalliance and a pleasant dinner. Afterwards, Cornelia was washing the dishes as Rita pored over the old account books that she had borrowed from Cosmo Chilton's office at 283 Commonwealth Avenue. Her interest in these documents was at first academic, the natural curiosity of a young CPA. They were a rare opportunity to study nineteenth-century accounting at her leisure. As a clan, the Chiltons had considered their position in the world of business to be of paramount importance, worthy of study not only for the history of commerce in a burgeoning nation but as the guide for future generations of Chiltons. Because of this self-aggrandizement, they had kept every scrap of paper, all carefully filed in Cosmo Chilton's old-fashioned office.

Rita had selected for close scrutiny a half-dozen oversized ledgers dating from the first four decades of the twentieth century. She was particularly concerned with the legendary losses sustained during the period of Norma Chilton's control over her part of the family empire. Rita found the character of Norma fascinating because she was a woman doing business at a time of total male domination. Rita somehow hoped to vindicate Norma of the stigma of failure. What she found confirmed her suspicions to an alarming degree but made her ponder over the abuses of power and success.

Rita pushed her horn-rimmed glasses onto the top of her head. She squeezed the bridge of her nose with her thumb and index finger as if she were trying to pull a difficult idea out of her brain. Turning to look at her lover, she said, "You know, Cornelia, according to these accounts, your aunt's companies didn't collapse during the Depression. In point of fact, most of them didn't make it into the thirties. They were liquidated in the late twenties, when the companies, all textile-related, were still viable and strong. A complicated system of cannibalization of assets was developed between subsidiary companies, leaving some weakened to a point of collapse. These were sold off. At the same time, the parent company grew briefly and disproportionately stronger. Stock values soared, and then Norma cashed in."

"Oh, Rita, how can that be? What happened to all the money? The whole family knows that Norma lost her money. Aunt Florence told me so herself, and people like Julia Chichester never lose an opportunity to harp on the lost fortunes and past glories."

"It was converted to gold."

"What was converted to gold?"

"The companies."

"What companies?"

"The textile companies that Norma inherited and then raped, her companies here in New England."

"That's ridiculous. Women aren't capable of rape, and Aunt Norma died a poor woman."

"Everything is relative, Cornelia, and the Chilton standard of poverty is a far cry from starvation. But rape in any language is violation, and that's just what Norma did to the hundreds of people who worked for her. She violated their trust and livelihoods, sucking them dry like a vampire and then discarding them as so much bothersome waste."

"You're right. I must confess, you have finally seen us for what we are. The Chilton blood boils with seething greed. We are powerless to disobey. And now—lust erupts inside of me, and I am compelled to violate you! Or should I say, again!"

"Go ahead and joke, but to me this is very disappointing. I hoped that Norma Chilton would be different from her male oppressors. I thought she might be competent and more adept at business instead of a self-indulgent and extravagant spendthrift. Well, clever and calculating she was, but the means to her end were as exploitative as those of the worst man. Although where it got her is a mystery, as she is unlikely to have spent nearly three million on sifting the dry sands of Egypt for moldering mummies."

"Three million?"

"Well, there's something that got your attention."

"You bet! Are you sure?"

"All I have to go by right now are these ledgers. They're remarkably detailed, but the trouble is that there are many entries identified only by cryptic initials, as well as a lot of overcomplicated transactions."

"But you said the money was converted to gold? Is that possible?"

"It was in 1929, but you couldn't do it today."

"Well if she liquidated her holdings she must have had a very good reason, although her reasoning does seem a bit warped. Maybe she saw trouble ahead and being the imperious Brahmin that she was, she wouldn't trust anyone but herself to guard her money."

The phone rang, cutting Cornelia short. She answered it. "Oh hello, Gyles. Yes, she's right here." Rita waved the receiver at Cornelia.

"Gyles, thank the Goddess! Rita has just discovered the most fantastic thing, which leads me to believe that Aunt Norma took it all with her! You know the old phrase, 'you can't take it with you'? Well of course nothing could be farther from the truth. After all, look at King Tut. I mean, really, he's been to Paris more times than I have, although I'll bet the poor stiff didn't see the Eiffel Tower, or the Ritz for that matter. Anyway, he went to get his bandages cleaned. Dear Goddess, can you imagine traveling on the plane with a three-thousand-year-old mummy? Although I guess they wouldn't exactly put him in first class. Anyway, I read it in a magazine. Tut went three times. So there you go. If you want the eternal, forget Helena Rubinstein. Cash in all your chips for gold, that's the way. I'll bet that's just what Aunt Norma did. Would you believe three million dollars?"

"Cornelia, Aunt Norma is buried in Cambridge, at Mount Auburn Cemetery," interrupted Gyles.

"So how do you know? Maybe—"

"She died at 283 Commonwealth Avenue," continued Gyles.

"Maybe, but—"

"No 'maybe buts.' You have Aunt Florence's letter saying so, and stating that Norma had lost her fortune. Besides, I saw her tomb in the mausoleum at Aunt Florence's funeral."

"Oh. But you don't really know if she's in there. And besides, it doesn't matter where she is. The point is, what's buried with her?"

That sounded to Gyles like nothing more than childish fantasy, and he said, "Unlike King Tut, I am fairly certain that Norma Chilton has not been rocketing around the globe. Not to get her bandages washed or her hair permed. Cornelia, what are you talking about?"

Cornelia handed the phone to Rita, refusing to answer her brother.

"Hi, Gyles. Rita here. This is a little bit complex to explain over the phone. Let me see, how shall I put it? Okay. I've been researching Norma Chilton's account books, and discovered that she didn't lose her money in the Crash of '29, but rather, she raped the companies she owned, liquidating all her assets in a series of complex transactions way before the Depression."

"If they were her companies, she was perfectly within her rights to use them as she pleased. What do you mean, 'raped'?"

"I would've thought that you'd have greater scruples than that, Gyles. I mean, she screwed the little guy. The workers in those factories. Screwed them out of their jobs."

"Well, I'm surprised to hear it, Rita. I was under the impression that Norma was the one who had been screwed. But if she anticipated the Crash, she was a lot better businesswoman than I ever supposed. So why are you so down on her? Aren't you a champion of equal rights for women?"

"Women's rights has nothing to do with ruining people's lives." Rita handed the phone back to Cornelia and stomped off to the kitchen.

"Hello?" said Gyles.

"Hello yourself, you male chauvinist," snapped Cornelia.

"Cornelia, what on earth is all this about? Three million dollars?"

"I don't know really, but Rita says Aunt Norma had all her assets converted to gold, which must mean one thing."

"Dare I ask what that might be?"

"I've already told you. She took it with her. Gold is incorruptible, eternal. She's buried with it."

"What makes you think that?"

"Well, there's the Egyptian jewelry, for one. And there are all those Egyptian artifacts at the MFA. She funded all those excavations for years, and besides—" Cornelia was grabbing for straws when her eye fell on the brightly colored architectural drawings of an Egyptian tomb that Rita had found tucked into the old ledgers she had been studying. Until this moment Cornelia had supposed these plans to be something of Norma's connection with the museum. Now she pressed this convenient if somewhat dubious proof into action. "I have the plans for the tomb right in my hand!"

"Right, and I'm King Tut. Little sister, that's the lamest excuse for fantasy I have ever heard."

Cornelia slammed down the phone.

"Hello? Hello?" Gyles replaced his receiver on its cradle and lit a Sobranie. He took a deep drag on the cigarette and as he exhaled, he relaxed into his club chair with a condescending shrug of disbelief. A moment later he sat bolt upright, momentarily reconsidering his sister's idea. But again, he dismissed the notion as ridiculous. Anyway, he had more compelling matters to contemplate. The whole drama of Wisner's death was too shocking and sad to really register. As far as his uncle's legacy went, it was too fantastic to be true. He certainly never expected an inheritance. Aunt Florence's house was a surprise, but at least a place that held fond memories, however distant. Gyles had not been raised with wealth. Privileged opportunity in education, yes, but when he was a child his Aunt Florence's house had been slightly shabby and certainly very frugal. Prep school had been Spartan, and Harvard was dependent upon scholarships and a small allowance from his mother's estate, and that had long since been spent.

Also, Gyles hadn't really liked his uncle, and that made the whole thing very disturbing. Although his own business was now dependent upon his credit at the bank, and he could certainly use substantial financing, he liked the idea that he was making it on his own, relying on his passion for and considerable knowledge of art and antiques. But he also felt responsible for Cornelia's career, because he had convinced her to join him in his venture. Now there was a new light on everything, and how would it affect their lives?

Gyles went to fix himself a drink. The bar was fitted into an old oak armoire. He took an ice tray from the mini-fridge and placing cubes into a crystal tumbler, he poured an inch of Glenfiddich on top. Resuming his seat, he rested his feet on the oversized ottoman.

While he sipped his Scotch, his thoughts returned to the other thorny matter, the Egyptian jewelry cases, which had reappeared on Wisner's desk. Val must have been telling the truth, or partially so, at least about Wisner removing the jewelry from 283 Commonwealth Avenue. Gyles could not clearly remember what the story had been because at the time it had seemed too bizarre. Val's guilt was easier for Gyles to believe than the idea that his seventy-five-year-old uncle was a cat burglar. Or was Gyles just using this as an excuse to push Val out of his life, to extinguish the spark the sensuous young man had struck in the twilight of Gyles's love life? There was a part of Gyles, a compelling, urgent core, which stirred as he held Val in his mind's eye. Suddenly, he leapt from his seat. He went into the bedroom to change into jeans and a sweatshirt.

He had to find Val. He didn't know where or how he would, but he told himself, "Just move, and don't debate it."

As he was putting on an old brown leather pilot's jacket, it occurred to him that Monique would know Lilly's telephone number. "I'll bet Val is still there." It might even be less complicated to ask Butch, who seemed like a regular guy. Well, in comparison to Monique anyway.

Gyles dialed and heard, "Hello. Château Lafarge. It's your dime, start talkin'."

Butch's bass rumble was music to Gyles's ears and his reply was correspondingly to the point. "Hi, Butch. This is Gyles Chilton. What's Lilly's phone number?"

"Won't do ya no good. Sh'ain't there."

"Look, help me out with this one. I'm looking for Val. He's still at Lilly's, isn't he?"

"Nobody's there."

"Are you sure?"

"Drove 'em all crazy today, and they ain't gettin' back 'til late tonight. Say, you wanna come over and listen to that Granados CD? We can mess around and talk about the first thing that comes up."

"Uh, not right now, Butch. I'm not quite sure I understand. Why don't you give me Lilly's number anyway?"

"Okay, if you wanna know, it's listed unda Lilly Linda LeStrange, 482-5587, but like I told ya, I drove 'em crazy."

"Well, I'm sure you do sweep all the boys and girls off their feet, but I think I'll give them a ring anyway."

"No, dope. I mean the Club Crazy. So don't be so fuckin' high and mighty. The whole troop are kickin' up their heels for Lilly's new show."

"Oh! Sorry I didn't quite get it. The Club Crazy? Where's that, Butch?"

"Yeah, that's not all you didn't get. 'Cause the kid's been pissin' an' moanin' up a storm since you dumped him. Lilly practically drags him to the club every night just to keep him off the street and outta trouble."

"What kid do you mean? Val? He's upset about me? Really? Where's the Club Crazy, Butch?" Gyles could hardly hide his excitement.

"You don't hafta sound so happy about it. The kid's a mess."

"No. Yes. Right. I mean, where did you say it was?"

"Five-ninety Congress Street. In Southie. Over the bridge past the Tea Party ship."

"Thanks, Butch. You really are a regular guy."

"Hey, watch your mouth, pal. I gotta reputation ta hold up." Butch hung up the phone and went back to watching The Dating Game.

Gyles grabbed the keys to his Jeep Grand Cherokee and dashed out the door, bouncing on his Reeboks. He arrived at 590 Congress Street and climbed four flights of dingy stairs. Somewhere in the hinterlands of gloom, down endless drafty hallways, could be heard a rhythmic entreaty of "One, two, three! Shuffle, shuffle, kick! Ball change, heel, and piqué, arabesque. That's it, girls and boys, get those gams into the air!"

A rehearsal piano drummed out a tune, leaning heavily on a syncopated beat. Gyles followed all this racket towards the Club Crazy. But nothing could have prepared him for what Lilly's minions had done with the Crazy space. The contrast between dim and worn industrial building and the brilliant and sparkling interior of a slick thirties nightclub was total. It was like being inside a diamond. All surfaces were polished and sparkling, with blue and silver mirrors. The ceiling was hung with a galaxy of mirror balls flashing laser beams of colored light in all directions. Silver lamé swathed the walls, hanging in thick, luxuriant waves. Horseshoe-shaped booths upholstered in faux zebra ringed the dance floor. The stage was a cave of crystal, like an enormous geode. On its boards stood Lilly's trademark: the ruby slipper, fifteen feet tall.

The dance floor was divided by a line of chorines who were being put through their paces by a tight little man with a penciled mustache and a rapier-like cane, which he used to rap out the beat. There were twelve dancers, and Gyles fixed on Val immediately. The boy's turquoise tights and fuchsia tank top were a riveting flash of color. Gyles's eyes traveled over his friend's body, stopping in fascination at the concave shadow behind his hip that dramatically sculpted the swell of his buttock.

"And again! Shuffle, shuffle, kick, ball change, heel, plié, freeze!" shouted the mustachioed choreographer above the piano. At this moment, on cue from the choreographer, the pianist rolled out a flourish up the entire keyboard, somewhat reminiscent of the styles of Rachmaninoff and Elton John, at the climax of which there appeared from the fly loft above the stage a massive figure, descending upon a swing, which was decorated to resemble a cumulus cloud with abundant silver lining. This nimbus was suspended by thick steel cables wrapped in pink velvet— wisely so, considering the load they were carrying. Diva indubitably, glamour personified, Lilly Linda LeStrange in full, glittering regalia warbled forth her song. "You may say life is real boring, one day following the next, no love, no joy, no adoring, not even very good sex. But I say, stuff it, don't rough it, enjoy! 'Cause into each life a little glamour must fall, yes, girls, into each life a little glamour must fall!"

As the last trumpeting notes of this scintillating refrain sounded, Lilly stepped from her cloud into the elevated heel of the gargantuan ruby slipper. At this juncture the chorines launched into a spirited tap dance, incorporating high kicks, cartwheels, and other gymnastic flourishes. This complex extravaganza was designed to be the proverbial showstopper. However, the terpsichorean gamboling of twelve chorines was no match for Lilly, no matter how artistic the choreography. Instead of descending the fifteen feet from heel to toe in a gentle and floating manner, as prescribed, the star hit the slide inside the shoe with the resounding thud of her ample posterior and rocketed downward with remarkable velocity and a prolonged howl of terror, abruptly halted by colliding into and crashing through the toe. This brought rehearsal of "Glamour Galore" to a halt.

During the ensuing pandemonium, Gyles walked over to where Val was toweling off.

"Hi," he began.

"What are you doing here? Slumming with the trashy show folk?" snarled Val.

"Actually, I came by to apologize." As Gyles spoke, his words were tinged with uncertainty.

"Yeah, really sounds like it."

"I did, Val, so stop being so damned obnoxious. I'm sorry, all right? I was wrong, okay? Apparently Wisner did take the jewelry. At least he ended up with it. If you say he forced you into helping him, I believe you."

"What do you mean, at least he ended up with it? Of course he ended up with it. He stole it! And if he forced me, you're sorry, huh? That douche bag had a loaded gun. If I'd given him an excuse to shoot me, who do you suppose woulda cared? He conned me for months about being super for his building. I thought I had a real job. I thought I could change my life, that I could be somebody. Someone decent. And that you—you—Oh, fuck. What a dope, huh? Just a stupid fuckin' hustler. That's me."

Val retreated beneath his towel, pretending to dry his hair, though he couldn't hide from himself the bitter tears that fell from his eyes mixing with the sweat from his forehead. He got angrier because of his tears, until he exploded with an ugly roar, punching a jagged hole right through the mirror-covered plasterboard wall.

Gyles jumped back. A slash of adrenaline raced through him like lightning, leaving a metallic taste in his mouth. Val stood stock-still and silent, his fist embedded in the wall, and small drops of blood oozed out of invisible cuts on his forearm.

The histrionics emanating from the bedraggled diva onstage came to an abrupt halt. Everyone shut up. All eyes in the Club Crazy were on Gyles and Val. Gyles moved with gentle concern toward his friend. He picked up Val's damp rehearsal towel, and covering his own fist, he carefully knocked the jagged edges of the battered wall away from Val's bare arm. Extracting the injured hand from the hole, Gyles wrapped the soft terry cloth around Val's cuts. Wriggling out of his leather flight jacket, he slipped it around Val's shoulders and guided him to one of the zebra banquettes in a corner of the club.

Seeing that no one was mortally injured, the rest of the company resumed their heated efforts to soothe the ruffled diva. Gyles carefully unwrapped the towel from around Val's arm to determine the damage. He was surprised and relieved to discover that the cuts were not serious, although he guessed that Val's fist would be painfully bruised. As he scrutinized the wound, he said in a shaky voice, "Val, I'm so sorry. I've been a real bastard. It wasn't you I didn't believe, it was me. I'm the one who's living a lie. I don't give a damn about the trashy jewelry. I never did. It was just an excuse for me not to have any feelings. I—I can change, and you can change too. You are someone decent, to me anyway. Val, look at me, please? I'm sorry. Please forgive me."

Gyles and Val came together with a kiss tasting of salted tears and pungent sweat.

CHAPTER 27

▼

Gyles led Val up the front steps of his building at 24 Union Park in Boston's South End. They had ducked out of the rehearsal at the Club Crazy and Val was still wearing Gyles's old pilot's jacket over his fuchsia tank top and turquoise tights. His left hand was wrapped with a towel as an improvised bandage.

The men stood before the heavy paneled front door, inset with windows of etched glass that had been painstakingly restored with their original floral designs. Val was surprised by a green scent of fresh mown grass, and he turned to follow that elusive trail. At the center of the square behind a Victorian iron fence, tall elm trees shaded a well-kept lawn. At each end of this park a fountain sprayed silver droplets, making gentle splashing sounds that echoed in the closed square created by the brick row houses all around. Below Val, on the sidewalk, two gym-toned men in almost identical running shorts and sleeveless shirts were walking their pair of pug dogs. They were also engaged in animated conversation, each on his own cell phone.

Gyles slipped his key into the lock of the front door and he held it open, politely standing aside for Val to enter. At that moment Gyles caught a glimpse of Val looking at the two men on the sidewalk and a pang of irrational jealousy shot through him. Val felt Gyles's annoyance as he passed inside the house. He was confused by the formal politeness of having a door held open for him, no one had ever offered such a gesture of respect. At the same time he was stung by Gyles's unfounded jealousy and these conflicting feelings put him on the defensive.

The lobby of Gyles's building was truly impressive and for Val it was more than a little intimidating. The walls were papered with a voluptuous William

Morris wall paper of intertwined foliage in rich coral pinks and shades of vivid blue. On the ceiling, hanging from an elaborate stucco rosette, was a brass chandelier of the aesthetic movement style fitted with iridescent glass shades. Against the left wall was a credenza of mind-boggling architectural embellishments including art tiles depicting the Arthurian myths and a lot of ebonised and inlayed wood. The ostensible function of this behemoth was simply to lay out the tenants' mail. Opposite that high Victorian conceit were the original parlor doors now leading to the first-floor condominium. These double sliding walnut panels stood nine feet tall and were surmounted by a pediment that incorporated carved wooden owls and unfurling fern fronds. Then there was the staircase, a structure winding up the entire five stories of the old house with a continuous walnut banister supported by turned balusters terminating in the lobby at a newel post of elaborate design and hefty proportions.

Val was overwhelmed by these grand decorations and as a consequence, oblivious to their charms. He, in turn, felt an irrational jealousy, fearing the competion of these alien things that Gyles apparently valued. The two men proceeded up the stairs compelled by an attraction they both mistrusted, creating a sense of danger that challenged their pride. In spite of himself, Gyles, following behind on the stairs, could not ignore the fluid musculature of Val's legs and ass so vividly accentuated by his thin turquoise tights.

Inside Gyles's second-floor duplex the two men were not any more at their ease. They avoided looking directly at each other and Gyles said,

"Have a look around. I'll get some Band-Aids and stuff for your hand." Gyles went about his errand and Val drifted towards the middle of the living room. This was a real home: comfortable, attractive and safe. Unlike the entryway downstairs, it was not too grand. Instead it had a well-worn serviceability that was not formal. At the same time the room was handsome in a bookish way. In fact, Gyles's living room could also be called a library because of his large collection of books that filled the painted shelves surrounding the room.

Val lowered himself into a comfortable-looking chair upholstered in what appeared to be a faded rug. He almost immediately got up again and walked to the window because the chair fabric was scratchy. This tiny incident of misjudgment further increased his unease. Would everything to do with Gyles look soft but turn out to be prickly?

Gyles returned from the back of the apartment carrying boxes of cotton balls, Band-Aids, and a bottle of peroxide, which he placed on the glass-topped coffee table in front of the large sofa. Val watched as Gyles cleared the table of art magazines and auction catalogs carefully arranging the first-aid articles. Val's curious eye caught a glimpse of life-sized birds perched on intertwining branches all made of burnished brass that served as the base of the coffee table. The table reminded him of a feature of Lilly-Land that incorporated cheap stuffed birds sprinkled with pink glitter and hanging upside down from a tacky ceiling light. But Gyles's table was really beautiful without the need to apologize with kitsch jokes.

"Would you like a glass of wine?" Gyles asked as he opened the oak armoire nestled in between two tall bookshelves on the back wall. Val was interested to see the inside fitted with a complete bar. "I have a Pinot Grigio or a Chardonnay."

"Can I have a diet Pepsi?"

"Oh, ah, I have...ginger ale or club soda."

"Club soda, I guess."

"Sure thing, have a seat but watch out for the club chair. Cornelia calls it my torture chair, although that may be a bit harsh." Gyles saw the confusion in Val's face, "I had it covered in an old Kilim rug, which looks terrific but turns out to be a bit abrasive."

Val cautiously circled the club chair looking mystified.

"I mean it..."

"Yeah, yeah, I get you, it's real scratchy."

"Anyway—come sit here by me and let me see your hand."

Gyles placed Val's club soda on a paper cocktail napkin on the bird table beside his own stemmed glass of Chardonnay.

"Well, come on, let's have it." Gyles urged.

"What do you mean?" Val frowned and retreated beneath the shock of blonde hair falling over his face as he gave all his attention over to the glass of club soda.

"Your hand, let me see your hand." Gyles replied in as neutral a tone as he could project.

"Oh yeah, you know, it's OK, let's just forget it."

"Val, please, let me disinfect the wounds and put on Band Aids. That is the least I can do after what..." he trailed off not wanting to remember or revive his doubts and suspicions.

Val didn't lift his head or look at Gyles. Instead he slowly unwound the damp terry cloth towel from around his punching fist. He was afraid the towel would stink because rehearsal had been a heavy work out and he had used it to mop up his sweat. Being this close to Gyles, Val could smell a deliciously elusive herbal scent that hinted at intimacy and arousal.

"So what's that cologne you're wearing, Polo or something?"

"Blenheim Bouquet. I found it at a small shop in London called Penhaligon's. Do you like it?" Gyles asked with more eagerness than he intended.

"Yeah, I guess it's like really cool."

At this point Val had unwrapped his hand and was trying to shove his grungy towel under the sofa with his foot. Gyles resisted his impulse to grab Val's injured hand and instead moistened a cotton ball with peroxide. Eventually after some moments of self-conscious hesitation as each man sipped his respective drink, Val held out his hand to Gyles. Gyles gently daubed the cuts with the moistened cotton and Val flinched from the slight sting of the peroxide but more from surprise than pain. Gyles took hold of Val's hand with protective care and Val tossed his heavy golden hair out of his eyes and looked at Gyles's face closely.

No one had ever cared for him like this before. Not the series of foster parents, not the reluctant school teachers, not the Johns on the street, not the tricks in the bars. Lilly tried, but always in a camp and over elaborate way. Lilly and Val were friends in desperation always getting by with mocking laughter.

What Gyles did now for Val was a simple act of kindness, but also a profoundly brave act in this time when the river of life, precious blood, could be teaming with virulent disease. But Gyles didn't hesitate, recoil or hide. He reached out with careful concern in the manner he had been taught. He thereby returned some of the nurturing riches that had been so freely given him, first by his family and then most especially by his first lover, John. John had so recently died of AIDS, a little less then a year and a half ago, that Gyles could hardly even think of him and certainly never talk about him. How could Gyles articulate, even to himself, that his very soul had been ripped out of him when John died?

Suddenly he felt in the presence of Val an unhoped-for chance. He cleaned the crusting blood from the bruised knuckles and covered the cuts with Band-Aids, and then he went to wash his hands and put away the medicine.

"How does the hand feel?"

"OK, thanks."

"I was relieved to see that the cuts are not very serious, but you'll probably ache from those bruises."

"Yeah, well, thanks again." Val was embarrassed by his outburst at the Club Crazy and wanted to forget all about it. The incident made him feel exposed and vulnerable. Part of it was his conflicted attraction to Gyles compounded by his own feelings of inadequacy. He figured he just wasn't good enough for someone like Gyles. He was also surprised to be having these feelings at all. He had never dared to hope for real love.

Gyles was frustrated by Val's withdrawn and sulky attitude, but at the same time he could relate to the protective distance that separated them. Although patching up a friend in need was a natural impulse, any admission of attraction or emotional involvement was difficult, even dangerous.

But their spontaneous kiss earlier this afternoon, forced by Val's outburst, put the lie to all of their fears. Between them there was already a connection no matter how static, abrasive, or incomplete. Sparks had flown from the friction of their encounter, searing their protective camouflage. Electric charges had pierced their armor. The inexplicable narcotic of desire had been tasted and ravenously devoured in one short moment, leaving a craving that could not be ignored.

Gyles resumed his place beside Val on the couch. But Val's heavy shank of shining hair covered his face again. Gyles placed refreshed drinks on the table and his hand reached out, on its own accord, and playfully parted the thick fringe hiding Val's eyes.

"Hello in there? Are you with me?"

"I think I'm falling! Catch me!"

They came together in a tentative embrace with delicacy and gentleness. Gyles held Val's face between his large hands with exquisite care. The warmth of his palms soothed Val's cheeks, and Gyles could feel the slight abrasive stubble of Val's invisible blonde beard. Gyles tipped Val's face upwards towards his own as he lightly brushed his open lips over Val's. Val reacted with a small quick gasp, inhaling Gyles's warm breath, which he held inside his chest until it radiated through his body like a magical essence. Val's hands hovered over Gyles's broad shoulders and then came to rest, at which point he reluctantly exhaled with a deep sigh and his lips explored the soft cushion of Gyles's mouth. Their tongues met with the poetry of love: reaching, pushing, probing, the mute verses of desire. Their bodies, perfectly rhymed couplets, moved together with the harmonious cadence of give and take. Val slipped out of his tank top and with one smooth movement he pealed Gyles's sweatshirt over Gyles's head. As their chests touched, Val swayed back and forth luxuriating in the texture of Gyles's chest hair against his own smooth skin. This motion excited his sensitive nipples, and he drew Gyles closer and closer feeling a power surge through him that knew nothing of caution. Val crushed Gyles's solid bulk in his strong, lithe arms with an overwhelming strength that he could not control. Gyles's only defense was to return the power so that the two men were in a desperate struggle to become one.

Their kisses grew frantic and slipped from mouth to chin, to ear and around the back of their necks where Val savagely chewed at the base of Gyles's skull and he could feel the short hairs raking through his teeth. This made Gyles growl with a sensation hovering between agony and release. Gyles retaliated by slipping around Val's neck with his tongue, where he tasted the salty sweat seasoning Val's clear skin. He relentlessly dove for the cave of Val's underarm where he nuzzled in the silken hair inhaling the patchouli-like muskiness there. This tickle torture made Val writhe with a lyric sensuality charged with passion, a dancing motion that described the whole shooting lust of men loving men.

Val wriggled free and grabbed at Gyles's ass, corseted beneath restrictive denim armor, and his long fingers dug into the crack between the iron-hard mounds of muscle. Simultaneously he returned to Gyles's mouth, which he entered with a pointed tongue. Gyles opened like a flower in the hot sun. His hands traveled the exaggerated length of Val's defined torso coming to a halt at the hard structure of the dancer's hips. He lifted them off the sofa where they had begun and he could feel his bicep's contract with the effort.

Standing tall together, locked in desperate need, they rocked their hips back and forth over the growing mass of their hard dicks, bulging beneath their disheveled clothes. They were enveloped in an electric buzz that traveled from the bottom of their feet to the top of their scalps, making their hair bristle.

Gyles forced them forward towards his bed.

CHAPTER 28

▼

After the debacle with the oversized ruby slipper, Lilly Linda had retired to her dressing room, where she lay on her divan heaving melancholy sighs and listlessly wagging her head from side to side. She rolled her truly astonishing eyes heavenward with the expression of a tortured martyr. This studied gesture gave reference to the melodramatic theatrical posters of Sara Bernhardt.

Betty the Bounder, who was trying to atone for her many transgressions by serving as Lilly's dresser, was deeply moved by La Diva's slumping spirit. So in an effort to revive her mistress, Betty got busy spritzing an atomizer of perfume about the room.

The unsuspecting Lilly gasped with allergic asphyxiation and exploded in a progression of sneezes that rumbled the walls of her dressing room, sending tremors reverberating throughout the theater. In the ominous quiet after this storm, La Diva recovered her composure well enough to inquire with her characteristic unladylike scorn,

"Betty, what the fuck are you spraying, insecticide or agent orange?"

"I'll have you know this is the very latest from Abruzio Dela Snozy. It's called Sewers of Paris."

"No, it's not!" screeched Lilly on the verge of panic. With Betty almost anything might be possible, but Lilly's skepticism would not allow the Bounder this degree of outrage.

"Give me that," she ordered, snatching the atomizer away. "Open the window and the hall door too," Lilly ordered as she scrutinized the offending bottle. "Not Sewers of Paris you slosh head, Soeurs de Paris—it means sisters of Paris."

"Oh, well, I thought, you know with *Les Miz* being so popular and all, that..." Betty's explanation trailed off in a vague direction.

"*Les Miz,* huh? So you thought I could use a little sewer water to cheer me up, is that it?"

"I got it at work. You really are lucky to have some, cause it's kinda hard to come by. So don't get so uppity. That bottle came down from the cosmetic floor 'cause the top was cracked. Otherwise it's very popular and expensive."

"How popular can second-rate perfume be? Even at Filene's Basement there must be standards. That junk smells like room deodorizer for a mobile home."

"Well that's gratitude for you! Here I go and risk my job supplying you with every fragrance on the market and all you can do is dish and bitch." Betty's visage dissolved with hot tears of rage and dismay.

"There, there," Lilly sympathized as she bestowed a couple of conciliatory pats on the Bounder's head. "I am sure you meant well, Betty, but so did Claus Von Bulow. Now put the plug in that jug and hand me my fan."

Lilly flopped back upon her divan, graciously accepting her oversized accordion fan. This accoutrement was really meant to fill an empty fireplace, but in the hammy mitts of La Diva it was a perfect fit. She soon stirred up the ether to hurricane velocity and cleared the room of all traces of Soeur de Paris. She did not, however, succeed in repairing Betty's wounded pride, tattered as it was by years of self-abuse.

Betty shuffled about the dressing room in a dejected and anguished manner, which really was a force of will on her part, because the environment surrounding La Diva was anything but glum. In fact, the gay and festive decor was guaranteed to bring cheer, even if our star had a tendency to be a bit snappy.

The most telling feature of this interior was a mannequin standing stiffly by the door with an eight-inch dildo sprouting from his forehead. Otherwise the dummy was clothed in an impeccably tailored three-piece suit of cheap tapestry cloth. This sculpture was known as the unicorn tapestry and had been the creation of Wally St. John, pronounced Sin Jin, for his thesis at the Museum School.

Wally had graduated with high honors, which had not surprised anyone as he had financed his education by peddling dope to his colleagues and some of his more avant-garde instructors. The grateful student body had voted Wally the most likely to succeed. Alas, this was not a prophecy to be fulfilled without some tribulation.

Lilly was wont to hang the odd bauble on the cyclopean pecker, which Wally frowned on, being a purist about his art. The rest of the room was an eclectic progression of styles. It appeared to have evolved over generations but in fact had been the work of a twelve-hour ecstasy trip. Wally had mistakenly been launched on this creative frenzy when in his usual hazy condition, he had ingested three hits of superior psychedelic. At the time, he had been innocently reaching for the chewable Chocks vitamins. This unfortunate blunder occurred on the first day of work on Lilly's new show, "Glamour Galore." The result was a smashing dressing room, but very little else. Wally had to hie himself away to the Arcadian retreat of McLean Hospital, where he was confined in rude circumstances until a friendly Cauli Flower Brother removed the invalid to his monastery on the banks of the Charles River in Cambridge. There Wally immediately went to work sewing costumes for a revival of the liturgical drama, "Beelzebub in Babylon."

Such was the history of Lilly's dressing room, where Betty pouted and sniveled even while she busied herself dusting a mirror framed by stuffed iguanas whose cured hides had faded to a delicate shade of puce. It is hard to imagine how Betty accomplished her dour attitude in the face of these helpful reptiles who held small light bulbs in their mouths, a flourish that was both illuminating and amusing. But weep she did and soon her misery was apparent even to La Diva.

"Oh Betty, stop your blubbering. I didn't mean anything by it. Go ahead and spritz if you must, but why not use that one you got me last week, what was it?"

"Poison?" You prefer Poison?"

"Well yeah, I thought that one was pretty good, spritz away."

Betty chose another atomizer from Lilly's dressing table and holding it aloft, she blithely spritzed the room. But even thus occupied, Betty couldn't shake the blues.

"Girlfriend, what is the matter now?"

"I'm sorry Lilly, it's Urna, Urna Flamanté. She's dead!" Now Betty really did start to holler and spout.

"Oh my God, you're right! And I have been asked to sing at her funeral." Lilly struck a pose of solemn reverence, pressing her hands to her bosom, allowing for a moment of silence. Betty's honker trumpeted a loud bray as she blew into her hanky and wiped her eyes.

"You're singing at the funeral? He was my boyfriend. We were in the seminary together."

"So?"

"So? They didn't ask me to perform."

"Oh Betty, get a grip!" On that dismissive cue Betty collapsed in a thrashing heap, having caught her three-inch spike in the hem of her dress, which had a dipping train in the back.

"Betty, stop that this minute! You're gonna hurt yourself." She stooped to pluck her dresser from the floor and without ceremony, flung her on the divan, which absorbed the impact with twanging complaint.

Lilly sauntered over to her vanity and, perching half glasses on her nose, peered into a magnifying mirror and ruthlessly plucked at her eyebrows saying, "Cheer up, Betty. I hear it's gonna be a swell farewell. I've already got Wally over at the monastery sewing the most heavenly black frock for me. You know, it's almost worth it to have him there. He can concentrate better. Why don't you read me Urna's obit from *Gay Windows?* You'll find the paper in my sewing basket beside you." Lilly's ubiquitous basket disgorged yet another handy item, and Betty read aloud with the aid of a slightly bent lorgnette, also fished from the same receptacle.

"OK, here goes: Signorina Urna Flamanté, legendary performer, expired Sunday at her home in Boston's South End. Signorina Flamanté had enjoyed a lengthy career on the boards of some of the more obscure venues of gaydom."

"I don't know if I like the tone of this."

"Oh go on, Betty. The piece was written by that smart-ass writer with the impossible Welsh name. what is it? Iorwerth Allison? Really! But never mind him, just read."

"Her tragic passing has considerably subdued the frivolous atmosphere of that famed music hall, 'Follies Derrière,' where she had been an abiding favorite. Urna's reputation was built on a fabled performance, in the distance past recalled by a privileged elite of that whimsical watering hole."

"I wonder what performance that might have been?" mused Lilly. Betty cleared her throat and continued.

"On that momentous occasion in a number entitled 'Fuego en los Huaraches' her tap-dancing frenzy reached such incendiary intensity that she literally charred a hole in the stage and vanished from sight with a puff of smoke and a shower of cinders."

"Jesus, that was a mouthful," bitched Betty.

"Ah the good old days. Yes, I remember it well," Lilly reminisced.

"Have you got a joint or maybe the smallest little drinky-poo? All this reading makes my mouth dry."

"Oh yeah, and a joint is sure gonna help that. No Betty, I think you better stick to booze. You can have one little sip from the carafe on the table beside you."

Betty didn't ask what the clear liquid might be when she lunged for the proffered decanter and poured herself a healthy tumbler. After a mighty swig, she smacked her lips with satisfaction and settling back upon the divan resumed her reading.

"Urna, the now celestial thespian, wheezed her last breath with impeccable timing while filming a revival of *La Dame Aux Camélias*. She has thereby been elevated beyond cult heroine to exquisite martyr by the national association of Female Illusionists. Her funeral is to be held at the Mount Auburn Cemetery. This will be the event of the decade. Attending luminaries are to include Risa Toosmelly, the famed hoof-in-mouth artist, amongst other international stars. The Gay Men's Chorus has prepared a medley of Urna's most famous ditties, to be climaxed by Lilly Linda LeStrange, who will dramatically intone the aria, "*O Terra Addio*" from *Aïda*, to the accompaniment of the Bronx Harmonica Orchestra."

"You know, Lilly, I've been asked to pick up Urna's ashes from that creepy Greenbrier Funeral Home in Watertown and I am just dreading the whole thing." Betty shuddered visibly as she polished off the gin in her tumbler.

"You're picking up the ashes?"

"Well you don't have to sound so surprised. You will remember I was Urna's boyfriend back when he was still known as Joey."

"Well I guess you can be trusted. But Betty, I'd lay off the sauce for at least a day before."

"No, that's not the problem, Lil. It's the funeral director, that hunk Nagib Iskander. I tricked with him once at Mount Auburn."

"Betty, have yourself another drink. There are some things best kept to yourself."

CHAPTER 29

▼

Gyles arrived at the Union Club, number 8 Park Street, home to a dignified and unobtrusive fraternity. They assume their position of leadership in the city by virtue of long standing. The members of the Club have always belonged to the first families of Boston, and their prosperity is supported by generational fortunes shrewdly tended and cultivated by lawyers of trust such as Eben Chichester.

Gyles climbed the old brownstone stairs and entered the glass-etched doors of the Club, with its Victorian designs of flower baskets and laurel wreaths,

"Hello, I'm Gyles Chilton, here to meet Eben Chichester."

"Yes, Mr. Chilton. Mr. Chichester rang up to say he would be slightly delayed and asked if you would kindly wait for him in the reading room."

Gyles followed this instruction and seated himself comfortably to wait. This lofty chamber was made bright with a rich red carpet and bayberry green walls trimmed with darker olive on plaster moldings. The atmosphere here was very clubby, with an odd assortment of brown and red leather-covered chairs and sofas. This tufted and commodious seating furniture was worn and cracked in the best tradition of serviceable shabbiness that generations of members had grown accustomed to and therefore fond of. Gyles hardly had time to take in the full measure of the room when his cousin Eben with purposeful and long stride came over the threshold saying, "Sorry to have kept you waiting, old man, but I had a minor crisis with the Foster-Filbricks up in Ipswich."

Gyles smiled, shrugged off the apology, and warmly shook his cousin's outstretched hand.

Eben continued, "It would seem that Catherine Foster-Filbricks, who is now ninety-three, has misplaced the deeds to Agawam Farms. She intends to give all

1500 acres to the Trustees of Reservations, and she is nigh onto being hysterical, fearing that the documents were consumed in the fire at the Great House." As Eben spoke, Gyles stole glances over his shoulder at the various portraits about the room. These included two of Chinese merchants in black robes and Mandarin regalia. They were exotic but familiar types in these surroundings, reminiscent of the China trade days of the early nineteenth century. That flourishing commerce had fleshed out the burgeoning fortunes of Yankee traders such as the Foster-Filbricks of Ipswich.

"I had to dispatch a posse of paralegal researchers on the rails north led by Miss Conger, my secretary, to assess the damage and mollify old Catherine."

Gyles, ever tuned to the possible trail of antiquities asked with seemingly casual interest, "What happened to the Great House at Agawam Farms?"

Eben answered, speaking to the reflection of his cousin in the large mirror over the mantel where Gyles was inspecting an elaborately carved ivory tusk, which enjoyed pride of place on the black marble shelf.

"The Great House at Agawam Farms was torched by warring factions within the Foster-Filbricks clan, who were outraged when the estate was inherited by Catherine, a widow without children."

Gyles filed this tidy bit of gossip in the back of his mind, knowing that similar stories of familial discord had led him to great treasures. He immediately envisioned a forgotten chicken coop with a slightly charred Chippendale highboy collecting dust.

Eben continued, "But I'm boring you. Let me take your coat and hang it up, and we can go up to luncheon." Gyles slipped out of his Burberry and handed over his hat.

"I say, where did you get such a magnificent bonnet?" Eben, who had taken Gyles's coat with good grace, held the hat aloft with awkward emphasis. Gyles realized that his cousin, who with Spartan vigor never wore so much as an overcoat in January, disapproved of such ostentatious flourishes as a felt hat.

After having deposited the hat and overcoat in a cavernous coatroom behind the front stairs, Eben suggested, "Why don't we walk up rather than take the elevator, and you can poke around and get a feel of the place. I trust you'll find the old digs to your liking. I had the idea of putting up your name for membership."

Gyles was taken aback and said hesitantly, "Gosh, I don't know, Eben, I'm not sure I would fit in."

"Nonsense. Of course you would. You are a Chilton. There have always been Chiltons at the Union Club. But take a look around and enjoy your lunch and give us a chance. The place may grow on you."

Leaving the front hall with its marble floor of alternating black and white squares, they walked up the sweeping staircase, which was covered with a vivid red carpet.

Eben's idea of a tour was not a lingering experience. Their progress up several flights was interrupted by brief excursions into reception rooms of mysterious purpose and fairly stark decor. Some of these were downright shabby, but others enjoyed a kind of institutional refurbishment that gave the pale impression of committee approval.

Eben and Gyles reached the fifth-floor dining room, where the lawyer pressed on without pause or ceremony to a small table by one of the floor-length windows looking out onto Park Street. From here, high above the tallest of the venerable elms across the street, one could see a good deal of the Boston Common. Gyles looked out over the park surrounded by the tall buildings of the city spread out beneath him, and he was strongly affected by the proprietary glow felt by all who were invited to witness the city from this vantage. Eben interrupted the moment with the pronouncement, "You must try the vichyssoise. It is by far the best starter, as they say in England."

Gyles ordered as he was advised, glad to surrender all initiative in this endeavor to his cousin, and he looked about the room. Like the rest of the Club, it displayed a comfortably worn if not battered interior. To the members it was evocative of the rough-and-ready atmosphere of a collegiate fraternity house or a no-nonsense officers' barracks. The atmosphere throughout the building was a self-satisfied mixture of grandeur and cultivated neglect. After the view the second most impressive feature was the vaulted ceiling of the dining room, with its handsome brass chandeliers and sturdy beams. All the wall paneling and other decorative woodwork, which enveloped the room with bewildering variety, had been painted white, although Gyles suspected the original intended look to have been baronial brown. A platoon of battered Chippendale chairs stood to attention at tables copiously draped with white damask and set with time-worn silver decorated with the initials "U.C."

An unremarkable but efficient waitress plodded about the dining room. She collected the order forms from Eben and leisurely returned with a half carafe of serviceable claret and two glasses. Eben poured the wine and lifting his glass proposed a toast. "To that grand old gent, Wisner Chilton. May he find as much comfort in the next world as he did in this."

Gyles sipped with cautious reserve the toast in memory of his great-uncle Wisner. The lawyer extracted an envelope from his jacket pocket.

"I was handed the most mysterious letter when I arrived just now by Reggie, the desk clerk. Apparently he has found it an advisable daily habit to read the obituary columns, because he offered me prompt condolences on the death of poor Wisner as well as this." Gyles peered at the missive with apprehension. "I read it quickly in order not to keep you waiting, but I can make neither head nor tail of it. What on earth do you think it means?" Gyles took the letter only after Eben wagged it at him insistently. It was an ecru envelope of thick, expensive stationery addressed in black ink with a wide nibbed pen. It read:

Wisner Chilton
Union Club
8 Park Street
Boston

Inside was one sheet of the same heavy stock embossed at the top with Wisner's monogram. Penned in the same old-fashioned hand was a cryptic inscription: The lotus path within the necropolis. From the tower of the mountain forest Anubis sits astride the tomb. At the gate he is looking back. With the ankh he will pierce the wedjat eye.

Eben said, "The handwriting is Wisner's, of course. I have become very familiar with his old-fashioned script, handling all of his financial affairs for many years."

Gyles read the note and, handing it back to Eben, said, "I have no idea what those lines mean. As far as I knew, Uncle Wisner was only interested in Chinese export porcelain and American Federal furniture. But this Egyptian thing seems to crop up everywhere right now. I think it really has to do with Aunt Norma. If you can believe it, Cornelia is convinced that the old girl has the treasure of the pharaohs buried with her. But it's all way before my time, and I know nothing about Egypt, so I'm as woefully ignorant as yourself."

Gyles made great show of his appreciation for the vichyssoise, which required some effort because the soup in question was just that, questionable soup. He feared he had already said too much about the strange note but hoped that by his frivolous tone and feigned disinterest the subject would be dropped. As an antiques dealer Gyles had developed a sixth sense for following the scent of jealously guarded treasures. He suddenly realized that he had been rather dense about the compelling quest being enacted right beneath his very nose. Until now his thoughts of the Egyptian jewelry had been simplistic. The mysterious appearance and loss several times over had fixated his attention on only the actual items, not on what they might represent or where they might lead. But Wisner's note changed everything. That message from beyond the grave, which spoke of the City of the Dead and that lithe, menacing creature Anubis, who sat upon a golden shrine and commanded a drama of obscure intentions from behind his shroud, must now be heard. For some instinctual reason, though, Gyles did not elaborate any more on the subject to his cousin.

Instead he lifted his wineglass and said, "To Uncle Wisner, a man of unexpected benefactions."

The rest of the luncheon was given over to Eben's colorful reminiscences of Wisner Chilton. The lawyer was a rich source of anecdotes about the elder relative, having served as his financial manager as well as shared the duties of several boards of trustees around the metropolis. Not the least of these was the vestry of the Church of the Advent on Beacon Hill. It was at that temple of high church Episcopalian gloom where, shrouded in clouds of frankincense, a solemn high mass was to be celebrated for their dear departed relation on the following Wednesday. An equally dignified interment was to follow at Mount Auburn Cemetery.

The lawyer's well-balanced monologue had skillfully teetered between affectionate levity and serious intent. He signaled the end of his performance by consulting a very thin gold pocket watch, which was secured to his person by a substantial gold chain threaded through the last buttonhole of his vest.

"Gyles old man, I must be off. I want to be in my office when Miss Conger calls about the Foster-Filbricks. With any luck she will have located Catherine's missing deeds. In the meantime, leave all the details of Wisner's estate to me. You have, I imagine, enough to occupy yourself with your new shop and your aunt's house on Commonwealth Avenue. I will see you next Wednesday at the Church of the Advent, and the following week Miss Conger will call you to schedule an appointment at your convenience. By then all the documents will be prepared, and we can discuss your financial future."

The ancient, pneumatic elevator of the Union Club lumbered to a bouncing halt. A distinctive grinding noise accompanied the opening of the door as the two cousins walked out into the entry hall. Eben retrieved Gyles's coat and hat.

He held the coat for his guest and discreetly mentioned, "One last thing I should report to you, Gyles. I dined last evening at the Harvard Club in the company of Police Commissioner Fitzgibbons. On behalf of the family, I thanked him for the diligence that his department exercised in searching for Wisner last week."

Gyles turned towards his cousin with perplexed curiosity as the lawyer continued earnestly.

"Fitzgibbons was relieved to hear that Wisner had been located visiting in Manchester-by-the-Sea, unbeknownst to us, his Boston relatives. He conveyed his condolences at the tragic passing of one of Boston's fine old gents, adding that he perfectly understood our concern. He assured me that the entire affair had been handled confidentially and without record."

Gyles was dumbfounded by this brazen fiction, but he recognized with some reluctance the necessity to suppress useless scandal. He was moreover uncomfortably impressed with the extent of Eben's power in the city, and he suspected this to be the secondary and more subtle intent of his statement. But with stubborn determination not to be intimidated, Gyles asked: "Eben, as a memento and example of Wisner's fine calligraphy, may I have the letter that was sent here?"

Without visible hesitation Eben reached into his pocket and handed over the envelope. "Of course, old man, it is yours by rights, being Wisner's heir."

"Thanks so much for a terrific lunch, Eben. Got to run. See you at the funeral."

Gyles tipped his hat to his cousin and made a swift exit down the brownstone steps, carrying more weight on his shoulders than when he had arrived. The lean and calculating lawyer studied the diminishing figure. From his pocket Eben extracted a hastily scribbled note, and as he read it a cunning smile played across his features. He complimented himself for the foresight of having made a quick copy of Wisner's cryptic message, but he wondered to what use Gyles would put the original.

CHAPTER 30

▼

Gyles entered his shop in a pensive and preoccupied mood. At first he did not see Cornelia, who was busily arranging American Beauty roses in a tall cut-glass vase.

"Oh Gyles, you just missed meeting Pat DeScenzo. I sent her out to Chestnut Hill to deliver some packages that Rosalind left here yesterday. I really think she's going to work out marvelously well."

"The only work that Rosalind could possibly do marvelously well would be heavy labor in the state pen."

"Not Rosalind, dummy, Pat, Pat DeScenzo, our new shop assistant. She used to work for Skinner's Auction House in Bolton, and she has a B.A. in art history from Wellesley."

"She sounds expensive to me. How come she left Skinner's?"

"I hope you haven't inherited Wisner's parsimonious reluctance along with his millions. Pat wanted to work with you. That's why she took the job, because of your sterling reputation."

"That's very flattering, but so far I have only inherited an enormous headache from Wisner Chilton. So don't count your chickens before next Wednesday, when after prolonged pomp and ceremony at the Church of the Advent and Mount Auburn Cemetery Eben will formally read Wisner's will. Even then it's not likely that Wisner's property will be in the form of cold, hard cash. The majority of it will undoubtedly be tied up in trust funds and other restrictions that one shudders to imagine."

"Gyles, you really are too bleak sometimes. I just told you that Pat came here because of your reputation in the art world. She's happy to be with us and accept a reasonable salary. She's only twenty-four. This is one of her first jobs. Now get over it!"

"Sorry, Corny, I know I should be jumping for joy. Val is back in my life, and it would seem that the shop will be in good shape financially."

"Val? I haven't even met the man, yet he keeps popping up like a jack-in-the-box. What gives, Romeo?"

"Nothing really. It's just that we spent the night together."

"And that's nothing?"

"Well, actually it's everything. But at this moment he's a little overshadowed. Look, Cornelia, read this and tell me what you think." Gyles handed his sister Wisner's cryptic note. She put down the thorny stemmed roses she'd been arranging and took up the equally barbed and enigmatic note: The lotus path within the necropolis. From the tower of the mountain forest Anubis sits astride the tomb. At the gate he is looking back. With the ankh he will pierce the wedjat eye.

"You know, Gyles, there's something going on here I don't get."

"I couldn't agree with you more, Corny. I'm in the same boat."

Then she asked, "Where did you get this?"

And he said, "Well, as you can see, it was sent to the Club, and Eben gave it to me, or to be more precise he showed it to me and then I asked to keep it. Eben confirms that the note is in Wisner's hand, but beyond that he can make nothing of it. It must relate back to Aunt Norma, although God knows how. Didn't you tell me you had architectural drawings of her tomb?"

Cornelia looked uncomfortable and said, "Well yes, I did say something like that, but it was really only a stab in the dark. Rita came across some renderings of Egyptian murals in the account books that we found in Cosmo's office. You were pressing me for proof of my theory about Norma's gold, so I just sort of put the two things together."

"Oh. So how come you sounded so sure of yourself then?"

"Well, you were being difficult with Rita. I do have my loyalties."

"Cornelia, you believed it when you told me. Maybe there's something in what you said. Where are these drawings now?"

"We returned them to the house, along with the ledgers."

"Good. Let's go. I want to examine those drawings, and while we're at it I think it's time to drag Anubis into the light of day. Something's going on here, Corny, some urgent quest. I can just feel it, and I think it's time we got to the bottom of it all."

"Hey, hold on, what about Pat? She'll be back in a little while, not to mention the mountain of work on my desk."

"You gave her the keys, didn't you? She is Ms. Efficiency, right? Leave her a note and tell her to call us over there. Now let's move it."

"All right, Gyles, but is there really such urgency? We do have other responsibilities."

"Fine. You stay here and arrange flowers. I'm going over to Aunt Florence's."

CHAPTER 31

▼

Eben Chichester paced the floor of his office impatiently. His right hand held a paper-thin cell phone pressed to his ear. As he listened to it ring on incessantly, he peered into a six-foot-long telescope made of highly polished brass that was mounted on a tripod of varnished mahogany. From the lawyer's aerie on the thirty-sixth floor of the granite and glass office tower, the powerful lenses of the instrument were focused on Deer Island in the outer harbor. Eben closely monitored the progress of the waste treatment plant being constructed on the island. This project was pledged to cleanse the waterways of the inner harbor by collecting the extravagant filth of the metropolis, filtering out the waste, and then, by means of a ten-mile pipe, sliding the collective excremental sludge off the edge of Georges Bank into the deep ocean. Eben had heavily invested the family trust funds that he manipulated in this multibillion dollar ecological delusion.

The phone was answered by a voice that labored to enunciate a language not his own. "Good afternoon, Greenbrier Funeral Home."

"This is Eben Chichester. Let me speak with Nagib Iskander."

"Will you please hold the line, sir?"

"Yes."

After a moment's pause Nagib's obsequious but ironic voice was heard. "Cousin Eben, always so very prompt and efficient. I hope that you were right and that your luncheon guest told you what we need to know. Although how you could persuade our young cousin to do so, I cannot imagine. But I forget, you have had such practice cajoling all of your old ladies."

"At least clients come to me willingly, Nagib. They profit by my administrations. And if I share in those profits, it is only just. On the other hand, people look to you with dread, because your ministrations are fruitless and profit only you. I do not recognize you as my cousin, Nagib. The middle-age indiscretions of Norma Chilton hardly qualify you for legitimacy."

"But, cousin, the only legitimacy of our family is indiscretion, from our beginnings as traders of slaves, rum, and opium. Where else was there to go in the fetid halls of profit except the logical conclusion, sewage disposal? I do wonder, however, if that endeavor is entirely equal to your acquired dignity."

Eben regretted the direction this conversation was heading, but, with all his lawyer's discipline, he was not exempt from the taunting barbs of Nagib—Nagib, who was born in shadow, wearing the stain of eclipse on his face, Nagib, who was consumed by revenge. Each man was stretched taut to the limit by his unscrupulous ambition.

"My concern, cousin, is with eternity," Nagib continued, "which you mistake for money, a simplistic definition but one you should be forgiven for, because yours is a relatively young dynasty in a country which was born yesterday in the eternal march of time. I am Anubis, I—"

"Please spare me the litany of your glories, Nagib, and let us get to the point. No, Gyles Chilton did not tell me what we want to know. I am convinced that he is entirely ignorant of our concerns, although his sister, who is apparently more attuned to the fantastic, has guessed that there is a tomb and that it holds a considerable treasure. At present Gyles has dismissed these notions as fantasy, but I think it is only a matter of time before she persuades him. However, an unexpected gift has come our way from a most reluctant quarter." Nagib made impatient rumbling noises. Eben continued, "Wisner, the old fool, has been both the problem and the solution, but in the end he has only outwitted himself. Apparently he had made contingencies, which he supposed would be insurance against any opposition from us. Or perhaps he, like you, was completely lost to arcane fantasy."

"So what is the point of the story?" interrupted Nagib.

"The point being," resumed Eben, "that Wisner apparently did find the inscription on the scarab, translated it, and then must have had it removed. The real danger of this venture never occurred to the pompous fool. Whatever dirt he had on you gave him a false sense of security. Although quite unbalanced himself, Wisner had the imagination to suppose that you were possessed of some sense of restraint and caution. That of course proved not to be the case when you drained his blood."

"He pumped his own blood down the sewer. I was kind enough to replace it. Unfortunately it was the wrong type and quite stale." Nagib argued his defense with a ghoulishness that masqueraded as humor.

"I must caution you about the literal absurdity that your ambition has driven you to, Nagib. You may be envious of our legitimacy, but the actual blood of our veins will not advance your cause one inch. Although you provided clumsy evidence, which I am sure you thought to be a brilliant explanation of the gaping holes left in Wisner's veins, the drug-soaked syringes you planted were an unlikely vice for a seventy-five-year-old pansy who had never taken any stimulants stronger than amontillado. It was a very trying afternoon for me with Perkins Wallace, who after having tended to Wisner's medical needs for the last forty years was loathe to accept the idea of death due to drug overdose.

"In the end your salvation came from another unlikely source, Gyles Chilton, who volunteered the information that Wisner paid male hustlers for sex. Thus it was assumed that these unsavory leeches were the source of the drugs. This was a scandal of gigantic proportions, which implied the extremes of all manner of perversion. Perkins Wallace was thus easily persuaded to save the Chilton reputation and sign a death certificate with the abridged truth of heart failure as cause of death."

Nagib replied to this lengthy narrative with obvious boredom. "Are you still dragging that corpse around with you, cousin? I have disposed of it twice over and found nothing of value there. What is the inscription on the scarab? What is the voice of the mother? Where is the tomb?"

The lawyer read Wisner's message: "The lotus path within the necropolis. From the tower of the mountain forest Anubis sits astride the tomb. At the gate he is looking back."

After a long silence, Nagib said in icy tones, "There is something more."

"No, that's all there was," lied Eben.

"Nonetheless, there is something more, because these lines speak only of the place. You thought Wisner was such a fool, and perhaps he was. But we shall see who the biggest fool is." Click.

The phone line went dead.

"Hello, hello, Nagib? You can't hang up on me. Nagib!" Rage snapped through the lawyer, and he hurled the sleek phone with all the power of a practiced backhand. The plastic instrument hit the densely grained rosewood paneling of the office wall and shattered, sounding like a small explosion. That unexpected disturbance brought forth the ever alert Miss Conger, Eben's executive secretary. She entered the office, closing the door behind her, in two steps, like the staccato movements of a practiced dancer.

"Yes, Mr. Chichester?"

As she stood alert and waiting, pad and pen in hand, her quick eye took in the shattered telephone on the floor. Eben, unnerved by his rare loss of control and further agitated by the presence of his unsummoned secretary, stammered momentarily, "Oh, uh, yes, something has come up, and I will be out for the rest of the afternoon. If I get a chance I'll check in with you later."

Miss Conger, who was privy to all the lawyer's affairs, was stung by this clumsy attempt to exclude her from his confidence, so she retaliated by saying, "Yes, Mr. Chichester. Shall I order a new Motorola phone?"

The lawyer snapped, "Don't bother me with petty details, Miss Conger. You can see that I am busy. Now good afternoon." He brushed past her and out the office door.

CHAPTER 32

▼

Gyles and Cornelia cut through the crowds on Newbury Street heading towards Commonwealth Avenue. Cornelia had to double step in order to keep up with her brother's long stride. They hurried along the boulevard beneath the canopy of leaves on the elms growing down the center of Commonwealth Avenue. Brother and sister were oblivious to the ivory and pink magnolia blossoms that billowed like celestial clouds along the sunny side of the boulevard.

But neither the delights of the season nor the bewildered greetings of Lucy Ann would divert the attention of Gyles and Cornelia as they charged up the front hall stairs of their aunt's house towards Cosmo Chilton's office. Gyles was the first to reach the tall mahogany door. Even his large hand was dwarfed by the massive doorknob.

Entering the room he was struck by the sense of order and stability that it exuded. The shelves held row upon row of black leather-bound ledger books of uniform size with gold-embossed lettering. The cabinets beneath held unbound papers, carefully arranged in drawers. Some of these documents went back to the eighteenth century. Old Cosmo, a prominent member of the Massachusetts Historical Society, had developed a keen interest in early documents and been an avid collector of them.

Gyles looked about and sighed for the great responsibility of having to dispose of or maintain Cosmo's collection, which was made all the more difficult by the strong sense of the industrial financier lingering in his office. His presence could be felt sternly admonishing his descendants to conserve and perpetuate a fortune wrenched from the raw and hostile wilderness by the genius of their ancestors, who were, in Cosmo's estimation, the righteous, pure, and chosen people of God.

Cornelia was oblivious to the emanations that had such an effect on her brother. She crossed the room to old Cosmo's monumental desk by the window. With some difficulty and a lot of clattering, she raised the arching tambour top. Cornelia picked up the stack of ledger books she had left there and took them over to the central table, where she opened one of the ledgers for the decade 1920 to 1930. From this volume she extracted three large sheets of thick rag paper.

"Gyles, tear yourself away from that desk and come look at these." Cornelia had spread out the gaudy colored paintings in an impressive display. "I can tell you whoever did these really was an expert," she continued. "They're flawless. The use of watercolor and the draftsmanship are perfect." Brother and sister gazed at the grotesque characters processing in profile along the pages. Half-man, half-beast, animistic gods sitting upon thrones, tended to and worshipped by long lines of faithful servants clad only in pleated kilts, stiff wigs, and peculiar curling beards. This parade was surrounded by dense columns of hieroglyphics animated with flapping birds, crawling beetles, slithering snakes, and crouching stick figures. All of these pictographs were also aligned with a myriad of mysterious symbols, as well as floating eyes and dismembered limbs. Bandage-wrapped mummies appeared in abundance, only their heads and hands unbound. They wore fantastic crowns, grasping in each hand a crook and a flail. Mummies on couches with lions' legs, mummies escorted on thin carved boats by animal-headed guardians. More mummies dragged on sleds by minions of worshipping nobles. Everywhere mummies were embraced and coddled and mourned over.

"But, Cornelia, these aren't plans for a tomb. They could just as easily be designs for a Ruth St. Denis stage set. At best they are some kind of archaeological renderings of the excavated material at the museum. Because photography was imperfect in the twenties, skilled artists were always employed to copy the discoveries, especially to record the colors that were lost to black-and-white film."

Cornelia stood silently glaring at her brother, her arms folded over her chest, her foot tapping. Her left eyebrow arched with exasperation. "Gyles, you are more than bleak—you are totally absent," she said with withering scorn.

But instead of arguing the point, she went to the desk, and after a moment of rummaging about she returned to the paintings on the table with Scotch tape and a pair of sharp scissors. Cornelia folded the vertical margins of each oblong page inward, forming quarter-inch flaps. Next she fit these folded corners into each other and fixed them together carefully with small hinges of Scotch tape. She gently stood the taped sheets up on their edges so they formed three walls of a little room. The figures with their hieroglyphics processed towards each other symmetrically, meeting at a door decorated with more hieroglyphics and a splendid golden mummy wrapped in linen, embraced by multicolored wings of vultures and hawks. Cornelia stood away from her handiwork and triumphantly proclaimed, "Theatrical it may be, but stage set it is not."

"Yeah, but—" began Gyles.

"Yeah but nothing. When was the last time you saw a sexy production of pharaoh's funeral?"

Gyles stooped to peer into the model his sister had constructed. He had not visualized the flat paintings as a room design. He was particularly intrigued by the central door, flanked by bunched reeds with lotus blossom capitals upholding a broad lintel carved with a winged orb. "Well, I must admit that it's interesting as far as it goes, but the theory is still a little flimsy." As if on cue, the paper room slowly collapsed onto the table.

"Say what you like, Gyles. The rest of the plans must be here," insisted Cornelia, "and we're going to find them."

"Okay, sis, you win. But I've got a hunch too. So you start looking and I'll be right back. I want to call Val, and then I'm going to pop upstairs for a closer look at our friend Anubis."

"Gyles! How can you think of sex at a time like this? I need your help. There must be hundreds of books here. You can't abandon me now. It was your idea to pursue this in the first place."

"Cornelia, I'm not thinking of sex, but I do think we could use Val's help. Like us, he has been unwillingly dragged into this business, and I think he deserves a chance to help untangle the mess. Besides, I promised I'd call. It won't take long. I'll be right back."

"Sure. Terrific. Go right ahead. Don't let me stop you." Cornelia waved her brother away with annoyed resignation. He responded by ruffling her hair and nimbly leaping to safety, avoiding by inches her lunging rebuke. As he danced out the door, he collided with Lucy Ann.

"Child, what in the name of God are you trying to do? Scare an old woman to death?"

"Gosh, Lucy Ann, I'm so sorry. I didn't see you."

"Child, you can't see forwards when you're facin' backwards. You're not at the gymnasium now, so walk like a dignified person and stop prancin' about."

"Wait a minute. What are you doing lurking outside this door anyway?"

Gyles was amused by Lucy Ann's curiosity; he was pretty sure that she had followed them upstairs and had been listening outside the office door.

Lucy Ann's buff tinted-cheek darkened with anger. "Don't you get fresh with me, boy. I am still big enough to take you over my knee. I brought you up to show respect where it is due, and that is right here and now!"

Gyles could not hide the laugh that Lucy Ann's ruffled dignity inspired. He tried to mollify her with some ill-conceived pats on the back.

But she brusquely deflected his conciliatory gestures and snapped, "Wipe that smile off your face, child, and go about your business." And with that she swept into the office, closing the door behind her.

Gyles shrugged off the scolding, pressed his ear to the door, and heard Cornelia say, "Oh Lucy Ann, you're just in time to help."

Satisfied that all was well, he skipped down the stairs to the phone in the front hall to call Val.

Just less than an hour later, Val stood on the front stoop of 283 Commonwealth Avenue ringing the doorbell. Lucy Ann emerged from Cosmo's office wiping her hands on an immaculate handkerchief. She had been relieved to have an excuse to leave the futile search to Cornelia. Lucy Ann had been curious to know what Cornelia and Gyles had been up to, but she hadn't bargained for the wholesale mess that Cornelia's increasingly frantic search would create. The plans had not appeared as easily as the young designer had supposed, and now ledger books were stacked and tumbled everywhere, except in their designated and proper place on the shelves. The doorbell rang again, long and loud.

"I'm comin', I'm comin,' keep your pants on," Lucy Ann muttered as she descended the stairs.

From behind her, loudly bounding down three steps at a time flew Gyles. "I'll get it. Don't bother, Lucy Ann, it's Val."

Another blast from the bell increased Gyles's enthusiasm, and he bellowed loudly, "I'm coming, I'm coming, I'm on my way."

As he charged past the affronted housekeeper, she wisely pressed herself against the wall, but she could not resist calling after him, "Gyles Chilton, what did I tell you about—" The rest of her scolding was lost to the boisterous greetings and warm embraces of the two men. Gyles practically dragged Val into the house, acting like a kid who has just been given his heart's desire.

"Val, it's great to see you. I've just made the most incredible discovery. It's really too fantastic." Gyles waved a thick handful of brightly painted pages in the air, and he clasped his free arm around his friend's broad shoulders, squeezing him with excitement.

Val was pleasantly baffled by Gyles's exuberance and allowed his substantial brawn to be affectionately lassoed. Catching sight of Lucy Ann coming down the stairs, he said, "Hi, Lucy Ann, long time no see."

"Hi, yourself. Gyles, what did I tell you about jumpin' up and down the stairs? You nearly killed me! Now go back upstairs and tell that sister of yours to clean up the mess she's making in the office."

Lucy Ann disappeared down the back stairs, having learned more in the past hour than she ever wanted to know about Norma Chilton's tomb. She was superstitiously disturbed by the reemergence of the woman she had thought herself well rid of for many years.

"Come on, Val, don't look so glum. Come on upstairs. I want you to meet my sister, Cornelia. We've been looking all over the house for these plans, and she's going to flip when she sees that I found them."

Val stopped short and shook free of Gyles's arm. Turning to confront the antiques dealer he said, "I read in the paper this morning that Wisner died yesterday. You knew that last night and never said anything to me."

"I was going to get around to it, but then it didn't seem an appropriate time. To tell you the truth, I just wanted to forget all about Wisner."

"So where did you go today, and what else do you not want me to know? Am I just the trick that comes in to take your mind off things?"

"It's not that, Val. It's not because I want to keep secrets from you. Listen, this is all new to me. I'm not used to being honest. No, not honest, I mean yes, but— I'm not used to sharing. I didn't want to burden you with my family problems. Wisner was not exactly my favorite relative on earth. It's even more complicated than that."

Gyles sat down on the stiff wooden bench on the front hall, shuffling the papers nervously in his lap. He motioned Val to sit beside him, but Val refused, leaning against the doorway in his typical slouch. Gyles told his friend all about the luncheon with Eben Chichester and the unexpected legacy from his uncle, the mysterious note and all the rest. Once he got started talking about the last twenty-four hours all the details poured out of him like water over a dam. He felt enormous relief by relating the whole story to Val, even the part about the supposed cause of his uncle's death and Eben's whitewashing of that scandal.

When he finished, Val surprised him by saying, "The night before last I was hanging out in the alley by the Lord Nelson."

Gyles interrupted abruptly. He shot up from the bench and paced the hall. "Val, how could you? The day before yesterday? I thought you were all finished with that. Butch told me that Lilly had you at the Club Crazy in order to keep you off the streets."

Val grabbed Gyles's arm and made him stop. "That's who I am, Gyles."

"That's who you were, Val. Last night you promised me."

"That was last night. I'm talking about the night before. Now shut up and listen."

The men's voices roused Cornelia's concern. She needed a diversion from the frustration of her search, so she stepped out into the hall. Looking below she saw Val charged with emotion, staring at her brother. Val's silken blond hair falling in his eyes did nothing to hide the struggle between hunger, hurt, and adoration as he compelled Gyles to listen to him. Immediately she saw what her brother was enthralled by. Val's utterly vulnerable but electric personality gave off visible sparks.

Val practically yelled at Gyles. "The night before last I saw Wisner in front of the Lord Nelson being gagged, handcuffed, and tossed into a black Lincoln with the license plate number DEA-20-8."

Gyles frowned at Val, as if he had not understood a word.

Val demanded, "Do you know what that spells if A is one and Z is twenty-six?"

"No. Why should I? And how come you remember license plate numbers?"

"It's a game we play on the street. Can you remember your trick's license plate number?"

"I should hope there were more important things to remember in life."

"When your life is important, Gyles, you can afford to remember. When your nights are full of hunger, your days are for forgetting. DEA-20-8 spells DEATH. Figure it out."

At first glance Cornelia decided that Val was absolutely right for Gyles. It was very much like her to grab at snap decisions, and the miracle of it was that she was oftentimes right. The two men were completely unlike, but even in opposition there was a lingering fascination, as if each had to push the other to see how he might react, testing their newfound love because neither could surrender to it.

Exhilarated by their powerful dynamic, Cornelia thought to divert certain disaster. To her it seemed obvious. Their burgeoning romance needed a little cultivation. Descending the stairs, she exclaimed, "Wisner was gagged, cuffed, and thrown into a black Lincoln with the license plate DEATH? Eight, fifteen, twelve, twenty-five, nineteen, eight, nine, twenty."

Both men turned to look at Cornelia. Val snickered at her outburst in spite of himself. Cornelia crossed over to Val, extending a firm and welcoming handshake, but even with heels on she had to look up at him.

"Hi, I'm Cornelia, and you must be Val. Gyles hasn't told me a lot about you, so I know you must be important to him. He's like that, you know, so don't get discouraged. Very repressed, very Boston."

"Cornelia!" exclaimed Gyles.

"We were brought up with such a stiff upper lip that it would take dynamite for Gyles just to crack a smile. And boy, you are dynamite. Eight, fifteen, twelve, twenty-five, nineteen, eight, nine, twenty."

Val and Cornelia exploded with laughter. Gyles looked down at them from what he hoped was the lofty heights of dignity but more closely resembled the confused state described in the old lyric "bewitched, bothered, and bewildered."

Val, snatching a look at Gyles, tried to control himself and asked Cornelia, "How come you know the number alphabet?"

"Oh, we used to play that game at prep school."

"Oh yeah," Val replied sullenly.

"Well, don't clam up on me. It's not my fault I went to a pissy elegant girls' school."

Gyles butted in. "What is eight, fourteen, twelve, la la la la la?"

Cornelia and Val giggled, and she nudged the blond boy, giving him the lead. Val said simply, "It spells HOLY SHIT."

"Really, Cornelia!" Gyles reacted with mock horror, and then he too broke up and all three laughed, not because any of this was so hilarious but because the whole mood of anger had been changed by the elegant interior designer's incongruous vulgarity.

Gyles recovered first and said, "If Wisner was abducted in front of the Lord Nelson the night before last by three men in a black Lincoln, then they must have been the ones who killed him."

"But who on earth would want to kill Uncle Wisner?" asked Cornelia. "And why? He wasn't the most delightful character on earth, but neither would he inspire any emotion stronger than mild revulsion. I know that's not very kind, but it's true."

"The old fart was up to some really weird shit," said Val bluntly. "You should have seen him when he stole that jewelry from here. He actually pulled a gun on me."

"So that story was true," mused Cornelia.

"Sure it was true. Do you think I'd make it up?" Val's anger flared.

"No, I don't think you would, but it's all so bizarre."

Then Gyles said, "I don't know what Wisner was up to with the Egyptian jewelry or if we'll ever know now, but look at these. These are definitely part of the same puzzle." Gyles waved his handful of papers above his head.

"Okay, Green Giant, let's have a look down here," Cornelia complained.

"Better yet, you and Val spread them out on the dining room table. I'll go to the office and retrieve the other three pages," Gyles ordered, handing the papers to Val as he raced up the stairs.

"I left them on Cosmo's desk," Cornelia called after him. "This way, Val," she directed, heading toward the formal dining room. Val pushed open one of the oversized oak pocket doors that separated the front hall from the dining room. Cornelia ducked under his arm into the darkened room.

"Val, push both doors all the way back, please. They'll slide completely into the walls. I'll open the shutters, and we can get some light in here."

Heavy Victorian drapes dripping with fringe and trimmed with braid covered the windows. Cornelia drew them apart by sturdy linen cords. Beneath the curtains, intricate wooden shutters barricaded the windows. These she folded back into their places within the deep window casings. Outside the window glass a Chinese magnolia tree was in full blossom. Its opulent display of flouncing pink flowers was so the over decorated dresses of the belle époque. Cornelia couldn't resist opening two of the windows to let in a breath of air and the soft perfume of the magnolias. Reluctantly she turned to face the Victorian magnificence of her grandmother's dining room.

On the eight-foot-long mahogany table, Val spread the bright Egyptian pictures down one side and back around the other. Cornelia did not interfere with his arrangement, but, following them around the table, she studied the triumphant parade in silence. Gyles came bounding in, waving the last three pages in triumph and toning his own trumpet like fanfare. "Ta-da!"

Val reached for the missing pages with simple authority. He unhinged the Scotch tape from where Cornelia had attached it and placed the pages separately on the right and left-hand side of the middle of the table. Gyles beamed at Val with reawakening pride. Standing next to him, Gyles brushed the silken blond hair out of his friend's eyes.

"Okay, love doves, break it up and let's concentrate on these."

"Cornelia," whined Gyles in mild protest.

"Can it, lover boy. Now, Val, why have you arranged these pages in this order? I don't mean to challenge you. At first glance they do seem to make sense this way. But what about those last pages? You've put them on opposite sides of the table, but they obviously form a gateway or door."

Val shrugged and looked a little apologetic when he said, "They're all numbered. I just put them one after the other."

"Oh! I didn't even think to look. Where are the numbers?"

"At the top of each page."

"Val's right," exclaimed Gyles.

"I feel like such a dummy. Oh well. Gyles, where did you find the rest of those pages? I tore apart the entire office, much to the horror of Lucy Ann."

"Inside the pylon with the statue of Anubis where I found the empty jewelry cases," he replied.

"You certainly have a thing for that creature. What did Val call him—Rin-Tin-Tin?" Cornelia shuddered slightly, thinking of her encounter with the menacing black jackal.

"Yeah, that was kind of a lame joke, but since then I looked him up." Brother and sister looked at Val with curiosity. "You don't need to look so surprised. Lilly bought *The World Book of Knowledge* at the Stop & Shop. She was going to study for an appearance on Jeopardy, 'cause she has this fantastic memory. But then she got involved with 'Glamour Galore' and forgot all about it."

"Who is Lilly, and what is 'Glamour Galore'?" asked Cornelia, completely bewildered.

Gyles explained, "You know Lilly Linda LeStrange. She was the headliner at the Dynasty Ball. Val is her, uh, roommate."

"She's my mother, not my roommate, but she used to be my father," interjected Val.

"Oh of course. How silly of me," declared Cornelia dubiously. "Unfortunately I missed her performance."

"Yeah, you OD'd on angel dust and had to be hauled out of the toilet by Monique," Val said mercilessly.

Now it was Cornelia's turn to bristle. "That's one way of putting it."

Gyles attempted to restore the peace by asking Val, "So what did you find out about Anubis?"

"I copied it out because I didn't quite understand it." Val handed a small, neatly hand-printed note on a filing card to Gyles, who read aloud:

"Anubis was an ancient Egyptian god of the dead, originally represented as a jackal. He was later depicted with a human body and a jackal's head. He was the god of embalming and the guardian of tombs. The Egyptians believed that during the ceremony before Osiris, by which a dead man was admitted to the underworld, Anubis weighed the heart of the dead against the feather of truth. Therefore he was a judge of the dead as well as their protector."

"Hey, look at this," Val interrupted with excitement. "Here's that exact scene." All three looked at the page that Val pointed out, and sure enough, a man's body wearing the head of a black jackal officiated at a tribunal before which a balanced scale held what they supposed must be a feather and a heart. Facing the inquisitors was a tightly wrapped mummy wearing a tiara of gold set with blue scarabs and the flaring head of a cobra. A false beard punctuated its chin. Gyles thought there was something very familiar about the face of the mummy. He searched his memory, surprised to recognize such an image. "You know, I think I remember having seen that face before, but I can't quite place where."

"If you recognize that face, you've been hanging out in strange places," Val commented derisively.

"Never mind the face. Look at the jewelry," Cornelia exclaimed with more than a little dread. "That's the crown that I wore to the Dynasty Ball and the earrings and the necklace and the bracelet. They're all the same, but in miniature."

"I wish I had a magnifying glass. The detail is amazing," agreed Gyles. "Yes, they do appear to be similar pieces, but we know the jewelry was pretty accurately reproduced, although the diamond eyes of the cobra were not strictly authentic."

"To hell with similar. I don't need any magnifying glass to see that this mummy is wearing my jewelry," Cornelia stated emphatically.

"Hate to say it, but it looks more like you were wearing the mummy's jewelry."

"I think Val's right, Corny. And I now know why the mummy's face seems so familiar to me, because it's a face I've seen a million times in the painting on the second-floor hall of Aunt Norma. That mummy is Norma Chilton. These were her jewels, and she intended Anubis, the guardian of the tomb, to protect her amulets until her death. But she couldn't bear to part with the treasure before her time. Wisner told me that she was a real problem for them at the MFA because she wanted to keep the exhumed artifacts that her patronage had afforded. Norma Chilton was possessive and controlling. She had been spoiled, indulged, and adored by her father, Cosmo, the archetypal Victorian patriarch. She had been his most cherished possession but wouldn't accept that role like her sister, Florence. Norma would never be complacent or obedient. She would not be owned by any man. Instead she would own and rule and hold the power. That's why she wanted Nagib Iskander to have the jewels. That's it. Wisner told me

Iskander became an undertaker. He would prepare her for her death—place the cobra tiara on her mummified corpse."

"Jeez, you sound like Elvira, Queen of the Night, on Creature Features," said Val with naive awe.

Gyles glared at Val, suspecting his friend of sarcasm. Cornelia, sufficiently recovered from her revulsion over her having worn the mummy's crown, added her own wisecrack. "Yeah, but he ain't got Elvira's tits."

"Listen, you two, this is serious," admonished Gyles. "Someone has killed Wisner, probably to get the Egyptian jewelry. They may just as easily have killed you at the Dynasty Ball, Cornelia, but fortunately you knew nothing about the real significance or value of what you were wearing."

"But we still don't know what was so important about it," said Cornelia. "And how would Wisner know anything about it either?"

"To use his own words, 'by virtue of having survived the vicissitudes of life's drama,'" Gyles said. "Of course he knew the significance of the jewelry. Why else would he set Val up in a situation months in advance to gain entrance to this house? Wisner knew just what he was doing. The important fact is that the jewelry is not what everyone has been after."

"I don't get it. If the jewelry isn't important, why was it stolen in the first place?" asked Cornelia.

"It's not that the jewelry isn't important, of course it is, but only partly. The other part must be the tomb where the jewelry was to go. I think you were right, Cornelia. Somehow she took it all with her."

"Well, I'm gratified that you think so, Gyles. I wasn't really entirely convinced myself, but anyway, where's the tomb? In the Valley of the Kings, maybe, in Egypt? I thought you were the one who said that Norma Chilton was buried at Mount Auburn Cemetery in a vault by Aunt Florence and the rest of them."

Val, who had been puzzling over the Egyptian paintings and Wisner's note, which Gyles had left on the table, asked, "So what is a necropolis?"

"A necropolis is a city of the dead, or another word for cemetery," explained Gyles.

"Well, that place you're talking about, there's a tower there," said Val, "and you can walk right up to it. I know 'cause one of my tricks took me there."

"What?" Gyles cringed with dismay.

"Yeah, it's sort of cruisey up there. I had this number who liked to do it outside, so he would drive us over there and we would make it in the bushes. He wasn't bad looking either."

"Val, spare us the gory details."

"Oh Gyles, it was just getting interesting."

"Cornelia, please. Save your unflappable liberalism for your own lover. Or to use the nautical phrase, stow it. Val, could you find this tower again?"

"It's not as if it's going to run away, you know. The thing's about a hundred feet tall."

"Well good, let's go. I've got my car parked a couple of blocks down the street."

"Hmmm, what have you got in mind, hot stuff?" Val growled provocatively.

"Hey, wait a minute, what about the paintings? Don't you think we should study the details first," suggested Cornelia, suddenly getting cold feet. "There seem to be some ominous-looking mechanisms here. What do you suppose these obelisks signify?"

"I have no idea, Corny, but I intend to find out. If you're uncomfortable with going to the cemetery, I understand." Gyles was determined.

"Okay okay, I'll go. But let me phone Rita first. We're scheduled to go to a BLAB potluck tonight."

"Blab potluck?"

"I know it sounds like a bunch of chattering dykes, but it stands for Bicycling Lesbians Around Boston and—"

"Cornelia, you can explain on the way, and you can call Rita on my car phone. Let's shake a leg. It will only be light for another couple of hours."

Gyles herded Val and Cornelia out the front door, and the three were still buttoning jackets and pulling on shawls as they proceeded down Commonwealth Avenue. A half a block behind them, a black Lincoln pulled away from the curb. Keeping a discreet distance, it shadowed the trio at a walking pace.

CHAPTER 33

▼

"Hello, Mr. Iskander? This is Achmed. I am following Mr. Chilton's Jeep now. He is with his sister and the hustler that the other Mr. Chilton hired. We are just entering Watertown on Mount Auburn Street, and there he is signaling now, and turning into the cemetery. Yes sir, I will stay a safe distance. No, I don't think they've seen me. Yes sir, I am armed. Yes, I understand. Circle back and wait for you at the main gate after I know the location." Achmed replaced his car phone onto its cradle embedded in the leather-padded dash of the Lincoln and made a hairpin left turn into Mount Auburn Cemetery, cutting dangerously in front of the oncoming traffic.

*   *   *   *

"Hello, Mr. Charlie? This is Lucy Ann. Put down that 'Lucy Ann Who' jazz and listen to me. I need you over here straightaway. My babies have got themselves mixed up with the past, and it's a heap more serious than they think. But, Charlie, you only know the easy part of that old story. Miss Norma, she ain't done with me yet. Lord protect us. But yet and still, nobody's gonna mess with my babies. That's where you're dead wrong, Charlie. This is my business 'cause I'm more part of this family than you can ever guess at. So get your butt in gear and drive that cab over here like the devil's chasin' you." Lucy Ann hung up quickly, before Mr. Charlie could waste any more time questioning the past she thought she had buried so many years ago. She returned to the dining room, and standing behind the drawn curtains so as not to be seen from the street, she scanned the avenue. Only five minutes before she had seen the swarthy looking stranger in the big black car following Cornelia, Gyles, and Val. She shivered to think who had sent that car.

Charlie's cab pulled up in front of the house, and he gave a friendly toot. Coming away from the window, Lucy Ann went quickly to the hall tree by the front door. She snatched her hat from one of the pegs, and catching a glimpse of herself in its central mirror, she was startled by her unusually pale appearance.

*   *   *   *

Lilly Linda LeStrange tugged at the black pearl buttons of her long kid gloves, struggling to cram her pudgy hands, thick wrists, massive forearms, and bulging biceps into the arm-length black leather that would complete her mourning. Having miraculously accomplished this feat, she turned her attention to straightening the seams of her black silk stockings. This was a more complicated maneuver, involving a kind of writhing convulsion to surmount the considerable girth of her equatorial regions. Lilly inadvertently jostled the companion beside her in the comfortable recesses of the 1938 Packard limousine, who was busily applying a particularly vivid shade of carmine lipstick to pouting lips.

"Woman, stop thrashing around like a pregnant armadillo and be still. Can't you at least try to act like a lady?" Monique Lafarge snapped with her typical lack of delicacy and then concluded by adding, "If you don't mind, I am trying to do my face."

"Girlfriend, if half a dozen plastic surgeons can't do you better, what makes you think another gallon of Revlon is gonna help?"

Lilly Linda's question ricocheted off the invisible armor of the dazzling showgirl but struck Butch right on the funny bone. His unguarded guffaw was audible above the busy traffic on Mount Auburn Street. Monique jammed the cap back on her lipstick, a prophylactic precaution that even she deemed necessary. With a deceptively casual, even bored gesture, she hurled the little metal torpedo at the giggling chauffeur. Butch's vanity refused to acknowledge this slight, except to glower at the two passengers in his rearview mirror, but as he stared at the glamorous thespians clad in deep mourning, he was bewitched by their aura of mystery, which gave blatant reference to the film noir of the 1930s. Butch ripped his attention away from the rearview mirror, and with the agility of a practiced daredevil, swerved the Packard back onto course. His abrupt downshifting was less fluent and caused the limousine to lurch as it careened on screeching wheels into the spiked iron gate of the Mount Auburn Cemetery.

* * * *

Rita Rosenstein drove her vintage Alfa Romeo like a professional racer, dodging in and out of traffic on busy Storrow Drive with steel nerve. She did not waste her time with foolish anger at the caprices of the average driver. She merely whipped around all obstacles with the surety of a serious competitor. She dashed over the gracefully arched Eliot Bridge spanning the Charles River just as the Harvard crew, with rhythmic strokes, pulled their needle-sharp scull over the chill waters and disappeared into the shadows beneath the bridge. Her diminutive race car came to a bracing halt at a light in front of the Buckingham Browne & Nichols School.

Poised like a jockey, her balance focused between her left hand on the leather-covered wheel and her right fist, which held the ball of ivory impaled on the Alfa's gearshift, she waited for the light to change. On green she took off, maneuvering the double S curve and complex intersection of merging speedways around the Cambridge Boat Club and the Mount Auburn Hospital. Her steel-belted radials neither screeched nor squealed as the Alfa's powerful engine rocketed her through the last seconds of a yellow light. Coming up on her left she saw the spearheaded black iron fence, behind which a jostling army of granite and marble tombstones competed for the vainglorious distinctions that death would not award unaided. Rita caught sight of the monolithic granite gate whose modified Egyptian motif was intended to reassure the bereaved with illusions of eternity. Downshifting, she slowed only enough to slip into the entrance of Mount Auburn Cemetery without pause.

* * * *

Nagib Iskander sat erect and motionless in the rear seat of his black Mercedes sedan, isolated behind thick tinted glass. All sounds of the mundane world were muffled and far away. Beside him on the black leather upholstery was the head mask of Anubis, alert and menacing guardian of the necropolis. In the front seat sat two grim and silent men dressed in black Armani suits. The mortician's trancelike stare was fixed upon the sedately rolling hearse that preceded his car. He whispered incantations from *The Book of the Dead* to the linen-wrapped corpse within. His words, like scalding steam, hissed and bubbled on his snarling lips. Traffic on Mount Auburn Street parted and withdrew, allowing the cortège to glide by and enter the gates of Mount Auburn Cemetery. The workaday world of the street shrank with reverence at the sight of the hearse and attendant black Mercedes. Nagib considered this deference his due, but far from being inured by the frequency of the public's recoiling, he became, with each year, more demanding of their cowering respect.

Inside the gates the cortège pressed on at the same moderate speed, winding around the smooth macadam roads, gently climbing the rolling hills and heading towards the Victorian Gothic chapel. This temple stood upon a leveled eminence surrounded by a host of impressive monuments grouped by dynastic genealogies behind lacy cast-iron stockades. The Mercedes came to a halt in front of the fantastically pinnacled chapel. Two grim attendants got out. One of the men opened the rear door for the mortician. Simultaneously, from the long black hearse two more men extended long legs. All four fanned out in front of the chapel and stood back to center, at ease but on guard.

Nagib emerged from his Mercedes and started across the lawn beneath the vaulted canopy of venerable oaks. He ignored the Christian Gothic conceit behind him as he proceeded towards a colossal granite sphinx crouching on a plinth of gargantuan proportions. This bestial god, tense with instinctive blood lust, posed a wordless riddle of inescapable death. Towards this ancient idol Nagib, now helmeted beneath the head of Anubis, marched. His arms outstretched in supplication, he fell to the earth, prostrating himself with ecstatic abandon. In his left hand he grasped a golden ankh; in his right fist, the chalcedony scarab, the heart of the mother.

*   *   *   *

Tatiana Sarkisian sat on a cold white marble bench wrapped in her black sable coat. Its luxuriant fur glistened in the spring sunshine. She was half hidden behind a veil of weeping willow branches that sprouted pale thin leaves. Beneath her oversized dark glasses, her olive complexion was aglow with determination as she exhaled dead blue smoke from her Dunhill cigarette. Tatiana's Rolls-Royce was parked in a discreet cul-de-sac a short distance away, screened from view by a verdant thicket of rhododendrons. As she waited she stared with contempt at a quarreling brace of ducks that defended overlapping territories on the shallow lily pond before her. Circling that decorative water, stood the tombs and mausoleums of Boston's powerful families, testament to the brevity of privilege.

This subliminal message fired Tatiana's resolve, as she greedily fondled the snub-nosed revolver in her pocket and drummed her sharp red nails nervously on the gun metal, now hot from her grasp. For the last couple of days she had come to the picturesque cemetery, its rolling hills richly decorated by the lavish stone markers scattered among the rare specimen trees, bushes, and flowers collected from the seven continents. Her interest, however, was not in the world-renowned arboretum. Nor was she attuned to the beauty of the stone architecture. And she was completely oblivious to the great numbers of migratory birds that beckoned to small groups of aficionados glued to their binoculars. No, her prey lay buried deep in the dark recesses of an obscure tomb.

So she sat on her bench waiting, because here they would all have to come eventually, all those who sought the tomb, all those who lay claim to its treasure-including the innocents, who were lured there by half-glimmers of truth. They would all converge here in the sacred grove.

CHAPTER 34

▼

Gyles's Jeep Cherokee swerved around yet another fluid curve on the macadam road. This endless maze of picturesque lanes fed a secondary system of footpaths with an encyclopedic collection of floral names, from amaryllis to zinnia. This design was intended to further the illusion of the infinite and, by implication, the eternal.

"Val, are you sure your tower is here? I don't see any indication of it, and we've been back and forth all over the whole place. I know this is at least the second time around for this hill, because I remember that angel holding the dead soldier." Gyles asked.

"Sure I'm sure. It didn't just walk away. It's just that everything looks sorta the same around here, with all these trees and stuff." Val's defense trailed off vaguely. The monument that Gyles had pointed out was a particularly sentimental white marble Pieta that depicted an androgynous but robust archangel draped in flowing robes. This seraph spread an enchantment of enormous wings protectively over the limp corpse of a spoiled youth whose uniform had been torn to pieces, presumably by the fury of battle, leaving his pallid musculature naked and lifeless.

Sitting in the back seat of the Jeep, Cornelia craned her neck to see the angel Gyles referred to, amazed that he could remember one from the other in this army of silent sentinels. One glance sufficed to incite her scorn.

"Yeah, I can see why you would remember that one. Ugh! All that male glorification of violence and repressed sexuality. I'm surprised the hero isn't impaled on an erect lance."

"Cornelia, really! That grouping is a direct reference to the deposition of Christ on the Ghiberti doors in Florence."

"Oh sure,Ghiberti I should have known."

"Look, there it is," shouted Val.

"Where is it?"

"What is it?"

"There, through the trees." Val pointed at a distant hill barely visible through the woods. An old tree must have fallen in a winter storm, because only at this angle could the tower be seen. The dark stone turret stood on a steep promontory. It looked like an enormous castle chess piece rising from a sea of green foliage. This was, without a doubt, the tower of the mountain forest.

Gyles jammed the gear shaft into first and took off. Driven more by instinct than by surety, he charged about the circuitous roads, seeking the most direct way upwards. Finally he found the steep hillside road leading to the tower but just then an abrupt change came over the placid spring afternoon. Rolling blasts of cold wind tossed the oak and maple leaves as branches were whipped back and forth by the bullying force of a gathering thunderstorm. Two jay birds, blown from their perch, flashed blue feathers and screamed with outrage. Ragged tufts of leaves were torn from the trees and sent flying through the air.

As the trees bent, glimpses of the tower could be seen looming above them. The voice of the storm grew in volume as if issuing an ominous warning to those who would presume not to cower beneath its fury. Still the Jeep climbed. A loud crack was heard, and an avalanche of crashing branches hurtled down on the road. Gyles stomped on the gas and swerved sharply to the left. The Cherokee leapt forward as the branches grabbed for it.

They came to a rocking halt at the bottom of the long stone staircase that led towards the tower. A tangle of yellow forsythia bushes overflowed onto the stone steps.

"Dear Goddess, are we still alive?" croaked Cornelia from beneath her oversized cashmere shawl.

"Nice driving, sweetheart." Val slapped Gyles on the back as he hopped from the Jeep and slammed his door shut.

Gyles was more shaken than he wanted to admit. He had driven up an almost vertical embankment in order to avoid the falling tree branch, and for a moment he had been terrified that the Jeep would flip over. He stepped down from the driver's seat, shaking his head in silent amazement. Inspecting the damage, he found only slight scratches made by the sharp branches.

Gyles helped his sister from the Jeep as Val fought his way through the forsythia bramble up the stairs and disappeared.

"Hey, wait for us, Val," Gyles called after him, and he pulled back the thick curtain of yellow blossoms for Cornelia to pass.

"If you think I'm going to play Ramar of the Jungle and ruin my new Kenzo shawl by charging up there, you are crazy."

"You know, Corny, you are such a sissy sometimes. What if this were a BLAB bike ride?"

"If this were a BLAB ride, I would have my Banana Republic outfit on so I could lounge comfortably on the well-furnished veranda of a quaint little bed and breakfast. Now run along and play in the bushes with your boyfriend. I'll take care of myself."

Gyles shrugged, ducked into the tangle of branches choking the stairs, and disappeared. Cornelia wrapped her shawl tightly around herself, and with frequent worried glances toward the wind-tossed trees, she slowly followed the road as it spiraled towards the peak of the tower mountain. Gyles emerged from the cover of the staircase onto a circular terrace paved with huge slabs of granite. The wind whipped round the stone tower so strongly that it slightly swayed the iron door that hung on massive stiff hinges.

Val was nowhere to be found. Gyles entered the twilight of the Gothic tower, where a fetid stench assailed him. The wind played the hollow tower like a huge flute wailing a lachrymose dirge. The damp, thick walls wept limey tears of dissolving mortar, forming stalactites that hung from the spiraling stone ceiling. Gyles's gritty footsteps echoed back an abrasive hiss, and around the second twist of the stone stairs the light failed altogether. Only plummeting drafts of cold wind indicated the direction in the darkness.

"Val," called Gyles as he groped up the stairs, but there was no answer.

Val had reached the middle-level balcony that encircled the outside of the tower. He checked this out quickly and went on with all the eager excitement of an overgrown kid. He came out on the top of the tower, which was surrounded by waist-high battlements. Leaning over the edge of these, he saw Rita's Alfa pull up to where Cornelia was walking on the road some sixty feet below. He wondered how Rita had got her sports car around the falling tree branch, and shaking his head with admiration, he said to himself, That broad's got guts. Val sat on the raised steel hood above the opening to the stairs, hugging one knee and rocking gently back and forth as the wind tossed his silken hair. He reveled in the power of the storm as it swept over the city spread out beneath him. In the gathering clouds there was an untamable energy that he could relate to. He gazed up into the nebulous, billowing mountains in the sky and wondered what it would be like to be up there. Gyles trudged up the last steps and out into the light.

"Oh, so there you are. Wow, what a view." Gyles stood in the center of the roof slowly turning, taking in the full measure of the vista. To the east stood the central city, its skyscrapers huddled together in a heap of glass, steel, and stone that dwarfed all other structures in a four-state radius. The Charles River whiplashed across the plain, the white steeples and turquoise cupolas of Harvard University decorating its banks. In the middle distance Harvard Stadium muscled its way to prominence, surrounded by Soldier's Field Parade. Over rolling hills the city spread its neighborhoods, shaded by a surprising number of trees and punctuated by church steeples, water towers, radio and TV transmitters, and the like.

Around the tower mountain a sea of turbulent leaves tossed in the wind, giving glimpses of the gravestones beneath the branches of the lofty old trees. Gyles sidled up to where the dancer sat and put his arm around Val's broad shoulders. Val untwined his arms from around his knees and took hold of Gyles at the waist, leaning his head back against Gyles's cheek. The lovers gazed without talking at the storm rushing in. The raw force of spring enveloped the two in an intoxicating bacchanal. Gyles breathed in deeply, filling his lungs with the fresh air and the faint musky scent of Val.

Val idly played with a bronze amulet that hung on a linen cord around Gyles's neck and asked, "What's this? I don't remember you wearing this before."

"It's some kind of a charm I found around the neck of Anubis, the statue behind the secret panel. It's called an ankh." Val dropped the ankh and tucked his hand beneath Gyles's belt, a movement more for protection than sensuality.

Footsteps and voices could be heard on the stairs, but the two men didn't budge.

Rita emerged onto the roof. She looked around quickly and called down the stairs, "Come on, Neil. They're both up here, just like I told you. It's just a little farther." Rita turned to face the two men. "Hi, I'm Rita Rosenstein. You must be Val." She offered a friendly hand, and Val awkwardly returned the gesture with his left hand because he didn't want to let go of Gyles.

"Oh I'm sorry, you two haven't met," Gyles said, stirring in Val's embrace.

"Well, now we have, so don't move an inch," Val admonished Gyles. "Hi, Rita, pleased to meet cha."

Rita checked out Val's hot grasp on Gyles, and she winked at Val knowingly. "You're smart to hold on to that one. He's a slippery devil."

"Rita," protested Gyles.

She turned back to the staircase and shouted more encouragement to the reluctant Cornelia. "Come on, Neil, I want you to see this before the rain comes." Rita stood at the edge of the battlements transfixed by the view. "Look at the Hancock Tower. Those dark clouds make it look like a bruised mirror, and you can even see the Tobin Bridge—down there must be the Arsenal Mall." Rita's attention swept over the horizon with eager recognition of some of the major sights. Cornelia, clutching the edge of the steel hood, peered out with trepidation. Rita, taking pity, reached out to assist her lover.

"Oh come on, Neil. You'll love it. Look, even Gyles likes it up here."

"Hey, Rita, I heard that. What do you mean, 'even Gyles likes it'?"

"Well, you're usually so caught up with all that dusty furniture."

"Rita, don't let go of me. Oh my Goddess. We're all going to be blown off the edge by the hurricane." Cornelia clung to Rita with panic.

"Okay, Neil, we'll stay just a minute," Rita said, and she wrapped both arms tightly around her lover. But Rita didn't really want to leave the tower. She was fascinated by the city spread out beneath them and exhilarated by the gathering storm. She sought to divert Cornelia's attention by asking, "So why are we here anyway?"

Gyles realized Rita's tactic and came to the rescue. "We have to answer a riddle that Uncle Wisner left us."

"I might have known it wasn't for the bird watching, and I'll bet that somehow this all relates back to antiques."

Val snickered and nudged Gyles in the ribs saying, "She's got your number, babe."

"This has nothing to do with antiques. That is, not directly."

"Oh Gyles, stop stalling. Of course it has everything to do with antiques. Show her the note, and let's get the hell off this tower before I scream."

"Okay, okay, Cornelia, calm down. Rita, you better read this. Wisner left it as some kind of clue, and I assume it refers to the cemetery and what can be seen from up here."

Gyles handed Rita Wisner's mysterious message. As he untwined himself from Val's embrace, he asked the dancer, "Can I see the binoculars?" Val handed over the small German binoculars Gyles had asked him to hold when they left the Jeep. Gyles scanned the cemetery, not knowing what to look for.

"Gyles, those are my opera glasses. Where did you get them?"

"Cornelia, you really are a nudge sometimes. Yes they're yours. And just this once I thank you for your general disorganization. You left them in the Jeep the last time we went to the ballet. I've kept them for you in the glove compartment."

"Well, if you're so organized and smart, what are you looking for?"

"I'm not sure. Anubis astride the tomb, I guess."

"Okay, Bosco, hand over the binos," Rita ordered.

"What do you mean?" Gyles demanded, considerably affronted.

"I mean, I've got a map and she's got the best eyes" was Rita's curt explanation.

"She does not. My whole life is visual."

"Yes she does. I know because she always beats me at target practice. She's a perfect shot." Rita admitted her defeat with pride.

"Well, archery is an entirely different matter," Gyles smugly pronounced.

"Not archery, you eleganza queen, rifle practice. BLAB sponsors rifle and handgun training, and your sister is a regular Annie Oakley with first-prize, one-hundred-percent bulls-eyes. So I know she has the eyes of an eagle. Now fork over the binos."

Cornelia accepted her binoculars with beaming triumph, forgetting for the moment her fear of the open tower. She too was beginning to appreciate the spectacular view. Rita spread out a map of the cemetery on the steel hood and enlisted Val's aid to hold it down and look for the Lotus Path.

"Where'd you get this map?" he asked, running his finger along the twisted lanes.

"I stopped at the gatehouse, where they have a whole rack of pamphlets and maps. I had to have some way of locating this tower. Wisner's message reads, 'The lotus path within the necropolis.' All the roads here are named for trees. The footpaths are all flower names. So it follows that the tomb must be on one of the paths."

"Here it is," cried Val.

Gyles leaned over his shoulder to see. Rita oriented herself to the map and view and then guided Cornelia towards Lotus Path.

"All I can see down there are some trees and some ordinary-looking tombstones. Oh, there's a white marble angel, and I can see one of those fancy iron signposts that name the paths, but I can't possibly read which flower it is. Mostly all I can see is leaves. The only reason that I can get a glimpse of anything below is because some of the trees aren't fully out yet. Wait a minute, there are two tall obelisks in a ring of weeping birch trees. All the rest is leaves." Giving up her search, Cornelia lowered her powerful opera glasses. She reached for Rita's hand, nuzzled gently against her lover's breasts, and both women gazed up at the billowing clouds. Gyles, determined to find the tomb and Anubis, was not about to give up so easily.

"Let me take a look, Corny." He focused the glasses on the area where they calculated Lotus Path to be. That was when he really appreciated his sister's strong vision. "Wow, you weren't kidding, Rita. Corny must have the eyes of a superwoman because all I can see is trees and more trees."

Cornelia beamed a silly smile towards Rita, who replied with a toying kiss to the tip of her lover's nose. "I guess that since Wisner's message was written, the mountain forest has grown up a lot," suggested Gyles.

"Or you can only see down there in winter" was Val's idea.

"I do see a hearse followed by a Mercedes limo. It must be a posh funeral, because there's a Lincoln following at some distance. I wonder who died."

"Gyles, give me back my glasses. You're giving me the creeps."

"Oh Corny, get over it. This is a cemetery, you know. I'm going to drive down the hill towards Lotus Path. Perhaps we'll spot Anubis. But first I want to go by Lake Auburn and pay a quick visit to the Chilton-Chichester tomb. There's something there I want to check out."

"Gyles, Cornelia and I will meet you at Lotus Path. I want to take my Alfa. I think we'll skip the house call to your illustrious ancestors. I'd just as soon stay aboveground, at least while I'm still breathing."

"Okay, Rita, we'll see you down there," Gyles agreed easily.

"Ciao for now," Val added gaily, waving good-bye with one hand. He slapped Gyles on the butt with the other as the antiques dealer disappeared down the steps of the tower and Val winked knowingly at Rita.

CHAPTER 35

▼

Along the normally placid byway on the shores of Halcyon Lake, surrounded by weeping willows and stately mausoleums, charged a puffing and panting dowager, whose black crepe skirt was hiked up above bony knees as she, with remarkable verve, chased down the tarmac hollering with unseemly gusto.

"Stop, stop, stop you motherfucker." The object of her desire was a rather shabby Boston cab traveling at a dangerous clip that would surely elude her. The hack squealed around a picturesque bend in the road and disappeared behind a phalanx of granite obelisks that stood twenty feet tall. From behind these same proudly erect monuments a vintage black Packard limousine motored sedately towards the disheveled widow. Throwing all caution to the proverbial breezes, the distraught dowager leapt upon this conveyance and clinging to its chromium with her high heels dug into the running board, she wagged a gnarled finger in the reverse direction and screeched, "Follow that cab!"

The occupants of the automobile were stunned into silence and unsure how to react to this desperate assault. All three gazed with reserved disdain at the undignified creature clutching the Packard. Then the apparition hollered at the driver with compelling pluck, "Step on it, dude. Floor it. The fuckin' cab's got the ashes."

Butch did not question the exact meaning of this ejaculation because he recognized Betty the Bounder by her bouncy red beard. Betty's unmistakable grimace could be glimpsed beneath a black velvet pillbox hat rakishly cocked to one side of her overlarge bouffant hairdo. The chauffeur, conditioned to obey many untoward directives, spun the heavy automobile around and roared after the disappearing taxi.

Regally ensconced in the backseat of the Packard, Lilly Linda LeStrange did not take kindly to being inconvenienced. Having already lavished half the day upon her elaborate toilette, she intended to make a stunning entrance at the funeral of the renowned female illusionist, Urna Flamanté.

Such was the import of the occasion that impelled Lilly Linda to prevent any delay to the proceedings. She would not stand for her own precision timing to be botched by the perpetually inebriated Betty, whose tiresome antics had caused mayhem and riot on more than one occasion. Lilly therefore flung open the left rear passenger door, which inadvertently caught the wind like a sail, slamming open upon the hapless creature clinging to the car.

"Betty, you silly bitch. Stop hollering like a whore in a cheap gangster movie and get inside this minute." To further emphasize her resolve to be obeyed, Lilly Linda prodded the hitchhiking Betty with the sharp point of her black lace parasol. This maneuver brought the diva dangerously close to the open door.

At the very brink of disaster, when Lilly was about to be launched in an unforeseen airborne plunge, Monique screeched, "Stop the car you dumb lug."

Butch slammed on the brakes with violence and outrage, bellowing, "Hey, watch your mouth, woman." The resulting whiplash action did eject the diva onto the tarmac, where the disheveled Betty also was hurled. Trust the Bounder to multiply her transgressions. Heaping insult onto injury, the silly bitch landed right on the deposed Lilly with a terrible thud. Lilly Linda was, however, formidably armored against all injury by her considerable girth. She took the fall with a minimum of damage but a maximum of indignacious hysteria. Butch dashed to the aid of the struggling and sputtering Lilly. First he plucked Betty from the heap, depositing that bag of bones without delicacy into the well-swept gutter of Halcyon Drive. A forlorn groan escaped the discarded carcass. Next, Butch exerted all his inflated brawn to raise the diva into a seating posture. But for Lilly to accomplish her full stature required the combined efforts of Butch, Monique, and Betty in addition to the larvic undulations of the lady herself, who of course was no lady at all.

Betty for all of her dithering delirium was still fixated on the long gone taxi. She imprudently urged the company, "We can't stay here wasting time. We've got to find that cab. You two stay here while Butch and I go after it." At this suggestion Monique took extreme umbrage. Drawing herself up into the rarified altitudes of her full and extended height, she glared down upon the cowering Betty and snapped, "Buzz off, Bitch. Butch goes nowhere without me."

"But the ashes, the ashes are in the cab. We've got to get them."

Moved to violent exasperation, Lilly bludgeoned Betty with her parasol and demanded, "What are you talking about you lush? We are going to the best funeral of the year and all you can think of is your fuckin' barbeque trash. I won't have it."

"No, no, Urna's ashes, they're in the cab," sobbed Betty. Lilly and Monique both screamed, "I don't believe you."

Butch broke in shouting, "Stuff it broads and let the Bounder sing." Then he turned on Betty, his gloved hands clenched in menacing fists, pressing into his sleek hips. He loomed over her, his black boots spread wide on the tarmac. As the Bounder whimpered, Butch growled, "I am waiting Miss Thing."

"I, I was supposed to bring Joey's, I mean Urna Flamanté's, ashes to the cemetery today. We had been lovers at the seminary together."

"Skip the history lesson and spit it out."

"I'm trying to tell you that I couldn't bring myself to leave poor Joey, I mean Urna, in that plastic box they gave me at the funeral home. So when I got him back to my apartment I looked around for something better to put him in where he would feel more at home. So I opened up my Raggedy Ann doll and emptied out the stuffing and filled her with Joey's, I mean Urna's, ashes. Well, all that took a lot of time so I was kinda late getting my own drag together. I had to do my face in the cab coming over here. Well, I got real flustered because I thought I had forgotten my money, and well, I got out of the cab and I forgot poor Joey." Betty, overcome with remorse, dissolved into a deluge of lamentation and woe. She attempted to anesthetize her pain with a handy gin bottle conveniently stashed in her purse, but Lilly grabbed the offending jug away from the blubbering Betty and sloshed the sauce onto the turf. Contemptuously the diva discarded the emptied receptacle with a shudder of revulsion.

"That does it. When we get through with this day, you are going to the detox hospital."

"But Lilly, I don't think I've reached my bottom yet."

"You are a half-assed idiot, Betty. You wouldn't know your bottom from a hole in the wall. Not only are you going to detox, but when you get out of it, it's AA from now on."

Betty uttered a convulsive sob and shook with horror. Contemplating a life on the wagon was to her a journey through hell. Butch, ever ready to lend assistance, plucked Betty from the gutter, propped her up and shook her out a bit.

Brushing off a smudge or two he said with platonic compassion, "Don't cry, Betty. It's really not so bad. I've been sober for five years now and there really is life after booze. I go to this cool gay AA meeting and you'll fit right in. It's a life second to none."

During this hiatus Monique had perched herself upon a nearby tomb that resembled a Roman bathtub. This monument was carved in sparkling white Carrara marble that was in dramatic contrast to her jet black mourning. The showgirl's black miniskirt displayed to great advantage her gorgeous gams, which were crossed at the thigh and swinging impatiently while she puffed, with studied nonchalance, at a joint of pungent reefer.

Butch turned a critical eye on Monique and bellowed, "Hey Mo, do ya mind? Smokin' dope in a graveyard ain't real ladylike you know."

"Sorry darling, I got bored. So why don't you get in the car and drive."

Lilly Linda exploded, "Wait a minute! How can we go to a funeral without a body? Betty's botched the whole deal and this was my big chance to break into the world of opera. 'Oh earth, farewell, thou veil of sorrow, brief dream of joy condemned to end in woe.'"

"Hey that's pretty good Lilly. Did you just make that up or what?" Butch was genuinely impressed.

"No I didn't just make that up, you numbskull. That's Verdi's Aida."

"Gosh, is she going to the funeral too? I guess everybody's gonna be there 'cept poor old Urna and it's all my fault."

"Shut up Betty and stop your blubbering. No, Aida is not going to be there. Aida is an Ethiopian princess who gets buried alive in a tomb. She's just a character in an opera."

"So why don't you go ahead with the part darling. We'll put you in the tomb and then there won't be any problem." With this suggestion, Monique crushed out her joint on the glistening grave where she sat, leaving a black blotch on the white marble.

"Because, to begin with dipshit, Urna Flamanté was cremated and her can of ashes was going to be stuffed into a niche in the Columbarium, a space not big enough to hold my left tit. However, now that you mention it, I think this will make a pretty good substitute." Lilly laid both hands on the chromium-plated headlight of Monique's vintage Packard and with the pith and brawn of a maniac, she yanked it off the car. The antique lighting fixture was remarkably urnlike in shape once wrenched from the fender where it had been mounted.

Monique sprang from her perch screaming like crushed steel in a five-car accident, "You stupid cunt. You've wrecked my car. I'm gonna kill you. Give me that headlight. A-a-a-r-r-r-gh." Her words dissolved into a barbaric screech of rage as she hurled herself at the diva with the ferocious intent of a rabid hyena. Fearlessly

Butch intercepted the vaulting chanteuse in the midst of her leap to kill. With the surety of a sadistic Apache dancer, he swung her around his shoulders twice and flung her with neat dispatch into the cushioned recesses of the vintage Packard. Lilly Linda, with studied grandeur, shoved the counterfeit funeral urn at Betty who, teetering dangerously from the impact, nevertheless clutched the substitute prop beneath her withered bosom as she whimpered vague protestations.

Extending one colossal arm tightly gloved in black kid, the diva pointed at the front seat and snapped, "Get in the car Betty and shut up. I've got a performance to give and you queens have fucked up long enough." So saying, Lilly Linda minced around the rear of the limo. Pausing briefly to allow the chauffeur to open the door, she wriggled into the Packard. Once installed there, she thrust an atomizer loaded with poppers beneath the nose of the subdued Monique. Off they spun down Halcyon Drive, slightly disheveled and a wee bit dazed.

CHAPTER 36

▼

Gyles parked his Cherokee in front of an impressive tomb sunk into the steep hillside that rose abruptly around Auburn Lake. Calling this duck pond a lake was a telling bit of pretension, equal to the grandeur lavished upon the dynastic repositories that enjoyed pride of place in this most exclusive dell. The few families resting here were all of fabled names, pillars of their community and fathers of their country. These were, however, private men of means and in the strictest Boston tradition; their illustrious names could only be glimpsed dimly through the grilled doors of their unmarked mausoleums.

Auburn Lake was cinched in the middle by a stone bridge that Val could not resist exploring. Standing on its arched span, he gazed about the landscaped water garden, truly impressed by what he saw. Tall willow trees drooped chartreuse curtains of fringed branches into the still waters. Azalea bushes burned with scarlet and purple blossoms. Delicate pink and white dogwood trees floated their flowers in the air. Lilacs filled Val's lungs with a funerary perfume, the essence of mauve, the color of mourning.

Intent on his purpose, Gyles approached the Chilton-Chichester tomb, where he inserted an oversized bronze key into the antique lock embedded in the heavy door. The mechanism moved stiffly but in good order as he knew it would, having recently used the key at his great-aunt Florence's funeral. Gyles was the direct heir and descendent of Cosmo Chilton, and as such, family tradition decreed that he be the holder of the keys. He had executed the responsibilities of this ceremonial office with the expected dignity, not realizing at the time what advantage this position would offer him. On the occasion of Florence Chilton's funeral, Cousin Eben had showed Gyles the keys, which were kept in old Cosmo's desk, inside a concealed drawer. When Cornelia had led Gyles to the office earlier that day in search of the tomb plans, he had checked on the keys. As he looked at them he had thought of the irony of locking up bones and dust. But Cornelia had interrupted his musings, and almost without intention he'd slipped the keys into the pocket of his tweed jacket.

Gyles had to lean heavily on the cold marble door of the tomb before it would swing inward. Once inside he was confronted by the spectral image of Cosmo Chilton glaring from the damp gloom. The patriarch wore an expression of stern rebuke for all those insolent enough to intrude on his brooding repose. This white stone portrait bust was mounted on a column of green marble. It was dimly lit from above by a small cupola set with stained glass that cast a blue light upon the mildew- and lichen-encrusted marble, adding a dolorous and morbid expression to the intended hauteur. At the foot of the pillar, the family mastiff lay guarding his master. This sculpture, also of white marble, was the cherished artwork of old Cosmo and represented the industrialist's favorite companion in life, a dog called Nebuchadnezzar.

Val peered cautiously in through the Gothic tracery of the half-open door. It made him shudder to see his lover inside the dim, stone-lined crypt. Standing stiffly beneath the high ceiling, Gyles was bathed in blue light that drained all color from his skin. From Val's perspective, the portrait bust of Cosmo Chilton was blocked behind Gyles, thereby eliminating all distractions except the names carved into the stone slabs that sealed the individual graves. The names made Val shake with horror: Gyles Buckman, 1837-1907; Gyles Chichester Chilton, 1892-1970; Gyles Sumner Chilton, 1840-1863; Gyles Elliot Chilton, 1920-1960; Gyles Ephraim Chichester, 1911-1981; etc.

"Gyles, Gyles," whispered Val.

"Oh Val, there you are. Well, what do you think of old Cosmo? Pretty scary, huh?" Gyles stepped away from the statue of his ancestor, and Val stared with shocked disbelief.

"Anubis, there's Anubis. Gyles, get the fuck out of there. That place is no good."

"Val, that's not Anubis, that's old Cosmo's dog, Nebuchadnezzar."

"Right, but man's best friend he ain't. Now Gyles, get out of there."

"But Nebuchadnezzar can't hurt me. He's really just a joke in the family. Aunt Julia thought he should be removed and loaned to the museum, because Nebuchadnezzar has become rather famous and she says it draws unwanted attention. But Eben wouldn't hear of it, because Nebuchadnezzar has a separate endowment, which of course he administers."

"You mean that a stone dog in a graveyard has a trust fund? Boy, that's sick."

"The sculptor was Hiram Powers, America's finest artist of the nineteenth century. The work receives periodic cleaning, but the really fantastic thing is that Cosmo's original endowment has grown to a considerable investment, while his oldest daughter, Norma, died in dramatically reduced circumstances. But now that story is in question too."

"Gyles, forget the dog and get out of there. Your name is written all over the walls. It's fuckin' creepy."

"Okay Val, that's very sweet of you to be concerned, but hold on a minute. I came here on a hunch, and I won't rest until I try it out."

"Gyles, if you stay here any longer you're gonna rest here forever."

"Okay okay, wise guy. Just push open the door all the way. I need as much light as possible." Gyles sorted through the keys attached to the ring on which the tomb door key hung. There was a series of small, flat brass keys, twelve in all. Added to the left side wall of the mausoleum was a cabinetlike structure made from marble. It was divided by small, square bronze doors marked with the names of departed family members. These held urns of ashes, a necessary space-saving device for the crowded tomb. The last interment had been Great-aunt Florence in number ten. He found key number eight and inserted it into the corroded lock of the sealed niche marked Norma Stebbins Chilton.

"Gyles, are you crazy? You can't dig people up from a grave. That's disgusting."

Gyles made a face at Val and shoved the key into the lock with stubborn force. He heard a faint click as he turned the key and then pulled the small door open. Inside, a graceful bronze urn stood remarkably free of dust and corrosion. It looked as if it had just been placed there, except the death date read, August 15, 1939. He reached for the urn and was surprised at its weight. He carefully grabbed both side handles and lifted his great-aunt's funeral urn out of her grave. He set it on the floor and stepped back.

He was suddenly overcome with conflicting emotions, which he had not even considered. His own mother and father were buried below his great-aunt, and although he knew they must be there, he had been able to block them out and had never consciously looked upon that place. Here was visible proof of the greatest loss of his life, the loss he never cared to admit. He could hardly even remember them. Now he stared at their names and he was angry, anger that erupted from long-buried reservoirs of powerlessness, grief, and loss. Like molten magma contained beneath a hardened surface, Gyles had concealed his explosive core even from himself beneath the suave and sophisticated polish that he had cultivated so meticulously.

All this pretense was shattered as he gazed at his parent's names carved into the dull bronze. Suddenly the game he had been playing with his aunt's treasure hunt filled him with revulsion and fury. Gyles kicked Norma's urn with a strength he had never before allowed himself to feel. He staggered off balance from the impact, and, feeling like he was going to throw up, he ran from the tomb.

The clanging reverberations of the crashing bronze struck Val like quick punches to the head. He curled beneath cradling arms until the noise subsided. Outside Gyles staggered towards a thicket of lilac bushes, where his confused emotions heaved between nausea and sobbing.

Val had always existed in the vulnerable turbulence of emotion. He had seen men explode or crumble when they had tried to approach that secret, forbidden place where all souls crave comfort. He had been battered by the crass disguise that love wore on the street, the mask of lust, the helmet of fear.

Val didn't need Gyles's explanation to know how to help his friend. From a core place of uncomplicated love, he drew courage to enter the tomb and retrieve the contents of Norma's battered urn. There in a dark corner lay an object of gaudy brilliance. Val reached for it cautiously. He held his hand palm open a few inches away, testing its palpable emanations, half-expecting to feel a burning heat. But it was not on fire, so he grabbed it and put it into his pocket.

Looking around the tomb, he was surprised to discover that the urn had not been shattered, and although the lid and vase were bent, apparently the urn had been empty except for the mysterious object. Val sighed with relief, having imagined gritty flakes of blackened bones scattered all over the crypt. He could hardly believe the comparative order of the stone chamber. He reached for the cup and lid, fitting them together as best he could. He quickly replaced the urn in its marble niche, but as he closed the door he saw the unmistakable image of Anubis etched on the inside surface. Val mumbled from memory the lines of Wisner's message. "Anubis sits astride the tomb. At the gate he is looking back." Sure enough, the black jackal glared with defiance at the door of the tomb, as if challenging the very light that dared to enter his realm of darkness.

Val slammed the small bronze door of Norma's grave shut, quickly turning the key. He hurried from the tomb, pulling the heavy marble door closed after him. Nervously he rattled the keys on their brass ring, searching for the right one to lock this prison of death behind him.

*   *   *   *

Tatiana Sarkisian crushed the butt of her half-smoked cigarette into the ash-tray of the dashboard. The thin white paper wrapper of her Dunhill burst beneath excessive pressure. She sat behind the steering wheel, her eyes never leaving the entrance to the Chilton-Chichester tomb across the placid waters of Auburn Lake. The engine of her Rolls idled with a snarling purr, like a panther stalking its prey. Her vigil had been rewarded when she spied Gyles's Jeep pull up in front of the tomb twenty minutes earlier.

Tatiana had known that someone would come to this place where all stories ended for the great family. She only needed to wait, because here it would begin again. Eternity was like that, perpetually circling back to where the seed had been buried. Old Nagib Iskander had taught his granddaughter Tatiana to study the fear of mortality that masqueraded as mourning and with unction and ceremony to induce tears, which would water her prosperity.

When her brother had the effrontery to throw her out of the Greenbrier Funeral Home on the evening of Wisner's death, she knew he was desperate and bound for failure. But she refused to be outmaneuvered or concede defeat. After all, Nagib's fanatic delusions had rendered him useless to her. She knew where the heart of the mother lay. She considered the Chilton-Chichester tomb the Oracle, where she would place her faith. That faith had been rewarded when the fool had arrived with the keys. Then the unarmed and innocent Gyles Chilton had stumbled from the tomb, choked, blinded, and overwhelmed by the power of exhumed grief. That repressed travail had given birth to the solution even without his knowing. But Tatiana knew, and she took up the scent like Anubis, hound from hell, jackal of the necropolis. She would chase her prey back to its warren and there rout out the prize. The blood lust of the predator suited her sleek greed, and she trembled with anticipation, wiping a bit of drool on the back of her gloved hand. She grasped the wheel tightly, following the Jeep at a barely controlled distance.

CHAPTER 37

▼

Val parked Gyles's Jeep behind Rita's Alfa on Eagle Avenue, where Lotus Path began. The place had not been difficult to find. He'd remembered the general direction from Rita's map. He had simply headed that way and eventually spotted Rita's sports car. Gyles sat in the passenger seat smoking one of his Sobranies. His eyes saw nothing. After his shock in the tomb, he had retreated into a sullen silence. The smoke from his cigarette poured from the open window and hung in the air of the now still afternoon. The promised storm had passed without breaking, leaving the atmosphere heavy with unresolved tension and unnatural quiet.

Val stepped down from the Jeep and opened the passenger door for Gyles, but he did not press his lover to get out. Instead he went to look for Cornelia and Rita. He saw the two women walking towards him before he could go halfway down Lotus Path, and he waited for them to approach.

"Hi, Val."

"Hi, Rita."

"This has been a wild goose chase," complained Cornelia. "There's nothing even remotely resembling a tomb or mausoleum on Lotus Path, not to mention that this is hardly a place Norma Chilton would end up, impoverished or not. It is really dreary and very common. My Goddess, it's just the wrong side of the hill."

"Hi, Cornelia," prodded Val.

"Oh hi, Val, I didn't mean to ignore you, but this is such a disappointment, and if things weren't grim enough already, there's a dreadful funeral going on at the other end of the path, with a huge vulgar Cadillac hearse and an enormous black Lincoln, and an even larger Mercedes with tinted windows. I mean, really."

The subtle points of Cornelia's snobbery escaped Val, but he did ask her, "What was the license plate number of the Lincoln?"

"Val, how the hell should I know what the license plate—" Cornelia stopped in mid-sentence and stared at Val, suddenly remembering what he had said about the license plate of the black Lincoln that had abducted Wisner.

"Was it DEA-20-8?" suggested Val.

"I, I, I don't know. I didn't see. You don't think it's the same car? We're not being followed, are we? No one else knows about the tomb."

"Cornelia," interrupted Rita, "we don't even know if there is a tomb. Val, you are intentionally scaring her with your nonsense. What is DEA-20-8 anyway?"

Val and Cornelia replied in unison, "Death."

"Would you please? Look around you—this is a cemetery. What do you suppose goes on here every day? Funerals. People are buried here all the time. A hearse and black limousines are naturally going to be here."

"No, you look around, Rita. Where's the open grave if there's going to be a burial?" Val pressed. "And if we're not being watched, who's the broad in the black Rolls that was practically leaning on our bumper coming over here?"

"My Goddess, Tatiana!" cried Cornelia. "Let's get out of here. Rita, suddenly I don't care where Aunt Norma is buried. This place frightens me."

"Well, finally you've come to your senses, Cornelia Chilton. This morbid obsession of your brother's is his business. Let him hang out in a graveyard if he wants to. He seems to like dusty junk and dreadful places. He should be right at home here." Rita took Cornelia's arm and led her away, but Val came to Gyles's defense.

"Hey, Miss Thing, why don't you cool it? Your little Barbie doll here is just as much to blame for any of us being here today. It was her lousy jewelry that started the whole fuckin' mess."

"Don't ever call me Miss Thing, you stupid queen. I am a woman, not an object."

"Rita, Val, please stop it and let's go." Cornelia took her lover's arm again and led the way back to where the Alfa was parked, but before they reached the car Cornelia turned around to Val and asked, "Do you really think I act like Barbie?"

"No, I'm sorry, but I got angry."

Cornelia flashed him one of her most charming and concerned smiles and linked her free arm in his. Rita rolled her eyes and tried to wiggle free, but Cornelia held on to them both. As they arrived at the beginning of Lotus Path, where the Cherokee and Alfa were parked, both cars were empty and the passenger door of the Jeep was wide open.

"Val, where is Gyles, anyway?" asked Cornelia.

"I don't know. That is, I left him here in the Jeep. He was sort of upset, and I thought it would be best to leave him alone for a while."

"What do you mean he was upset? What happened?" Cornelia let go of Val's and Rita's arms. Val stammered, and Rita stood, arms akimbo, glaring sternly.

"I don't really know. He sort of lost it. He got sick. I mean, he kicked the pot and started crying. Well, I mean, he opened one of those graves and then he went berserk."

"What did he say to you?" asked Rita sharply.

"He didn't say anything to me. You wouldn't understand. Sometimes guys don't tell about stuff that bothers them. It was enough that I was there. He didn't have to tell me nothing."

Val hung his head, looking at his sneakers. He kicked the sand at the side of the road, avoiding the women's eyes because he couldn't explain what he understood about Gyles.

"Well, he's around here somewhere. I can smell his Sobranie," declared Cornelia as she realized the change in the weather. "It's funny how still everything is now, as if some force was sitting on us and compelling silence in order to listen."

In defiance and fear of the unseen presence, she slammed the Jeep door and marched off in the direction of the cigarette smoke. There was a stand of huge weeping beech trees in a rotary formed by the intersection of the roads nearby. The oversized trees spread thick blankets of bronze-colored leaves hanging from knotted silver branches like the arthritic fingers of a fantastic monster.

Cornelia disappeared into this dense foliage. Val and Rita scurried after her, not wanting to be left alone in each other's company. Inside the thicket was a twilight world of lofty, dim spaces. The trees dominated completely, and nothing else would grow beneath them. The thick curtains of leaves formed cathedral spaces of druidic secrecy.

In the midst of this sacred grove, half shrouded and jealously guarded by the huddled trees, stood a domed temple of Renaissance proportions and basilicalike design. The architect of this conceit had exercised all the strength of his imagination with brute force. There was a certain pagan excess to the pile of granite. It started with a classical temple fronted by a pillared portico. This was surmounted by a dome worthy of Michelangelo, sheathed in green copper and crowned by a cupola decorated with elaborate detail. Two obelisks, seventeen feet tall, stood as tireless sentries at the front of the building.

This was a mausoleum like no other at Mount Auburn. On the broad front steps sat Gyles, smoking his Sobranie and staring off in a daze. Cornelia maneuvered her way through the leaves and clinging branches. She brushed herself off and, looking up, gasped at the extravagant monument.

"Gyles, Gyles," she called her brother back from his abstraction.

"Oh hi, Corny. Pretty fantastic pile, ain't it?"

"Gyles, are you okay? Val said you were upset, that you went to the family tomb and saw something that disturbed you." Gyles looked at his sister, his head hanging to one side as if what she had said weighed him down. "Actually, he didn't say all that, but I thought that's what he meant."

"I saw Mom and Dad. I mean their graves. I just got so angry. I had forgotten about them, and I was caught off guard."

As Gyles looked at his sister, huge tears welled up in her large green eyes and ran down her face. He was immediately drawn out of himself by her pain. He tenderly held her face with both hands and rested his forehead against hers. He whispered, "We never talked about it. I'm sorry."

She said nothing, and their tears flowed together. There was rustling and a crack of branches. Rita wrestled her way through the trees, followed closely by Val. The two of them stood awkwardly silent, staring at Cornelia and Gyles. Although Val and Rita realized they were intruding, their protective concern would not allow them to withdraw. Rita, fishing for a distraction to relieve her embarrassment, looked up at the mausoleum and read aloud the name carved in the stone over the tall bronze doors.

"Si-buna. Sibuna. Sibuna? S-I-B-U-N-A. A-N-U-B-I-S! An-u-bis. Anubis! This is it! It's not hidden at all. It's the biggest mother in the whole place. Just look at it."

Cornelia and Gyles looked up and saw the name that Rita had read. "At the gate he is looking back," quoted Gyles. "It means the name is backwards. Anubis is the guardian of the western gate, so he naturally faces from east to west or from right to left. 'At the gate he is looking back.' And Sibuna then spells Anubis. Rita, you're right! Holy shit. No wonder it cost a fortune, it's more like a bank than a tomb."

Gyles, jarred from his melancholy by the grandeur of Norma Chilton's indulgence, strode boldly up the stone stairs to the tall bronze doors beneath the pillared portico. There he stopped abruptly, daunted by the staunch refusal of the doors to budge. He cursed himself for his stupidity. How was he to get in? With childish frustration he rattled the oversized ring that hung from a lion's mouth emerging from the door. The noise echoed inside the stone chamber, mocking him like the laugh of a madman.

Val stepped up to where Gyles was fuming. The dancer reached for the antique dealer's hand. Holding it in his own, he opened the clenched fist and placed on his lover's palm the gaudy object that had come from the urn marked Norma Chilton. Gyles flinched with surprise and would have dropped it had Val not been supporting his hand.

"It came out of the urn when you kicked it. There were no ashes, only this. It's what you need now."

Gyles's thick eyebrows knitted with concentration as he stared at the gold key in his hand. The long, cylindrical shaft was mounted with the image of Anubis surrounded by the great ennead, the nine gods of Egypt, all in minute detail and bright enameled colors. Cornelia stepped up to the door, and taking her brother's hand stared at the key with amazement. "Dear Goddess. It's the same workmanship as the cobra crown and the other jewels."

Rita joined the others and stared at the key. Slowly she put her arm about Cornelia's waist, no longer protesting the quest she now knew they all must face together. Gyles turned to face the doors, where beneath the lion's head he found the keyhole. Easing the golden key into the dark slot with gentle reverence, he twisted it. A screech issued from the long-closed lock, startling them all. The bronze doors swung slightly inward on their own weight, and a stale ammonia stink wheezed from the tomb. Again they recoiled. Gyles held his handkerchief to his nose and mouth while he shoved both doors wide open. A demonic cloud of shrieking creatures swarmed out at them. Everyone screamed and fled.

After a short time there was quiet again, and Gyles called out to the others, "It's only bats. They're gone. Come back and see. This place is unbelievable." Val cautiously peered from behind the shield of leaves where he had dived for cover. Above him he heard rustlings and high-pitched squeaks. He realized the bats had settled in the upper tree branches. With a shudder rippling through him, he quickly stepped from his hiding place. Hearing the same noise, Cornelia screamed and leapt into the air from where she had been cowering beneath a thick curtain of leaves. She landed in Val's arms, proving the amazing providence of chaos. But she was not at all comforted by her rescue. She wasn't alone in her confusion. Val had not expected to land a prize the size of Cornelia. It was only his dancer's training that allowed him to keep his balance long enough to break the fall that was inevitable from such a collision.

Rita emerged from the foliage grumbling pettishly but was stopped short when she caught sight of Cornelia sprawled over Val and she had to control a spasm of jealousy. Cornelia brushed herself off, discovering she was remarkably unscathed by this latest debacle. She faced Val, said, "Thank you." and marched off to the mausoleum.

*   *   *   *

The bronze doors were opened wide, allowing a view of grandeur conceived without modesty. When she first caught sight of the interior Cornelia slowed her pace. Transfixed by what she saw, she walked up the blue granite stairs and passed slowly between the Corinthian columns that supported the high portico. She stood on the threshold, gaping with awe, and she reached for her shawl to pulled it up and cover her hair.

Gyles stood in the center of the room, dwarfed beneath the swelling dome. Straining to see the magnificent polychrome and gold mosaic that entirely sheathed the inside of the dome, he bent back his head. Even in the late afternoon light the effect was dazzling. Formed by a myriad of small glazed tiles, the mosaic depicted a lush garden, Eden regained, a place abundant with plant and animal life and watered by streams and cascading rivers.

Cornelia's attention was commanded at a more earthly height by a more spiritual subject. She was enraptured by an angel depicted in layers of opaline stained glass, creating an image of three-dimensional holography. This angel appeared to emerge from the mists of time. If there ever had been a convincing image of the Goddess, this was it.

Val poked his head around the corner of the open door and said, "Wow. Pretty classy joint. No wonder you people think so much of yourselves."

"You've at least got that one right," Rita grudgingly agreed from the other side of the doorway. "I've never seen a more grotesque waste and oppressive extravagance."

Cornelia sighed and swallowed her exasperation against Rita's unwarranted attack on her family, denying as it did the profound beauty of the chapel. Cornelia had trained herself to hear the fear and intimidation that lay beneath Rita's rash bluster, as Rita knew the depth and seriousness beneath Cornelia's decorative frivolity.

Val entered, slowly looking around and above. He circled the center space, his eyes never resting. In slow motion and with sweeping arcs, his head took in the spacious marble chamber.

Gyles caught Val by the hand and wrapped his arm around the dancer's shoulders. Pointing above them, he told his lover, "This is one of the most magnificent mosaics I've ever seen. It reminds me of the ceiling of the great choir at Saint Paul's in London."

"Gosh, it reminds me of the Public Garden in springtime. You know there are a lot of ducks there too."

Gyles found Val's comparison both apt and charming, and he squeezed his friend's shoulders.

"So where's the Egyptian tomb and all the other booga-booga?" asked Rita, striding over to where Cornelia stood staring at the angel window, which constituted almost the entire back wall.

"Well, it's not here, Rita, but look at her. Isn't she beautiful?"

"Stunning if you go in for flapping females wafting about in their night-gowns."

"Rita, shut up," said Cornelia in her sweetest tone. But Rita was right. There was not a hint of Egypt in the cool classicism of this Renaissance Revival interior, constructed with several colors of highly polished marble reaching a height of twenty feet. An arrangement of pilasters, arches, and freestanding columns topped with Corinthian capitals supported the dome. At its fullest height the vault was pierced by a cupola that rose another ten feet and was in turn capped by a smaller dome coated in gold and painted with blue stars.

"Where's the Egyptian tomb?"

"I don't know that I really care," mused Gyles, half to himself.

"Gyles, what do you mean? You know something's going on here. This is it. But this is not all. I mean, it's a lovely chapel and I'm thrilled to discover it and proud of its beauty, but there must be more. There's just got to be. What did Wisner's note say? Do you have it with you still? You had it when we were all on top of the tower."

Gyles sat down on the marble steps leading up to the altarlike casket that lay beneath the angel window. This chilling receptacle was made from imperial red porphyry, and its heavy stone lid had spiraling ends like rolling scrolls. The upper edge of the casket beneath the lid was decorated with a low-relief frieze of unfurling acanthus leaves.

Val stood behind Gyles, leaning against the cold stone tomb in his usual slouching pose. With one finger he followed along the leaf design, delighting in the undulations of the sculpture.

After searching all his pockets for Wisner's note, Gyles finally came across it in the breast pocket of his jacket.

"Here it is," he said, now weary of the perplexing puzzle. He read the now familiar message aloud. "The lotus path within the necropolis. From the tower of the mountain forest. Anubis sits astride the tomb. At the gate he is looking back. With the ankh he will pierce the wedjat eye."

"Apparently we've gotten as far as the inside of the tomb, so the pertinent line now is the last," reasoned Cornelia, pacing in front of the red stone casket before which her brother sat.

"What on earth is an ankh and a wedjat eye?" demanded Rita.

"An ankh is like this," said Gyles, holding up the amulet that hung around his neck. It was a medium-sized metal cross that had a loop above the horizontal arms instead of the vertical post of Christian martyrdom. "It's a sign of eternity."

"Oh yeah, I've seen those before. All the punks with dyed black hair and nose rings wear those. Yuck! I hope that doesn't mean they're eternal. Where did you get such a thing anyway?" Rita asked.

"Well, it's a long story, but suffice it to say that it came from around the neck of a statue of Anubis in my aunt Norma's bedroom."

"Boy, you people get weirder all the time. So what's the wedjat eye?"

"I'm not really sure, but isn't the wedjat eye the amulet depicting an eye heavily ringed with kohl and a funny curling teardrop trailing down from the bottom lid?"

"I don't know, you tell me. Is it or isn't it?" Rita countered Gyles's rhetorical question. But before Gyles could reply, Val nudged him sharply with his elbow.

"That hurt," protested Gyles, twisting around to frown at Val.

Val mimed a jabbing thumb towards a point dead center on the red porphyry casket, where his finger had been idly playing. They all stared at a plain round disk that interrupted the luxurious acanthus leaf frieze. There, etched deeply into the precious marble, was the wedjat eye, its dilated pupil staring, a black negative space beckoning, daring, and calling to fulfill the inescapable destiny that had drawn them to the very edge of the grave. A long, awful silence punctuated this discovery.

Gyles's expression was so intense he scared Val, who said nervously, "I sort of was messing around, and I found it."

"Boy did you ever!" Gyles exclaimed. He realized that each one of them had contributed a piece of the puzzle. Even Rita's skeptical inquisitions had helped grind away the shaft concealing the hidden kernel that lay buried beneath them. His hand clutched the ankh hanging on his chest. No one said a word. He lifted the amulet up and bowed his head, releasing the cord from around his neck.

He stared at the ankh in his hand. How did it come to be there? Had he brought it or had it brought him? Why had he taken it from the statue of Anubis to begin with? What was the compelling attraction? Unlike the other Egyptian jewelry, including the gaudy key to this grand mausoleum, the ankh was plain, even ordinary. Was that the secret of the amulet, to disguise itself as mundane, so that the uninitiated, the unwary, and the unguarded would be drawn into its exact and prescribed drama? What was reason and what was happenstance, and did these questions matter?

Gyles, the hereditary holder of the keys, had acquired this most important key not by primogeniture from his ancestor Cosmo Chilton but from a more ancient and powerful source. One for whom Anubis had been the messenger. Anubis, the guardian of the western gate.

Gyles obeyed the summons. With the ankh he pierced the wedjat eye. He twisted it as he would any key, and sure enough, it turned. He could feel a light resistance to his motion, but no protest or sound greeted the release of the lock. Neither did the lid budge. He studied the casket, wondering what to do. The stone lid must weigh a great deal, and he did not want to risk hurting himself or the others by wrenching the casket open. After all, it stood a good four feet from the floor of the mausoleum. If the monolith were carelessly upturned, it might crash to the floor, and how would they replace it? What if the desiccated corpse of Norma Chilton lay inside the imperial stone grave? With this last thought he was frozen with fear and revulsion, painfully remembering his reaction in the other tomb.

Cornelia, frustrated beyond her own similar fears, could no longer wait for her brother to act. She stepped up to the casket, and, without regard for the superhuman effort that would be required to lift the lid, she gave it all her strength, grunting like a champion weightlifter. To everyone's surprise, the stone swung upward easily, thrust by bronze arcs emerging from the walls of the casket. These armatures were sturdily bolted to the inside cover. The quick swing of the lid knocked Cornelia off balance, and she lurched over the edge, her upper body falling into the negative space of the casket.

The two men and Rita gasped as Cornelia teetered on the brink of the grave. She had moved so impetuously that none of the three could have stopped her. Now they all lunged to the rescue, but Rita brusquely deflected the men's efforts and retrieved her lover with her own capable and sturdy arms.

"Good Goddess, Neil. Please, please be careful," begged Rita as she guided Cornelia to sit on the steps before the casket.

"Ree," whispered Cornelia.

"What is it, Neil, what is it?"

"Ree, there are stairs."

"Hush, sweetheart. You've had a shock." Rita rocked Cornelia in her arms.

"Holy shit, she's right. The thing's full of stairs," Val exclaimed.

Gyles roused himself from where he hovered about his sister and Rita. Reluctantly he peered over the edge of the open casket. Cornelia wriggled free from her lover's solicitude. Standing on tiptoe next to her brother, she also stared inside the casket. A long, narrow flight of stairs descended into the thick darkness.

"How could you possibly have lifted that slab of stone, Cornelia?" Gyles asked, as if trying to avoid the beckoning stairs.

"I don't know. It didn't seem like any weight at all. That's why I fell in. I was psyched out to press the biggest weight of my career. I did everything J.J. taught me. Breathe out, straight back, think tall. But when I pushed the damn thing, it just flew up as if it weighed nothing."

"Who's J.J., Cornelia?" asked Gyles.

"J.J.'s my trainer at the Woman's Space Health Club. Did you think I was born with this body?"

"I must admit that I haven't given it much thought."

Gyles played with his moustache, contemplating the open casket. Val, ever more direct, took hold of the lid and pulled it down several inches. The stone slab traveled on the sturdy bronze arcs receding into the walls of the casket. He pushed the opposite way and the lid rose easily, stopping on its own volition, having swung open about eight inches, bringing with it a comparable length of the bronze armatures.

Val was about to repeat his experiment with more confidence and greater strength when Gyles clamped his fist on his wrist. "Val, don't do that," he commanded.

Val shook free of Gyles's grasp and snapped back, "Chill out, man, this ain't the military, you know."

"Sorry, Val, but look." Gyles pointed at the inside surface of the lid. Its polished red porphyry was incised with the portrait in profile of Anubis. Beneath the crouching omnipresent jackal was the warning Twice opened I shall be, and then closed for all eternity. Gyles read the line, and then, thinking aloud, he said, "I'm sure that these are Norma's words. And she meant them. The lid must weigh a quarter of a ton at least, but it is easily manipulated by some kind of counterweight system attached to these bronze armatures. The whole mechanism is very clever. We should be on our guard."

"Yeah. Maybe your sweet Aunt Norma is going to come up from the grave and grab you by the throat." Val mocked Gyles's warning because he was still stung by his sharp command.

"Yes, Val, I'm beginning to believe Norma Chilton might cause anything to happen if it suited her purpose."

"You're crazy. The old bitch is dead and gone. You're afraid of this thing closing on us? Fine, let's jam it so it can't close."

Val spun around, spotting one of several bronze standard lamps positioned around the chapel. Before Gyles had time to protest, Val took up the lamp, inadvertently tearing loose a dusty electrical plug from an outlet in the wall. He remarked with wonder, "Geez, the joint is wired for electricity. Maybe Norma Baby is hanging out in a freezer in the basement."

Gyles realized that Val's bad jokes were only cover for a mounting fear they all felt. As he brought the lamp towards the casket, lowering it horizontally, the alabaster bowl that formed a shade for the light bulb began to teeter. Gyles caught it before it fell and smashed.

"Val, you've got a great idea. Just hold on one second, huh?"

Gyles unscrewed the bulb, disengaged the opaque stone shade, and laid them safely in a corner. By the time he had looked up, Val had already wedged the length of the lamp inside a corner of the casket. Gyles inspected the brace carefully before he nodded his approval. Then he turned his whole attention to the staircase and said, "Okay, Corny, if you want to go first, I can give you a leg up."

"Over my dead body. Cornelia is not crawling into any grave, and that's final."

"Rita, you may think that's final, but the dead don't stay put around here. So you won't make a heap of difference," Val wisecracked.

"Rita, it's okay, I want to go. But, Gyles, why don't you go first? We'll follow."

"Okay, Sis, have it your way. I was just trying to be nice," Gyles said as, with one long leg extended, he climbed into the casket. Bending almost double beneath the red stone lid, he was careful not to disturb the lamp wedging the casket open. As he descended into the darkness, he called back, half-joking, "I don't suppose anyone brought a flashlight."

Cornelia called down to him, her voice echoing against the stone passage. "Feel on the wall for a light switch. If there's electricity up here, there must be down there."

"That's ridiculous. Who pays the light bill, Norma Chilton?" snapped Rita.

Cornelia responded, "Well, Rita, you're probably right after a fashion. For example, the Chilton-Chichester tomb is endowed several times over. It's called perpetual care. Even Nebuchadnezzar has a separate fund."

"Who the hell is Nebuchadnezzar?"

"Oh never mind, it's a long story, and now that I think of it, you'd only be outraged."

"Cornelia Chilton, don't patronize me."

"Rita, shut up and give me a boost."

"Oh nice, now I'm supposed to shove my lover into the grave."

"Rita!"

Cornelia scrambled over the wall of the casket, stepping in Rita's reluctantly proffered hand. She reached back over the edge to help Rita up. The accountant's Birkenstocks slipped on the polished stone, and Val assisted from behind with a friendly push.

"Hey! Watch it Buddy."

"Excuse me, I was only trying to help."

"Rita, come on, take my hand," called Cornelia.

The narrow stairs led straight down into the cold, dark crypt. As they descended, a damp, musty smell enveloped them. The stairs stopped abruptly, leaving the four in a chamber filled with black ether. No walls or ceiling could be felt. With eyes wide open, they could see nothing but empty and complete darkness.

A voice said, "This must be what it's like to be blind. I can't see anything. Where are the lights? Give me your hand, I'm afraid I'll get lost."

"We're already lost. Gyles, what happened to you?"

"I'm here looking for a light switch."

"Wow! Who's that?"

"It's me. What happened to the walls? This place must be enormous."

"Can anyone see?"

"I can make out the top of the stairs, but that's all."

There was a sputtering noise accompanied by blue sparks, and then a tiny blue flame lit Gyles's face. Deep shadows carved a fearsome visage from his familiar features. The flame flickered and died, plunging them into total darkness again.

"Damn, my lighter went out," cursed Gyles, his frustration fed by fear. He tried again. The same sputtering was heard. This time the flame stayed. He held the light above his head, trying to visualize the crypt, but the dimensions of the chamber were too immense and the light was swallowed before it met any reflective surface. In fact, the light was hardly strong enough to illumine the four souls huddled together in the darkness.

Gyles said, "You all stay here. I'm going to try to find a wall and hopefully the light switch. If I don't succeed, we'll have to come back another day with flashlights."

"Not me," contradicted Rita. "Once I get out of here, I'm never coming back."

As Gyles inched his way into the thick darkness, Val retraced his steps up the stairs, quickly playing a hunch.

"Oh great, now both of them have left us alone in a blind grave. Cornelia, if you ever wondered why you should never trust a man, remember this moment."

"Rita, I'm scared. Hold on to me. Where are you?"

"I'm right here, Neil. I'm not going to leave you."

Just then a flash of dazzling light filled the space with a noiseless explosion and instantly vanished. Rita and Cornelia flinched, covering their eyes with their hands. Behind the shield of their tightly closed eyes, they could not escape the demonic hallucinations that were imprinted inside their minds' eyes. A host of animistic creatures strutting in procession with white mummies encased in bandages. Gyles stood frozen with horror, not daring to move. In the lightning flash he had been confronted by a pantheon of zoomorphic images, whose brilliance burned into his brain and then disappeared into the darkness. The lights came on again, and this time they stayed. Gyles rubbed his eyes and squinted, trying to adjust to the light.

Scrambling down the steep stairs into the crypt, Val saw Gyles at the edge of a fall and screamed, "Freeze!" The two women screamed and clutched each other. Gyles lurched back, tripping on them, and all three went sprawling on the dusty stone floor.

Val scurried down to assist, saying, "Geez, I'm sorry I scared you, but look."

Gyles, Cornelia, and Rita pried their eyes open, blinking against the light. As their pupils began to adjust, they all froze in silence. They were in a round, vaulted stone crypt. The stairs ended on a round stone platform about ten feet in diameter. Beyond this platform an abyss gaped.

Gyles tried to recover from the shock of having nearly plummeted to his death, asking Val, "How'd you find the light switch?"

"It was simple. I went back upstairs and shoved the lid of the coffin open all the way, like you wouldn't let me do before. I guessed that would trigger the lights, 'cause Lilly's closet has the same thing. That's how I figured it."

"Of course. Lilly has come to the rescue once again. Why didn't I think of that?" Gyles threw up his hands, weakly disguising his own chagrin.

Cornelia picked herself up off the floor and stared with disbelief at the murals that covered the circular walls of the crypt. They duplicated the gaudy picture-graph designs of the tomb plans found in Norma Chilton's ledger book. A procession of animal-headed gods in bright, flat colors densely covered the walls.

Between the figures were columns of hieroglyphic writing, animated with flapping birds, crawling beetles, slithering snakes, and crouching stick figures. All of these picturegraphs were also aligned with a myriad of mysterious symbols, including floating eyes and dismembered limbs. The stiff bodies in profile had a supernatural vitality. They defied decay, and the ancient gods obsessively tended to the tightly wrapped mummies. As the four stared at the walls, they felt above them a deep rumbling which grew in volume.

"What the hell is that?" demanded Rita, grasping Cornelia's hand. "It sounds like chanting voices."

"Sounds more like rap music to me. It's probably some jerk up there with a boom box" was Val's idea.

"Val, darling, is it really very likely for a rap enthusiast to be lounging around a mausoleum in Mount Auburn Cemetery?" asked Cornelia delicately.

"Well, Miss Hoity Toity, you've got a hustler, a queen, and two dykes here already. I'm expecting almost anyone," Val retorted.

The rhythmic drone grew louder, compelling their silence, and now words could be discerned. "Praise to Ra when he riseth in the eastern part of heaven. Behold Osiris, Ani the scribe who recordeth the holy offerings of all the gods. Who sayeth, 'Homage to thee, oh thou who has come, Khepera, the creator of the gods. Thou resteth, thou shineth, making bright thy mother crowned queen of the gods.'"

As they listened with disbelief to the fantastic words of the droning chant, a figure of a man began to descend the stairs. He wore only a white pleated kilt and sandals. His body was hairless, and his flawless skin was the color of desert sand lit by moonlight. His powerful build showed taut and defined muscles. Above bulging shoulders he wore the black hooded mask of Anubis, with pointed snout and erect ears. The haughty eyes glared at the four friends. He bore down on them, a giant standing almost seven feet tall. Behind the half-naked Anubis appeared a procession of men incongruously dressed in black suits. Two of them bore a litter on their shoulders that carried a weight not yet discernible from below.

Gyles assumed a position in front of the others and demanded, "Who are you, and what are you doing here?"

From behind the mask an equally authoritative reply was heard. "I am Anubis, guardian of the western gate, weigher of the heart and judge of the dead."

"Watch out, Gyles, this queen's lost her marbles and could be dangerous," warned Val.

Gyles ignored his friend. Not bothering to contradict the absurd character before him, he cut to the point of the matter and demanded, "Anubis, is it? Well, why are you here?"

"You put up a brave front, cousin. You might have been a worthy opponent, but there is no more time for sparring. I came here to bury the mother, queen of darkness, source of the river. She will flood our lands with the water of life, and I will reap her golden harvest."

"Are you aware of the fact that you are on private property?"

Anubis and his minions did not exactly retreat or quaver in response to Gyles's question. Rather, they came forward, crowding the circular platform at the base of the stairs. It was Cornelia who realized first what was on the litter that two of the scowling men carried.

"Good Goddess, they've got a body. No, it's a mummy. All wrapped in bandages. And it's wearing my cobra crown!"

As the last of the men descended, Val made a move to dash up the stairs, but the figure of Anubis snatched him back. Like a predator pouncing on its victim, he caught Val by the scruff of the neck, and, holding him in a vicelike grasp, he dragged him off the stairs and dumped him in a heap at his feet.

"Cower, slave. Prepare yourself for attending the queen of darkness for all eternity."

With bravado that wouldn't quit, Val dished, "Geez Louise, this queen's gotta be on crack."

"Silence," bellowed the black jackal.

Rita was the next to confront the gruesome parade of men who had invaded the crypt.

"Listen, I don't care what you're up to, but this woman and I are leaving here right now, and don't try to stop us because I know karate." To prove her point, she gave a savage upward kick to the towering animal-headed man blocking the stairs. He dodged her kick and missed being hit in the groin by fractions of an inch. Rita's foot flew into the air, throwing her off balance. She fell sprawling on the stone floor, narrowly missing the edge of the platform. Her Birkenstock rocketed across the room. Slamming against the wall, it disappeared into the abyss. After a count of three, the sandal could be heard hitting the unseen depths below. Cornelia dived for her lover and held on for dear life. Two of Anubis's guards reached into their jackets and pulled out loaded and cocked revolvers.

Anubis turned to Gyles. "Cousin, I must congratulate and thank you for having opened the tomb so long sealed. Pity Wisner did not live to see this day. Foolish man. He tried to hide the heart of the mother from me. Now even eternal rest will be denied him, because Eben Chichester burnt his carcass. I would have made him a beautiful mummy, like I did for Grandmother." The towering demigod leaned over Cornelia gloating and continued, "You were right, cousin, that is the cobra crown that you so lately wore, but your great-aunt was jealous of your beauty, and she sent me to fetch her regalia back."

Gyles interrupted the ghoulish monologue and asked, "Why do you call us 'cousin'? Who are you?"

"Because we are of one royal blood. I am Nagib, grandson of Norma Chilton and Nagib Iskander." The voice behind the mask grew in volume. With one swift movement the giant wrenched the jackal head from his human shoulders, revealing a livid face drenched with sweat and splashed with a curse. The man raised his arms in a sweeping gesture and bellowed, "I am he who tends the dead, the keeper of the western gate. The one who weighs the heart and judges the soul. I am Anubis."

"Get over it, Mary, you're nothing but a dog, and your skirt's too short." Val's quick jab made Gyles laugh nervously.

This irreverence inflamed the towering demon, who, with one powerful arm wearing a golden circlet above his bicep, snatched the ankh that hung around Gyles's neck with such force that he snapped the linen cord as if it were a thread.

"With the ankh I will pierce the wedjat eye," bellowed Anubis triumphantly. He dropped to his knees at the center of the drum platform. There, carved into the paving stone, was another magical weeping wedjat eye. The man-jackal thrust the ankh into the pupil of the eye and twisted it with vicious strength. It rotated, and he pulled out a stone plug and set it aside. One of his minions handed him an instrument. He snatched it greedily and shoved its metal shaft into the enlarged hole. This tool had a perpendicular handle about three feet above the floor. It took two men to crank the mechanism. As Anubis chortled hysterically, the men worked up a fast sweat.

A stone bridge about two feet wide inched across the dark space. Cornelia recoiled at this inanimate erection probing the empty moat. She sensed its irrevocable defilement of the virginal emptiness, and she intuitively knew that there was only one way over this bridge, to hell and no return. The stone monolith collided with the opposite curved wall and ground its way into a dusty slot with complaint and crude force. On the wall where the bridge came to rest was a painted doorway filled by two wooden doors painted with vertical lines of hieroglyphics and a splendid golden mummy wrapped in linen bandages, embraced by multicolored wings of vultures and hawks.

Anubis covered the length of the narrow stone bridge with three long strides. He burst through the wooden doors and disappeared into a dark passageway. The suited henchman grabbed Gyles and Val and shoved them towards the bridge.

"Oh no, I'm not going nowhere with that nut, especially not—"

"Val, shut up, this is certainly no time to argue," shouted Gyles.

"Hey man, chill out. Whadda ya think they're gonna do, shoot me?"

In swift response to this dare, there was a terrible explosion, and searing white fire burned Val's shoulder. Cornelia screamed, and Rita roared, "Any of you bastards touch her and you're dead!"

Val, gritting his teeth, swallowed the sob of terror in his throat. Clasping his bloodied shoulder with one hand, he hissed at his assassin, "Fuckin' asshole."

Gyles moved swiftly towards his lover, not really comprehending what had happened, but Val shook himself free. He barked angrily, "It's just a scratch. The bastard's a lousy shot. But I guess that means we're going this way."

With the grit and guts of a lonely street hustler, Val swaggered over the bridge.

CHAPTER 38

▼

The shot echoed through the crypt, reverberating against the hard stone walls of the mausoleum above. An acrid smell of gunpowder rose from the open porphyry casket. At the same moment, Mr. Charlie's cab came to a screeching halt between Gyles's Jeep Cherokee and Rita's Alfa Romeo.

Lucy Ann burst from the cab, saying, "They're here, I knew it. Come on, Charlie, don't drag your butt now. We've gotta go after them."

"Lucy Ann, baby, hold on. I can't leave my cab here. This ain't our sort of place. They don't want us here. Come on back now, and leave Mr. Gyles and Miss Cornelia to their own business."

"Charlie, I know you mean well, but God help me this is my business. You say they're not my babies. You're right. Mine were torn from me by that hateful woman. These kids are all I have. I'll follow them into hell and drag them back if need be."

"Lucy Ann, you are a black woman. Those people are white. Don't you know better? They ain't children, and they ain't yours."

"No, Charlie, there are things about this family you don't know. Things I thought died with Miss Norma years ago. But that woman won't stay dead. She won't leave me alone. That bitch was my mother, and she wouldn't even admit it. I'll be damned if she's going to ruin their lives too."

Mr. Charlie was too surprised to move. He watched as Lucy Ann charged ahead, her long legs swinging beneath her full skirt. Before he could decide whether to follow, she had disappeared into the thick foliage. Charlie lit a Lucky Strike and prepared himself to wait.

Lucy Ann knew exactly where she was going, although she had not been to this place for over fifty years. During the last years of Norma Chilton's life, the increasingly reclusive woman had made Lucy Ann drive her to Mount Auburn Cemetery time and time again. They always went to the same place, the immense and forbidding mausoleum. There the grand dame draped in black veils would enter and spend an hour alone. When she reemerged, she would make Lucy Ann pull the tall bronze doors shut and lock them with the pagan key. On the return journey to their house in Back Bay, Norma would swear Lucy Ann to secrecy about their errand. It was the nature of Norma Chilton to be obeyed, and so the young girl did as she was told.

Lucy Ann walked up the stairs of the mausoleum to the bronze doors. Fifty years peeled away from her life in a flash. Fifty years of acquired armor, the shield of forgetfulness. She felt the unreasoned fear of a young girl return. The powerful presence of Norma Chilton bore down on her, and she began to buckle beneath the weight.

But in defiance she cried aloud, "Woman, the love you could have had freely you are not going to take from me now. I curse you and blame you. You are dead, now get aside."

Lucy Ann pushed the door open. She hugged the handbag hanging from her shoulder beneath her elbow. She could feel the weight of her small revolver beneath the soft leather of her purse, but she was not sure whether this gave her more or less courage.

As Boston had grown tougher in the sixties, Mr. Charlie had insisted that Lucy Ann be armed. He took her to buy a gun and showed her how to care for it and how to shoot it. As Lucy Ann stared up at the stained glass angel above the open casket, the obvious reference to resurrection struck her. She was shaken by the idea that her gun might have no effect against the power unleashed in this cold and lonely tomb. But the memory of secret shame filled her with anger again. She proceeded into the empty chamber, and her footsteps echoed a mocking ghostly response. Bracing herself for the worst, she peered into the open casket and was startled to see the staircase leading down to the crypt.

Again her resolve quailed at the thought of descending into a grave, and she called out, "Norma Chilton, you are a twisted and stingy woman. I said I would go to hell and back, and bitch, you better believe it."

Having thus rallied the courage of a righteous crusader, Lucy Ann hefted her aging self over the edge of the red porphyry casket, descending the steep steps into the unknown.

*   *   *   *

A black Rolls-Royce stealthily eased by the Checker Cab parked beside Lotus Path. The cabbie sat pensively smoking his Lucky Strike. He was so surprised by the quiet sedan suddenly right beside him that he did an exaggerated double take. But so awed was he by the beautiful machine that he hardly noticed the driver. She, however, took careful note of Charlie, the empty Cherokee, and the Alfa parked there also.

Tatiana circled the area of Lotus Path. At the other end from the waiting cab, she passed the empty cortège. The vehicles parked beside the road were all too familiar to her.

"Nagib has gotten here first. Well, let him do the dirty work." The woman behind the wheel narrated her observations aloud to herself. "He longed for the glory of eternity, and he should be given what he wants. Tiresome, foolish, deluded Nagib. I have something for you that will link you with the heart of our mother forever." A cramped twitch disturbed the smoky beauty of Tatiana, the closest she would come to laughter that afternoon. Her Rolls-Royce glided by the rotary, where, through a cover of overgrown weeping beech trees, she caught a glimpse of a green copper dome crowned by an ostentatious cupola.

Tatiana immediately parked in the shadow of a thicket of rhododendrons. She went to the trunk and opened it. Tossing in her sable, she slammed the lid quickly and walked towards the tall beech trees, her long stride stretching the tight skirt of her black Chanel suit. She fumbled with her clutch purse, jamming in a snub-nosed revolver. Without looking back she activated the car alarm from her key ring. Its screeching reply was not musical.

Standing in the thick cover of beeches, Tatiana strained to hear a distant droning, which she could not identify. Perplexed but emboldened by the deserted aspect of the mausoleum, she approached the half-open doors. The droning became an audible chant. She could make out a phrase or two. "Glory to Osiris, Un-nefer the great god within Abydos, king of eternity, lord of the everlasting." The voices came from a distance, so she felt safe to peer inside. Seeing no one in the upper chamber, she proceeded directly to the open casket and looked into it. Suddenly the chant stopped, and she froze listening. A rumble of angry voices could be heard, but still at some distance. She judged the moment to be right, and with awkward determination she wriggled over the edge of the casket and disappeared down the stairs.

*   *   *   *

Eben Chichester arrived in the vicinity of Lotus Path, driving his diesel-fueled Mercedes, which left a trail of stink in the otherwise clear spring air. After scanning the area closely, he drove to where the empty hearse and accompanying limousines were parked. As he pulled in back of the Lincoln, his three male passengers got out, all dressed in dark suits. The first man pulled a flat, shiny aluminum strip from the sleeve of his jacket. The thin, flexible metal was about two feet long and two inches wide. He inserted the strip between the window glass and the tight rubber gasket of the Lincoln's driver's side window. The man pulled upward fast, and the chromium knob of the door lock shot up. The second man opened the door and slipped behind the wheel, where he jabbed the ignition with a series of small metal probes. The engine turned over and began to hum. The first and the third man repeated this routine with the hearse and then the Mercedes with the tinted windows. When all three automobiles of the cortège were started, Eben gave a nod, and the procession glided forth sedately and without haste.

Eben then drove around to the other end of Lotus Path, where he parked his Mercedes behind Gyles's Jeep and got out. He walked up to Mr. Charlie's Checker Cab and said, "Hi there, I'm Eben Chichester."

Mr. Charlie crushed out his Lucky and replied, "Afternoon, Mr. Chichester."

"You're Charles Jennings, aren't you?"

"Yes sir. The very one. But everyone calls me Mr. Charlie."

"That's it. Charlie. Weren't you at one time my great-aunt's chauffeur?"

"Lord, Mr. Chichester, that time's been and gone long past. Seems like nothin' you don't know." Mr. Charlie shifted uncomfortably on the beaded seat cover of his cab. Sweat oozed from his forehead.

"Yes, Charlie, I like to keep informed. I have a message for you from Lucy Ann."

Charlie interrupted the lawyer. "You've seen Lucy Ann, Mr. Chichester?"

"Yes I did. And she says you can go on without her. Gyles will give her a lift home."

"Lucy Ann told you that, Mr. Chichester?" asked Mr. Charlie, wiping his forehead with an immaculate white handkerchief and stalling for time.

"Yes, Charlie, and here's something for your trouble." The lawyer palmed a folded twenty over to the cabbie.

"Oh no sir, there's no charge for Lucy Ann. She and me go way back."

"That's from me, Charlie. I know how hard you work, and I don't want you to miss any more business. Now so long, see you in the city."

Mr. Charlie reluctantly started his Checker and eased on down the road. But he didn't like to leave Lucy Ann behind. When he could no longer see the lawyer in his rearview mirror, he doubled back up the hill to a spot not far away and pulled over to the side of the road.

Eben Chichester returned to his Mercedes, and reaching inside beside the gear shaft, he disengaged his car phone. He dialed a number, and, leaning against the driver's side door, he listened to a pleasant voice say, "Good afternoon, Mount Auburn Cemetery, Office of the Director, this is Miss Townsend."

"Good afternoon, Miss Townsend. This is Eben Chichester. Is Bill in?"

"Oh yes, Mr. Chichester. Mr. Kirkland is in his office. Will you please hold one minute?"

"Yes, thank you, Miss Townsend."

There was a brief pause, and Eben tilted up the rearview mirror to check his perfectly knotted silk tie.

"Hello, Eben, is that you?" a hearty voice greeted the lawyer.

"Yes, Bill, I hope all goes well with you, old man. Will we see you in Nahant this weekend for the regatta?"

"Wouldn't miss it for the world, Eben, although my poor old tub hasn't a chance against your rig."

"Oh well, we shall see. I haven't got your crew either." Eben demurred easily. Modesty was a pose he could well afford. "Bill, I would like you to do something for me. I'm here at Mount Auburn with my young cousins on some family business."

Bill Kirkland interrupted. "Uh, by the way, terribly sorry about Wisner. Seems like all the great men are going now."

Eben's left eyebrow raised with silent protest against this generous assessment of his recently departed uncle. But he replied with honeyed hypocrisy, "Thank you, and how right you are." He allowed a moment's silence, steering the conversation into the wind before he shoved the tiller in the opposite direction, coming about on a tack that would steal the wind from his challenger's sails.

"Bill, there's a Checker Cab loitering in our neighborhood. I'm sure he's a perfectly harmless fellow, but not our sort, don't you know. I wonder if you could send over someone from security to help him find the most direct way to the front gate."

"Of course, Eben. Glad to be of assistance. These things do happen in an institution as large as ours. I'm terribly sorry you were bothered. We're open to the general public, but I'm glad to say we still have jurisdiction. Tell me where you are."

Eben replied with intentional evasion about his own whereabouts. "The cab is on the back side of the tower mountain. Your man can't miss him."

"Should I give orders for my man to stay in the area?"

"Not necessary, old man. In fact, we prefer to be left alone. That's the point, you see. Delicate time with families, as you know. So thanks awfully. My best to Marge. Bye, Bill."

Eben Chichester liked to tie up loose ends before they became entangled in the rigging. Because of his shipshape discipline, he rarely lost a race. Satisfied that his course was plotted in safe waters, he sailed towards that harbor of the soul, the mausoleum of Anubis, where he expected to breeze across the finish line and claim his prize.

*   *   *   *

Gyles and Val had been slammed up against a wall. They stood there cramped and aching, but they did not dare move and had long since stopped complaining. The flesh wound on Val's shoulder throbbed as his bloodstained T-shirt dried, sticking to the raw skin. Cornelia and Rita were similarly positioned, hugging a rough stone wall. Bruises began to stain Rita's skin. All four of them stood behind the pylon-shaped shrine, on which lay a golden casket in the form of a mummified pharaoh. The precious metal of the casket, polished to a high sheen, glowed beneath the ceiling lights. The whole casket was inlaid with semiprecious stones: turquoise, carnelian and lapis lazuli. Their contrasting colors of green, red, and blue represented the protective wings of vultures and hawks. The golden mummy's hands were crossed over its chest, grasping a crook and a flail. The smooth, eternally young, aureate face, with its eyes encircled by inlaid obsidian was the likeness of Norma Chilton. On her chin was a fake braided beard of gold. She wore a wig-like headdress of gold, inlaid with stripes of lapis lazuli, while above her forehead reared the menacing heads of a flared cobra and a bald vulture. On the floor before this idol lay the bandaged, wrapped body of Norma Chilton, wearing the cobra crown and other bright jewels. Before her knelt the mortuary priest Anubis, droning his magic spells. Above him stood five men dressed in black suits repeating antiphonal refrains, their eyes glazed in trance.

*   *   *   *

Lucy Ann crept down the long, unlit passageway from the circular crypt beneath the mausoleum, following the chant. As she approached, the supplications grew to a fevered pitch. Her heart pounded with revulsion at the demonic spells that reverberated off the stone walls. They conjured almost visible images of human-animal monsters. The chants droned on. The air was thick with an animal smell. Feeling faint, she reeled into the stone wall of the narrow passageway.

As Lucy Ann neared the end of the hallway, the chants suddenly stopped. She shrank back into the cover of the thick darkness, looking ahead into the womb-like chamber. She could see a half-naked man with the head of a black jackal, kneeling before a golden idol lying on an altar. Behind his horrific presence she saw Cornelia and Gyles with their friends. In their faces she read the desperate and resigned fear of the condemned. Without hesitation LucyAnn reached inside her purse, grabbed her gun, and pulled it out, pointing it at the back of Anubis. Nagib stood motionless, his chant finished. There was an uneasy silence.

"Now, cousins, the time has come for the queen to lie upon her tomb and hear her mourners weep. What an honored position you do enjoy. Perhaps your sacrifice will serve to recompense our stern and jealous ancestor for the loss of her beautiful golden casket. Yes, here she will rest at last, but her legacy through me will rise and flourish, I who have suffered in shadows long enough without the benefit of the illustrious name Chilton. Now I will reign supreme. Here from my bank vault I will withdraw this sizeable deposit. I claim this collateral against my defaulted inheritance." Nagib stroked the surface of the golden idol with a gloating lust that sent shivers of excitement through his body.

Sweat and tears burned Lucy Ann's eyes, and her fear threatened to overcome her. She squeezed the trigger of her Colt automatic again and again and again. Deafening explosions inflated the darkness of the passageway. She screamed and stumbled forward into the burial chamber. The towering man-animal staggered backwards with arched spine, his arms outstretched and flailing as if he were impaled. The jackal mask fell from his shoulders; he twisted half round and collapsed in a broken heap. His head lay smashed on the stone floor in a growing pool of blood.

Lucy Ann stared in horror at the birthmark and screamed, "My son, I've shot my son!" Tidal waves of anguish broke over her.

Cornelia, released from her invisible bondage by the strength of love, dashed to the sobbing Lucy Ann. The others, not so quick to recover from their shock, stood undecided, looking at the five men in black floundering in the wake of their leader's sudden death. At that charged moment, when opposing parties stared at each other in limbo, there emerged from the passageway a tall and coldly beautiful woman in a black Chanel suit. She stepped forward, pointing her snub-nosed revolver at her brother's henchmen, and hissed at them, "Drop your guns, swine. Get over against the wall. I'll be needing all of you to carry out the gold, so for the moment you're safe."

Cornelia rocked Lucy Ann in an awkward embrace. The older woman still sobbed and cried out, "My son, my son, I've shot my son."

Tatiana hissed, "Shut up, you silly woman. You haven't shot anyone. I shot Nagib. Your bullets hit the gold mummy. Look, there, embedded in the cheek and in its leg. But never mind, it's the thought that counts. You said he's your son? I suppose with a face like that you wouldn't make a mistake. Well, that makes me your daughter. Life is full of little ironies. But if it's any consolation to you, Nagib was full of shit. If he had known you were his mother, he would've left you here to rot with the rest of the family. He was such a family man. And while we're on that subject, have you seen your mother recently? Doesn't she look lovely, party hat and all? Well, granny, where you've gone the party's over, so I'll relieve you of your finery."

Tatiana stepped over the corpse of her brother and snatched the cobra crown from the gruesome mummy. Her last act in this world was not her most flattering. Nagib, leaking his life onto the stone floor, was briefly resuscitated by a bitter jolt of hate. Drawing a gun from his pleated kilt, he shot Tatiana at point-blank range through her chest, where her heart should have been.

No one screamed. No one cried. The tall beauty fell without grace onto the linen-wrapped corpse of her grandmother. In a cramped and contorted fist, she clutched the cobra crown. An acrid smell of gunpowder mingled with the cloying scent of French perfume.

Gyles seized the advantage of this moment, and, moving out from behind the gold coffin, he snapped, "Rita, go to Cornelia. Val, come with me."

Avoiding the piled bodies before the altar, Gyles went to Lucy Ann's side. He and Val roused the older woman and fairly dragged her down the passageway. Rita and Cornelia ran after them, never looking back, leaving behind that awful tomb where secrets of greed, revenge, and jealousy had so long fermented.

The five men converged on the mummy, fixated on the greed engendered so deeply in them by Nagib. Each laid hold of the gold sarcophagus. They heaved the weight onto their shoulders, but the designs of Norma Chilton were far-sighted and her intentions to possess and hoard were not to be thwarted. The great weight of the sarcophagus had held the gates of the tomb open. When that weight was lifted, it tripped a mechanism that released tons of stone into motion. A thunderous rumbling noise was heard. The earth shook, and dust fell from cracks between the huge slabs of the ceiling, a rush of stale air compressed within the chamber pressing hard on the pallbearers' ears. With one final and deafening crash, two immense blocks of granite fell into the dark passageway, blocking all hope of escape.

Gyles crawled out of the red porphyry casket, dusty, disheveled, and dripping with sweat. He reached back and took hold of Lucy Ann, where she had collapsed on the narrow stairs. Val, supporting from below, lifted the older woman to the top of the stairs. With a strength born from sheer panic, he charged up the remaining steps. Cornelia and Rita scrambled at his heels. Gyles yanked each of them out with a ferocious brutality. They staggered from the open casket, chased by a cloud of dust. The stones below roared with fury. The vainglorious dome above shuddered with anger. The four witnesses to nightmare and death ran from the tomb, carrying Lucy Ann among them.

The beech trees shrouding the mausoleum seemed to crowd closer, the last barrier to freedom. They lay Lucy-Ann on the lawn between the granite obelisks that had inexplicably shrunk from their former height. Gyles ripped off his tweed jacket and bunched it up as a pillow for her. The oversized key to the mausoleum fell from his pocket into his hand. Startled by the dead weight of it, he threw it as if it were a burning coal. Once again following the providence of chaos, it fell at the feet of Eben Chichester, who had insinuated himself into the clearing. The lawyer grabbed the key and slipped it into his own pocket.

"Gyles, Cornelia, what is going on here?"

The group hovering about the prostrate Lucy Ann experienced a collective jolt of fear.

"Eben! What are you doing here?" Gyles volleyed.

"Never mind me. I've had business to attend to here at the cemetery. You will remember that I am a proprietor of this institution. I saw your cars parked nearby, and I came to see if I could be of assistance."

"He's trying to say that he wants to know what's up." With the resilience of youth, Val's spunk had bounced back quickly.

"I am not trying to say anything, young man. I have already said it. What's going on?"

"I'm not exactly sure how to answer you, Eben. You'd better look for yourself."

Gyles pointed ominously at the half-open bronze doors of the mausoleum. The lawyer went inside.

As he disappeared behind the doors, Rita said, "He won't get far, and he won't see the worst. Too bad, because that man could use a lesson in humility. But at least you got rid of him for the moment."

However deserved, humility was not the reward to greet Eben inside the mausoleum. The richness of the tomb held no fascination for him. He crossed the broad marble floor towards the open casket. Not hesitating at all, he easily propelled himself over the edge, holding a handkerchief to his mouth and nose to filter the dust. He descended the steep stairs into the crypt. The Egyptian murals on the circular walls below were to him no more than cartoon nonsense, completely defused of threat. He saw the stone bridge leading to the painted doorway, from which clouds of dust were still streaming. He secured his handkerchief with a knot behind his head so that his hands were free to balance as he crossed the narrow bridge. On reaching the far side, he strained to see inside the dark passageway. Not three feet away was a dead end, blocked by a solid wall of granite polished to a glasslike surface, which reflected the lawyer's shadowy image. He felt both relief and regret at this sight.

Eben Chichester had joined forces with Nagib Iskander only after Nagib had purchased a block of Chilton Savings and Trust Bank stock that brought his holdings perilously close to a majority. But Eben, who prided himself on knowing all the details of Chilton-Chichester business, had been woefully ignorant of the machinations that had fermented so long in Nagib. When the full extent of the mortician's delusions of Egyptian deity became apparent to the lawyer, he was appalled. When the collusion of Norma Chilton and her improbable lover, Nagib Iskander, Sr., were revealed to Eben, he was dumbfounded. When the family relationship of Nagib Iskander, Jr. to the Chiltons was reluctantly accepted, Eben was repulsed and moved to desperate action.

The lawyer had planned a showdown with the mortician, from which he intended to emerge the victor. To this end he had cleared the area of the single uninvolved witness, Mr. Charlie. All means of escape and transportation for Nagib and his thugs as well as the gold treasure were eliminated by the removal of the cortège vehicles, which had been returned to the Greenbrier Funeral Home by Eben's own discreet hirelings. Any trail leading to the tomb would thereby be eliminated also.

That left Eben alone to enact a timely, if somewhat melodramatic, rescue of his young cousins. They would without question be grateful for their deliverance from the clutches of the crazed mortician.

Eben had never killed anyone before, at least not in civilian life, and he was rather looking forward to the experience. He did not doubt his success, coming with intent to kill and a powerful semiautomatic. He had wondered if it would be like hunting mountain goats, as he had done in Montana last autumn. The method would be the same, stalking the unsuspecting game and firing without warning from a concealed position. But explaining all of this legally might prove too dangerous, so he decided it would be best to let sleeping dogs lie. What better place for them than in an obscure tomb, apparently totally unrelated to any of the missing persons? Surely no one would disturb them there.

Staring at his dim reflection in the polished granite, Eben realized that he would not have the bittersweet satisfaction of personally eliminating his hated rival. But there were some compensations. Primary among them would be not having to pretend alliance with that presumptuous upstart. Bastards are always such lingering problems.

Eben did not know all the luck that had befallen him this day, but neither did he waste a moment in idle speculation. He would learn all he needed to know about the events in the inner tomb later from Gyles. Now it was imperative to clear the scene of his cousins and their associates. One thing Eben was sure of: no living soul would escape from behind the granite monoliths blocking the passageway and therefore neither would Norma's gold. Ah well, it was really Nagib who had been desperate for that crutch to support his thinly stretched ambitions. Perhaps some time in the future even this prize could be retrieved.

He retraced his steps up the stairs, trying not to laugh aloud. After emerging from the casket, he pulled the bronze lamp from where it jammed the porphyry lid. Grasping the edge with both hands, he saw the warning cut deep in the blood-red stone, and he read aloud: "Twice opened I shall be, and then closed for all eternity."

He replied to this imperial threat with irony and relief. "Well Norma, you have protected your treasure thus far. I trust that your words will prove true now." He slammed the heavy lid down upon his great-aunt's tomb and yanked the ankh from the keyhole. Holding it, he remarked aloud, "Quite ingenious." He marched towards the tall bronze doors. Once outside he pulled them shut one after the other. A final hollow slam reverberated inside the empty tomb, dying reluctantly in a diminishing echo.

CHAPTER 39

▼

The gala opening of "Glamour Galore" was scheduled for a Saturday night in June. It also happened to be the night of the blue moon. So as the saying goes, only once. And this evening was just that—once in a lifetime. The already fabled follies were to be enjoyed this special night by a glittering crowd of notorious revelers before the general rabble were allowed to witness this superb entertainment at subsequent performances for $22.50 a clip.

Although Cornelia's costume was calculated to knock 'em dead, there was about her finery no reference to Egypt, ancient or otherwise. Neither was she wearing any jewelry. Instead she was decked out in a 1950's Christian Dior strapless evening gown. Her voluminous voile skirts fluffed out over rustling peach taffeta petticoats of countless layers. Her twenty-four inch waist was tightly cinched by a belt three inches wide and encrusted with sparkling rhinestones. The bell of her skirt brushed the floor in a circle five and a half feet in diameter, showing the sharp points of her pink satin pumps. Floating above this dream skirt, her bodice was a miracle of simplicity, cut and sewn from iridescent peach silk satin. It followed the V-shape of her tiny torso, hovering on the daring edge of her blushing décolleté. Around her swanlike neck was tied a lace ribbon the color of dawn, secured with a bow at the back. Her chestnut hair was piled on top of her perfectly formed head, frothing at the crown around a spray of peach-colored orchids. Her makeup was deceptive and enchanting, with one slight indulgence—a dusting of silver glitter on her high cheekbones.

She was escorted into the club on the arms of Rita and Gyles. Both wore identical white tie and tails of impeccable tailoring. Their haircuts, also identical, shone with brilliantine like black lacquered helmets. As the three celebrities entered the Club Crazy, Cornelia floating on ahead, there was a spontaneous standing ovation from an audience of equal dazzle. The interior of the Crazy space was filled with all manner of glitterati. Youth had a monopoly on the proceedings, and if this bunch didn't blush naturally, they at least had enough sense to buy the cosmetic equivalent and liberally apply it. Subtle modesty was not the objective. Tonight all seats were booked for the breathless achievement of glee.

Cornelia floated on the ether of admiration toward the faux zebra banquette, front row center on the dance floor. A waitress, whose sparkling black spandex body suit displayed to advantage every nuance of her gymnasium-sculpted body, whooshed towards Cornelia's table on roller blades. Her elaborate flourishes were reminiscent of the muscle-powered contortionism of a Midwestern baton twirler. As the waitress's routine dragged on, she managed to enthrall everyone in the assembled company except Cornelia, who stood waiting for her table to be pulled out so she might complete her entrance and be seated. This simple act was eventually accomplished by Gyles, who without pride and with a certain amount of wry amusement withdrew the linen-draped table onto the edge of the dance floor.

Rita glared at the pirouetting waitress and said, "Okay Sally, rip your eyes off my gal's tits unless you want to die young."

"Rita, please!" Cornelia thumped the banquette beside her, urging her lover to sit down.

"Oh, I'm not Sally. I'm Collette. I'll be your waitress this evening," offered the girl as she mopped her brow, blotting the exertions of her performance with a napkin snatched from Rita's place setting. Collette was momentarily brought to her senses by Rita's murderous expression. The girl hid the offending napery behind her back, tucking it into her elastic waistband.

She nervously straightened the tablecloth and said, "Oh, sorry, I'll get you a clean one."

Gyles attempted to rescue the peace by asking, "Collette, while you're at it, would you please bring us a bottle of Dom Pérignon and three fluted glasses?"

"Well sure, I'll try. But just in case they don't have that, do you have a second choice?"

"Yes. A loaded gun and a bottle of gin," retorted Rita.

Collette trilled a nervous giggle and asked, "Are you serious?"

Rita moved off the seat to strike, but Gyles and Cornelia held her back as the skating waitron beat a hasty retreat.

Gyles lit a Sobranie and exhaled a huge sigh of relief. Looking about the Club Crazy, he was amazed again by the expensive rehab that had transformed this old loft building into a slick Art Deco nightclub. The prismatic blue and silver mirrors affixed to every surface, contrasting with the luxurious waves of silver lamé, swathing the walls, was breathtaking. Above all this the ceiling was hung with so many revolving mirror balls as to give the effect of being in the Milky Way, as laser beams of colored lights flashed in all directions, filling the air with effervescent sparkle.

Three long tiers of scalloping banquettes rose above the dance floor opposite the stage. Each was upholstered with faux zebra and was large enough to accommodate six people. Behind the tiers of seating there was standing room only, corralled by a serpentine bar against the back wall. The bar was presided over by an eager fraternity of mixologists radiating sex appeal like overfed furnaces.

Cornelia fished in her beaded purse for her compact. She located the enameled vanity and extracted it with studied nonchalance. She popped open the lid, which was decorated with a leaping gazelle of sleek proportions, and studied her reflection in the small mirror. But what she was really up to was practicing surreptitious flirtations in the glass as she had seen in an old Jean Harlow movie. She maneuvered the mirror in her hand, scanning the crowd behind her, searching for some sweet honey who might pluck a heart string or two.

As with many an intended flirtation, the results were unexpected. In her mirror Cornelia saw the flushed visage of Rosalind Wortheley. The greater part of this tragedy was that Rosalind had seen Cornelia's clandestine vamping and knew exactly what the decorator was up to. As eloquent proof of Rosalind's acumen, she wagged a scolding finger at Cornelia and gave her an exaggerated and lewd wink. Rosalind had propelled herself from the banquette where she was ensconced with her husband and a party of suburban refugees. In response to the gathering crowd, this bunch wore a collective expression that closely resembled that famous David drawing of Marie Antoinette on her way to the guillotine. As Rosalind charged towards her decorator, Cornelia snapped closed her compact with deep chagrin.

Leaning close to her companions, she warned, "Don't look now, but here comes Genghis Khan's mother-in-law." This remark made Gyles and Rita twist around and stare, a movement rapidly reversed as they sought with desperation some rug to crawl under. Rosalind was dressed to kill in a wildly expensive outfit by that misogynist designer, Moslem LaCrock. In her bouncy and fluffed-out miniskirt with matching vest, she looked like a cross between Dale Evans and Margot Fonteyn portraying the dying swan. This costume involved a lot of lurid green and cherry red, along with cheap gold chains and an alarming collection of mismatched buttons. Rosalind loomed above the party cowering on the banquette. When it became apparent that this was not a bad dream and the professional beauty before them was not likely to disappear on her own volition, Cornelia decided that the better part of valor was to recognize her old school chum.

Seeking the proper greeting, she floundered about until she hit upon the not-too-ingenious statement "Oh Rosalind, there you are. Don't you look—"

Gyles whispered, "rabid—"

Cornelia shouted, "Ravishing! Ravishing! Ravishing!" Each time she pronounced this word she attempted to apply a more convincing delivery.

"I heard you the first time, Cornelia. Thanks a lot. But at least I can afford an original designer gown."

"Original," agreed Gyles, nodding his head too many times.

Rosalind plunked herself down next to Rita and wriggled in close to shmooze with Cornelia. At that moment Collette arrived with the bubbly and three fluted glasses. Hefting these on her overdeveloped arms, along with a wine stand and bucket sloshing over with ice water, she went into a spin so energetic that the party shrank back in terror. But the skating waitron came to a neat halt, beaming with pride, arms thrown wide with a gesture of presentation. The Dom Pérignon nestled into the ice bucket standing beside the table.

"Oh, Dom! My absolute favorite," Rosalind enthused.

"Better bring us another bottle, and put two more on ice, Collette, and see if you can scare up some more glasses. I'll open this one." Gyles waved Collette away on her mission of mercy.

"Sure thing, mister." Off the waitress whooshed, only too glad to help Gyles spend his inheritance. The antiques dealer distributed the bubbling flutes to the three women.

Rosalind got down to business. "Well, my dear, I must tell you, not a word of this to a soul. You didn't hear it from me, but Farag Sarkisian has gone away with Dottie Major!"

"What? Did he kidnap her?" asked Gyles.

"Say, who're Dottie Major and Farag Sarkisian?" demanded Rita.

"No, silly, he didn't kidnap her. Farag Sarkisian is Tatiana Sarkisian's very hunky husband. Dottie went willingly. They eloped, or whatever you say with married people. Dottie is my cousin. She's married to Bubba Major. He's the president of the Chase Manhattan Bank."

"So?" Giles question intended to dismiss the gossip, but Rosalind sailed blithely onward.

"So? Women who are married to bank presidents don't elope with furriers, no matter how hunky they may be. Men can be so dense sometimes."

Rosalind directed this last aside at Rita, but then retracted her statement with apologies when she looked for the first time at the accountant sitting beside her. With slight misgivings she mistook Rita for a man. The professional beauty paused with confusion, and Cornelia, seeing this, took mischievous delight in introducing Rita as her lover to Rosalind.

"Oh well, yes," sputtered the gossip. "For a minute there I thought you were a man. You know you look really cute like that."

"Never mind, Rita, she says the same thing to me," cut in Cornelia.

"Now where was I?" asked Rosalind.

"In the fetid halls of betrayal and deceit?" suggested Gyles.

"Yes," she said with a little sigh, "that's it—no! I mean, oh, now you've got me all mixed up. Men are so holier than thou, don't you think, Rita? Oh now I remember, Tatiana will die when she finds out that Farag ran away with another woman."

Rita's eyes bore into Rosalind with disgust, and she said, "She already has died, but it was not from the lack of a husband. Women can be pigs just like men."

In response to this disclosure, Cornelia choked on her champagne. Gyles whisked his sister's glass to safety and gently thumped her on the back. Raising the flute in a toast, he said, "I'll drink to that, Rita. Go on and let her have it."

"Let who have what, Gyles? What do you mean she died already, Rita? She can't have heard the news yet. Dottie only called me from Rio this afternoon," Rosalind whined.

"Where Tatiana is now, news travels fast," concluded Rita.

Cornelia, desperate to change the subject, asked lamely, "So what brings you to the Club Crazy, Rosalind? I wouldn't have thought it exactly your cup of tea."

"Don't be silly, Cornelia. You're not the only one who's hip, you know. George is the angel for 'Glamour Galore.' How do you think Miss LeStrange can afford all of this?" Here Rosalind made a grand gesture indicating the renovated expanse of the Crazy space. "Oh there's my darling now, flagging down his muse. I must be off. Drop by our table. Too-da-loo!"

"Dear Goddess. George Wortheley is a backer for Lilly Linda LeStrange and the Fab Chorines at the Club Crazy? Is nothing sacred?" Cornelia was appalled.

"Wow! I'll bet that's a story in and of itself, but one that will have to wait for another time," Gyles narrated. Then he concluded, "Oh here comes Collette with reinforcements. You know that girl is beginning to grow on me."

"Yeah, like green fungus," Rita sneered.

"I wonder where she learned to skate like that." Gyles's musings were interrupted by the rocketing arrival of Collette. While gliding smoothly round the table, the waitron ministered to their several needs, distributing clean glasses, a new bottle of bubbly, a supply of swizzle sticks mounted with wriggling hula girls—unasked for, inappropriate, but amusing nonetheless. From somewhere she produced a bowl of peanuts and an immaculate napkin folded with origami complexities in the form of two kissing swans. This sculptural ephemera she presented to Rita with one of her usual spinning frenzies, and then she whooshed away.

Cornelia, trying to keep the waters calm, gushed, "Oh Rita, look. Collette brought you a peace offering. She really is trying to be sweet."

"But, like Sweet-'N Low, she's a bit phony."

"Rita, lighten up!" Gyles exclaimed. "I saw you ogling her hot buns."

Ignoring Gyles's remark, Rita lifted her glass in a toast and said, "To close calls: May they all be long distance from now on." The three friends sipped their wine with serious intent for a while, studying the festive crowd about them.

Gyles topped their glasses again and asked, "Say Rita, what did you mean about close calls?"

"I meant the next time you get a brilliant idea of groveling about a graveyard with your mummified ancestors, I hope that I'm a long distance away."

"I'll drink to that," Cornelia agreed, and after a delicious slurp she asked, "Gyles, what did Cousin Eben say when you told him what happened in the tomb?"

Before he replied, he refilled their glasses again and then, checking over his shoulder for any would-be eavesdroppers, he leaned close to the table and his companions, saying, "First of all, he said that discretion was absolutely imperative regarding this matter. Those were his exact words."

"I can hear him saying that," confirmed Cornelia.

"Second, he said for us to put this unpleasantness behind us and let him deal with all the details."

"I think he's absolutely right about that too," agreed Cornelia.

"Eben says the Sibuna tomb has no legal connection to the Chilton family."

"What's the Sibuna tomb?" asked Rita.

"You remember, that's the actual name inscribed on the mausoleum. It's Anubis spelled backwards. It also is the name registered in the Mount Auburn records. Naturally, there is no other identification of the Sibuna family, but, more importantly, there is no history of the tomb's construction, although a considerable endowment exists for perpetual care of the mausoleum."

"Trust Eben Chichester to check that detail," Rita remarked.

"He also told me that there will be no loved ones looking for Nagib Iskander, with the exception of his legion of creditors, who may provide in and of themselves a plausible reason for his disappearance. In any case, he could have disappeared as easily from his own house as from anywhere else. There's nothing to connect him with the cemetery that day, or at least no evidence exists anymore. Certainly nothing connecting him to the Sibuna tomb, as Eben insists upon calling it," Gyles finished.

"I'm beginning to get the picture. Our powerful cousin has pulled a number of strings, and I'm not sure whether I feel safe and relieved or more afraid than ever."

"Cornelia, don't be afraid. It's to Eben's advantage for the family in general to flourish as he manages all our monies, making himself a tidy and well-earned profit in the process. In us he has perfect clients, because through Wisner we are now substantial shareholders at the bank."

"You are, Gyles, yes," Cornelia corrected him.

"No, Corny, both of us. I instructed Eben to divide Wisner's estate between us evenly. That way I don't have to feel guilty about dragging you into the pitfalls of self-employment with our new business. And besides, I don't believe in primogeniture."

"Oh Gyles, yes, I'll be happy to relieve your conscience of that intolerable burden." Cornelia kissed her brother on the cheek and proposed a toast. "To one swell guy, my brother, Gyles. May Chilton's Interiors and Antiques long flourish."

"Chilton's Antiques and Interiors," corrected Gyles.

"Sure thing, partner." Cornelia clinked glasses with high spirits. By this time the three friends were pleasantly flushed by the wine.

"So what was Nagib Iskander up to anyway?" asked Rita.

"That is a story that may be buried forever with Norma Chilton and her unfortunate grandchildren."

"Don't forget the five horsemen of the apocalypse." Cornelia shuddered at Rita's reminder of Nagib's henchmen.

Gyles took up the narrative. "The gist of the modern version of that saga is that Nagib Iskander was trying to take over the Chilton Savings and Trust Bank. He sunk himself into debt, mortgaging his real estate empire to the hilt. He apparently was also doing a brisk business in ancient Egyptian artifacts that

Norma and Nagib Sr. had somehow kept for themselves from the excavation she patronized. Decades ago they had plotted a complicated scam involving a fire at the Chilton East India Wharf, where incidentally Wisner had worked one summer inventorying the artifacts. These valuable items were supposed to have been destroyed in the blaze. But in reality the best of the collection had been removed to the Greenbrier Funeral Home, where they've been ever since. During the last several years, Nagib Jr. has been hawking the goods on the international art market to bolster his floundering enterprises.

"Eben learned all of this in the last couple of days from private reports discovered in Wisner's papers. It all seems rather desperate, but not nearly as incredible as Nagib's pursuit of Norma's golden mummy sarcophagus to support his crumbling real estate empire."

"But I thought he was an undertaker, not a powerful real estate tycoon," Cornelia said witheringly.

"That, dear Cornelia, is the typical WASP disdain that urged our cousin towards the ruthless ambition that was his undoing."

"Well I'm sorry, but somehow I don't feel responsible for that maniac."

"No, I don't mean to imply that you should be." Gyles gulped his wine and continued. "The ancient history of the Chilton-Iskander saga is a bit murkier, but I can tell you from having studied all the plans to the tomb—"

"So that's where they went," interrupted Cornelia. "I was going to burn them."

"We are of one flesh and one mind, Corny. That's just what I did. But first I couldn't resist an evening's perusal. From what I could gather, the place was full of booby traps, like the pit I almost fell into. But the final irony was, the casket was in fact made of lead with a gold wash. The plans clearly show that.

"Cousin Eben grilled me over and over about the gold sarcophagus. He knew of its existence, perhaps from Wisner's papers, but still I found it puzzling. Eben seems to know at least a little bit about quite a lot. He wanted all the details I could provide, which was to be expected considering the supposed value of the sarcophagus. But at the time of our meeting I hadn't yet studied the plans myself. So I didn't know very much about the sarcophagus and certainly nothing about its gold content except that it looked impressive. As I told Eben, it was the most terrifying moment of my life, and my attention was not on items, gold or otherwise."

"Well that's amazing," Rita could not resist remarking.

Cornelia jabbed her lover with her elbow.

"Watch out, Neil," Rita threatened.

"So the sarcophagus wouldn't have done any good for Nagib or Tatiana?" asked Cornelia.

"I'll bet Norma did it to lure her unfaithful lover Nagib into her eternal embrace. It's amazing what hetero women will do to catch a man."

"I think you read that accurately, Rita, because the most impressive of the traps was the closing of the tomb that was triggered by lifting the gold casket. Apparently when we dashed out of the burial chamber, those five men tried to take the gold for themselves. By the way, Rita, there were only four horsemen of the apocalypse, not five, but your point is shudderingly well put."

"Hey, what's another body or two in that pile of carnage?" Rita's dismissal of the gang with her jaundiced remark shocked even herself. They all swizzled the sauce sheepishly, and Gyles refilled their glasses before he continued.

"The two obelisks standing in front of the mausoleum were positioned over the passageway leading from the circular crypt to the burial chamber. The tripping mechanism beneath the gold casket released those tons of granite to fall straight down a distance of five feet, blocking the entrance forever."

"Geez. Sounds just like Raiders of the Lost Ark," a familiar voice exclaimed. The three friends huddling on the banquette jumped as if jolted by electricity.

"Val!" exclaimed Gyles. "Thank God it's just you!"

"Well thanks, that's a nice way to say hi." The dancer pouted above them. His arms folded over the fuchsia-colored tank top that struggled to contain his elegant and defined bulk. The rest of him was poured into a pair of blue jeans whose pockets would not have allowed room for a thin dime.

Stumbling all over himself, Gyles asked, "Aren't you going on? I thought the curtain was about to go up."

"Oh terrific. First I'm treated like an extra in a silent film and now I'm being told to go dance for my supper. Well, as it happens, I'm not on till the second number."

Rita read Val without mercy. "You know, Val, you really are touchy sometimes. You've got a big chip on your shoulder. Why don't you sit down and have a little bubbly?"

"Oh! Coming from you, Miss Serenity, that's a hot one." Val slouched his weight from one hip to another.

"Hey Val, park your ass over here and shut up." Gyles thumped the banquette beside him and handed his lover a fluted glass of sparkling champagne.

"Well I never!" the dancer camped and plunked himself down practically in Gyles's lap, planting a loud smooch on his boyfriend's lips. He prompted Gyles, "So go on already, what happened then?"

"That's it really. I guess Norma was going to make sure that she took it all with her, no matter what the cost. But she didn't trust Nagib Iskander. She apparently kept the location of the tomb a secret, only posthumously to be revealed by the jewelry, which had an encoded message on the back of the chalcedony scarab. This scarab they called the 'heart of the mother,' which is some reference to *The Book of the Dead*. But Norma, ever jealous of her treasure, wouldn't give up the jewels of Anubis until too late. At that moment the only person around was Aunt Florence, who unwittingly put the whole quest to sleep by locking the jewels in Cornelia's safety deposit box. She was supposed to send them and the statue of Anubis to Nagib Iskander. I can't blame her for not fulfilling this rather bizarre deathbed request. So the matter hibernated until the half-instructed neophyte Nagib Jr. and his sister, Tatiana, both smoldering with jealousy, revived the quest of greed with corrosive results on their characters. Like the sorcerer's apprentice, their half-learned magic was in the end their undoing."

"Wow, you should write a book, Gyles. That all sounds real spooky." Val was truly amazed.

"Spooky is just the word for it, pal," Cornelia agreed, "but that's only half the story. Wait till you hear what Lucy Ann told me. Lucy Ann's earliest childhood was spent in South Carolina with a kindly old woman known to her as Mama. Mama's Christian name was Liberty. Liberty had been the daughter of a fugitive slave whom Norma's grandmother, Bedertha Chilton, had helped escape to freedom before the Civil War. That slave's name was Sally. Liberty had found her way back to South Carolina sometime around the turn of the century. But she had always kept in touch with her mother's patroness, Mrs. Chilton of Boston. Norma Chilton took advantage of this gratitude, turning favor into debt, which she called to account when she deposited Lucy Ann, a newborn infant, with Liberty.

"Hold on a minute Neil. So Norma's grandmother was Bedertha Chilton and she helped to free the slave Sally?"

"That's right."

"And Sally's daughter Liberty brought up Lucy Ann as a small child."

"Yes, that's it, Rita." Cornelia continued, "Fifteen years elapsed, and out of the blue Norma Chilton returned to reclaim Lucy Ann. Not as a repentant mother longing for her dear babe Lucy-Ann is Norma's only daughter—but because she found herself in need of a personal maid."

"Gee, what a tough break. Poor old Lucy Ann has been really kicked around!" Gyles was very disturbed, and no one else dared to comment.

"LucyAnn was brought up in ignorance as to her true identity. She was also ignorant of the fact that she had a brother. This boy, however, was not unknown to her. He was the acknowledged son of Nagib Iskander, the constant companion of Norma Chilton. Both father and son visited frequently at 283 Commonwealth Avenue. The boy was old Nagib's pride and joy and an honor student at Groton Academy. That must have been a lonely place for the son of a Saracen mortician, and Nagib Jr. bore the unmistakable likeness of his father's handsome dusky complexion and strong features."

"I sorta know how he musta felt," said Val. "I never really fit in either."

"LucyAnn was the only person his age who looked remotely like him. They were frequently together, so they fell from loneliness into love. That desperate loneliness climaxed one afternoon in LucyAnn's tiny bedroom in the attic of 283 Commonwealth Avenue. Their passion spent but not savored, they were discovered by the avenging Norma, who shot and killed her unacknowledged son."

"What a monster Norma was!" Gyles was aghast and Val put a protective arm around his shoulders.

"The name of Nagib Iskander, Jr., was quietly withdrawn from the lists of Groton, much to the relief of the conservative administration. They did not inquire as to the boy's future.

"Nine months later, in a conciliatory gesture towards old Nagib, Norma delivered to his doorstep in Watertown the two innocent children who were later known to us as Nagib and Tatiana."

"Boy, Cornelia, I didn't know all of that. What am I saying? I didn't know any of it! But how did you piece together all those details, like old Sally, the fugitive slave?"

"I didn't piece together anything. Lucy Ann did. She's told her share of white lies too. One of them was that she never went into Aunt Norma's bedroom after she died. Lucy Ann knew about the secret panel and the statue of Anubis, although she didn't understand or care about its significance. She was looking for Norma's extensive diaries, which she knew all about because Norma spent a lot of time writing in them. Not being a person of modest persuasion, our great-aunt was given to quoting herself or reading lengthy passages to any and all who she could get to listen. She had intended her diaries for posthumous publication, a project her sister, Florence, had little enthusiasm for. Knowing her tormentor's intentions, Lucy Ann began to burn the many volumes after Florence's death."

"And a good thing too," Rita approved.

"Her one act of revenge, poor darling. But even Lucy Ann was seduced by Norma's endless chronicle, and she read the diaries before she burned them. That's where she learned about her true parentage and all the rest."

"Wow, Cornelia, sort of like Roots, huh? You tell a story even better than Gyles." Val's applause resonated with his unguarded enthusiasm.

"What did you expect?" asked Rita with pride, giving her friend a hearty squeeze. Without thinking Rita asked, "So how's the old girl getting on now?"

"Old girl?" asked Gyles, laying it on thick. "Is that politically correct lingo, Rita?"

"Stuff it, pal, you know what I mean. Lucy Ann, how is she anyway?"

"Well I never," flounced Gyles.

"Ha ha," Rita warned flatly, "your brother is a regular riot, Cornelia."

"Lucy Ann is remarkably well, I'm happy to say. Gyles and I have decided that our Aunt Lulu is the rightful heir to 283 Commonwealth Avenue, and she was thrilled by the idea and accepted with alacrity. She immediately told us of her longtime fantasy of running the house as a bed and breakfast. She wants to keep it exactly as it is, which will give the old place the unique advantage of being a living history museum of no small importance. We both think it's a great idea with a strong future. Gyles asked Aunt Lucy if she would like the Chilton Savings and Trust Bank to be her financial backer, but get this. She told him she'd consider it, but first she wanted to consult her accountant, Rita Rosenstein, and maybe shop around."

Rita beamed with pride at the idea and casually sipped her champagne.

Gyles winked at Cornelia and said, "Oh, that reminds me, Val, Aunt Lucy wants me to sound you out about joining her staff. It seems she was very impressed with the work you did managing and maintaining the apartment house next door to her. She needs someone young and strong, and, as she puts it, 'Customers like to see a handsome face around.' So what about it?"

"Awesome, man! Does that mean I've got a real job?"

"Sure does, hot stuff. Hope you'll still have time for me."

"Gosh, I don't know. I'll have to think about it, Gyles." Val, seeing Gyles's deflated expression, added, "I mean of course I've got time for you. It's the job I don't know about. Do you think I'd be good enough?"

In a rare moment of unguarded laughter, Gyles gushed, "Oh sweetheart, you're the best."

There appeared on the dance floor before the assembled company the requisite jester for all gay functions, the nun with the bushy beard. This superior sister had abbreviated her habit to miniskirt length, preserving her modesty by a densely layered collection of black lace petticoats flouncing over scrawny legs that were immodestly clad in black net stockings. Her altered habit was intended to resemble the wide swing skirts of country square dance styling. Completing this image the demipenitent wore steel-pointed high-heeled shit-kicking cowboy boots.

With a high-pitched screech, she entreated the audience, "Hee haw, get down, pardners." She then launched into a spirited and sultry line dance of complex shuffling choreography to the twangy wailings of Patsy Cline over the sound system.

"Good Goddess, it's Sister Scena Finale with the latest line dance direct from Dallas. I can't just sit here. Come on, let's shuffle," Cornelia exclaimed.

"Sister Scena Finale indeed," muttered Rita as she reluctantly wriggled off the banquette.

Val yanked Gyles to his feet saying, "Come on, cowboy, let's boogie."

The dance floor was immediately flooded. They all plunged in, including Rosalind Wortheley, who was immortalized in the international gay press by that sleazebag photographer Popper Ozzie.

He thrust a little brown bottle under the nose of the professional beauty, saying, "Just one sniff and you'll be bored no more, honey. I get a kick out of you." Popper Ozzie snapped numerous shots of Ross as she reeled in the haze of amyl while trying to follow Sister Scena's shuffle. Rosalind's bright-eyed beauty was never more daringly portrayed than in the resultant photos.

The company at large was coming together with the coordinated and very cool understanding of Sister Scena's dance when there was an abrupt halt to the proceedings. This hiatus was signaled by a deafening scratch of needle being dragged off Patsy's disk. In the ominous and ensuing silence, the unmistakable bellowing of that chanteuse extraordinaire, Lilly Linda LeStrange came from behind the fringed silver Mylar curtain.

"Get that bitch off the dance floor. You queens have fucked up enough. I have a performance to give."

Val took his cue reluctantly. Planting a juicy smooch on Gyles's cheek, he leapt into the wings of backstage and disappeared.

Lilly's pronouncement brought the multitudes grudgingly to their senses. All returned to their respective seats, having been convincingly reassured of the imminent arrival of the diva. Impressed by her public's fickle sense of amusement, Lilly Linda did not keep the fans waiting any more. There sounded an impressive overture from a seventeen piece band with a contrapuntal composition that would have been the envy of John Williams. Wave upon wave of silver-fringed Mylar curtain peeled away, advancing deep into an enormous crystalline cave, like the inside of a huge geode. The band became visible, backlit and silhouetted against a sparkling cityscape. They played the snappy tunes with such zip and pizzazz as to twitch the beat in everyone's feet, whipping the audience into frothy ovations and squeals of glee.

From the wings a single muscle-bound he-man lumbered onstage wearing naught but a glittering thong girding his considerable loins. He staggered beneath the weight of a fifteen-foot-tall red-sequined high-heeled shoe. This act of brawn brought down the house. The hulk, glistening with sweat from his exertions, dumped his load upon the stage and treated some of the more easily amused spectators to a brief routine of flexing pectorals. He was, however, urged to concede the limelight by Lilly Linda herself, who hurled abuse as well as a can of diet soda with lethal marksmanship.

The strains of a haunting melody were played by the band, now strengthened by a string section twelve strong. The extravaganza of this production was unlimited, and the fans hummed along in appreciation. From above there appeared a dream cloud of vast proportions, suspended by stout cables wrapped in pink velvet. Perched upon this nimbus was the diva indubitable, glamour personified, the resplendent Lilly Linda LeStrange in full glittering regalia, warbling forth her ballad benign. She enunciated her lyric profound:

"You may say life is real boring, one day following the next, no love, no joy, no adoring, not even very good sex. But I say stuff it, don't rough it, enjoy! 'Cause into each life a little glamour must fall, yes, girls, into each life a little glamour must fall!"

As the last trumpeting notes of this scintillating refrain sounded, Lilly stepped from her cloud into the elevated heel of the gargantuan ruby slipper. At that moment there appeared onstage the twelve Fab Chorines, who wore outfits of minuscule proportions. Without delay they launched into their spirited tap dance, which included gymnastic flourishes that left the audience panting for more. Lilly, with the confidence and grace of a queen supreme, descended the steps inside her ruby slipper, showing to great advantage her zaftig undulations encased in a blinding silver-sequined sheath, which had a small flaring skirt at the ankles, sewn from tissue called "rain from heaven." In her deep cleavage she wore a tiny Mexican Chihuahua named Pepé, who yapped tentatively now and again. Lilly sashayed to stage front center in the midst of frantic, kicking chorines and dramatic crescendos from the band. Her audience in one voice screamed with glee as they all sang a rousing chorus of "Into Each Life a Little Glamour Must Fall."

The End

0-595-33025-8